BROOKHAVEN

a novel

g l y n n   y o u n g

T. S. Poetry Press • New York

T. S. Poetry Press
New York

Tspoetry.com

Cover photo by Dave Hoefler.
 https://unsplash.com/@iamthedave

ISBN 978-1-943120-76-5

Young, Glynn
        [Fiction. Historical romance. Civil War.]
        Brookhaven: a novel, by Glynn Young
        ISBN 978-1-943120-76-5

All quotations are taken from poems by Henry Wadsworth
Longfellow. Public domain.

for bruce roquet and chris paton,
who left us too soon but will always be part of my heart

BROOKHAVEN

1

This memory brightens o'er the past,
As when the sun, concealed
Behind some cloud that near us hangs,
Shines on a distant field.

—from "A Gleam of Sunshine"

September 1915

Elizabeth Putnam smoothed her skirt for what must have been the tenth time. Sitting ramrod straight in the chair outside John Osborne's office, she recognized the movement of her gloved hands as nervousness, not unlike that of sitting outside her dean's office a short two years before. But she still kept smoothing her blue skirt, which, according to the latest fashion, reached just above her ankles. Her long-sleeved white blouse was covered by a kimono jacket, which fell several inches below her waist. A blue velvet boater, complementing the blue of her skirt, sat atop her pinned-up hair. She looked both business-like and fashionable.

At her side was the book Mr. Osborne had asked her to read. *Confederate Spies and Saboteurs in the Civil War: A History* was well written, she had to admit, but she was not interested in a subject she considered ancient history. The war had ended 50 years before, and she had no idea what had possessed Mr. Osborne to have her read it as a pre-assignment. Pre-assignment for what? And shouldn't the books editor be handling this?

She was half afraid she knew what was coming. She was the only woman reporter working in news at the New York *World*. Nellie Bly and Ida Tarbell notwithstanding, women writers in general newspapers and magazines were still an oddity, at best barely tolerated by their male colleagues.

She'd seen the looks of amusement, scorn, and even leering when she'd been introduced in the newsroom. She'd felt the daily humiliation of her assignment editor giving her the dregs of stories to report—and expecting her to be grateful. She'd smile, grit her teeth, hold her tongue, and do the assignment. She was capable of far more. And, slowly and grudgingly, she was being assigned more substantive stories.

She was afraid the newspaper would move her to something less challenging, like the society pages. That's the place many of her male colleagues told her she'd likely end up. What she wanted was to be sent to Europe, to be the first woman correspondent covering the Great War for the World. She did not want to be writing notices about society weddings, fashion, or books on history, no matter how well written they were.

As she sat waiting for Mr. Osborne, she thought of her father and how proud he was of her. She sat a little straighter. She considered the trust Mr. Osborne had placed in her, working with the city editor to assign her to write human interest stories. As young and inexperienced as she was, in less than a year she'd moved from doing rewrites and obituaries to becoming one of the most read reporters at the *World*. She just wished she received these assignments more often.

The door to his office opened, and the city editor and national editor filed out. Both men nodded at her.

"Miss Putnam?" Osborne beckoned her in.

A brief period of small talk was followed by a question.

"You've read the book?"

"Yes, sir, I did. Am I to write an article about it?"

Osborne shook his head. "No, not exactly. Tell me what you thought of it."

"The Civil War wasn't my forte in college," she admitted. "Of course, we studied it in American history, but I know about as much, or as little, as any other person might. A great deal has happened since the war ended, and it seems to have largely receded into the history books, except, of course, the golden jubilee of the war's end celebrated this past spring. But this is very well written; Professor Seale is a very engaging writer."

"Littleton Seale," Osborne said, "is one of the leading Civil War historians alive today, easily among the top two or three in the country. He's been teaching at the University of Mississippi for more than 25 years, and, from what I hear, he's one of the most popular lecturers at the school." He paused. "Was there anything that particularly struck you?"

Elizabeth knew this must be a test; she'd prepared for the possibility by reading the book twice. "Well, there was one very curious chapter." When Osborne nodded, she went on. "About the Gray Wisp."

"Ah," Osborne said, smiling. "And why was it odd?"

"He never names who it was," she said. "Everyone else is

identified by name, but not the Gray Wisp." She hesitated, unsure if this is what he wanted to talk about. "And yet, it was clear that Seale knows the man's identity, and, in fact, it's also clear that he's interviewed him. The alternative is that Seale made it all up, and that doesn't fit with how careful he is to document everything."

"You've put your finger on what most everyone who's read and written about the book missed," Osborne said. "He knows who the Wisp is, yet he never identifies the man."

"Could he be the Wisp himself?" she said.

"No. He wasn't even 10 when the war started. As desperate as the Confederacy became for soldiers, they didn't conscript young children, or children that young." He looked briefly out the window. "I should confess that I have a personal interest here, Miss Putnam. Many years ago, because of a kindness by General Grant, my mother-in-law and my wife met the Wisp. They traveled to the South with her in-laws two years after the war to meet him."

"What connection could there have been to your family? I understood both you and Mrs. Osborne are from Pennsylvania."

"We are," he paused. "The identity of the Wisp remains one of the Civil War's greatest mysteries. For 20 years after the war, speculation was rampant. All kinds of fanciful theories abounded. Some said the Wisp was a child. Or the Wisp was a young slave. Or even that the Wisp was actually several people. He was responsible for any and every Union defeat or setback after Gettysburg. Every officer who wrote a memoir claimed to have met him or speculated about his identity. His activities supposedly drove President Lincoln to distraction.

Some said the Wisp didn't really exist. But as you read in Professor Seale's book, the Wisp was a real person. And he was just one man, operating as part of a small band of spies—and the only member of that band to survive the war.

"He seemed to have arisen from nowhere in mid-1863, and he played crucial roles in helping keep Gen. Lee's Army of Northern Virginia fighting in the field. He helped trick Gen. Meade after the Battle of Gettysburg; Meade had Lee and his army by the throat, but he didn't know it, largely because of the Wisp. And then Lee had astounding information about the Northern armies, because it appears the Wisp periodically embedded himself among the Union troops.

"It's one question that should have been asked but never was. How could he move so freely among Northern soldiers? Even Seale is somewhat coy and less than forthcoming on the topic, and I suspect it has to do with the man's identity.

"There's more. He played a crucial role at the Battle of the Wilderness in 1864. A group of Union soldiers didn't know it, but General Lee and his top officers were holding a conference alongside a road when federal troops suddenly emerged from the woods nearby. Lee told Gen. Grant later that it was the Wisp who warned them and suggested they quietly mount their horses and leave.

"Here's another story that isn't in Seale's book. At Appomattox, Grant asked Lee to introduce him to the Wisp. Lee did so, but only on Grant's word that no retribution would be taken. When they met, the Wisp gave Grant a saddlebag that contained letters and a wallet, including a considerable amount of money." He paused. "That saddlebag belonged to my father-in-law, a man I never met. He'd been mortally wounded

in a cavalry charge at Petersburg, a few days before Appomattox. His horse took him into the woods, dumping him almost next to the Wisp, who was working as a messenger
between Lee and his officers and had concealed himself
among the trees when the cavalry charge began. My father-in-
law was believed to have deserted; the Wisp told General
Grant where his body could be found. Grant dispatched a
staff officer to search for the body, which was exactly where
the Wisp said it would be. The general personally brought the
saddlebag to my mother-in-law in Philadelphia, telling her the
story.

"My wife, then a child, was with her mother and her in-
laws when the general visited, and she remembers her mother
telling her that he apologized to the family for having suspected my father-in-law of desertion. Then he told them about
the Wisp. It was very strange that, months later, my mother-
in-law somehow knew who it was. Grant didn't have to tell
her."

Osborne cleared his throat. "She never told my wife how
she knew. All she said was that my father-in-law had met the
man in 1863, and that the same man—the Wisp—had saved
his life sometime later. In the summer of 1867, my wife, then
five years old, traveled with her mother and her father's parents south to meet the Wisp and thank him personally for his
kindness in returning the saddlebag. My wife does not recall
the name of the town or even what state it was in. But she has
a very strange memory of the trip. She says she remembers
meeting her father. Except she couldn't have, because he'd
been dead for two years by that time. The only thing her
mother ever said later was that she had never realized how en-

twined the Wisp's life had been in my father-in-law's life and her own, even before the war.

"The mysterious Gray Wisp saved my father-in-law's life *and* his reputation. Far from being a deserter, he had heroically led a cavalry charge ordered by his incompetent senior officer. The Gray Wisp had witnessed the charge, and he was the last person to see my father-in-law alive and hear his dying words.

"This may be ancient history, Miss Putnam, but the story of the Wisp and who he is needs to be told, and I'm asking you to find the man and write the story. From Professor Seale's account, the man is clearly still alive, or he was when Seale talked with him. How Seale knew the man's identity may be a story in itself." Osborne smiled, but it quickly faded. "It is also a personal story for me and especially for my wife. She grew up with the legend of her father and the Gray Wisp. She was an only child; the war put short work to growing the family. I would write it myself, but my responsibilities here do not afford the time required. So, I'm asking you, because I know that if anyone at the New York *World* can write this story, and write it well, that person is Elizabeth Putnam. What I fear is that it may be beyond even your prodigious capabilities."

"Mr. Osborne," Elizabeth said, "what was your father-in-law's name?"

"John Haygood. His parents' names were Jacob and Ann Haygood. And, yes, that's the founder of the Haygood Department Store of Philadelphia and a multitude of other businesses. The family fortune and business interests largely, but not entirely, passed to other Haygood relatives. Until their deaths, Jacob and Ann adored my wife, their one and only grandchild. They, too, met the Gray Wisp, and they, too, remained silent about anything to do with the man." He smiled. "As you might imagine, my wife's memories of her father are very faint, except for that odd memory from the trip. She's read Seale's book as well, but just so you know, she's said nothing to me about trying to find the Gray Wisp. She believes that chapter of her father's life is forever closed." Osborne smiled. "I would like to answer those questions for her. And to publish a cracking good story."

"The answers might not be entirely welcome," Elizabeth said.

"True," he said. "But I think she'd like to know what really happened."

2

In vain we look, in vain uplift
Our eyes to heaven, if we are blind;
We see but what we have the gift
Of seeing, what we bring we find.

—from "Moonlight"

October 1915

Elizabeth was on the final leg of her train journey from New York. She'd traveled first to St. Louis and then south to Memphis. She would soon be arriving in Oxford, Mississippi. It had been three weeks since her conversation with John Osborne.

She smiled to herself, remembering how clever the managing editor had been to gain her agreement to take on the story. He'd raised the possibility that she would fail to learn the Confederate spy's identity, because it had been beyond the efforts of so many others. When he told her that many reporters and researchers had tried and failed over the years, all he had to say was that they'd all been men.

Osborne was aware of her strong opinions about women, including what she often said was the moral necessity, and the moral obligation, of giving women the vote. Even *hinting* at the idea that she was somehow lesser because she was a woman was usually the minimum required to create a passionate argument.

A year earlier, she'd been hired by Mr. Osborne directly. Elizabeth had graduated from Smith College in May of 1913, determined to enter the world of journalism. She'd sent more letters than she thought possible to newspapers, magazines, and literary journals all over Boston, New York, Philadelphia, and even Chicago. She received five responses, all form-letter rejections, all saying no positions were currently available.

In the meantime, she'd lived with her parents in Boston. She knew they, and mostly her mother, often despaired of what would become of her. They'd hoped for a well-connected marriage, like the ones her older brothers had made, but Elizabeth had politely yet firmly rejected all comers. She was not interested in marriage, and not any time soon, if ever. She often told her mother she did not need a man to feel completed. She was interested in a career in the newspaper business. And in equal rights for women, starting with the vote.

She'd finally made a bold move and approached the managing editor of the Boston Globe at church, asking him to give her an opportunity to work for no pay as a trial. At first he declined her offer, but she persisted and finally overcame his objections. He initially assigned her rewrites of others' work, and then one afternoon unexpectedly sent her to cover a barroom brawl that had spilled into the streets of Boston's Irish district. She reached the tavern as the police arrived with their truncheons and had to dodge a few crashing bodies, thrown beer bottles, and even a policeman's billy club.

Elizabeth talked to the police, who were only too happy to speak with the attractive young reporter from the *Globe*. She interviewed the tavern owner and a barkeep, who put her on to the cause of the fight, an 18-year-old bar maid named Mary O'Donoghue. Two rivals for her affections had come to blows, drawing in their supporters and friends. By the time the police broke it up, more than 40 men and six women were battling in the bar and outside in the street, the bar was a shambles, and Elizabeth had seen more blood spilled than she'd seen in her entire young life.

She found the bewildered bar maid cowering in near shock in a storage room behind the bar. She escorted the girl to a café across the street, buying her a cup of strong tea and then, when she saw the girl eyeing the food at other tables, a thick sandwich of ham and cheese. And Mary O'Donoghue told Elizabeth her story.

By 4 p.m., Elizabeth was working feverishly at one of the communal typewriters; she didn't have a desk or a machine of her own. She first wrote the news story, which wasn't the most newsworthy of subjects; fights in taverns were a common-place, even with more than 40 people arrested. Then she worked quickly and diligently in writing the story of Mary, giving both stories to the city editor.

Elizabeth waited while he read them. When he finished, he looked at her, stood without speaking, and walked to the managing editor's office. Fifteen minutes later, the door opened, and the city editor walked over to her. "We're running both stories tomorrow," he said, without adding anything else.

It was a sleepless night. She was waiting on her parents' front porch when the paper was delivered at 5 a.m. Her story about Mary was on page one, at the bottom which was usually reserved for human interest stories. It included Elizabeth's by-line.

She was over the moon. Her mother was horrified, realizing that her daughter, a young woman from one of the most socially prominent families of Boston, had voluntarily placed herself in the middle of an Irish brawl. She ordered Elizabeth not to return to the newspaper, but Elizabeth ignored her mother and went anyway. What she found there, however, seemed a wall of ice. The other reporters pointedly ignored her. The city editor nodded and refused to speak to her. She was finally called to the managing editor's office, who told her she had produced a wonderful story, one of the best in the paper that year, but that they would not be able to pay for the work and he could not let her work for nothing.

Elizabeth was devastated. She went home and locked herself in her room, only then giving into the flood of hot tears that had been threatening to spill. She refused her mother's entreaties to eat and tried to ignore the condemnations for doing such work, that she not only had no job, but she would also be shunned now by polite society.

When her father, a partner at one of Boston's largest law firms, returned from his out-of-town business trip, he took his daughter to the Parker House, where they had a magnificent lunch and each a piece of the restaurant's famous Boston Cream Pie. He talked with her at length, urging her to press on with her dream to work in the newspaper field. "It is a marvelous story, Elizabeth," he said, "and I'm not saying this because you're my daughter. You have a gift, and you must use it. Your mother and I would both love to see you settled and with a family, but I read that story, and it was so good I nearly wept."

Two days later, a telegram arrived at the Putnam house. It

was from John Osborne, managing editor of the New York *World*, who'd seen the story and, in his words, was "bowled over." He asked her to come to New York for an interview. She went and was offered a job, a paying job, and a week after the interview, her parents accompanied her to New York, helping her to settle in a highly-recommended hotel for young women. Her mother was in a state near hysteria at the idea of her daughter alone and working in New York City, but Elizabeth knew she'd accepted her decision.

She'd told her father of the trip to Mississippi, asking him to say nothing to her mother unless pressed. She knew what her mother would think of a young woman traveling alone by train all over the country, even if it *was* 1915.

The train pulled into the small Oxford station. The stationmaster himself retrieved her two trunks from the baggage car, setting them on the platform. She arranged with him to have them delivered to the Oxford Hotel, where she'd reserved a room. Elizabeth then walked to the university, was directed to the History Department, and was informed by a receptionist that Professor Seale had just left for his last lecture of the day. The auditorium was in the building next door, and soon Elizabeth quietly slipped into the large room and took an empty seat at the back. Professor Seale's subject for the lecture was the First Battle of Bull Run, also known as the Battle of Manassas.

"And that, ladies and gentlemen, concludes our class for today. Let me remind you about the short test on Wednesday, and that your mid-term essays are due next Friday at 2 p.m. That's one week from today, and not a minute after. I know that poses no hardship, since each of you has already been diligently at work." The news was greeted with the expected loud groans. Professor Littleton Seale smiled.

The large lecture hall came alive with the noise of young men and women shifting from their seats, conversations starting up or resuming, and the happy sounds of students knowing their classes were over for the week with nothing standing in the way of their plans for the weekend, except perhaps that essay. A few students came up to him with questions and observations but finally left, and he began to gather his lecture notes.

"That was quite a lecture," Elizabeth said. "You should consider the speaking circuit."

Seale looked up. The young woman who'd spoken with a cultured Northern accent was only slightly older than his students. She wore an attractively tailored suit, with the loose-fitting jacket perfectly aligned with the dress that flowed from a slim waist to her ankles. Her large-brimmed hat was worn at a slight angle, set off by two small feathers. She wasn't what his male students would call "keen," a description he was still not entirely sure the meaning of, but she was certainly attractive, with an interesting face filled with intelligence.

"I've come a long way to meet you," she said. "New York, in fact. My name is Elizabeth Putnam."

He shook her extended hand. "And what, might I ask, is there about a history professor at the University of Mississippi that would induce a young woman to travel all the way from New York?"

She smiled. "Your book, *Confederate Spies and Saboteurs in the Civil War*. It's made quite the splash in publishing circles.

My newspaper editor had sent me to St. Louis and Memphis to cover other stories, and he said that as long I was in the region, I needed to go to Oxford and meet the famous Professor Littleton Seale."

He smiled. "Ah, I see. A newspaper reporter."

"You say that like I have some infectious disease." She smiled as she handed him her business card.

"Not at all," he said, looking at the card. "It's only that I'm not accustomed to newspaper reporters sitting in my lectures. Shouldn't you be out looking for stories on murderers and thieves?"

"The press does cover serious subjects, Professor Seale," she said. "Although, I admit, more than a few lurid ones are thrown in to attract readers. But I was wondering if I might make an appointment to talk with you about the book? I've read it; in fact, I've read it twice. And I've discovered I'm not alone in believing that this is almost a work of autobiography."

Seale laughed. "I was 10 years old when the Civil War ended, Miss Putnam, so it's hardly a book about myself."

The young woman frowned lightly. "I'm surprised, Professor. It seems so personal and immediate that I was sure you were writing about your experiences." She smiled again. "Still, your subject is fascinating, and I'm certain our readers will enjoy a story about the author. And my editor has told me not to return to New York until I've interviewed you."

Seale stood quietly for a moment, considering her and her request. "All right, Miss Putnam, we can speak. I'll escort you to the faculty lounge; we can talk there and avail ourselves of coffee and tea."

3

Tell me not in mournful numbers.
Life is but an empty dream!
For the soul is dead that slumbers,
And things are not what they seem.

—from "A Psalm of Life"

The October afternoon would have been considered warm in New York, but it was cool in northern Mississippi. Elizabeth could see the tree leaves just beginning to consider changing color; she'd left behind a growing riot of red, yellow, and orange in New York.

"Is this a day trip," Seale said as they walked, "or do you intend to stay for a time?"

"I have a room at the hotel," she said. "I wasn't sure how long it would take me to find you, and whether or not you had the time to talk."

As they walked, she covertly glanced at the man walking next to her. She knew he was 60, having been born in 1855. He was about two inches taller than she was, so his height must have been about 5 foot 8. His silvery gray hair oddly made him seem younger; she thought it might be the longish style he had. He was an attractive man, with almost merry eyes, full mouth, and a well-proportioned nose, but he wasn't what her Smith friends would call strikingly handsome. His accent was what might be called "cultured Southern."

He escorted her into the administration building, to a spacious first-floor room. Several men were talking, and they all looked at Professor Seale and her as they entered.

"This is Miss Elizabeth Putnam from New York," Seale said, introducing her to his colleagues. "She happened to be passing through Oxford and stopped by to ask me about my book." The men nodded and smiled; two shook her hand and greeted her formally. But Elizabeth could see she was a definite oddity in a room where women might not usually be seen. She also noted that he hadn't introduced her as a reporter.

"Coffee or tea?" Seale said.

"Tea, please," she said. He walked over to a sideboard and was soon back with a tray of two cups of tea, a glass container of sugar with a matching small pitcher of milk, and spoons.

"Please, help yourself, Miss Putnam."

They talked, mostly about the book. But she was surprised that Seale seemed interested in her as well, asking questions about her background and education.

"How did you become interested in the subject of spies?" she asked him.

"It started with my research on the war itself," Seale said. "While there had been several books about spies on the Northern side, the only ones I could find on the Southern side were about Southern belles in hoop skirts, spying on Yankee generals. And most of those read like badly written fiction. But I knew there were spies for the South; they simply weren't well researched. I began to read and talk with colleagues and historians at other schools. Slowly, the idea for a book came together."

"You devote an entire chapter to the Gray Wisp," she said. "Was his work well documented?"

It might have been her imagination, but she thought she saw the professor take on a more guarded look.

"No," he said finally, "it wasn't. He was one of the most famous, or infamous, spies of the war on either side, but very little is known about him. There are some vague references in several official Confederate government papers, but nothing definitive. A few officers, especially on the Union side, claim to have met him or someone like him. If you read the various memoirs, he was supposedly seen over all the war fronts, from east to west. It would have been physically impossible for him to be in as many places as people claimed, and often at the same time. I think he became a talisman of a kind."

"You made that clear in the book, and then you say he operated in the eastern theater of the war, especially Virginia, Maryland, and Pennsylvania."

He nodded slowly, and now Elizabeth was certain that Professor Seale was weighing every word. "That's where the most credible reports place him," he said. "He seems to have been closely connected to General Lee."

Elizabeth decided it was time for greater candor. "My editor in New York tells me that his mother-in-law, because of a kindness by General Grant, traveled from Philadelphia to somewhere in the South, specifically to meet the Wisp. She never spoke of the place or the meeting. All she ever said was that she'd no idea how bound up her husband and even she herself had been with the man."

Seale stared intently at her. "Her name was Mrs. John Haygood, if memory serves."

He'd surprised her. "You knew Mrs. Haygood?"

Seale shook his head. "No. I met her once, when I was 12."

Elizabeth felt the steadily building excitement of a story. "Her son-in-law, John Osborne and my editor at the New York *World*, said the Wisp saved both her husband's life *and* his military reputation. And he's read your book so many times, and that chapter in particular, that he's convinced you know the Wisp and actually talked with him for the book." She paused. "It sounds like you do know him."

"What are you asking me for, Miss Putnam?" Seale said. "This doesn't sound like an interview about the book."

"I'm asking you to provide me an introduction to the man. I want to interview him. And I know my editor and his wife would like to meet him."

She expected the professor to refuse outright and to ask her to leave. Instead, Seale stared at her for a moment, and then he removed a calling card from his pocket and scribbled something on the back, handing it to her.

"I don't know if that's possible," he said. "But if you come by my house tomorrow at 10 a.m., I should have an answer. So you know, if there's agreement to do what you're asking, the man who was the Wisp does not live here in Oxford or anywhere close. Travel would be required."

"Do you think he might agree?" she said.

"I don't know what's possible. But I will have a better idea by tomorrow."

At the hotel, as she dressed for dinner, Elizabeth considered Seale's responses. He acknowledged that the Gray Wisp was a real person but not living in Oxford. She had seen a flicker of his eyes when she mentioned Mrs. Haygood, and then he admitted he knew exactly what she was talking about. And he was not surprised at all when she mentioned General Grant.

She was convinced he knew that story but, for whatever reason, had declined to include it in his chapter about the Wisp.

Before going downstairs for dinner, she reread part of that chapter. And then she looked at the biographical information about Professor Seale. He was a native Mississippian, it read, born in Brookhaven. After she was seated in the dining room, she asked her waiter, who told her he was a university student "studying history under Dr. Seale," about Brookhaven.

"It's about 70 miles south of Jackson, ma'am," he said. "It's the county seat of Lincoln County. I have an uncle by marriage from there."

"A county named after President Lincoln?"

He smiled and nodded. "It happened during Reconstruction. Pike County was split into two counties, and some pieces added from other counties, with the new county named for the President."

"Did Brookhaven have any particular role or importance in the Civil War?" she said.

"My uncle told the story many times," the waiter said. "It almost missed the direct impact of the war, until Grierson's Raid in 1863."

"Grierson's Raid?"

"It was a group of Union cavalry that traveled from Tennessee to Baton Rouge, tearing up railroad tracks, and burning Confederate supplies and some large planters' homes.

It was a diversion by the Yankees that allowed them to confuse the Confederates and cross the Mississippi south of Vicksburg almost unnoticed. Grierson and his troops avoided Jackson and almost missed Brookhaven, but for some unknown reason they turned eastward at the last minute and rode into the town. My uncle said they burned the railway station, but the fire spread to other buildings on the main street. With all the mayhem, only one civilian died, an old gentleman who owned the town's primary general store."

Elizabeth smiled. "I'm surprised you're so knowledgeable about it."

He grinned. "You should know my uncle. And Professor Seale was there, a mere boy when the raid happened. He's talked about it in his class. I'm sure the story grew over time into a legend, but the professor is very meticulous about sticking to facts. And if you're from the South, you know your Civil War, or at least the stories handed down about it." He laughed. "I think we're still fighting it."

4

All these scenes I do behold,
These, and many left untold,
In that building long and low;
While the wheel goes round and round,
With a drowsy, dreaming sound,
And the spinners backward go.

—from "The Ropewalk"

Promptly at 10 the next morning, Elizabeth walked up the steps of Professor Seale's home. It had been a short walk from the hotel, with directions provided by the desk clerk. The house was in the Queen Anne Style, with a wraparound front porch, two stories, and an attic level. It was painted a cheerful yellow with black trim.

Even before she rang the bell, the door opened, and Professor Seale welcomed her and ushered her inside.

Standing behind him was a woman who was obviously his wife. She was about five foot four, with solid gray hair done up in the old-fashioned Gibson Girl style, held together by a beautifully enameled clip atop her head. She had clear blue eyes and dimples in her rosy, very lightly powdered cheeks. Her dark blue dress had a high neckline and extended to her ankles. This might be a small university town in Mississippi, but Mrs. Seale obviously kept up with women's fashion.

"Miss Elizabeth Putnam," the professor said, "this is my wife, Beatrice. I've told her about your story, and she's been very eager to meet you."

"Welcome, Miss Putnam," Mrs. Seale said, in a heavily Southern but clearly upper-class accent. "Welcome to Oxford, and welcome to our home."

They escorted Elizabeth to the parlor, and a servant woman brought tea.

"Miss Putnam," Mrs. Seale said, "this is Hetty. Hetty, Miss Putnam has come all the way from New York."

Hetty nodded and smiled, quickly turning and leaving the room.

"Has she been with you long?" Elizabeth said. She could see that Mrs. Seale had spoken directly to the woman.

"Hetty was born deaf," Mrs. Seale said. "She's very good at reading lips, and Littleton here knows sign language. She's also very shy with strangers."

"Growing up," Professor Seale said, "I had an aunt who was born mute. Her youngest brother, who was also my uncle but close enough in age to be like a brother, learned sign language, and he taught me most of the signs. Hetty came to us about 20 years ago; she'd been a student at the Mississippi School for the Deaf and Mute in Jackson. She'd graduated, and my uncle had asked if we might employ her."

"She's a wonderful cook," Mrs. Seale said. "They teach all the students there a skill or trade. Her mother had died, and her father found himself unable to care for her. She's really become part of the family."

"Miss Putnam," the professor said, "I promised you an answer to your request. I should mention, first, that I did call your editor in New York, to verify that you were indeed who you said you were. This is no reflection on you, but I needed to make sure. Then I telephoned the man who was the Gray Wisp, and he's agreed to your interview. He's old now, and while he doesn't need or particularly want the publicity, he'll meet with you. I think he understands he's part of history, a history that will be lost with his eventual death, unless he tells his story. And I've convinced him that you may be the one to tell it." He paused. "His name is Sam McClure, by the way."

"That's wonderful, professor," Elizabeth said. "Thank you so much for arranging this. You sound as if this possibility has happened before now. Have others sought interviews?"

"You're the third reporter to call, Miss Putnam," Mrs. Seale said. "Littleton has served as something of a screen, and you're the first he's felt comfortable with."

"I might add, Miss Putnam," Professor Seale said, "that the previous applicants all were clearly looking for what they called a 'scoop;' they were more interested in personal fame for learning the identity of the Gray Wisp. You were very straightforward when we talked, and I detected a certain level of professional disinterest. While it sounds like a contradiction, that disinterest tells me that you will write a better and fairer story than someone interested in personal glory or sensationalism."

"Professor Seale," Elizabeth said, "why aren't you telling the story yourself? You might have included it in your book."

"Because I'm too close to it, Miss Putnam, too close. I doubt I could have impartially told the story had I revealed the man's identity."

Elizabeth wasn't sure what that might mean but sensed now wasn't the time to pursue it. "I believe you said travel would be involved?"

Seale nodded. "Yes. And Beatrice will accompany you."

"That isn't necessary," Elizabeth said, surprise in her voice.

"Miss Putnam," Mrs. Seale said, "you'll learn shortly why we're so protective. The man once known as the Gray Wisp has been a huge influence on my life, on Littleton's, and on every member of our family. He was very young when he went to war, too young to be conscripted, in fact, and it was his fate to be the only male surviving sibling. His two older brothers both died in the war. And not long after he returned, his father suffered a stroke, and he found himself head of a large extended family. That family included Littleton, his four sisters, and his mother; another sister-in-law and her two daughters; and the sister who was mute. Before and after his father's stroke, he also became responsible for several members of two other families."

"Sam McClure is my uncle," Professor Seale said, "but he's also much more than that. My father died at Shiloh along with one of Sam's brothers. I was seven. When Sam returned from the war, he was still only 15. He became head of the family at 16. For me, and for my sisters, he served as a replacement father. He made sure I attended Vanderbilt and then Yale. He escorted each of my sisters and Beatrice here down the aisle at their weddings. He provided the food on our table, he held my family together when my mother died too young, and he saw us through very difficult days after the war. The plan had been for him to attend Harvard and become an attorney, or perhaps even an actor, but he had to set those dreams aside to care for the family."

"An actor?" Elizabeth said.

Professor Seale nodded, smiling. "Sam found school boring, except for the recitation of poetry. There's likely no one on the planet who can recite Longfellow from memory like Sam can. And he used his emotive and acting skills when he went to war. They are what helped make him so successful as a spy.

"None of us knew he'd been the Gray Wisp, until that day in 1867 when the Haygoods arrived, wanting to meet the man who saved John Haygood's life at the Battle of the Wilderness and later his reputation. The rest of the family learned Sam had been the Wisp the following year, when General Lee visited Brookhaven specifically to see Sam. He blurted it out, assuming the family knew. It was a considerable shock, because of the stories that had attached themselves to the legend of the Gray Wisp."

Two days later, Elizabeth took the Monday train to Jackson, Mrs. Seale seated next to her. Elizabeth chafed a bit at the idea of a having to travel with a chaperone (or perhaps watchdog), but she found Mrs. Seale a pleasant and informative traveling companion.

"How did you and Professor Seale meet?" Elizabeth said.

Beatrice smiled. "When I was seven, my family moved to Brookhaven from Alabama. We met at Sam's house. Littleton was four years older, but I had this huge crush on him from the time I first saw him. He knew me and my family, but I was so much younger that he probably just saw me as some little girl. Which I was. Years later, when he came home from Yale with his Ph.D. and a job offer at the university in Oxford, we sat next to each other at his welcome home dinner at the McClures. Littleton remembered me, and of course I remembered him. And we talked, and then, when he began teaching, he'd write letters. He wrote the most wonderful letters. He'd come home to see family, and I suppose me as well. And one time he arrived with a ring and asked me to marry him."

Elizabeth smiled. "That's a lovely story."

"The times were hard," Mrs. Seale said. "But Sam held it all together." She smiled. "Our firstborn is named for him, and the three boys who followed all have Samuel as their middle name."

"He helped your family, too?"

"We were part of his family," she said. "But that's more his story to tell." And then she fell silent.

"What can you tell me about the family?" Elizabeth said.

The older woman smiled. "Sam's father Franklin was married twice. The first time was to a Margaret Fletcher. They had four children, Martha, who was Littleton's mother; Hugh, who died at the Battle of Franklin near Nashville; James, who died with Littleton's father Jarvis at Shiloh; and Cora Beth. She's the one that was born mute.

"Franklin was an officer in the Mexican War, and sometime after hostilities ended, he paid a visit to his commanding officer in Philadelphia. It was there he met the officer's daughter, Louisa Williamson, and they were married after something of a whirlwind courtship. He was 45 at the time, and Louisa was 17, younger than Franklin's two oldest children. I'm afraid there were some bad feelings about the surprise of it all. Without saying a word of warning to anyone in the family, Franklin returned to Brookhaven with a young bride who was already with child. Sam was born in 1850; he was the only child from the second marriage.

"From what the family has said, including Littleton, from a very early age, Sam could track anything in the woods; he often says he feels more at home in the woods than in the town. And his skill with horses was and still is amazing. It's as if by instinct they know to trust him. He was five when he rode his first horse, a stallion that the menfolk said was too wild to be ridden. But with Sam, he was as docile as could be."

"If he was born in 1850," Elizabeth said, "he would have been 11 when the war started?"

"That's right," Mrs. Seale said. "And he had just turned 13 when he and a friend ran off and enlisted."

"Thirteen?" Elizabeth said, amazement in her voice. "The Gray Wisp enlisted at 13 and was 15 when the war ended?"

Mrs. Seale nodded. "I know it sounds impossible, but that's what happened. It was more common than most people remember." She paused. "A lot of children fought in the war on both sides."

5

He was a valiant youth, and his face,
like the face of the morning,
Gladdened the earth with its light,
and ripened thought into action.

—from "Evangeline"

They changed train lines in Jackson; a different railroad would bring them to Brookhaven.

"The southbound won't be too crowded on a Monday," Mrs. Seale said. "Now, if this were Friday, it would be packed, with all the legislators and students heading to New Orleans for the weekend."

"I take it that New Orleans is a popular destination?"

"It's quite something to see," Mrs. Seale said. "Now, you might want to note that the railroad is part of Sam's story. I don't think he'd mind me telling this small piece. Are you familiar with Grierson's Raid during the Civil War?"

Elizabeth nodded. "A student mentioned it Friday. It was in 1863?"

"That's right. A cavalry unit of about 1,700 came down through the center of Mississippi, part of a diversion General Grant had ordered to help him cross the Mississippi south of Vicksburg. It was too large for small Confederate units to take on, and too small to order a large army to chase it or confront it. Littleton has often said it was a brilliant tactic, even though it brought considerable woe to Mississippi.

"Part of what they did was tear up railroad tracks, often for several miles. The point was to disrupt the supply lines to the Confederate army defending Vicksburg and armies in the east. Track was torn up, stations burned, and sometimes large plantation homes and warehouses full of cotton were burned as well. There was little resistance; the able-bodied men were elsewhere in the army, with only old men, boys, and women left to defend towns and homes. Surprisingly, there were few civilian deaths."

"I believe the student said there was only one person died in Brookhaven," Elizabeth said.

"There could have been considerably more, if it weren't for luck," Mrs. Seale said. "The Union troops came riding into town from the west. The townspeople were surprised; the report had been they were riding southward toward Port Gibson. The word of their impending arrival came with only minutes to spare, and about 500 townspeople, many of them women, grabbed whatever firearms they could find and stood waiting. Grierson had his troops ride right through the crowd; they made straight for the train station and set it afire. A wind came up and the fire began to spread to adjacent buildings. Then Grierson ordered his men to stop feeding the fire and start fighting it. Their intention had been only to burn the station, but they managed to burn several other buildings as well."

Mrs. Seale shook her head. "But, as you mentioned, there was only one death. That one death, however, was consequential. It was Sam McClure's grandfather. Like his grandson, he was also named Samuel. Sam adored the man, whom

I believe was 75 at the time. Yankee soldiers came into the McClure's general store, right across the street from the burning train station. Samuel struggled with them to stop them looting what few goods that were for sale. An officer pushed the old man, who fell and hit his head. He died in Sam's arms; the boy was all of 13. Four days later, Sam and a friend made their way to Jackson and enlisted."

"He wanted to avenge his grandfather's death?"

Mrs. Seale shook her head. "It's more complicated than that, I think. The war had come home. Sam was never one for vengeance, then or now. Even he knew the death had been an accident. But, young as he was, he felt compelled to do something to defend his home and his family. And so he enlisted. He was a tall boy, and so was his friend, Nate, who enlisted with him. Recruiters were getting desperate to fill quotas, so if you said you were 16, that was sufficient. By the time his father got wind of what had happened, Sam had already been sent to the east. That is a huge part of Sam's story. He was 13 years old, and he was wanted by none other than General Robert E. Lee himself for the Army of Northern Virginia."

"How did General Lee know about the boy?"

"General Lee knew his father, Franklin, who'd served with Lee in the Mexican War. Sam's father had a significant reputation from that war, and he and Lee had continued to correspond for years after. In those letters, Franklin had told Lee all about Sam, his tracking abilities in the woods, his hunting exploits, and his skill with horses. Franklin's own experiences in the Mexican War played a role as well, and I'm afraid I don't know more than that. But for whatever reason, it was all very important to General Lee, and his staff in Richmond was alerted by telegraph that Sam had enlisted. Lee had him sent to Richmond." She patted Elizabeth's hand. "And there, my knowledge runs out. Littleton knows more but will rarely talk about it. I was surprised as anyone at that book chapter on the Gray Wisp, because it was more than I ever heard Litt say about Sam's history. I do know that he and Sam had been talking, and that Sam agreed to the inclusion of the general information. Oh, goodness me, I've talked your ear off so long that we're almost in Brookhaven. Sam said someone would meet us, but he didn't say whom."

It was 3 p.m. when the train pulled into the small station, comprised of a ticket office, small waiting room, and an open-air platform. Several passengers alighted, and Mrs. Seale directed the attendant to their baggage.

Families were greeting relatives, men were shaking hands, young children were weaving around adults. And then she heard Mrs. Seale. "Why, look. It's Sam."

Elizabeth looked up. Walking towards them with a huge smile on his face was perhaps the handsomest man she'd ever seen. He was six feet tall, she guessed, with high cheekbones, blue eyes so dark they seemed almost black, and a dimpled chin. His wavy, longish black hair was parted down the middle and touched his collar. He was broad-shouldered but slender. He wore a white dress shirt and bow tie but without a coat. And pushed pack a bit jauntily on his head was a boater with a red-and-blue-striped band. She would guess his age to be mid-to-late 20s.

If this is Sam McClure, Elizabeth thought, *he hasn't aged in 40 years. And he's gorgeous.*

"Aunt Bea!" he said, as he threw his arms around Mrs.

Seale and lifted her in the air.

"Samuel David McClure," Mrs. Seale said, laughing, "put me down this minute!"

He set her down gently. "I'm so glad to see you, Aunt Bea, that I got carried away."

"Now," she said, smoothing her skirt, "I want to introduce Miss Elizabeth Putnam of the New York *World*."

Sam turned to Elizabeth, smiling. "Miss Putnam," he said, taking her hand, "it's a pleasure."

"You're Sam McClure?" Elizabeth said, knowing her face likely betrayed the shock she was feeling.

He looked at her puzzled, and then at Mrs. Seale.

"Oh, my," Mrs. Seale said, laughing, "I thoroughly confused you. This is Sam McClure III, Sam's grandson."

Young Sam joined Mrs. Seale in laughing, and Elizabeth followed.

"I'll arrange with the attendant to have your trunks delivered," he said, "and then we'll drive to Papa's house."

"Oh," Elizabeth said, "I should stay at a hotel in town."

"Papa told me to bring you and Aunt Bea to his house," he said. "Your rooms have been readied. And I'm afraid you'll find all hotel accommodations unavailable because of the county fair starting Wednesday. It's Lincoln County's major event of the year, and people are already arriving."

"I can't impose on your grandfather," Elizabeth said.

"It's no imposition, Miss Putnam," he said. "And if you need transportation, my house is across the street from Papa's." He looked at Mrs. Seale. "Papa just bought a new Oldsmobile 42 touring car, and it's a dream to drive. He won't drive it, of course, he still prefers his horse, but he has me and everyone else serving as his chauffeur. After I see you and Miss Putnam to his house, I need to fetch him at the sawmill."

After speaking to the attendant, Sam escorted them to the waiting car. Elizabeth didn't know much about automobiles, but she knew this one was not unlike her father's 1914 Cadillac Touring Car. Sam started to help Mrs. Seale into the front seat, but she shook her head. "I'll never get used to these things, Samuel McClure, so let me sit in the back. Miss Putnam can share the front seat with you."

Sam looked at Elizabeth and smiled with a questioning turn of his head, and she nodded. He helped Mrs. Seale into the rear seat, and then Elizabeth into the front seat. He pointed to McClure's General Store across the street.

"It's more of a farm and feed store now," he said, almost shouting over the noise of the automobile engine. "The main general store is a few blocks from here." With a brief lurch, they were soon motoring their way through the streets of Brookhaven.

6

There are things of which I may not speak;
There are dreams that cannot die;
There are thoughts that make the strong heart weak,
And bring a pallor to the cheek,
And a mist before the eye.
And the words of that fatal song
Come over me like a chill:
"A boy's will is the wind's will,
And the thoughts of you are long, long thoughts."

—from "My Lost Youth"

They drove through what to Elizabeth looked like many small towns in America. The cluster of businesses in downtown soon gave way to churches, small corner shops, and residences. They turned onto Cherry Street, and soon Sam steered into a graveled drive leading to a very large mid-to-late Victorian house. Like the Seale's house in Oxford, it was painted a light yellow with black shutters and trim and had a formal garden in front. It was easily the largest house on the block; the home occupied a double lot.

"This is Papa's house," Sam said, and then he pointed across the street to a bungalow. "I live there, just across the street, so I'm available if you need anything." He walked them up to the porch and opened the screen door. "Miss Sophie! Guests are here!"

"I'm coming, young Sam," a voice called from within the house.

There appeared a heavy-set black woman, a bit on the short side, Elizabeth thought, with snow-white hair and a huge smile on her face. She would guess the woman to be in her 50s.

"You must be Miss Putnam," she said, extending her hand. "I'm Sophie, and we welcome you to Mr. Sam's house."

"Thank you," Elizabeth said. "I hope I'm not inconveniencing anyone."

"Not at all, young lady," Sophie said. "And Miss Beatrice, we haven't seen you since June. You better come more often, or you'll forget what we look like."

Mrs. Seale laughed and then hugged her. "I'm so glad to see you, Sophie. And it has been too long. Littleton sends his regards, and he's rather in hopes that, when he comes this weekend, he might find Miss Sophie's red velvet cake."

Sophie laughed. "He would, that boy. He was always one for the sweets. Now, all of you come in, and young Sam here will show you to your rooms. I expect you'd like to freshen up."

As Sam escorted them up the stairs, he explained that the men from the station would bring their trunks directly to their rooms. As they reached the second floor, he nodded toward a door on the left. "Aunt Bea, you and Uncle Litt when he comes are there. And Miss Putnam, you're across the way here on the right." He opened the door.

It was a spacious, airy room, and she saw it faced the deep backyard filled with trees and small gardens, including what was obviously the kitchen garden. The furniture was old-fashioned but solid and well-cared for; it included a fourposter bed with a canopy and an armoire for her clothes. Sam nodded toward another door. "Your bathroom is through there."

"My bathroom?"

"Papa had indoor plumbing installed about three years ago, which, I understand, made him an immediate hero with the women of the family. And now I must be off to fetch him at the sawmill."

Minutes later, Elizabeth heard a knock at her door; the men had arrived with her trunk. She offered a gratuity, but the men refused, saying it had been taken care of. It took her some time to unpack, but when she finished, she changed quickly from her traveling dress.

It seemed a boisterous, personable family, she thought, very unlike her own quiet, reserved, and always proper Bostonian family at home. The house was large; she quickly counted six bedroom doors on this floor. And she could see from her window that a one-story extension had been built from what was likely the kitchen. Whatever the extension was, it had its own fireplace; she could see the chimney.

For several minutes, she worked with her notes, writing down the main points of what Mrs. Seale had said on the train as well a few brief jots about young Sam. The size of the house and the reference to a general store, a farm and feed store, and a sawmill suggested the family was very well-to-do, at least by Brookhaven standards.

She had just finished her notes when she heard something of a commotion from downstairs.

Descending the stairs, she saw young Sam standing in the foyer with an older man of almost the same height, perhaps slightly shorter. She stopped part way down the stairs, surprised at how much the young man and the older man resembled each other.

Young Sam's older counterpart had what she could only call a silver mane of hair. His beard and moustache were silver as well, and he had the same dark blue eyes of his grandson. Like young Sam, he was broad-shouldered but slender. He looked up the stairs and saw her. His broad smile suddenly faded into something almost hidden and expressionless. Something about her appearance, she thought, had surprised him.

She knew immediately this was the man once called the Gray Wisp.

He stood there, staring at her, to the point that young Sam and Mrs. Seale both could see it, as could Sophie standing by Mrs. Seale.

To break the awkward silence, she resumed her downward steps. Sam gave his head a shake as if to collect himself. And then he resumed his smile.

"Miss Putnam," he said, taking her hand as she offered it, "I'm Sam McClure. I apologize for my momentary silence. It's my pleasure to make your acquaintance. I trust my family have welcomed you, and your room meets your needs?"

His voice was deep; the man's presence suggested a lion-like strength she'd encountered only with her father. It was a gentle strength but a solid, enduring one. This man was like an oak, she thought, and she understood what both Professor Seale and his wife had meant when they described him. He seemed almost courtly, but she knew from reading the book and from the physical presence she was now experiencing that he was fully capable of the work attributed to the Gray Wisp. He would make a true friend and a formidable enemy.

"Mr. McClure," she said, "I'm delighted to meet you. Everything has met my needs perfectly; everyone's been most kind. And I thank you for opening your home to me."

"I hope you don't mind," he said, "but we're going to pull you right into the family and have our supper in the kitchen. It's where we usually have our meals; the dining room is reserved for Sunday dinners and formal occasions." He offered her his arm, which she took, and escorted her to the kitchen.

The table was large enough to seat at least 14. The kitchen was bustling with several people, and Sophie was handing off dishes to a young black woman, whom she'd later learn was named Patsy. Another woman, who was white and likely in her 60s or 70s, was pulling a pan of dinner rolls from the oven. A third woman of about the same age was pouring water into glasses.

"Everyone," Sam McClure said, "if you haven't met Miss Elizabeth Putnam of the New York *World* newspaper, now you have. She's our guest, and I'm giving her full authority to talk with all of you about what she's writing for her newspaper." He proceeded to introduce the people present. The two older women shared the last name of O'Brien, as did two teenaged boys who had bounded in from the yard and started roughhousing with young Sam. The kitchen was chaotic with greetings for Mrs. Seale, general conversation, and Sophie giving last-minute orders to Patsy.

The room went silent, however, when the older woman who'd been pouring water started using her hands to speak to Sam McClure. Elizabeth knew it was signing language, and she could tell by the expression on the faces of young Sam, Sophie, and Mrs. Seale that they understood the signs being made.

"Yes, Cora," said the older Sam, "I know. I was struck by the same thing."

"I didn't even realize it until Aunt Cora just said it," Mrs. Seale said. "But she's exactly right."

When Elizabeth realized that everyone in the room was staring at her, she blushed. She wasn't sure what to say or how to proceed.

"Miss Putnam," the older Sam said, "we're being discourteous. What has surprised us all is how much you resemble my late wife."

"My goodness," Sophie said, "I missed it until Miss Cora said it. She looks just like Miss Janie."

"Let us say grace and eat," Sam said. "Young Sam, will you give the blessing?"

"Yes, Papa."

Still surprised by Sam McClure's words, Elizabeth focused on the words prayed by his grandson, and she knew what she was hearing was coming directly from the young man's heart.

After dinner, the family dispersed; Mrs. Seale said she had letters to write. The older Sam suggested they talk in his study.

The room could hardly be called a library. No walls were lined with bookshelves; no tables were waiting for someone to set volumes down to study. Instead, it was a smallish room, with two chairs in front of a mahogany desk, and a side table containing framed photographs. Above the table was a painting, a portrait. At first it startled her; she did indeed resemble the woman in the painting. This must be, she thought, a portrait of the young Jane, Mr. McClure's late wife.

A bookshelf was positioned near the desk, and only one shelf had books, the others being crowded with files and loose papers. The books were the Bible, a biblical commentary and dictionary, and a leatherbound set of the complete works of Longfellow that looked well read.

"Mrs. Seale told me about your love for Longfellow," Elizabeth said.

"Warned you, did she?" he said, grinning. "Please be seated, Miss Putnam. And I promise not to recite any poems."

This man, she thought, was charming. He could poke fun at himself. His voice seemed ideal for recitation or even acting; Mrs. Seale had been right. Before she left, whenever that was, she'd ask him to recite a poem.

"I know," he said, "that interviews are usually a series of questions posed by the reporter or interviewer. But I'd like you to consider an alternative. I don't think I can explain what I did in the Civil War without explaining what happened before, and what happened after. My life isn't easily compartmentalized like that; I don't think anyone's life is. I will, of course, answer any questions you might have, but it might be better if I explained it like I was telling a story. It will all be true, or as true as I can remember it. It was, after all, fifty years ago.

"Now, I'd love to be able to do it all at once, but I have the work at the mill, the stores, and the stables. We will need to take breaks or, if you'd like, you can accompany me and see what it is I do, because the work is part of the story as well. You're also free to talk with family members, including Sophie and Patsy, because I consider them family. You might want to talk with some of our customers and friends and our church pastor. I think you should get to know Brookhaven a little bit, because to know Brookhaven is to know the Gray Wisp. And I don't believe this story can really be told chronologically. If I did, I'd likely leave out the best parts. Does this sound reasonable to you, or were you expecting to conduct a traditional interview and then return to New York?"

"I have no expectations, Mr. McClure," Elizabeth said. "I have questions, of course, about what you did in the war, and what a lot of people claimed you did. I like what you're suggesting, but I already feel like I'm taking advantage of your hospitality."

McClure smiled. "We always have guests here, Miss Putnam. Sophie and Patsy can handle far more than a young woman and Beatrice, and Litt when he comes. We have family flowing in and out, from Pennsylvania, Louisiana, Texas, and even Brazil. When Sophie needs help, she's not shy about asking for it. We also have two housemaids, Margaret and Harriett, sisters, in fact, not here right now because they've been tending to an ill brother. I expect them back tomorrow."

"And young Sam is your chauffeur?"

McClure laughed. "Young Sam is that, but he also happens to be an outstanding attorney, a graduate of the Harvard Law School and editor of the *Law Review*. He graduated first in his class and scandalized his parents when he turned down half a dozen job offers in big Eastern cities to come to Brookhaven. He works with a law firm here, Foster Perkins. You can probably tell by his accent that he was born and raised in the north. My son, Sam's father, and my daughter-in-law live in Pennsylvania, and that's where Sam and his brothers were born and raised. But he spent almost all his summers and many holidays here, and this is where he decided he wanted to live and work. But you should ask him about it."

She stared at the elderly man for a moment. "All right, Mr. McClure, let's do this the way you've suggested. From what you're saying, I'm going to end up with more than a story about the Gray Wisp in the Civil War."

He smiled. "Yes, you will. Far more. And I apologize again for my surprise. As you can see from the painting here, you do remind me of my late wife Jane. And not only in features. When he called, Littleton told me I might be surprised when I met you, and while he didn't say why, he was right. From the time she was very young, my Jane had some very set ideas about life, and I suspect you do as well."

He was quiet for a time before speaking. "As you know, Miss Putnam, every story has a before, a during, and an after. I think it's how we make sense of the stories we hear, to organize them that way. Novels are like that, generally. The news stories a writer such as yourself write seem somewhat different, as you start with the most important point first. Other kinds of newspaper and periodical stories, the ones that aren't really about news, follow a more before-during-after approach."

Elizabeth nodded. She was surprised that he understood news and story writing so well.

"But life isn't that way, is it? The before, during, and after all become jumbled up in real life. Tonight at supper, you may not have noticed how slowly my sister Cora Beth and Leorinda O'Brien ate, and they ate every last morsel on their plates. I do the same, and my children do as well, because they learned from us. Young Sam, on the other hand, eats quickly, although he, too, rarely leaves anything on his plate, likely because he enjoys Sophie's cooking so much. My generation eats as it does because we remember the years when food was scarce."

"I noticed that when I ate with Professor Seale and Mrs. Seale in Oxford," Elizabeth said.

"There was a time," McClure said, "when you could never take food for granted, first during the war and then the first years afterward. Common things like coffee and salt disappeared. At the end of the war, basic foodstuffs like flour and corn meal commanded prices that would astound you. At table, we ate slowly and sparingly, to make food last as long as possible. Those were learned habits never forgotten. That's just a small example of what I mean when I say before, during, and after stay jumbled up in real lives."

He smiled. "I could start my story anywhere, but I think the best place to start might be a few months after the war ended. We can talk for a bit tonight; I know you've had a long day and need your rest. But perhaps we'll make a brief start and then continue tomorrow. You will have to accompany me on my business rounds."

7

This is the place. Stand still, my steed,
Let me review the scene,
And summon from the shadowy Past
The forms that once have been.

The Past and Present here unite
Beneath Time's flowing tide,
Like footprint hidden by a brook,
But seen on either side.

—from "A Gleam of Sunshine"

February 1866

He never thought he'd miss those days of sitting astride a horse in the woods in the rain, chewing moldy hardtack for his meal. As he cut four-year-old niece Angelina's already small piece of stewed rabbit, the memory of the hardtack, and the rain, brought a smile.

He also thought he'd never smile about that time.

"Now, chew it well," Sam said. "It'll last a mite longer." He slipped a piece of rabbit from his own plate onto hers. Angelina was a pretty child, with the large brown eyes of her father and the rounded face of her mother, Sam's half-sister.

He glanced around the long table. The entire family was

there, and two guests who'd become like family. His father had insisted they maintain their Sunday meal tradition, even if to call it a meal was stretching the definition.

The table was crowded. His sister Martha and her five children, four girls and a boy. His sister-in-law Emily and her two daughters. His sister Cora Beth, the sister he loved most dearly, eating in her permanently muted silence. His father and mother. Their guests, who'd become regulars at mealtimes: Lydia Pettigrew, the doctor's widow who lived two houses away, and Leorinda Russell, the schoolteacher who boarded with Mrs. Pettigrew. Of the 15 people sitting at the table, 12 were women. The three males were Sam's father Franklin, Sam himself, and almost-11-year-old Littleton Seale, Martha's oldest child and only boy.

"We might have some of the stew broth left for your corn-bread," Sophie said. She was standing in front of the stove, stirring the cast iron post. Her two children, Belle, 12, and Daniel, 8, sat at a small table in the corner, eating the same rabbit stew.

Littleton and Daniel had become Sam's shadows, accompanying him around town and to the woods when hunting, and working with him at the various McClure businesses.

Sam, the only child of Franklin's second marriage, was the one son left bearing the McClure name. He felt it as a burden, simultaneously light and heavy. Light because, not yet 16, he felt he had time. All he needed to do was to find someone. But also heavy, because of what he'd learned during the war, about his father and himself.

The children vied to sit next to Sam at mealtimes. They idolized him and considered him a war hero even in defeat.

Most of all, they knew he always shared what was on his plate. His mother would gently reprove him, out of earshot of the children. "Sam," Louisa would say, "you're too thin as it is, and you need your strength."

He'd smile and nod. "I know, Mama, but they're so hungry." He'd also manage to slip a small portion to Belle and Daniel.

The rabbit in their stew was courtesy of Sam and the two boys. With bullets in short supply, Sam had fashioned bows and arrows for himself, Littleton, and Daniel, and taught the boys how to use theirs. Three or four mornings a week, before school if it was a weekday, Sam and his nephew awakened early to hunt in the woods owned by the family outside Brookhaven. Daniel would follow, too shy and perhaps too uncertain to keep an even pace. It was late February, and success had been spotty this winter, their first after the war. It was a hard winter for the McClures and the townspeople of Brookhaven, almost as hard as that of 1864-65, and it wasn't because of the cold.

Sam concentrated on his own small plate of rabbit soup —too thin to call a stew—and a small piece of cornmeal bread. They all ate slowly, to make the food last. As spare as the meal was, the adults knew the family was eating better than most in Brookhaven. Before the war, Sunday after-church dinner had been a feast—fried chicken and ham, vegetables, fruits, breads, grits, and two or three cakes or pies. But that was then.

"I have news."

Sam looked down the table at his mother.

At 34, and despite the privations of the war, Louisa

Williamson McClure was still a beautiful woman. She wore her golden-brown hair pulled back in a bun, emphasizing her high cheekbones and pure complexion. She, too, had become thin; they all had. But, in her case, the thinness accentuated her innate beauty.

"I've had some wonderful news," his mother said, looking down the table at her husband. "I've heard from my mama. The letter came Thursday."

Louisa was Franklin's second wife. His first wife, Margaret, had died giving birth to Cora Beth. Margaret had caught a case of measles, and the weakening after-effects had lingered to the end of the pregnancy. She'd died; the baby had survived. The child was mute, however, likely a result of her mother's illness.

Cora Beth was six years older than Sam, and there was no one in the family closer to him. She'd loved and cared for him as long as he could remember, a partial balance to the resentment, and sometimes more than resentment, the other children had aimed in his direction. When he was a child, Cora Beth had always stood between him and the bullying of his older half-siblings.

Sam wondered why his mother had waited three days to tell them her news. A quick glance at his father told him Franklin already knew.

"Mama wrote the letter almost a month ago," his mother said. "She'd finally received one of mine. She says that the family is well, that Papa's rheumatism is a bit worse but he's still managing the farm. My brother Edward is well, although he suffers a pronounced limp from his war injuries in Georgia. It's been six years since I've seen my mama and papa and my brother. Now that the rail lines to Jackson and Atlanta have finally returned to regular service, it is my intention to make an extended visit. Mama said they're wiring the funds for travel."

The room became very still. Even the younger children stopped eating. Louisa's family lived in Pennsylvania, outside Gettysburg. The McClure family lived in Brookhaven, in southern Mississippi, operating, or trying to operate, a sawmill, a grist mill, and a general store. With the state and the South still buried under the economic and social devastation of the war, and under military occupation, conditions were unsettled at best.

Sam and his sisters looked at his father. At 62, Franklin McClure was 28 years older than his wife. In 1849, three years after the death of his first wife, Franklin, an army officer and veteran of the Mexican War, had traveled to Philadelphia, accepting an invitation to spend time with his former commanding officer and his family. Colonel Jared Williamson had a rented townhouse in Philadelphia and owned a large, prosperous farm near Gettysburg. As Franklin explained to the family, he and the Williamsons' only daughter, Louisa, had had a whirlwind courtship. Four weeks after meeting, they'd married. He'd been 45 to her 17. He brought her home to Brookhaven, not having told the family he'd remarried. Two of his children, Martha and Hugh, were older, and James was only two years younger, than their new stepmother.

Louisa had already been with child—Sam.

The family's surprise had quickly given way to unspoken resentment, aimed at Louisa and then Sam after he was born. The McClure siblings also shared murmured words, suspecting Louisa had already been carrying Sam when she married their father. Louisa maintained that Sam had been born premature, but his size and general health dispelled that notion for the rest of the family.

Sam, who'd turn 16 in April, didn't favor either of his parents, except for his mother's dark blue eyes. Louisa said he looked like her father. He had wavy, black hair, dimpled cheeks, a tall, slender build, and an overall appearance so pleasing that his father often said half the girls in Brookhaven were smitten, and the other half shortly would be. The beard he'd grown out of necessity during the war was now kept neatly trimmed.

"Well, Louisa," Franklin said, "I know you've missed your mama. Have you considered that, while rail lines may be repaired, travel conditions are still uncertain?"

The family understood his meaning. They'd all heard the stories of bands of former Confederate soldiers, deserters, freed slaves, and escaped criminals wandering the countryside. Many of the stories were likely unfounded and exaggerated, and the presence of federal troops was helping maintain order to some degree. But there were still rumors of atrocities, real and imagined.

"I have, Franklin," she said. "I've talked with Mr. Haynes at the rail station, and he said that the trains will continue to have federal soldiers for protection for some time to come."

Sam knew his father could not forbid anything his mother asked for. He could also see that Franklin was struggling not to stop her.

"You will need to have some kind of escort, if you're set on doing this."

"Mama has wired funds to Brookhaven Bank, and I've already talked with Mr. Jenkins there. I'll arrange for the train tickets for me and Sam," she said. "He's old enough to serve as my escort."

The silence around the table deepened.

Then Martha, the most forward of all the McClure siblings, spoke. "You would have us starve to death?"

Young as he was, Sam had become the family provider, hunting and fishing for food, working with his father to manage and make repairs at the two mills, and helping his sisters with the store, which had finally begun to see a slim trickle of new supplies. Losing Louisa and the work she did in the house and the store was one thing; losing Sam, even for a few months, could be catastrophic.

"You will not starve to death," his mother said. "Franklin can still hunt, and Littleton will help as he helps Sam now."

"If Daddy won't say it," Martha said, "I will. There's no ammunition available, and Papa does not have the strength for the bow and arrow." Which happened to be true; while still a tall and striking man, Franklin McClure was aging rapidly. The loss of two of his sons and his son-in-law in the war had taken a toll, emotional and physical. The entire family, including Louisa, knew how much he'd come to rely on Sam, something of a surprise development since he'd never shown himself close to the boy.

"Mama," Sam said, "I cannot go with you."

"Of course, you can," Louisa said. "It will only be for a few months."

"Mama," Sam said, "I am needed here. Papa and the family need me. We have a good possibility for the sawmill and grist mill to fully resume operations, and I'm needed to help put food on the table. And given events in Jackson, this is not the time for me to go to Pennsylvania."

The state's political conditions were approaching upheaval. President Johnson had accepted Mississippi's re-admittance to the Union, but the Radical Republicans in Congress had been outraged. The state was trying to reinvent what many saw as a form of slavery—indentured service that would tie former slaves to their owners. Johnson, a Southerner, had accepted it; Congress had not. Johnson would not likely be able to withstand the anger coming from the Radical Republicans, who wanted the former slaves fully freed—and the South fully punished.

The McClure family had not owned slaves. That and Franklin McClure's army service in the Mexican War were the only reasons that Union army officials had not confiscated or destroyed the family's two mills, although federal troops had heavily damaged the sawmill's steam engine. While very few had owned more than one or two slaves, many people in Brookhaven and the surrounding area *had* been slaveowners. The Pettigrews had owned two, a woman who cooked and cleaned and an older man who did maintenance work around the house, cared for the yard, and drove Dr. Pettigrew's buggy. Once her slaves left, Mrs. Pettigrew had wandered about the house for days, almost in a daze, until Franklin and Louisa sat down with her and worked through how she would manage going forward. They arranged for the schoolteacher to board with her and for both Mrs. Pettigrew and Miss Russell to take their dinners and suppers with the McClures.

"If you won't say it," Louisa said, addressing Sam but glancing at Martha, "I will. Your brothers and sisters were nothing but mean to you as a child. They resented me marrying your father, and they resented you in turn. Save for Cora Beth, it was nothing but meanness."

Martha's eyes flashed anger. Emily's eyes flashed alarm; her own experience with her husband and the family underscored the truth of Louisa's words. Cora Beth, understanding every word, looked close to panic.

"More to the point, Samuel," his mother said, "you have not seen your grandparents in almost six years. And you'll be back before anyone knows you're gone."

"But I did see them, Mama," Sam said. "I saw them right before the Battle of Gettysburg. And Grandfather told me I was a traitor, that he disowned me from the family, and that I was no better than any of the other Southern vermin swarming his farm. And he said that I was now dead to the family."

What had been the silence of surprise at Louisa's news gave way to the silence of shock at Sam's.

8

For there are moments in life,
when the heart is so full of emotion,
That if by chance it be shaken,
or into its depths like a pebble
Drops some careless word, it overflows,
and its secret,
Spilt on the ground like water,
can never be gathered together.

—from "The Courtship of Miles Standish"

October 1915

Elizabeth finished dressing for the day and went downstairs, greeting the two Sams and Sophie.

The Tuesday morning light promised good weather. She'd had a comfortable night's sleep. She'd smiled as she used the bed-step to get into the old-fashioned and very high four-poster, wondering how many feet had stepped there to do exactly the same thing. She doubted any of them could be as tired as she was. She'd fallen asleep almost immediately.

Sam McClure had stopped the story the previous evening right at a cliffhanger ending. "We both need our rest," he'd said. "You especially, Miss Putnam. You've been traveling and must be tired."

He'd been right, but she didn't really notice it until he interrupted his story. "You're a terrible tease, Mr. McClure," she'd said. "To stop right at that moment!"

He'd laughed.

As they ate breakfast, Papa Sam had explained about the family.

"My sister Cora Beth," he'd said, "is my only living sibling. She's 71 now. She married Seamus O'Brien back in 1866; I'll let her and Seamus explain how it happened that Cora married a former Yankee soldier and an Irishman to boot." He smiled. "Actually, I should say that you'll need me or young Sam here to help understand, unless you know sign language."

She shook her head.

"The other woman at dinner last night," he said, "is Leorinda O'Brien. She's widowed now, but she married Sean O'Brien, who was Brookhaven's primary physician for decades. Leorinda had been our schoolteacher. Sean and Seamus were brothers, and Leorinda and Cora Beth were married in a double wedding. Seamus is almost 80, and you'll never meet a better storyteller. He wasn't here yesterday because he was seeing to a mare birthing her foal; Seamus operates our stables outside of town and is one of the finest horsemen in the state of Mississippi. Young Sam here will drive you, likely this afternoon."

Elizabeth looked at young Sam. "Can you afford the time from your law practice?"

Young Sam nodded. "My workload is light this week; most clients are anticipating the county fair and don't want anything, including lawsuits, to interfere. Next week will be busy; I have several court appearances on Tuesday and Wednesday."

They finished eating and soon walked to the automobile.

"You and I will sit in the back seat, Miss Putnam," Sam said, "so we can talk and not distract our chauffeur. I can tell you a bit more as we drive to the sawmill."

April 1863

Sam never talked about the war. What little the family knew was that the 13-year-old Sam had run away with his best friend Nate Cohen and enlisted in the Confederate Army in Jackson. The army had established a conscript camp at Brookhaven, but the boys were too well known there. Instead, they'd enlisted in the 9th Mississippi Rifles. Both boys could shoot well and had brought their hunting rifles. Sam, as his uncle in Pennsylvania and the family in Brookhaven well knew, had been born with a mind, and a nose, for hunting. He could sense almost anything in the woods; he could read even obscure tracks; and he inerrantly knew where to find game and deer. At 9, he led a group of men hunting a bear that had been terrifying farmers' cows, and he found it. His hunting and tracking skills were uncanny. And from the time he first sat on a horse at age five, Sam's skill with horses had become almost legendary.

What Sam didn't care for was school. Louisa had taught him to read by age 4, and the boy seemed to prefer educating himself through books. He attended school because his parents, and especially his mother, adamantly accepted no alternative. And he liked the teacher. But he would never be a scholar.

"He's the brightest pupil in my school," Miss Russell had

said to Franklin and Louisa, "but he simply will not apply himself. His mind is always in the woods." She had paused, carefully choosing her words. "He has something of the wildness of the woods in him, as if it's in his blood."

From the time he was barely able to understand the words, Louisa had read to him. She read stories and poems, fables and fairy tales. He'd squirm as she read; she often wondered if he was listening or not. That is, until early in 1856, when he was not quite six years old. Her mother in Pennsylvania, knowing how much Louisa enjoyed the poet, sent her a copy of *The Song of Hiawatha*, recently published by Henry Wadsworth Longfellow. Louisa thought it might be a bit beyond Sam's grasp, but as soon as she started reading, he sat quietly and unmoving, his eyes riveted on her face and listening in rapt attention.

She read it to him in two sittings. When she finished, he very politely asked if she might read it again. She did. And then she found her earlier poetry volumes by Longfellow, and soon Sam was listening to *Evangeline*, *Hyperion*, *The Belfry of Bruges*, *The Golden Legend*, and Longfellow's *Ballads*. She tried other poets, but Sam would begin to fidget and become easily distracted. It was only Longfellow who captured his interest.

She debated long and hard about reading one group of poems, and then decided to do so, quietly warning Sam that only she and he could share them, and that he wasn't to talk about them with anyone else. These were *Longfellow's Poems on Slavery*. By this time, Sam was reading on his own, although he still enjoyed listening to his mother recite. He kept her secret about the slavery poems.

When the package from Pennsylvania arrived that in-

cluded *The Courtship of Miles Standish* arrived, eight-year-old
Sam asked if he might read it to her. Louisa was stunned.
He read the poem in a strong, clear voice, thrilling his mother.
That fall of 1858, when Miss Russell held the annual scholars'
night at school, an event Sam had never previously partici-
pated in (nor had he been asked), he shocked his parents and
everyone else in the audience by reciting a long section of the
poem, almost performing it as an actor might. The next year,
he did the same with *The Song of Hiawatha*, and the following
year, the last one before the war, he recited *Evangeline*. His
recitation, more a performance, was so good that he had many
in the audience moved to tears.

The boy clearly had a gift. But he never recited publicly or
mentioned Longfellow's poems on slavery, keeping his promise to his mother. Public sentiment in Brookhaven was not
wildly in favor of secession, but Longfellow's poems on slavery were deemed a significant threat to the social order.

When Sam left with Nate for Jackson, he took Louisa's
slim volume of *The Song of Hiawatha* with him, tucked inside
his shirt. She wouldn't notice it was gone for weeks.

In Jackson, the enlisting officer gave both Sam and Nate a
skeptical glance but made no objections to their obvious
youth. Conscription down to age 16 had been the law in the
Confederacy since the previous year, and he had a quota to
maintain.

Nathan had been Sam's best friend since they'd been tod-
dlers. The Cohens were one of about 20 Jewish families living
in Brookhaven, a large community for such a small Southern
town. Nate's father, Benjamin Cohen, was a highly regarded

tailor and operated a kosher food store on the side, managed by his wife and oldest daughter. Nate was the youngest of four children and the Cohens' only boy. He was two days older than Sam.

While the Jewish community and its individual members were rarely if ever mistreated, a distance still existed with the larger Christian population. Sam, often facing bullying within his own family, crossed that distance easily, gravitating to the friendly, outgoing, and often hilarious prankster Nate. Except for the six months Sam spent with Cora Beth at the school for the deaf and mute in Baton Rouge, Sam and Nate had been almost inseparable.

With other boys their age, they played games in the woods, swam in nearby creeks, and sat side-by-side in school. Both boys were secretly sweet on Miss Russell, the schoolteacher, but for Sam, she was the only reason to attend, other than his parents. Nate was more academically minded.

Born in 1850, the two boys had just turned 11 when the war started. Their games changed to military battles between North and South. All the boys in their group wanted to be Confederates, so they took turns for which side they played.

The games stopped on April 30, 1863.

That day, the rumor of federal cavalry slicing its way down central Mississippi from Tennessee became reality. It was a campaign designed by Gen. Grant's staff to distract the Confederates from the federals' planned crossing of the Mississippi near Vicksburg. The 1,700 strong cavalry troops under Major Benjamin Grierson left La Grange, Tennessee on April 17 and arrived in Baton Rouge, Louisiana on May 2. In between, they brought disruption to a part of Mississippi that had largely been spared. The federals cut telegraph lines, tore up railroad tracks, burned warehouses full of military supplies and cotton, occasionally set fire to large plantation homes, told slaves they were free, and fought surprisingly few skirmishes. The troops stayed on the move, keeping the perplexed and thin-on-the-ground Confederate forces off guard as to their goal and intentions.

What the raid was teaching the people of Mississippi was that no Confederate force in the field seemed able or willing to stop the federals.

The day before the raid, the townspeople had relaxed. Word had passed that the federals were riding to the west and south, bypassing Brookhaven. Franklin McClure, relieved with the reports, decided to make his planned ride to Hattiesburg, to discuss a logging contract. He wouldn't return until the day after the federals left.

About noon on April 30, Grierson and his troops arrived in Brookhaven from the west. The soldiers had almost bypassed the town when they unexpectedly turned east. They made their way to the station of the New Orleans, Jackson, & Great Northern Railroad and set it afire while they tore up track.

The plan had been to burn only the station, but a sudden wind whipped the flames to adjacent buildings. Grierson ordered his troops to help fight the blaze. One of the buildings caught by the fire was the Cohens' tailor shop.

Sam and Nate had been across the street at the McClure general store, both still angry at Sam's grandfather having prevented them from joining the citizens confronting the federals. When the boys saw the fire and Nate's father calling for help, they rushed to the Cohens' store and began moving as much merchandise and sewing equipment as they could. Louisa McClure had been helping her father-in-law Samuel (for whom her son was named) hide their more valuable merchandise in the store's cellar when she heard the commotion. She ran to the street to see the two boys dashing in and out of the Cohen store, now burning from the rear.

"Sam!" Louisa screamed, trying to stop him from running in and out of the burning store. He either didn't hear her or ignored her. She fell to her knees in the middle of the street, moaning his name.

The two boys kept darting in and out of the store, with flames engulfing the second story. They came tumbling out for the last time together, carrying Mr. Cohen's sewing machine between them, Nate's father, his arms full of fabrics and tools, finally stopped them from going back in. With the other buildings adjacent to it, the small store soon collapsed with a roar.

That was when Sam saw four soldiers break off from the group fighting the fire and enter the McClure store. Followed by Nate, he rushed past his mother and bounded inside.

An officer and three soldiers were struggling with his grandfather, who was trying to stop them from looting the already sparse wares. Sam cherished his 76-year-old Grandpa McClure, who'd taught him to hunt and track, shoot a rifle, whittle, and all the practical skills a boy needed to learn. It was said that the grandfather's legendary hunting skills had skipped a generation and found a home in young Sam. There was no adult, including his mother, to whom Sam was closer.

The officer finally shoved his grandfather, who fell, hitting his head on the corner of the counter cloth goods. The act startled the soldiers into almost freezing in place. Sam rushed to his grandfather's side and knelt. The blood was pouring from his grandfather's temple. Sam grabbed a bolt of cloth from above him and tried to stop the bleeding. He looked up to see his mother come through the front door of the store.

"Mama!" he said. "Help me!"

Louisa didn't hear him. She was staring at the Union officer.

"Mama!" Sam said again, his voice reaching almost a scream. He could feel his grandfather's blood flowing through his fingers.

The officer had turned back from the door. "Louisa?" he said.

Sam screamed again at his mother, who seemed oblivious to anything except the Union officer. He felt his grandfather's body go limp in his arms. He stared at the face he knew and loved so well.

Sam didn't utter a sound. He looked back at his mother, who seemed not to have understood what was happening. He then looked up into the distress of the clean-shaven officer's face, who was staring openmouthed at Sam and his grandfather. The man looked back at Louisa, and then he returned his gaze to Sam. The soldiers still in the store seemed frozen in place. No one moved.

Sam and the officer stared at each other for what seemed far longer than the few seconds it was. Then the man seemed to shake himself and then ordered the soldiers to drop everything and leave the store. As he left, he stopped, and looked back at Sam, still staring at him. His gaze fell upon Louisa, who seemed struck speechless.

"I'll come to see you," the man said to Louisa. "Where do you live?"

"On Cherry Street," his mother said. "No. 212."

The man nodded. "I'll come tonight. Stay at home. The streets won't be safe."

Sam's mother nodded, and then the man turned and left. She stared at the door for a moment and then finally turned to Sam. He was still holding his grandfather's lifeless body.

"What happened?" she said, bewildered.

Sam's grandfather was the only casualty of Grierson's Raid in Brookhaven. But several federals had been wounded, some seriously, by a small band of Confederate soldiers.

Before the war, Sam's father had purchased the small building next door, planning an expansion of his own store. But the war had stopped those plans. When Franklin returned to Brookhaven the next day, he saw the Cohens' belongings piled on the wooden sidewalk in front of McClure's Store. He told Mr. Cohen to use the vacant building for his food store and tailoring business.

The federal troops stayed the afternoon and spent the night in Brookhaven, many at the hotel a block away from the store. Some houses were commandeered, and their owners dismissed for the night; the McClures' large house on Cherry Street had been a tempting target but the body of Sam's grandfather being laid out in the parlor was a powerful deterrent. Word had spread of the old man's death, and the townspeople heard that Major Grierson had been furious with the officer and the soldiers.

After supper, Sam was the only member of the family who saw his mother slip quietly out the front door and sit in the darkness on the front porch. Muffled sounds of what sounded like a drunken celebration could be heard coming from the center of Brookhaven.

The deaths of Sam's older half-brother James and his brother-in-law Jarvis Seale at Shiloh had been a terrible blow, but the deaths were at a distance. James left behind his wife Emily and two young daughters, while Jarvis's wife Martha now had five children to rear alone.

Sam could almost pretend that Jarvis and James were still alive and fighting somewhere. While he'd never been close to James, Jarvis had always been kind to him "("the best of the Seales," his father Franklin often said) and appreciative of Sam's hunting skills.

His grandfather's death was close and far more personal. The boy was devastated. And angry with the Union officer, and angry with his mother. He slipped out the back of the house, made his way around to the bushes next to the front porch, and waited. His mother sat a bare five feet away. He heard the Union officer arrive, and he listened to their conversation.

Grierson's Raiders left the next morning, a Friday. Sam and Nate sat side by side in the McClure parlor, his grandfather's open coffin in front of them, as people came to pay their respects. Cora Beth sat on the other side of the room. Nate was keeping up a steady stream of whispering, but Sam was barely responding.

"Nate," Sam said, "I'm going to enlist."

"What?" Nate said.

"I'm going to enlist."

"Enlist?" Nate said, whispering. "Sam, we're 13. Even with conscription, we have to be 16. And everyone knows us at the camp."

"I'm tall enough to pass for 16," said Sam. "I can go to Jackson and enlist. I can fight back. He paused. "Well, I'm going to do it. I'll tell Mama and Papa I've gone hunting." Sam began to consider the ramifications, not the least of which would be his mother's response. Then he thought of his grandfather bleeding in his arms, and how his mother had ignored his cries. How she'd stared at the Union officer, and how she agreed to meet him. And what they said.

Nate waited until Cora Beth stood and left the room. "All right. I'm coming with you. We can say we're hunting for a couple of days. We've done that before. Sam, hold on. Tonight's the Sabbath. And you have church on Sunday and the funeral. We'll have to wait until Monday."

"Nate," Sam said, "you don't have to do this."

"They burned our store and killed your grandfather," Nate said. "I'm coming with you."

"They might separate us," Sam said.

Nate shrugged. "If they do, they do." He grinned. "The Yankees won't know what hit 'em."

On May 4, three days after the raiders left Brookhaven, and the day after his grandfather's funeral, Sam and Nate quietly left their homes before dawn and caught a ride with a farmer taking a wagonload of hay to Jackson.

They enlisted with the 9th Mississippi Rifles. They walked to the general army camp outside of town, met their officers and fellow enlistees, and got down to the business of training, which amounted mostly to marching, throwing themselves on the ground and firing a rifle, and knowing when and to whom to salute. The camp was rife with reports that General Grant had crossed the Mississippi with an army and won a battle at Port Gibson.

Sam didn't want to think about what home was like. He knew his family and Nate's would be frantic when the boys didn't return from hunting.

"We'll have to let them know," he said to Nate. "Maybe when we leave Jackson."

On May 6, their lieutenant asked if anyone in their unit had knowledge of or experience in the border states like Maryland or possibly southern Pennsylvania. Sam timidly raised his hand. From 1854 to 1860, he and his mother had spent six weeks almost every summer at his grandparents' farm near Gettysburg. His uncle Edward would take him horseback riding, and by the time Sam was 6, was taking the boy on overnight hunting trips in the region. Sam had learned not only the terrain but a lot about the people who lived there and what their farms were like.

"Put your hand down!" Nate said, whispering. "They'll send you someplace."

It was too late. The lieutenant called Sam to the side and asked him what he knew. Unknown to Sam, raising his hand initiated a series of telegraph messages between Jackson and Richmond.

The next day, Sam was called out from the camp training.

"Get your kit," the lieutenant said to Sam. "I have your orders."

Sam rushed to their tent on the campground and grabbed

what few belongings he had. Nate came running up.

"Sam, where are they sending you?"

"I don't know," Sam said, grabbing his pack. Nate hurried with him back to the parade ground. "When the time is right for you, get word to your parents, and ask them to speak to mine. I'll try to get word, somehow."

They reached the lieutenant, who'd been waiting.

"Where am I going, sir?" Sam said.

"It's confidential, soldier. Come with me."

Sam looked and nodded at Nate. The two boys held each other's gaze, nodded at each other, and then Sam turned and followed the officer.

On May 8, Nate's unit left with two others, bound for General Bragg's army in Tennessee. All others remained with General Pemberton in Jackson, with rumors of an imminent departure for Vicksburg.

9

Toiling,—rejoicing,—sorrowing,
Onward through life he goes;
Each morning sees some task begin,
Each evening see it close;
Something attempted, something done.
Has earned a night's repose.

—from "The Village Blacksmith"

October 1915

"Your mother knew the Union officer," Elizabeth said.

Sam McClure nodded. "An old beau, from when she was a girl."

They'd arrived at the sawmill. What Elizabeth had been expecting was a relatively small building, with a waterwheel for producing power. Instead, she saw a large enterprise, not a sprawling manufacturing complex but close enough. Wagons and even a few trucks were arriving with large trees while others were departing empty.

"We have a rail spur," he said, noticing her attention on the empty wagons. "That's how we ship finished wood from the mill, except for local orders."

"How many people work here?" she said. The sign simply read McClure's Sawmill.

"About 150," Papa Sam said as the car entered the mill yard.

"It's Brookhaven's largest employer," Young Sam said. "And the largest lumber mill in Mississippi."

A thin, bespectacled man hurried up to the car. "Mr. Sam, the foreign gentlemen are here. They're waiting in your office."

Sam stared at the man for a moment. "They're a mite early. They weren't expected until tomorrow." He turned to Elizabeth, smiling. "Miss Putnam, I apologize, but young Sam here and I have a meeting that wasn't supposed to happen until tomorrow. This is Philip Burton, the mill's office manager. Mr. Burton, might I prevail upon you to escort Miss Putnam on a tour of the mill? She's a newspaper reporter from New York, and I'm giving you authority to answer any and all questions she might have."

"Of course, Mr. Sam. I've had coffee and tea brought to the gentlemen."

The elder McClure nodded his thanks, and the two Sams walked into what Philip Burton told her was the mill's executive offices.

"Well, Mr. Burton," Elizabeth said, "you're apparently stuck with me. I hope I'm not keeping you from important work."

"Not at all, ma'am," he said. "Please come this way."

Elizabeth followed him to an office area where two other people were working. He introduced her, explaining the role of the bookkeeper and something he called a scheduler. "He manages the deliveries for the incoming logs and the outgoing lumber, as well as the crews sent to various forest areas."

She could see across the open office area to where the two Sams were meeting with what looked like well-dressed foreigners.

Burton followed her gaze. "They're from Europe," he said. "England and France specifically. They're about to sign a contract for lumber to be shipped for the war."

"Doesn't France have forests?" she said.

He nodded. "They do, but too many of them are in war areas and under German occupation. This is their fourth trip to Brookhaven, and likely it will be the final one. It's a significant piece of business for Mr. Sam, and it will be a boon for the town. A major expansion will be getting underway in the next few weeks, and we'll be doing a lot of hiring. Probably a hundred new jobs. And no one pays as well in the state of Mississippi as Mr. Sam. Come with me to the window that overlooks the yard."

Elizabeth wasn't quite sure what to expect, but she could see that, even with what seemed a whirlwind of activity, what Burton called "the yard" was immaculate.

"It's so clean," she said.

"It is," he said, "but it's not what you need to see. Just watch for a while."

She watched newly arrived trucks being unloaded. Off to one side, men were stacking bundles of lumber on to flatbed rail cars. Food was being delivered to what must be the lunchroom. Barrels were being rolled from what Mr. Burton identified as the milling house. "Wood chips and bark," he said. "We grind it for use for all kinds of things."

She'd been watching for several minutes when surprise registered.

"The black men and the white men are working together," she said.

"Most people don't expect that," Burton said, "for a state like Mississippi. Now I don't want you to think this is some kind of racial heaven. It's not. Black men do the lesser jobs and they're paid less than whites. If they did the same work, there's not a white man anywhere in the state who would work here, no matter how good the wages. What's happened, though, is that the men have learned to respect each other. Mr. Sam pays the best wages in Lincoln County and in the state, so he gets good people. A lot of people around here weren't happy at first, but it's worked, at least so far. It started during the Reconstruction years, and then everyone thought things would go back to what they were before the war. They didn't know Mr. Sam. He wasn't even 20 years old when he first stared down the Klan; that was in front of the black American-Episcopal church. They've come here a few times over the years, and he's faced that down, too. He can't change what he doesn't control, he says, like the schools. But for what he does control, he treats people well, and he pays them well."

"People must think it's a scandal," Elizabeth said, almost shocked at what Burton was telling her. "They don't even do this in the North."

"It took some getting used to," Burton said. "There was a time when a group of the white workers said they wouldn't work with blacks. But Mr. Sam had a secret weapon, and that's the wages he pays. If you can get work at the McClure Sawmill, you can provide for your family the rest of your life. Even when times get hard, like they did back in the panic of '93, he kept everyone on wages, doing all kinds of things, until business finally improved. Two banks failed, all kinds of businesses shut down. But Mr. Sam saved his businesses, and he saved Brookhaven. People don't forget that kind of stewardship. That's what he calls it—stewardship. And he tells people who apply to work, if you can't abide my rules, no one is forcing you to work here."

He smiled. "Once a group of white men decided to walk out, because they refused to work with black men. They were all back, every one of them, within about 90 minutes."

"What changed their minds?" Elizabeth said.

"Their wives. They came back so quick you would've thought they'd never left."

She walked with Burton on a tour of the mill; some areas she could only see from several yards away because of safety concerns, he said. She watched large logs being offloaded from trucks, moved onto conveyor belt-type machinery, and guided towards the saws. It was noisy, and Burton communicated by pointing. Otherwise, he would have been shouting.

He showed her the rail spur, with empty flatbed cars waiting on siderails. Then he walked her to a large, cleared field at the rear of the property. "This is where the expansion will happen," he said. "Mr. Sam bought the land years ago, but he allowed it to sit idle other than for some sharecropping."

"He seems quite the businessman," she said.

Burton nodded. "You should see the stores in town and the racehorse stables. Once he figured out that automobiles were here to stay, he began to shift from horse-drawn transport to mechanical. But he loves horses. His brother-in-law, Seamus O'Brien, manages the stables and the racehorse business for Mr. Sam. Seamus is almost 80, but you wouldn't believe it to meet him."

"How long have you worked here, Mr. Burton?" she said.

"Going on 34 years, ma'am. I started when I was 16, back in January of 1881."

When they finished the tour, Mr. Burton found Elizabeth an empty desk so she could write down what she'd heard and seen. She already had so many pages filled that she'd likely have to find a store in Brookhaven for another pad or diary. She could see what was already happening. This wasn't just a story about the Gray Wisp and the Civil War. It was a story about a family, and people, and a town, and the change that came upon them like a whirlwind. And it was people like Sam McClure who had steered them through it.

She wondered about Young Sam. Where were his parents in all of this? And she thought he'd said something about brothers as well.

The door to the meeting room opened, and she could see that the discussions or negotiations must have gone well. Everyone was smiling and shaking hands.

"You drive a hard bargain, Mr. McClure," a man with a British accent said, "but a fair one. We did fine work today." And then they left; a car was waiting for them in the mill yard.

Sam turned to Elizabeth. "I trust you haven't been bored to tears, and that Mr. Burton gave you a proper tour?"

She smiled. "He did, and I've been sitting here making notes."

"We're driving to the Brookhaven Hotel for lunch," he said, "something of a celebration for the signing of that contract. Mr. Fitzgibbons and Mr. LeBlanc had to leave immediately, unfortunately. But we can celebrate among ourselves, and we can continue our discussion."

Elizabeth bid Mr. Burton goodbye, thanking him again for the tour. She and the two Sams made their way to the automobile in the mill yard.

"It's only three miles," Sam McClure said. "But we can talk on the way."

10

And the mother at home says, "Hark!
For his voice I listen and yearn;
It is growing late and dark,
And my boy does not return!"

—from "The Fiftieth Anniversary of Agassiz"

April 1863

Neither the McClures nor the Cohens realized their sons had left to enlist. The boys often hunted together, and they often spent a night and sometimes two in one of the small camps scattered throughout 300 acres of dense forest owned by the McClures. It wasn't until the second afternoon that Louisa became even mildly concerned. Something tugged at her about this supposed hunting foray, so soon after her father-in-law's funeral. She'd assumed that Sam wanted to take his grief to the woods, where he'd shared so many experiences with Grandpa Samuel. On Thursday morning, she walked from the McClures' house on Cherry Street to the Cohens' house several blocks away. Ben Cohen had yet to reopen his business, and the storefront on Railroad Avenue was still closed.

Louisa McClure and Miriam Cohen were more acquaintances than friends, despite the close friendship of their sons. Louisa worked hard to hide her feelings; she had manners, after all, but she didn't care at all for the friendship her son had with Nate Cohen. The Cohens seemed nice people; it was their religion she had problems with. She'd grown up with her father often thundering about the Jews.

She found Mrs. Cohen in about the same state of mind as she was. They got hold of their husbands, who went together and spent most of Thursday checking the forest camps. Mrs. Cohen and Louisa began to call upon friends of their sons. No one had seen the boys; no one knew anything. None of the forest camps showed signs of recent occupation, their husbands reported.

By Thursday evening, both mothers were frantic and the fathers seriously concerned. Four days after the boys had left, after yet another sleepless night of worry, Franklin had the presence of mind to find Cora to see what she knew.

Grierson's Raiders had left behind six wounded federal soldiers and a doctor to attend them. The Union doctor had asked Dr. Pettigrew where he might find nursing assistance. While Cora had no training in nursing, Dr. Pettigrew had seen her many times at the Brookhaven hospital, tending to wounded Confederate soldiers. No one else in Brookhaven was willing to attend to the wounded federals, but she agreed to help. Cora walked daily to a small house near the western edge of Brookhaven. The group had been sequestered there by the town sheriff, pending their recovery and the arrival of Confederate or Mississippi forces to take them into custody. She helped care for the soldiers by changing their dressings, bringing them meals, and helping write letters that might be posted to families.

One particular soldier made her smile whenever she was

around him. Seamus O'Brien, a young Irishman, had literally just stepped off the boat in New York when he and several others were almost bodily carried to a recruiting office. In return for their service with the Union army, they would be granted American citizenship. Through a long, tortuous route he didn't quite fully understand, Seamus found himself in Jacksonville, Illinois, and assigned to a new cavalry unit being formed under Major Benjamin Grierson. Perhaps it was experience with horses that had triggered it, him having been a groomsman at an estate in County Cork.

Seamus had hoped to join his older brother Sean, who had come to the United States in 1857. But Sean, a trained physician, had met a wall of prejudice against the Irish, even one with a prestigious medical degree from Dublin. In New York City, Philadelphia, and Boston, he was sometimes politely and sometimes rudely turned away from hospitals. He'd even seen signs in shop windows, reading "No Irish Need Apply." Sean had gone to Atlanta, half-expecting to find the same animosity. Instead, he'd been welcomed by hospital administrators often desperate for trained physicians. He'd been working at Atlanta's main hospital when the war started, and he signed up as a medical officer with the Confederate army.

Seamus told Cora all about his brother and the possibility that they might find themselves on opposing sides in a battle. He also called her his silent angel, as he cracked jokes and flirted with her while she tended to the wound in his leg.

When Grandfather Samuel's coffin was placed in the McClure parlor, Cora had sat for a time with Sam and Nate and seen them whispering. She'd heard just enough to know what they were talking about, but she hadn't taken it seriously.

"You have an idea, though, don't you?" Franklin said, when he questioned her.

She shrugged and wrote on a chalk slate that she wasn't certain. She then wrote a single short sentence, since Sam was the only family member who knew sign language.

"They talked about enlisting."

Franklin rushed to the Cohens' house to tell Ben. When he told Louisa what Cora had suggested, his wife took to her bed. The two men went to the Confederate conscription camp outside Brookhaven, but no one there had seen the boys. The officer in charge told them that Sam and Nate would have been refused enrollment at the office there, but they might have gone to Jackson, where they wouldn't be known.

At four a.m. on Friday May 8, Franklin set out on his horse for Jackson. Ben Cohen wanted to come but had the Sabbath starting that evening. Franklin brought a change of clothes; he had no idea of how long it would take to find the boys and if they indeed had gone to Jackson, the closest enlistment center.

If the rumors swirling in Brookhaven were true, it might be a dangerous trip. Grant's army was supposedly moving toward the capital.

Arriving in Jackson by late afternoon, he immediately saw the signs of panic in the streets. Townspeople were packing wagons and almost anything that moved, fleeing to the east. He started at the general enlistment office, but it was closed except for a black man cleaning up. He told Franklin that if the boys had enlisted, he would need to check with the officers at the camp, but they'd been ordered to break camp and move to Vicksburg. Franklin found a hotel without trouble;

the manager asked him to leave his key at the front desk, as the entire staff was leaving. He stabled his horse and found a tavern that was still open and serving food.

Early the next morning, he arrived at the camp. It was in general chaos, and no one wanted to take the time to tell him what might have happened. A Lieutenant Morrison finally helped him, checked the rosters, and said that both boys had enlisted with the 9th Mississippi Rifles. Nate had left with his unit the previous morning, ordered to the Confederate army in eastern Tennessee.

"And my son?" Franklin asked.

"I'm sorry, Col. McClure," the lieutenant said, "all I can say is that he left a day earlier than Private Cohen."

"I don't understand," Franklin said. "Why can't you say more? Weren't they in the same unit?"

"Private McClure's orders were marked confidential. He was separated from the 9th Rifles. Even if I knew where he was sent, which I don't, I couldn't tell you. And sir, I don't have to tell you, but you need to leave Jackson as soon as possible. Grant is due at any time, and a battle is highly likely. If the federals prevail, I don't have to tell you what will happen here, and to anyone left."

The only additional piece of information the lieutenant had was that Sam had been sent by himself, unattached to a unit until his arrival at his assigned destination. Neither the assignment nor the destination was known.

Hours later, reaching Brookhaven, Franklin first rode to Ben Cohen, telling him what he knew of Nate and Sam.

"I'm not sure how to explain this to Louisa," Franklin said, "when I don't know myself. The officer didn't seem to know either, only that Sam had been sent as an individual to some unnamed destination."

"What would Sam know," Ben Cohen said, "to get himself singled out like this? He's only a boy."

Franklin pondered the question for several moments. "It might be," he said, "because he's familiar with southern Pennsylvania and the Maryland border area. It's where his uncle took him hunting. But I have no inkling of why that might be important." He paused. "Ben, people were fleeing Jackson. Grant's army was approaching, and they said a battle would happen at any time. I don't know how to find out anything else. At least we know the boys weren't sent to Vicksburg."

When Franklin told Louisa what little he'd learned about Sam, he was surprised at her utter lack of emotion.

She'd simply nodded. "I have to assume he's dead, Franklin," she said. "My beautiful boy got himself caught up in the ridiculous cause of allowing rich planters to keep their slaves."

"Louisa," Franklin said, "we both know how hard he took the death of my father. We know that's what led him to enlist. It had nothing to do with rich planters or slavery, and everything to do with how much he loved his grandpa. It was my father who died, an old man who posed no threat to anyone, killed by a Union officer even if it was an accident. And I believe you're discounting Sam's resourcefulness."

"It doesn't really change anything, though, does it?" she said. "He'll still end up dead, so I should accept it and get on with my life." And she'd turned from him and walked to the kitchen. She told her husband nothing about the Union officer.

11

Each heart has its haunted chamber,
Where the silent moonlight falls!
On the floor are mysterious footsteps,
There are whispers along the walls!

And mine at times is haunted
By phantoms of the Past,
As motionless as shadows
By the silent moonlight cast.

—from "Aftermath, The Haunted Chamber"

October 1915

"My father told me what had happened when I came back from the war," Sam said. They were seated in the dining room of the Brookhaven Hotel and had ordered their meal. Elizabeth noticed how deferential the maitre'd and their assigned waiter had been. Even the hotel manager had stopped by and welcomed them. She also noticed how intently Young Sam was listening, and she suspected he was hearing much of this story for the first time.

"Some weeks later," Sam said, "guilt got the better of me, and I sent Mama and Papa a letter. I couldn't tell them much; there was a veil of secrecy wrapped around what I was doing.

Both wrote back, as did my sister Cora Beth. I wrote several more letters, but the Confederate postal service being the condition it was, and rail and road travel so disrupted, those three letters were the first and last I received from home. When I eventually saw Mama again, she told me that a letter I wrote to her and one to Cora Beth did arrive three months later, but those were the last the family received." He shook his head. "I must have written dozens more, but they were never delivered. Cora Beth said she wrote a letter a week for the rest of the war, but I only received that first one. You can't imagine how hard it was, hearing names called out for mail from home, and not hearing your own."

February 1866

Sam's words at the dinner table had caused mouths to hang open.

"So, you see, Mama," Sam gently said, "I can't go with you to Gettysburg. I would not be welcome."

"Mama said nothing about this in her letter," Louisa said.

"Did she mention me at all?" Sam said.

Louisa sat, not answering. Sam could she was trying to remember what the letter had said. Surely there had been something about the Williamsons' only grandchild?

"No," she said finally. "She didn't." She paused. "What did you do to cause Father to speak like that?"

"I was fighting for the Confederates, for one thing," Sam said. "For another, I told General Lee and his staff to use Grandfather's farm as their field headquarters."

Franklin was closely watching the exchange between

mother and son. He'd never seen Sam disagree with his mother before, and he was stunned. And not once had the boy ever talked about his experiences in the war. He'd had no idea that Sam had been anywhere near Gettysburg or the commanding general of the Army of Northern Virginia.

An additional thought registered. Not even 16, his son was no longer a boy. He'd become a man.

Late Sunday afternoon, following the discussion at dinner, Sam, Littleton, and Daniel sat in the kitchen near the still-warm stove. All three were carving arrows needed for hunting, Sam inspecting and helping the two younger boys improve their carving skills. Cora was sitting at the table with Emily's two daughters, mending socks and shorts and a pair of pants Littleton had snagged on a thornbush during a hunting expedition two days before.

Louisa had not spoken to Sam since his words at dinner. He knew she was upset, both with what he'd told her and the fact he wouldn't escort her to Pennsylvania.

His mother appeared at the kitchen doorway. Sam looked up and could see the bright patches on her cheeks, a recognizable sign she was angry.

"What was a 13-year-old boy doing to advise General Lee on where to place his field headquarters?" she said. "I didn't realize they had been that desperate for men or military intelligence."

Sam considered her words and her concern and refrained from the sharp response he wanted to make. "It was my assignment, Mama. They needed someone who knew the area, as General Lee had determined to invade the North. He told me they'd be moving toward Gettysburg. I told him about the area, the terrain, the town, and the farms. The best headquarters location for all concerned was Grandfather's farm, and I told him that."

"He knew it was your grandfather's farm?"

"Yes, Mama. I told him."

She stood motionless, staring at Sam. Then she spoke.

"I understand why Father said what he did, and I have to tell you, Samuel, that I concur with him." She turned her back to leave, and then turned and faced him again. She turned and spoke once more. "You were my beautiful boy when you left. And it was a stranger who returned." And then she left.

He stared at the empty doorway, not saying a word. He finally turned his attention back to the arrow in his hand, then looked up to see Cora Beth staring at him.

"Don't take her words to heart," she said in sign language.

"She might be right, Cora Beth," Sam said. "I do feel like a stranger." He shook his head. "She doesn't understand. If Lee had headquartered anywhere else, Grandfather's farm would have been ravaged."

A week later, Louisa left for Jackson, accompanied by the mayor who had business in the capital. The mayor said he would find her an escort from Jackson to Atlanta. Other than her husband, she did not speak to anyone in the family, including her son, before she left.

While the McClure house on Cherry Street was large, it was also currently filled with family. James's widow, Emily, and their two young daughters lived with McClures, as did Littleton, his mother, and his four sisters. Two of Littleton's sisters shared a bedroom with Cora, the other two with their mother. Sam and Littleton shared the smallest bedroom, more a screened alcove on the second floor, while Franklin and Louisa had the largest bedroom.

After marrying Jarvis, Martha and eventually her children had lived with the Seales. As the war continued, food became increasingly scarce. The Seales had operated a blacksmith shop, but with so many horses taken for the army, there was little work, and they had closed it in 1864. In the last months of the war, with food in short supply, the Seales decided to leave Brookhaven for Texas. Martha's in-laws had informed her that there wasn't enough food for her and the children to accompany them.

Thrown on the mercy of Franklin and Louisa, her father had welcomed them, even though the McClures, too, were on very short rations.

The oldest daughter in the family, Martha doubted what the Seales had told her about food, although many staples were in short supply for everyone in Brookhaven. She suspected that her mother-in-law saw the opportunity to remove Martha's sharp tongue from the Seale family circle.

There had been no word from Sam since right after he'd left to enlist. The last letter they received had been mailed from Virginia, and then nothing. The following year, the fall of Atlanta to Sherman's army had disrupted rail and postal routes. They didn't know if Sam was alive or dead, but the entire family, except for always hopeful Cora Beth, feared the worst.

The Cohens had had a similar experience with Nate, but for different reasons. Their son had been taken prisoner during the Second Battle of Franklin in Tennessee in late November of 1864, the same battle in which Hugh McClure had died. Their hopes for a parole or a prisoner exchange had been dashed when they received word from Nate's commanding officer that he and the other prisoners were believed to have been sent to a prison in Illinois. The officer in his letter didn't explain how he'd heard this. Nothing had been heard of Nate since then.

No one in Brookhaven knew anything about prisons in Illinois for Confederates. Ben traveled to Jackson and asked the Union authorities there. An officer told him of two prisons for POWs, one at Alton, near St. Louis, and the other Camp Douglas, near Chicago. The officer was more informed about Alton.

"It was a state prison that closed some years back," he said. "We reopened it in 1862 for captured soldiers, bushwhackers, and people deemed traitorous." The man had paused. "Mr. Cohen, it's known for overcrowding. We've heard stories of dysentery and smallpox. It may be just rumors, and nothing could be as bad as what we hear tell of Andersonville in Georgia or Palmyra in New York. I hate to tell you this, but I don't want to give you false hope." He paused. "If it's any comfort, Alton is considered better than Camp Douglas, which is right next to Lake Michigan."

Ben returned to Brookhaven and told Miriam and his daughters that Nate might have been sent to a prison near St. Louis or Chicago, but no one knew anything about it. He did tell Franklin McClure what he'd learned, asking he say nothing to anyone, especially Louisa or Miriam.

"This is a terrible burden to carry, Ben," Franklin said.

"But I will carry it with you." The two men, who'd previously been nodding acquaintances in the street, had become close friends, bonded by a common concern for their sons.

By the end of the war, the McClures, the Cohens, and the rest of Brookhaven knew that law and order had generally broken down in many parts of the South. Mississippi had experienced the same disorder for the past two years. Roads were unsafe and said to be filled with soldiers-turned-bandits, Confederate deserters, freed criminals, and bands of freed and previously runaway slaves, although no such groups had been spotted locally. Rail service had stopped, with so many destroyed tracks and stations. Postal service would not be re-established for months. A federal military commander oversaw Mississippi, and what order there was came from the federal troops mostly centered in Jackson and Vicksburg. Both Franklin and Ben, and many of the older men in Brookhaven, had formed a militia to patrol and make sure the town and surrounding environs were kept safe from marauders. Franklin and a few other men had planted vegetable crops on the McClure farm, rotating guard duty to protect the hoped-for food from thieves of all types, human and animal.

October 1915

"It was a dark, dark time," Sam said, as they ate in the hotel restaurant. "The great Confederate dream had died. Many people thought God had turned his back on the South. The economy was in ruins. The social order was destroyed. It was true even in Brookhaven, which had been largely spared physical destruction beyond what had happened during Grierson's

Raid. Banks had failed. Foodstuffs were in short supply, except for what families could grow themselves. Then came the scavengers, the carpetbaggers and the scalawags, with the corruption and outright theft that went on during military occupation. With all that and the upheaval in the social order, it's no wonder that the Lost Cause became a kind of religion.

"The only bright spots were the churches. The McClures, with our Scottish ancestry, were good Presbyterians, and I will tell you, Miss Putnam, this family clung to our church, Brookhaven Presbyterian. That was true even in the prewar years. And it was more true after. Because I returned on a Sunday, I knew exactly where I would find them."

Elizabeth felt deeply moved by Sam's words. He wasn't inspired by sentiment, she knew; this was coming from some inner part of his heart. She glanced at Young Sam, who'd been staring at his grandfather, listening as intently as she had. He turned his eyes to her, and suddenly she understood the connection between the old man and the young one. It was more than a name. Sam McClure and his grandson shared a soul.

She wondered about the middle Sam, the one, Young Sam had told her, who lived in Pennsylvania. Without knowing the man or his story, she sensed that he was not part of this bond between grandfather and grandson.

"Do you know these stories?" she said to Young Sam.

He shook his head. "Some of them. And none to this detail. Your talks with Papa here are partial revelations for me. I'm most heartily sorry that I missed the one last night. He rarely talks about the war."

"Don't pay attention to his nonsense, Miss Putnam," Sam said. "He knows the important things. Now, I think I might like to have some dessert today. I wonder if they have any of their apple pie left. I highly recommend it."

As they ate dessert and sipped coffee, Sam touched Elizabeth on her wrist. "You know, Miss Putnam, you've been asking all these questions and listening to this old man here ramble on. But you've said hardly a word about yourself. Perhaps we should interview you as you're interviewing us."

She smiled. "I'm too young to have much of a story, Mr. McClure. I was born and raised in Boston. My father is an attorney. I have two older brothers, Charles and James, whom we call Jamie. Charles is an attorney, working in my father's firm, and Jamie is a doctor."

"Would that be Stevens, Frost & Putnam?" Young Sam said.

She nodded. "Of course. You went to Harvard Law School. You probably heard of them."

"I interned one summer with them," Young Sam said. "I was assigned to Mr. Frost's staff, but I worked with your brother and father on several occasions."

"And you can tell her the rest of the story," Sam said. "She'll likely hear it eventually."

Elizabeth noticed that Young Sam slightly reddened.

"I was offered a position when I graduated from law school," Young Sam said. "And it was a wonderful firm; I truly enjoyed the people and the work. But my heart was here in Brookhaven, which I know wouldn't make sense for most law school graduates. But this is where I wanted to make my life. Because Mr. Frost was out of town, I spoke with Mr. Putnam, your father, about my intention to settle in Brookhaven." He glanced at his pocket watch. "And I need to get the Buick.

I left it with the mechanic to fill it with petrol. If we dawdle too long, we won't have time for the stables. If you'll excuse me, I'll see you both in a few minutes."

They watched him leave the dining room.

"The stables?" Elizabeth said.

Sam nodded. "We'll drive out to where Seamus and Cora Beth live. Seamus manages the stables and breeds some of the finest racehorses in the South. The property used to be the McClure grist mill, but it was a dwindling business with the big flour boys gobbling up the market. We converted the property to raising horses. Seamus had married Cora Beth in 1866."

Elizabeth nodded.

"They were two young men from Ireland. Sean was a surgeon in the Confederate Army under General Bragg, and his younger brother Seamus fought for the Union. He rode with the Grierson's Raiders, and he and several other Union cavalrymen were wounded and left here with a Union doctor. Eventually, there was a prisoner exchange. But Cora Beth had tended to the wounded men, and Seamus came back after the war to find her. He'd also told his brother about Brookhaven, and Sean settled here even before Seamus's return."

Sam laughed. "Seamus is the only Yankee veteran that people here tolerate. I exaggerate a bit, but even now, at 79, he's one of the best-loved storytellers in all of Lincoln County."

"Is Sean still alive?" she said.

Sam shook his head. "He died about four years ago. He was seven years older than Seamus, and he'd developed heart trouble over the years. His oldest son Aidan took over his father's medical practice, and Aidan's boy is finishing up at the medical school at Tulane in New Orleans. Leorinda, who was my schoolteacher, is 80 now and she lives with Aidan and his family two houses down from us on Cherry Street. She often shares meals with us."

He looked at his pocket watch. "Young Sam will be along shortly. I don't think he'd mind me telling you what he left out. I believe I mentioned last night that he had several employment offers. They were all excellent, well-known and respected firms. He told me that the one from Stevens, Frost & Putnam was the best offer, and he was sorely tempted. But he had set his heart on Brookhaven. I played no role in his decision, and in fact didn't know any of this until some months after he arrived. It caused a significant upset in his relationship with his parents, especially his father."

"I hear a sense of regret in your words," Elizabeth said.

Sam smiled. "Not for the decision he made. I've been thrilled to have Young Sam here. In an odd way, it's like finding my youth all over again." He hesitated, as if gathering the right words. "David, and that's what we call my son, the middle name we all share, David and Young Sam have not had an easy companionship. David is much closer to Young Sam's two younger brothers. David had a difficult relationship with me and his mother, but it was for different reasons. In Young Sam's case, he and his father are like oil and water. They love each other, of course, but they never got along. When Young Sam was born, David didn't know quite what to do with a child and a son."

He hesitated again. "David is very different from most people. He has a brilliant mind, but for a very long time, we and his doctors could see something was wrong. He hated to be touched, even by his mother. He was frightened of the forest, which mystified me, because it's the place I usually felt most at home. And still do. David would pitch terrible tantrums, terrifying his mother and driving the entire family to despair. He didn't speak like most people, his speech patterns being jerky and usually loud. He'd be fascinated for hours with the most inconsequential things, like lining up his toy soldiers. He also had a habit of blurting out things that were true but should have been left unsaid. We seriously considered having him institutionalized at the asylum near Jackson, and it was only Sean O'Brien who convinced us it would be a mistake.

"It's another long story, but, when he was six, my mother took David with her to Gettysburg. She'd been living there with her parents since the end of the war. Her father died in 1871, and it was her and her mother on the farm. She had an older brother, the uncle I hunted with in Pennsylvania and Maryland, but he had stayed with the army. David lived with her there. I don't know exactly what it was, but it was the best thing that could have happened, for him and for us. The cost, however, was permanent estrangement from us.

"My daughter-in-law Amy, David's wife, is a Gettysburg girl. We adored her from the beginning. She accepted David with all his limitations and his brilliance, and she's worked very, very hard with him. I know there must have been days when she was at her wit's end. Young Sam was born during that time. For seven or eight years, he was their only child. It was a difficult time for the entire family. And then something seemed to happen with David. It was as if he settled, still with many of his problems, but settled. And he was better. Joseph and Michael were born a year apart, and David took to them like you'd expect a father to do. He tried with Young Sam, tried to make some kind of amends, develop some kind of relationship, but I think too much had happened between them. David and Amy knew about the offer from your father's firm, because the letter arrived at the house in Gettysburg. David thought it was addressed to him and opened it. When Young Sam declined the offer and said he was moving here to Brookhaven, David erupted and likely said some things I'm sure he later regretted.

"Miss Putnam, my son is a professor of mathematics at Gettysburg College, and he is a brilliant mathematician. He's published papers and textbooks and given lectures all over the Northeast. And I haven't seen him in more than 20 years. He will not come to Brookhaven; he didn't even attend his mother's funeral. And I am not welcome in Gettysburg. Amy would bring Young Sam every summer, and then the younger boys when they were old enough. Until his internships, Young Sam spent every summer here, not Gettysburg. When he turned 10, he began taking the train by himself to come here. He even came here the summer after his year-abroad study in Germany in high school and the year he spent there in Germany during college. He's so fluent in German that the family he boarded with thought he was lying at first about being an American. Because of the ugly scene over Young Sam rejecting the job offers, he and David have not seen, spoken, or written to each other in more than two years, and David has not allowed Amy and my other grandsons to visit. And it breaks my heart. Almost everything relating to my son breaks my heart.

"When I went to Gettysburg for the anniversary of the battle two years ago, David would not see me. Amy and the two boys visited at the camp that had been set up, but David took a sudden trip to New York."

He shook his head. "So, yes, you have rightly sensed regret in my words."

"Did you and your wife have other children?"

"Two beautiful girls, Edith and Helen. Edith and her husband Todd have four boys; they live in Texas where Todd has gotten himself involved in the oil business and done quite well. Helen and her husband Carter live in Shreveport, where Carter is a banker; they have two girls and a boy. So, with David's three, I have 10 grandchildren and I'm soon to become a great-grandfather, with Helen's oldest boy about to become a father. Both girls and their families come every summer for a big family reunion." He laughed. "I call them girls, but Helen is 40 and Edith is 38. David is 47."

He stood. "Young Sam will be waiting for us in front of the hotel. And we can talk more as we drive."

12

The faces of familiar friends seemed strange;
Their voices I could hear;
And yet the words they uttered seemed to change
Their meaning to my ear…

—from "Hawthorne"

September 1865

Sam returned to Brookhaven on Sunday, Sept. 3, a week shy of five months since he left Appomattox. He came from almost due east, following the road from Monticello in neighboring Lawrence County. He'd spent the night beside a stream near Monticello and awakened early, Sophie and her children still sleeping. He bathed in the stream with a small sliver of lye soap and trimmed his beard with the use of scissors and a small mirror. He changed from his traveling clothes to ones that approximated Sunday-go-to-church clothes. Sophie and the children were stirring by then, and he went walking through the woods while they readied themselves.

The four rode the wagon into Brookhaven, Sam's horse Tag tied by the reins to the wagon's side. It was Sunday morning quiet in Brookhaven, with what few people were on the streets hurrying for church. They made directly for Brookhaven Presbyterian. Knowing this was exactly where the family would be on a Sunday morning, he tied the horse's reins to the hitching post in front of the church and told Tag to wait. Sophie said she and the children would remain in the wagon. Sitting at the church door was Marcus Wheelwright, a longstanding church elder taking his turn checking guns and keeping an eye out for strangers in town during Sunday worship service.

"Stop right there, young man," Wheelwright said in a commanding voice. "Your rifle and your gun stay with me. They're not allowed inside during worship."

"Yes, sir, I understand," Sam said. "How are you, Mr. Wheelwright?"

The man frowned. He didn't recognize this tall, rather gaunt young man with a neatly trimmed beard. The young man's clothes were almost too good for him to be a returning soldier, who'd usually arrived in town in little better than rags. Wheelwright glanced at the horse and the wagon with three black faces staring at them.

"It's Sam, Mr. Wheelwright," Sam said. "Sam McClure. Is my family inside?"

Wheelwright's mouth fell open. He jumped up and embraced Sam. "Well, praise the Lord, Sam. No one knew what had happened to you. We'd heard you were—." He stopped.

"Dead, I'd imagine," Sam said, smiling. "Not quite."

Wheelwright nodded toward the wagon. "And who might they be? Since the end of the war, the ones still in Brookhaven worship at their own church."

"They're a family needing to get to Vicksburg, sir. They'll wait here, if you're obliging."

"Get inside, boy," Wheelwright said. "You know where

your family sits. Sixth and seventh pews from the front on the left. I'll keep an eye on your companions."

Sam nodded his thanks and quietly opened the church door.

The congregation was just finishing a hymn. Sam looked on the left side and spotted his father, with his mother sitting next to him. Simply seeing them brought tears to his eyes. Cora Beth was next to his mother, with Littleton next to her in the aisle seat. Behind them sat Martha and Emily and his nieces.

The pastor had stepped up to the pulpit, preparing to start the sermon, when he saw Sam standing by the door. The man stared for a minute, recognized the young man, and then glanced at the seated McClures.

"I don't think the Lord will mind," he said, smiling, "if we wait a few moments before I start the message for today." And he nodded toward Sam.

Littleton was the first to turn his head. The boy saw what he thought was a stranger standing at the back. He frowned and stared hard. And then he almost flew from his seat and ran to Sam.

Franklin and Louisa both frowned, perturbed by Littleton's sudden move. They turned to see the boy throw his arms around a stranger and begin to sob.

Cora Beth turned and then stood. She, too, suddenly ran toward the rear of the church. The congregation began to murmur loudly.

Franklin and Louisa both stood. Louisa gasped and made her own dash to the back. As she reached Cora Beth and Littleton clinging to the stranger, she stopped. This was not the boy she'd known. Before her was a tall, thin young man sporting a beard. She saw from his eyes that he seemed older than what his obvious youth suggested. Watching the mother and son, the congregation grew quiet.

"Mama," Sam said, tears in his eyes.

The next thing Louisa knew was that her son's strong arms were holding her close.

Franklin, recognizing his son, held himself in check to prevent running to the back as well. He walked quickly to the rear.

"Papa!" Sam said. "Papa!" And Franklin, overcome with emotion, found himself holding his son, the son he'd feared was dead.

The church service eventually resumed, and Sam joined his family, sitting between Cora Beth and Littleton. Behind him, Martha and Emily and the girls kept reaching forward and touching his shoulders, his back, and his head.

For days afterward, the family had dozens of questions, but Sam answered very few. He said he had served in the east, with the Army of Northern Virginia. He said he'd been paroled and discharged at Appomattox and had to make his way home, often stopping to work in a swap with farmers for food and shelter. "I plowed and planted a lot of cotton and corn seed," Sam said. "By the time we reached southern Alabama, I was helping to harvest the first of the early corn." He said he'd been given the horse, a three-year-old he called Tag and previously owned by a dead plantation owner. "It was more a case of Tag finding me," Sam said. And someone had given him the clothes of a husband killed in the war.

No, he didn't see violence, or much of it, on the roads, he said. They were often in the company of other soldiers making their way home, at least in the first few weeks. Some days it was hard to find food; local people were rightfully suspicious of anyone they didn't recognize.

"What did you do in the war, Sam?" his mother said. "Were you infantry, cavalry, rifles? They said you enlisted with the 9th Mississippi Rifles, but that you were ordered elsewhere almost immediately."

Sam didn't answer for a time. He shook his head. "Maybe another time, Mama. I did a lot of things."

Another time would never come. It wasn't long for the family to realize that Sam wasn't willing to talk about his wartime experiences.

He explained the presence of Sophie and her children by saying she'd been a slave in North Carolina, and he'd agreed to see that they got to Vicksburg, where her husband had been sold three years before.

From his own experience in the Mexican War, Franklin felt a touch of fear in his heart. He knew that Sam's reticence suggested that his son had been involved in activities that didn't lend themselves to easy explanations. He suspected, again from his own military experience, that Sam might have been messenger boy, spy, scout, courier, or some combination of all of them. Or something darker, like sharpshooter or assassin. Something like what had happened in Mexico.

It was only Littleton, sharing the same alcove bedroom, who had a small glimpse of what Sam had done in the war. Littleton would often awaken to the sounds of Sam moaning in his sleep. The boy would rise and touch Sam's shoulder, stepping back after learning the first time that Sam would immediately jump out of bed. He'd stand there, drenched in sweat and shaking. The first couple of times it happened, Littleton had been terrified. He was used to it now, and it seemed to be happening less than at first.

"I'm sorry to have awakened you," Sam would say. "It was bad dreams."

"From the war?" the boy said.

"From the war," Sam said.

"You talked about a fire," Littleton said.

Sam was quiet and then shook his head. "It doesn't bear mentioning, Littleton."

Right before Christmas, Sam walked to the store one morning as he now usually did to open for business. He saw a thin, almost emaciated figure sitting outside the front door. At first, he thought it might be a vagrant who'd spent the night on the bench. But the figure turned and looked up into Sam's face, and then stood.

"I was waiting, hoping you'd come home. Or that Mama and Father were still here."

It was Nate Cohen.

13

I pledge you in this cup of grief,
Where floats the fennel's bitter leaf!
The Battle of our Life is brief,
The alarm,—the struggle,—the relief,
Then sleep we side by side.

—from "The Goblet of Life"

May 1863

At the enlistment and training camp in Jackson, the lieutenant had first walked Sam to the mess tent, where he was given a package of rations. "Eat sparingly, private. It's to last you until Atlanta."

The lieutenant himself accompanied Sam to the Jackson train depot. "In Atlanta," the officer said, "you'll be met at the station by a Major Armstrong, who will ask for your orders. He'll give you further instructions."

"Yes, sir. Sir, how will I know Major Armstrong?"

"He'll find you."

Sam had ridden the Jackson-to-Atlanta line many times with his mother, when they made their way to Pennsylvania for their annual six-week visit. From Atlanta, they would travel to Richmond and then Washington, D.C., where they would change trains for Philadelphia. The final leg was from Philadelphia to Gettysburg.

The train from Jackson was crowded with military officers, a few families, and businessmen. In Atlanta, as Sam stepped off the train and looked around, he saw a man signal to him. Sam walked over and saluted. That station was crowded, with two trains having just arrived.

"I'm Major Armstrong. Your orders, soldier?"

Sam handed him the still-sealed envelope. The major opened it and withdrew another envelope. A message was written on the outside.

"Track 3," he said. "You're to take the train to Richmond. Major Colby will meet you when you arrive." He handed Sam another box of rations and what Sam could see was some type of train pass. "Show this to the conductor when he comes through for tickets. I'll walk you to track 3 now. My orders are to wait with you until you board and the train leaves. We have at least an hour. Meantime, you might fill your canteen from the water spigot."

Sam followed the officer. Atlanta's station was considerably larger than Jackson's. The last time he had been through here was the summer of 1860, that last visit to his grandparents. He remembered the station's three tracks.

Waiting for the call to board, Sam watched the busyness of the station. Atlanta had been a major hub before the war, and now it was even more important, with food, weapons, and other wartime supplies for the Confederate armies moving both north to Virginia and west to Tennessee and Mississippi.

"Recently enlisted?" Major Armstrong said.

"Yes, sir, about a week ago."

"I'm not sure what it is you have or know, private, but they're moving heaven and earth to get you to Richmond.

Do you have family in the military?"

"A brother died at Shiloh, and another brother is with General Johnston in Tennessee. My father was an officer in the Mexican War."

The officer nodded. "Perhaps your father is the connection. Those Mexican War veterans are a tight-knit bunch." He paused. "Would your father happen to be Franklin McClure?"

Surprised, Sam nodded. Before he could ask how the man knew, the conductor shouted out the first call to board for Richmond. Major Armstrong shook Sam's hand and told him good luck.

"Thank you, sir," Sam said. "Thank you for the rations."

Sam boarded and found a seat. Through the window, he could see Major Armstrong waiting. As the train began to move, the man smiled and nodded.

After about an hour, the conductor came through the car, collecting tickets. When Sam handed him the pass, the man's eyebrows went up.

"Well, this is a surprise," the conductor said. "Soldiers usually ride the freight trains, in boxcars or flatbeds. You must be something special to someone."

"They haven't told me, sir," Sam said. "All I know is that I'm going to Richmond."

"Very unusual," the conductor said. "Very unusual. If you need anything, I'm the man to check with."

Two days later, just outside Petersburg, Virginia, the engineer guided the train on to a sidetrack, and there they sat, for two hours, until another train headed south passed by them. The journey resumed, and an hour later, Sam's train reached

Richmond's main station.

It was dark, about 8 p.m., when Sam stepped down from the car and looked around. His fellow passengers were either met by people waiting or hurried out of the station. No one came forward like Major Armstrong had in Atlanta. Sam walked to the mostly deserted reception hall and looked around. He wasn't quite sure what to do. He had very little money, and his food rations were just about gone. He was thinking he might have to spend a hungry night on one of the station's benches when an officer came hurrying from the street.

"I'm sorry, soldier, for my delay," the man said, returning Sam's salute. "I'm Major Colby. They told us your train would be delayed at least three hours, but I can see I was misinformed. And you're Private McClure?"

Sam nodded. "Yes, sir."

"Come with me."

They exited the station, and the major led Sam to a waiting carriage, one that was nothing like the hauling wagons he was used to. It was a shiny enameled black with red cushioned seats. A black man in a top hat and evening coat was driving.

"Back to Franklin Street, Noah."

"Yes, sir," the driver said.

"You have your packet of orders?" the major said, turning to Sam.

"Here, sir," he said, handing him the envelope.

"I know this must seem rather mysterious," Major Colby said, "but there's a good reason, which you'll learn shortly. When the telegram arrived from Jackson, saying you'd enlisted, we were immediately alerted. When I told the general, he was surprised, because he thought you might be too young, and I can see he wasn't far wrong."

Sam was becoming more mystified, and he wondered if he might be still foggy from the trip. "The general, sir?"

Major Colby smiled. "I'm not being very clear, am I? You know almost nothing about this. We're riding to General Lee's house on Franklin Street, where he lives when he's in Richmond. I'm a member of his staff and one of the guests he and Mrs. Lee are hosting tonight for dinner. The general served with your father in the Mexican War, and they'd been regular correspondents right up until the war started. He'd even offered your father a commission in the Confederate army, but Franklin declined, saying he could not fight against either the United States or Mississippi. Which meant he would sit out the war and risk being caught between both sides. But, in his letters, your father had told him quite a bit about you, your hunting and tracking skills, what he called your 'citizenship of the woods,' no matter where the woods were, and your knowledge of Maryland and Pennsylvania. That's what brought you here, private.

"And the general is anxious for your arrival. President Davis and several members of the cabinet are his guests tonight, and General Lee is trying to convince them that he should take the war into the Yankees' territory."

Sam felt almost terrified. He'd had no inkling of what this was about, except for what the officer in Jackson had said about Maryland and Pennsylvania. He thought about his grandparents in Gettysburg.

"We'll stop briefly at General Lee's," Major Colby said, "and then you'll go on to my house, a few blocks away. That's where you'll stay for the time being. Then we may go on to the camp at Fredericksburg. You've been assigned to my command, and I'll explain more tomorrow. Tonight, General Lee wants to meet you."

October 1915

Young Sam drove the Buick through wooden gates with an "O'Brien Stables" nameplate in the centering arch. They went down a road with fenced pastures on both sides, and several horses in each. The road turned through a small grove of trees and came to a stop in front of what Young Sam called "the house."

But what a house.

Elizabeth could see immediately that this had been the main building for the grist mill. It reminded her of many brookside mills she'd seen in New England, but it was larger, with a wide front porch and what must have been a side structure added later. Nearby were two large barns and a building that Sam told her was both a stable and a business office.

Coming down the steps of the porch were an elderly couple. Elizabeth recognized Mrs. O'Brien, Sam's sister Cora Beth, and knew the man must be her husband, Seamus O'Brien. He had snow-white hair, might be 5 foot 7 inches in his boots, and was as attractive now as he must have been when he first came to Brookhaven during the raid in 1863. He had beautiful dark brown eyes.

"I see, Sam, that the leprechauns didn't mislead you into getting lost," Seamus said, a huge grin on his face. "And Cora Beth didn't say a word about the reporter being such a beauty.

Now don't pay me any mind, Miss Putnam; I've had the Irishman's gift of gab since I was born, and my brother Seamus, the good Lord rest his soul, would have told you how I drove my dear mother and father to distraction with all my jabbering." He reached for her extended hand then tucked her arm under his. "If I wasn't so much in love with my Cora Beth, I'd be more than willing to run off with you to New Orleans." Seeing her almost shocked surprise, he laughed. "And remember to ignore what are clearly the ravings of an old Irishman."

"The leprechauns have clearly trained you well, Mr. O'Brien," Elizabeth said. "Why do I suspect that there's a very clear-eyed businessman behind all your blarney?"

"Oh, she's a delight, she is," Seamus said. "Young Sam, you might want to think about convincing her to stay in Brookhaven. You know, Miss Putnam, you could do a far sight worse than Young Sam here, good-looking young buck that he is."

At that point, Cora Beth stepped towards them, her hands moving rapidly.

Young Sam, blushing with his uncle's words, translated. "Aunt Cora Beth says you are to pay him no mind, he's full of nonsense, and he's always saying outrageous things."

"Seamus," Sam said, still grinning, "might we prevail upon you to take Miss Putnam on a tour of the stables? I'll have Young Sam accompany you, to make sure you don't get too out of line or flirtatious. As capable as she seems to be, I think an escort might be appropriate."

"I will be glad to, Sam," Seamus said. "And now I know that when I die, I won't need to go to heaven, because I just experienced it here today."

Elizabeth and Young Sam laughed. Cora Beth shook her head at her husband, but Elizabeth could see her smile. They'd been married almost 50 years, and she was certainly used to his ways. The kindly twinkle in his eyes told Elizabeth that Seamus O'Brien was a total gentleman.

Sam stayed with his sister while Seamus walked with Elizabeth and Young Sam to the stables and extended operations. In a very businesslike voice, an abrupt change from his previous playfulness, he explained that they had between 30 and 40 horses at any given time that belonged to the business, and another 20 they boarded and trained for others. O'Brien Stables had earned a reputation for excellent racehorses and breeding stock.

"Uncle Seamus won't mention," Young Sam said, "that he's also known for his scrupulous behavior in a business that has more than its fair share of shady operators. You should tell her about some of your customers, Uncle Seamus."

"Oh, tosh," the Irishman said. "We have good customers from all walks of life. We treat everyone the same."

"You do," Young Sam said, "and your celebrated fair and honest dealing has brought customers like kings from Arabia and the former Prince of Wales from England, who's now the king. And his horses have won the Kentucky Derby three times and a host of other races."

"That's amazing," Elizabeth said.

"We have good horses," Seamus said, clearly embarrassed by his great-nephew's words. "That's what it is. People can see the quality." He covered his embarrassment by launching into the details of the operation. They toured the barns and he explained how they used each of the business's six fenced pastures.

They entered the stables.

"How did you get started in this business, Mr. O'Brien?" Elizabeth said.

"I was a horse trainer on a big English-owned estate in County Cork," Seamus said. "We survived the potato blight, but so many people died that the English lord who owned the place couldn't find enough workers for the fields, potatoes and otherwise. He finally closed the entire estate, and I decided to follow my brother Sean to America. By that time, the Civil War was on, and I walked off the ship in New York into the welcome arms of the army recruiters. We were offered decent pay and, more importantly, citizenship, in return for service. Because of my background with horses, I was sent to a cavalry unit being formed under Major Benjamin Grierson. Are you familiar with Grierson's Raid?"

"Yes," she said. "Several people have told me about it, including Mr. McClure."

"I was one of the wounded federal cavalrymen who were left behind with the unit's doctor. A local girl, by the name of Cora Beth McClure, was recruited to care for us. I'd been wounded in my leg; even now, I can tell you when rain's on its way." He smiled, remembering. "She was like this silent angel. The doctor told us she was mute, but he said she was not deaf, and we were to mind our language and manners. I had an edge on the others; she'd never met an Irishman before, and I could get her smiling and laughing, silently, of course. When the war was over, I returned to Ireland to see my mother and father and the rest of the family, and then I came back, traveling from New York down to Brookhaven. I was determined to marry her, and I knew Sean was already here. He told me she lived two houses down from him and was still unmarried. And that was that.

"But to your question directly, it was Sam who financed the horse operations. He'd closed the grist mill when the big flour companies began to dominate the business. And there was this prime property, with lots of space for pastures. To this day, I don't know where he found the money; times were desperately hard, but, somehow, he did. And he's made a tidy profit off his investment, if I do say so myself." He paused. "Do you ride, Miss Putnam?"

"I'm not a horsewoman, Mr. O'Brien," she said. "But I took lessons in boarding school and in college, and I occasionally ride the horses in Central Park in New York."

"That's splendid," he said. "After we have some refreshment back at the house, Young Sam here is going to take you for a ride through the property so you can see it all properly. You ride side-saddle, I expect?"

She nodded. She could see that Young Sam was as surprised as she was, but he quickly nodded in agreement.

"Young Sam," Seamus said, "is one of the best horsemen I've seen anywhere. There's only one perhaps better than he is, and that's his grandfather. But it's a close race. The two of them have a way with horses that's absolutely astounding."

"You a great teller of tales, Uncle Seamus," Young Sam said.

"That is no tale, as you well know. Now, let's see to our tea."

14

Be still, sad heart! And cease repining;
Behind the clouds is the sun still shining;
Thy fate is the common fate of all,
Into each life some rain must fall.
Some days must be dark and dreary.

—from "The Rainy Day"

March 1866

Three days after Louisa had left for Gettysburg, Sam and Littleton went hunting.

It was early when they left Cherry Street, together riding Sam's horse Tag. Daniel had stayed home in bed, his mother keeping a watchful eye over what was a bad cold. The weather had turned bitterly cold, with snow falling overnight and light snow continuing. Both Sam and his nephew were bundled up against the weather but still feeling the cold. Sam allowed Littleton the choice of where they'd enter the woods, and the boy had nodded toward the area closest to the property's farmhouse.

Before the war, Sam's brother James had lived in the farmhouse with Emily and their daughters. It was something of a family division of labor, with James on the farm; Hugh at the sawmill; Jarvis at the gristmill; Louisa, Cora Beth, and Martha at the store; and Franklin, and often Sam accompanying his father, moving back and forth among all three. But in early 1863, with social order beginning to fray, Franklin had moved Emily and the two granddaughters from the farm to the house on Cherry Street.

Sam and Littleton rode to the farm and tethered Tag to a tree next to the woods. The snow had finally let up. They'd just entered the woods when Sam stopped them, holding his finger to his lips. He pointed.

Twenty feet away was a deer, a large stag. Sam had seen does and fawns in the woods before, but rarely a stag. The animal was magnificent.

Sam hesitated for barely a second. He quickly set what he considered his strongest and sharpest arrow in the bow. Littleton did the same with his bow, but he signaled that he knew that Sam would shoot first.

The animal turned his head toward them just as Sam released the arrow. A second later, Littleton let his arrow fly as well. The animal staggered and then went down.

They ran over to the deer. Just as they arrived, the animal shuddered and then was still.

"A clean kill," Sam said. "A fine job of it, Littleton. The deer didn't suffer. Now, I need you to ride Tag home and tell Papa, Martha, and Emily. Tell Papa to bring the wagon and stop at the Cohens' store to get Nate. It's going to take the four of us to get the deer into the back of the wagon and home. And Nate will help me hang him in the smokehouse."

"Will we eat deer tonight?' Littleton said.

Sam laughed. "No. We have to get him hung, and then I'll gut him. Then we have to get past the stiffening. We don't do the butchering right away unless you want to eat what tastes like shoe leather. I think the weather will hold for a few days, and about Monday we'll start the butchering. Believe me, he'll taste a whole better if we age him a bit. Now go get Papa."

He hoisted Littleton into Tag's saddle and then leaned towards the horse, speaking in a low voice. "Tag, take Littleton home, and bring him back."

Sam believed the horse understood every word he said, although he wasn't completely certain. But Littleton and Tag were off.

When the boy had left, Sam dragged the deer carcass to the open ground next to the woods. And then he waited.

An hour later, Franklin and Nate arrived with the wagon, Littleton following on Tag.

Eyeing the deer, Franklin looked almost spellbound. "Oh, Sam," he said finally, "what a beauty. We haven't had deer meat in three or four years."

"Nate," Sam said, "we're sharing this with you and your family. I need your help to lift this boy into the wagon and get him hung once we're home, and we'll need some guidance from you or your father on butchering him according to your custom."

"My mouth's watering already, Sam," Nate said.

After some maneuvering, the four of them got the deer into the back of the wagon.

Emily, Martha, Sophie, and the children were waiting, along with Nate's father. They all watched the deer as Sam and Nate pulled it from the wagon and then hung the animal in the smokehouse. Under Mr. Cohen's direction, Sam quickly sliced the stomach and removed the organs and intestines, placing them in large, clean buckets brought by Martha and Sophie, who served as the family's cooks. And then he used a strong stick and propped open the deer's now eviscerated stomach.

"The temperature's near perfect to let it hang," Franklin said. "What a blessing, Sam; you did a great thing here."

"Littleton, too, Papa," Sam said. "We both fired arrows. Without Littleton, it wouldn't have been a clean kill, and the animal would have suffered."

Franklin tousled his grandson's hair. "Good work, boy."

Littleton beamed.

While the others remained to admire the deer, Sam walked with Martha and Sophie back to the house to wash up.

"Do you know what it would mean to Jarvis to know you've taken his son in hand?" Martha said.

Sam smiled. "I loved Jarvis, Martha. He was always kind to me. And he taught me a lot about hunting. I'm just passing on to Littleton what Jarvis would have done himself."

"You're doing a lot more than that," she said. "You've become Littleton's father, and you're keeping us all alive." She paused. "Louisa was right. We were mean to you, Sam. You really do owe us nothing for how we treated you. You would have been perfectly justified to go with her to Pennsylvania."

Sophie heard every word but kept silent.

"This is my family, Martha," Sam said. "It's where I belong."

"Is there a girl who's caught your eye yet?" she said. "I noticed a few of the girls giving you the eye in church last Sunday, and then you were surrounded after service."

Sam shook his head. "Given the war, the pickings for young men are a bit slim. If you're single and breathing, you're an attraction. But there's no girl. Not here in Brookhaven, anyway."

"Whoa," Martha said. "That sounds like there is someone."

Sam was quiet for a moment. "No, not really. There was someone I met, but it wasn't possible, for a number of reasons. Do you need help with the innards?"

Sophie smiled to herself. She knew who Sam was referring to.

The deer meat and organs passed the Cohen family's kosher test, though it was a reminder of how sore the topic of food had become between Nate and his parents. But that night, the Cohens joined the McClures for a feast of the organ meat.

Nate had returned from the prison in Alton profoundly changed by the experience. Like Sam and his war experiences, Nate wouldn't talk about prison with his family. What they knew, however, was that Nate no longer kept kosher or attended worship at the synagogue.

"If I'd kept kosher in Alton," he said to his parents, "I'd have starved to death."

He was more forthcoming with Sam. In late January, the two had taken the McClure's wagon to the woods, to gather firewood. They talked while they rode and worked.

"I blessed the name of Doc Pettigrew more times than I could count," Nate said. "Remember how we both howled when he gave us the smallpox vaccine?"

Sam grinned. "I do. We were convinced we'd die. We ran a fever for a day or two, but that was it."

"It saved my life in Alton, Sam," Nate said. "We had two outbreaks, and they wouldn't send for medical help. There were two Jewish brothers from St. Louis imprisoned with me, and they both came down with it. A crooked competitor of their father's wholesale business had accused the family of Southern sympathies, and the two sons were railroaded into Alton. The older son was almost recovered from the pox when the dysentery hit. It killed him two days later. The younger son nearly died of the pox. Nobody would help him. I tried to keep him drinking water, kept him as cool as possible. I convinced a guard to bring some extra water and a little food, and to get a note to his father in St. Louis. The guard smuggled in some medicines and food, and it must have cost Mr. Stein a fortune in bribes. But it saved his son. We were packed in like fish salted in a barrel—3,000 of us in a prison built for 250.

"The winter was a nightmare. No fires were allowed. No way to keep warm. No coats or gloves. We used these thin cotton blankets from our beds to wrap ourselves in. More than a few prisoners died from exposure.

"And when I came home, almost the first thing my parents asked me was if I'd kept kosher. If I'd a place to go, I would've walked out. The guards and the commandant at Alton would have laughed if I'd asked to eat kosher."

They chopped and gathered wood for two straight hours and then rested. Sam could tell that Nate needed to talk more.

"When the war ended and we were released, Joseph, that was the younger brother, was too weak to walk out on his own, so I carried him out. The Stein family was waiting. Mr. Stein asked me where Judah was, and I had to tell him that his son was dead and buried in an unmarked grave with hundreds of other men. I rode home with them; Joseph was near out of his mind and wouldn't let anyone but me nurse him back to health. He was too weak even to feed himself. You saw how bad I looked when I came home, like somebody's bad drawing of a scarecrow. I looked worse, like walking sticks, when we were freed in June.

"I stayed with the Steins six months. They were a well-to-do St. Louis family and lived on one of those private streets. They didn't keep kosher, and I didn't care. Just to eat real food again was a miracle.

"From time to time, Mrs. Stein would ask if I wanted to write my parents. I said no, and I didn't have a good reason. The Steins told me I could stay as long as I wanted, but once Joseph had mostly recovered, I knew it was time to go. Mr. Stein paid for my passage on a steamboat to Vicksburg." He shook his head. "They were brokenhearted over Judah, but they kept thanking me over and over again, calling me Joseph's savior. Joseph remembered more of what went on than I thought he did, and he told them."

"You did save him, Nate," Sam said. "Even in that hellhole, God was there. You were God for Joseph."

"I don't believe in God anymore, Sam," Nate said. "That and my not keeping kosher is causing real problems with my parents. I think they try to understand, but they can't imagine something like this. I can't talk with them about it." His voice broke. "Father's handed me an ultimatum. I have to follow family rules or leave. He's given me until Spring."

"Nate," Sam said, "don't leave Brookhaven. I need you here. If a family break comes, come stay with us. The farmhouse needs someone to live in it, and I'll talk to Papa. And maybe your father will come around."

Nate Cohen stood staring at Sam. He couldn't speak. Tears filled his eyes. He finally nodded.

October 1915

"Does Nate still live in Brookhaven?" Elizabeth said. She sipped her second cup of Cora Beth O'Brien's very good tea.

Sam shook his head. "In late 1867, about eight months after Janie and I married, Mr. Stein came down from St. Louis to find Nate. They'd apparently kept exchanging letters, and he knew that Nate had been shunned by his family. He came to ask him to consider living with them in St. Louis. Their son Joseph had physically survived prison, but he lived as a perpetual recluse. I think the Steins hoped that Nate might help cure their son. It was a big ask of Nate to give up his life here, but as he told me, he felt like he had no family life left in Brookhaven. He accepted Mr. Stein's offer, and he left for St. Louis about a month later."

He shook his head. "I have to tell you, Miss Putnam, that Nate leaving about broke my heart. But his prospects were much brighter there than here. The Steins had a large home on a private street; it was a well-to-do Jewish neighborhood. Nate lived there the rest of his life. He continued to care for Joseph after the Steins died; the two were like brothers, almost twins. Nate did marry a Jewish girl he met, and she and their children lived in the Stein household as well. He never returned to Brookhaven, but I usually found a way to visit every two years or so. He'd been the best man in our wedding, and I was the best man in his."

"Is he still living?" Elizabeth said.

"No," Sam said. "Nate died in 1909. It was his heart, the doctors said. Joseph had died the year before, and I think it took some kind of toll on Nate. The man had never married; Nate and his family had become Joseph's family. One of Nate's sisters still lives here in Brookhaven, and she maintains correspondence with Nate's widow and children in St. Louis."

The group sitting at tea fell into a silence. The family, and even Elizabeth, knew that this was something Sam felt deeply, something with a combination of joy and pain, memory and childhood. Sam was looking away, staring through a window, and Elizabeth felt his growing loneliness in old age, as people he knew and loved passed on.

Sam cleared his throat. "After Mama left to visit her folks in Gettysburg, she never returned except for once. It was in 1874, when our oldest David was six. After she left in 1866, I'd written a ream of letters, but she never responded."

15

We spake of many a vanished scene,
Of what we once had thought and said,
Of what had been, and might have been,
And who was changed, and who was dead;

And all that fills the hearts of friends,
When first they feel, with secret pain,
Their lives thenceforth have separate ends,
And never can be one again…

—from "The Fire of Drift-wood"

September 1866

September 9, 1866

Dear Mama,

I hope this letter finds you and the folks there well and in good health. I do not know what your plans might be for returning to Brookhaven, but I thought you would want to know that Papa has suffered a stroke. He was working at the sawmill when he suddenly fell down. Mr. Perkins from Perkins Farm was there with his son Jeremy, and he sent Jeremy running to Doctor O'Brien. This was the 4th of September. I apologize for not writing sooner but things have been rather busy here with all the upset.

Doctor O'Brien says Papa is stable, and that it was a medium-size stroke. His left side has some paralysis, especially around the mouth, arm and leg. Papa is having a little difficulty with his speech, but he's already a little better from when it happened. He's confined to bed for the moment, but Doctor O'Brien says we will need to be getting him up and about soon. The doctor is not one for long bedrests.

I should tell you about Doctor Sean O'Brien. He was a surgeon in General Johnston's army, while his younger brother Seamus was a federal soldier in Grierson's Raid. Seamus was one of those federals left behind whom Cora Beth helped to nurse. Doctor O'Brien was on his way to start a new life in Texas, but his brother told him to visit Brookhaven. He did, and then he stayed. We're mighty grateful to have him; there's been no doctor in town since Dr. Pettigrew died, as you'll recall. He says his brother went back to Ireland to see family but that he's expected to return and come to Brookhaven.

He is a very fine doctor, with a medical degree from the University of Dublin. He's been keeping close watch over Papa, and he's been boarding with Mrs. Pettigrew and using old Dr. Pettigrew's surgery, so he is close at hand. He thinks Papa will make a decent recovery, but there will be some changes.

Everyone here is well. Nate Cohen is now living in our old farmhouse and is growing a little cotton and some vegetables. He is estranged from his family, and it has much to do with not keeping Jewish customs. He had a very hard time in the prisoner camp in Illinois. I'm still hoping his old sense of humor comes back.

I am well. We covet your prayers. And I hope I will see you soon.

Your loving son,
Sam

Nov. 13, 1866

Dear Mama,

I hope this letter finds you in good health and good spirits. I have received no response from my last letter, so I'm not sure if you received it or not.

Papa is slowly on the mend from his stroke. Doctor O'Brien had hoped he might make a speedier recovery, but it has been very slow; the stroke may have been more severe than we first thought.

As you might imagine, the biggest problem for Papa has been the loss of his privacy. He is dependent upon us for his personal needs, as he is not yet able to navigate the stairs for the privy. Littleton has been a great help to me in this regard.

Cora Beth helps Papa eat; he is now able to sit at a table in your bedroom for his meals. He can hold his fork and spoon with ease, but she or one of us must help with his knife, as his left side still suffers some paralysis.

You would be interested, and I hope pleased, to know that Cora Beth is engaged to the brother of Doctor O'Brien. As I mentioned in my previous letter, he was one of the federal soldiers left behind after Grierson's Raid, and she had cared for him and the others. When the war ended, he returned to see his family in Ireland. He came back to the United States, and he is a full citizen because of his war service. As I mentioned before, he was the one who sent his brother the doctor to Brookhaven. His name is Seamus, and he is a fine fellow. I like him very much. When he arrived, he first found his brother, and then he came looking for Cora Beth. After a time, he met with Papa and asked his permission to marry her. He had learned sign language, and that's how he proposed to her. The wedding is planned for Christmastime.

We may have two weddings; Doctor O'Brien has been courting Miss Russell, the schoolteacher.

As I mentioned in my October letter, Nate Cohen produced a good harvest of vegetables and cotton at the farm. We have been blessed with a flood of corn, potatoes, melons, cabbages, and more. We have shared the bounty with the Cohen family and others, but the Cohens are still estranged from Nate, and they will only accept the food from me. I think they know that their son is helping to provide their nourishment.

I hope you receive this, and I hope you might consider returning to us soon. Papa asks daily if I've heard from you.

Your loving son,
Sam

Dec. 26, 1866

Dear Mama,

I hope this letter finds you well and in good health.

I hope you had a fine Christmas.

We had a double wedding on Christmas Eve. Doctor O'Brien married Miss Russell, and Seamus married Cora Beth. It was at our Presbyterian Church. The O'Brien brothers, being Catholic, didn't seem to mind. We were able to help Papa attend. Nate and I carried him down the stairs in a chair and out the front door to a waiting carriage. He was unable to walk down the aisle, so I had the honor of giving both brides away. We must have made a fine sight, with me in my best suit and a bride on either arm.

I don't think I've ever seen Cora Beth so happy. Seamus is so tender and loving with her. To watch him follow her with his eyes is a wondrous thing. You will like him; he has a keen sense of humor, and he tells fine stories. He's also helping to take some of the work from me; he's been helping to manage the sawmill, allowing me more time for the grist mill and the general store. Even though he fought for the Yankees, the people here have grown quite fond of him and his stories.

Our political situation is getting very serious. The Reconstruction government in Jackson is apparently set on levying ruinous taxes, especially on former plantations. It is quite a thing to see former slaves occupying positions of authority. That is a development that's very difficult for many people to accept. Many say we're being treated like a conquered people, and I suppose that's what we are. The vote has been taken away from anyone who served in the Confederate government or military, which is not a problem for me since I'm not old enough to vote anyway.

Littleton, Daniel, and I have been hunting, and we've gotten several game birds and another deer. Litt and Daniel are becoming quite the experts with the bow and arrow. Ammunition is becoming more plentiful than it was a year ago, for which I'm thankful. I'm not very proficient at making my own bullets. We still have shortages of some things, but it's eased considerably since you were here.

Mrs. Pettigrew has some additional guests, Miss Octavia Jane Montgomery, late of Windhaven Plantation in Alabama, and her young cousin. I escorted them to Alabama from north of Greensboro, North Carolina, where they had been visiting relatives and became stranded by the war. Traveling with Miss Montgomery and a young girl, plus Sophie and her children, slowed my return to Brookhaven considerably. We were just talking about our great adventure, and the sudden realization of how much we went through together made us thankful to God for his protection.

Miss Octavia lived with her family in Alabama, but her father died at Chancellorsville and her mother from a fever. Her oldest brother was captured at the Wilderness and died in a prison in New York. Her other brother, who served under General Bragg, tried to manage the plantation but taxes and loss of their slave labor were ruinous. Their plantation, one of the largest in southern Alabama, was sold for debt and back taxes. He has gone on to an offered position in Brazil, down in South America. Miss Octavia told him she and their cousin, whom we call Honeybee, would settle in Brookhaven.

Papa sends his love. He still asks me daily if I've heard from you. We miss you.

Your loving son,
Sam

April 14, 1867

Dearest Mama,

I hope this finds you well. I'm of two minds about my letters to you. I hope you're receiving them, but I also hope yours in return are getting lost or mislaid. We've heard nothing here, only that mail service now appears to have been regularized.

In my last letter, I should have been more forthright about Miss Octavia Jane Montgomery, and I do ask your forgiveness. When she arrived here with her brother and young cousins, her brother explained to me that she was insistent on coming here rather than accompanying him to Brazil. She was coming here because of me. After we arrived at Windhaven in Alabama, it was a very hard thing for me to leave her. And yet too many things seemed to stand in our way, not the least of which being her coming from a very wealthy, slave-owning family. Their wealth had been destroyed by the war, of course, and her brother had no interest in trying to keep the plantation together, which he said was impossible without the slaves. I'd never spoken to her of my feelings, but it was likely not too difficult for her to see. What I didn't realize was that her feelings for me were just as strong.

You are now an official mother-in-law. Janie, as I call her by her middle name, and I were married on April 9, my birthday. It was very bright and sunny. Mrs. Pettigrew, Mrs. O'Brien (formerly Russell), and my sisters made a great fuss about the bride, and she was indeed beautiful. As her brother had moved on to Brazil some months back, Seamus did the honors of escorting her down the aisle. Nate was my best man, while Cora Beth served as matron of honor. The house across Cherry Street that is owned by Mrs. Pettigrew was vacant, so we have established our household there, with Janie's cousin from North Carolina. Honeybee's family lived near Greensboro, where Janie and her grandmother had gone to help her sister during her confinement. Due to various circumstances of illness and the war, the little girl was left an orphan. She traveled with us to Alabama, when I escorted Janie home. When I met the family after Appomattox, Janie's grandmother was dying from a cancer. We buried her there in the family plot at the plantation.

Mama, I love her very much. I know I am only 17, and she is 16, but she makes me feel a complete person. I hope you will love her as a daughter. When we met, she was still trying to learn how to dress herself without the help of slaves. She now churns butter, builds a fire in the stove, cooks, and can make flapjacks over an open campfire. She minds her young cousin, and she helps Martha and Emily in the store. The experiences we had on the way from North Carolina to Alabama created a bond between us that I doubt could ever be broken.

Our home is also quite convenient for me to continue to care for Papa. He's doing well, but I'm afraid his paralysis may be permanent. Littleton has been doing his grandfather a great service, and a great service for me as well. I love that boy like he's my own.

Your loving son,
Sam

October 1915

"It just struck me. Littleton. That's Professor Seale," Elizabeth said.

Sam smiled. "The very same."

"You think your parents somehow emerged fully grown,

because that's how you know them," she said. "You hear stories about their youth, but you think they're really talking about someone else."

"We were all young once," Sam said. "We all had the hopes and dreams and the fears that come with being young. The war interrupted all of that for our generation, or perhaps a better way to say it is that the war, mostly by necessity, reshaped and changed what those hopes, dreams, and fears were all about."

Seamus, Cora Beth and Young Sam were listening, saying nothing. They'd never heard about the letters, or the full story about Nate Cohen.

"You were 16 when your father had his stroke," Elizabeth said. "The responsibility must have been huge, and you were still teenaged."

Cora Beth began speaking in sign language.

"My Aunt Cora says," Young Sam said, translating, "that while all the family helped, the heaviest burden fell on my grandfather. My great-grandfather died in 1867, and Emily in 1870 of a ruptured appendix. Martha died in 1874 of a stomach cancer. We had a house full of children and teens and precious few adults. And there was all the corruption and upheaval of the Reconstruction to contend with."

"Seamus and Sean were there," Sam said, "and I can't tell you how much I came to depend on the two Irish brothers, as we called them, and on Cora Beth."

The entire group was silent.

"On that rather somber note," Seamus said, "I think it's time Young Sam here took Miss Putnam on a horse ride. We still have light left, but we won't if you wait much longer."

Seamus escorted Young Sam and Elizabeth back to the stable.

"I think I'll saddle Eva for Miss Putnam," Seamus said. "Eva could do with some air. She's a nice mare, Miss Putnam, gentle as a lamb." He motioned to the young groomsman who stood waiting instructions. "And I assume you want Galahad, Young Sam."

"I don't think Galahad would let me leave on another horse," Young Sam said.

Elizabeth watched Young Sam walk over to a stall containing a magnificent black stallion. The horse was snorting and shaking his head, which he lowered to accept Young Sam's hand. "I better be the one to saddle him, though."

"Galahad is Young Sam's horse," Seamus said to Elizabeth while Young Sam saddled the horse. "He's high-spirited and can be a bit rough to handle, but he's like a bosom friend to Young Sam. He would have made a fine racehorse, but there are only three people he'll let on his back—Young Sam, Sam, and myself. There was some thought to selling him, but then Young Sam moved here to live, and Sam decided to keep him. Young Sam takes him for a run three or four times a week, and it's like watching a man and a horse become one being. I've not seen anything like it since Sam rode his horse Tag after the war."

The horses were ready. A step was placed next to the mare for Elizabeth to reach the saddle, but she couldn't figure out how to lift herself side-saddle. She turned around, and suddenly met Young Sam. His hands around her waist, he lifted her up to the saddle. Their eyes locked about two seconds longer than they should have.

"Thank you," Elizabeth said, feeling the blush on her cheeks.

Securely seated on the mare, she followed Young Sam on Galahad. They trotted toward the woods, and soon she saw a parting in the trees that revealed what was a wide bridle path. Seamus watched them leave, a smile on his face.

For a time, they rode in silence. Then Elizabeth spoke.

"Your grandfather said that you spent two years in Germany, one in high school and one during college. It must have been exciting. What part of Germany?"

"It was Heidelberg," Young Sam said. "On the Neckar River, a tributary of the Rhine. I spent my junior year in high school or what the Germans call 'gymnasium,' and my junior year of college at the university."

"Where did you stay?"

"Both times with the Mittelstein family. Dr. Mittelstein is a professor of chemistry at the university. He and his wife had signed up to serve as a host family for study-abroad students. They had three children. Wolfgang was the oldest; he was working in the Foreign Ministry in Berlin, and he still does. Paul was the second child, and almost exactly my age. I think it was because of Paul that I was matched to the Mittelsteins. Because he was the middle child, he was called Mitti, or German for 'middle.' Mitti Mittelstein. Their youngest was Annaliese, who was two years younger than Mitti. I'd applied to a program sponsored by Gettysburg College, where we lived and where my father taught and still teaches."

"Did your parents escort you to Germany?"

"No. I was 16, so they believed I was old enough to take myself, since I'd been taking the train by myself to Brookhaven since I was 10. It wasn't like the excitement of Papa Sam's experiences at 16, but I took the train to New York, made my way to the steamship line, and sailed on the S.S. Heimatland for Hamburg. The voyage took six days, and then I took a train south to Heidelberg. The Mittelsteins met me at the station."

Elizabeth smiled. "Did you already speak German?"

"I'd taken German for three years, so I leaned in the direction of textbook fluent. But it was more than enough for me to travel and live with the Mittelsteins. Germans are always surprised when Americans speak their language. My time with the family greatly helped my language skills because they didn't speak English and I had to build upon what I knew. It was the same for my classes at gymnasium. At university, my major was German history and literature, and everything was taught in German." Young Sam touched Galahad's mane lightly.

Elizabeth felt intrigued by Young Sam's foreign travel and asked him if it was a good experience.

"It was wonderful," Young Sam said, "both with the family and in school. And the family liked to travel between school terms, so I got to see some of Austria, Italy, and Berlin. The best part, though, was that Mitti and I became best friends. The family had me share his room. We were in the same classes in gymnasium, and he immediately included me in his circle of friends." He smiled. "Mitti is gregarious; he attracts people and friends like flies. I was a fish out of water, a foreigner, and naturally shy to begin with. Mitti opened up life for me."

"What is the family doing now, with the war? Do you stay

in touch with them?"

Sam didn't immediately respond. When he did, the affectionate tone she'd heard when he had been talking about his German friend had shifted to something more formal. "We still write regularly, but the war has made it difficult. Letters to and from Germany and America are channeled through Sweden or Switzerland. The time lag is often months." He paused. "To answer your first question, Wolfgang is still in Berlin with the Foreign Ministry, the last I heard. Annaliese is working for a convalescent hospital in Heidelberg. And Mitti is somewhere on the western front, with the German Army." He paused again. "I've had one letter from him, and a few notes passed through his parents. I write to him in care of his parents in Heidelberg, and they forward my letters. Contributing to the time lag is that all letters to and from Germany are checked by the censors."

Young Sam smiled. "I was able to return a small bit of their hospitality. The summer before my junior year in college in Heidelberg, Mitti came to America, and I met him when the boat docked in New York. He stayed with me for a week in Gettysburg with my family, and then we took the train here to Brookhaven, where we spent the rest of the summer. We had a wonderful time, and he and Papa got along famously. At summer's end, we traveled together back to Heidelberg."

He looked away. "I miss him. I miss him terribly. I worry about him being at war, and I pray for him every day, Miss Putnam. I pray for his family, too. I know that Germany is the aggressor nation in this war, but I love the Mittelstein family. They opened their home and their hearts to me, and being a part of their family, even for a short time, was something I'll always be grateful for."

Elizabeth felt that something was being left unsaid, but it would be rude to probe. She sensed that he found something with the Mittelsteins that he didn't have with his own family.

"You didn't really tell us much about yourself and your family," he said, startling her from her thoughts.

"You noticed that, did you?" she said. "I've been trying to be the professional journalist, maintaining my distance and detachment, and I've discovered that the McClure family and its extensions are making that rather difficult. Beyond what I've already said, I'm hoping to be assigned to cover the war in Europe, so now you know why I'm so interested in your background. I can tell you that I am the despair of my mother, who wants to see me married into one of Boston's Brahmin families and settled with children, instead of pursuing a working career. I covered an Irish bar brawl in Boston, and the story horrified her and likely put me beyond the pale for Boston mothers seeking suitable wives for their sons.

"My father is more supportive, but he's conscious of my mother's feelings. My brothers think of me as something of a tomboy. And the entire family finds some other place to be if I start talking about the vote for women. Does that tell you enough?"

Young Sam laughed. "It tells me that you might find riding Galahad here to be something of a tame experience. Ah, we've reached the end of the trail."

The trail ended in a clearing next to a small river. The late afternoon sun filtered through the tall pine trees, dappling the gently flowing water. The silence enhanced the beauty of the view.

Elizabeth felt a quiet and solitude she'd rarely experienced. She looked at Young Sam's face, and she saw he was experiencing something similar.

"It's the East Bogue Chitto River," he said. "As the name implies, there's also a West Bogue Chitto. They come together just south of here and merge, continuing on to the south. This particular spot is perhaps my favorite in all of Brookhaven."

"It's beautiful."

"And it's often a fight to keep it that way. Papa has had an untold number of offers for the land on both sides of the river here. The city fathers would love to see it developed. But he's determined to keep it as he's always known it, and likely as it has always been." He cleared his throat. "The county fair begins tomorrow. Opening ceremonies are at 3 p.m. I know it sounds rather bland and humdrum, but it's really not to be missed. If you'd like, I'd be glad to escort you. Papa doesn't go until the fireworks on Saturday night, but the rest of the family usually manages to be there most every day."

"I'd be quite honored to be escorted by you, Sam," she said.

It wasn't until they were almost back at the stables that she realized she wasn't sure if this were simple kindness to a guest or if it was more like a date. Young Sam had said nothing about seeing anyone, but that may have been simple reticence. She decided to consider it an invitation to a guest, but she knew she wouldn't mind if it were an actual date.

After dinner back on Cherry Street, the family members present all remained at the kitchen table, to hear Sam continue telling his stories to Elizabeth.

16

Into the darkness and the hush of night
Slowly the landscape sinks, and fades away,
And with it fade the phantoms of the day,
The ghosts of men and things, that haunt the light.

—from "Ultima Thule, Night"

May 1863

Major Colby escorted Sam up the front steps of the house on Franklin Street. A tall black man in formal livery opened the door and nodded. "I will inform General Lee you're in the library," he said.

The major directed Sam down a short hall and to a doorway on the left. The room wasn't large, and it seemed almost filled by a desk and a table. Books were stacked on shelves, and the walls were filled with framed pictures, but it was the table that drew Sam's attention. It was covered with several unrolled maps, held open by small metal statues and a bust of a bald-headed man (Major Colby would tell him later the bust was of Cicero, the famous Roman orator).

Within minutes, two men appeared in the doorway. Sam had seen enough likenesses of both that he immediately saluted.

General Lee smiled. "At ease, soldier. Welcome to Richmond." He shook Sam's hand. "Do you know President Davis?"

"No, sir," Sam said, "although he lives not far from us in southern Mississippi."

Davis shook Sam's hand. "Lived," he said, glancing at Lee. "I understand my home has been occupied by the federals around Vicksburg." He looked closely at Sam; Davis and Sam were exactly the same height, with Lee only slightly shorter. "General Lee says you're his secret weapon for a proposed campaign. I did not expect someone so young."

Sam, somewhat perplexed at the description, looked at General Lee.

"Private," Lee said, "I have some maps here that I need you to see. I am not familiar with the region, but I need you to look and tell me the best places to move and position an army."

"I know nothing of military strategy, General Lee," Sam said, "But I can speak to the terrain."

Lee led him to the table by the desk and unrolled several maps. The top map showed the central Pennsylvania and Maryland border region. Sam studied it and then looked at General Lee.

"I don't rightly use maps, sir," Sam said. "This one seems a fair reflection of the region I'm familiar with, but I know the land more from the ground level."

"All right," Lee said, pulling a map from underneath. "What about this one?"

It was a hand-drawn map of the Gettysburg region. Sam could see it was detailed enough to denote farms, woods, and roads. He could also see a diagram of the town. His eyes went directly to where he could see his grandfather's farm, west of the town out the Chambersburg Road.

"Our projected path will lead us up the Chambersburg Road and into Gettysburg," Lee said.

Sam looked up. Lee, President Davis, and Major Colby were all staring at him intently.

"Is something wrong, Private?" Lee said.

"The map is approximate, sir," Sam said, "only roughly accurate." He pointed. "The woods here, along Seminary Ridge, they're not as close to the Emmitsburg Road as this suggests. Some of the farms are shown with the wrong names, and a couple of them are missing. And the woods at the south end of Cemetery Ridge are larger than this here. I know, because I've hunted them with my uncle."

"Your uncle?" said President Davis.

"Yes, sir. My grandfather's farm is a mile or so west of Gettysburg," Sam said. He swallowed. "It's out the Chambersburg Road." He placed his index finger on the map. "Right here."

"It's a shame, General Lee," President Davis said, "that you didn't have Private McClure here with you at Chancellorsville."

Lee and Major Colby had begun to smile, but Davis's words put a chill in the room.

By 11 p.m., Sam and Major Colby were riding in General Lee's carriage to Major Colby's rented home a few blocks from Franklin Street.

"You must be close to starved," the major said. "I should have said something to Mrs. Lee."

"I am a mite hungry, sir," Sam said.

"My wife, Alma, will arrange something in the kitchen.

For the time being, you'll stay with us; a few more of my men are with us as well."

"Sir," Sam said, "could you tell me what your unit does?"

"We're a special group, Sam," Colby said. "Officially, we're listed as the 2nd Virginia Rangers. General Lee and his staff simply call us Colby's Rangers. We do surveillance, reconnaissance, run messages, and occasionally infiltrate the enemy's ranks. To put it shortly, we're spies for General Lee."

Colby paused. "While President Davis was unaware, General Lee and I were testing you tonight. We knew about your grandfather's farm, and we knew that map was inaccurate. We wanted to see how you'd respond, knowing full well that you'd see both the risk to the Gettysburg area in general and your grandfather's farm in particular. It was unfair of us, of course, but we needed to test your loyalty, and to see if your geography and directional skills were everything your father said they were."

With all that had happened in the past few days, Sam wasn't quite sure how to respond. "Did I pass the test, sir?"

"You did, indeed. It was something of a risk, with President Davis being there, but General Lee remembered your father's surveillance and espionage skills well enough to suspect you had at least some of them. And he needed to impress Davis with the informational resources we had available for heading into the North."

The carriage stopped at a two-story townhouse, smaller than General Lee's but of similar design. Colby stepped down from the carriage, and Sam followed.

"Sir," Sam said, "my father was a spy?"

The major smiled. "You didn't know? I was part of his

unit in the Mexican War. He trained me." He paused. "Sam, you seemed extremely familiar with the farms in the Gettysburg area. Would your grandfather's farm make a suitable field headquarters? That sounds better than you might think. General Lee forbids destruction or looting of any farm where he establishes his field quarters. It would offer your grandparents considerable protection."

Sam nodded. "It's the largest farm and farmhouse in the Gettysburg area. It could easily accommodate the general and his staff. But I suspect my grandfather would be furious."

"No doubt," Colby said. "Now, let's see if Alma can find you something to eat."

The next three weeks passed in a blur. Sam spent three nights at Major Colby's house ("Enjoy it now, Sam," Major Colby said; "You won't have many opportunities to sleep in a bed with a roof over your head"). Four other members of Colby's unit were staying there as well, men older and considerably more experienced in warfare than Sam was.

When Major Colby introduced Sam, one of the men, Caleb Willingham, nearly spat. "Since when do we conscript mere boys, Major?"

"We don't," Colby said. "Sam here has knowledge of Maryland and southern Pennsylvania, which is more than any of the rest of us have. And Caleb, I'm assigning you to take him under your wing to train him."

Willingham turned red in the face but said nothing. Sam didn't relish the upcoming training.

They started in the small back yard of the Colby house. They drilled, they practiced closequarters fighting, and Willingham showed him the quickest way to kill a man with a knife. The man might have been furious with his assignment, but he took to it faithfully. The man was sparse with his words, but Sam became his captive audience for what soon became almost non-stop training. Sam was also introduced to his horse, and the others were surprised at how quickly the animal took to the boy.

The day before they learned their next mission, Colby's Rangers discovered their new recruit had more depth and skills they than they could have imagined, completely changing the Rangers' perception of Sam.

They were practicing hand-to-hand combat in the Colby's rear yard. Using a short stick for a knife, Caleb Willingham unexpectedly grabbed Sam from behind with a stick at his throat. Willingham found himself flat on his back, the wind knocked out of him, and staring at the sky.

"What the heck just happened?" one of the Rangers said, staring at Caleb and then at Sam.

Major Colby has been standing on the rear porch, watching. "Sam, did you just do what I think you did?"

Sam stared at the man on the ground. It had happened so fast, the response had been so immediate, that Sam at first wasn't sure what to say. He offered his hand to Willingham, helping him stand when the man accepted it.

"Where did you learn that, boy?" Willingham said, after catching his breath.

"I can hazard a guess," Colby said, stepping down from the porch. "There's only one other time I've seen a maneuver like that, and it was Big Tom, that Cherokee Injun who stuck to your father like his shadow."

Sam slowly nodded. "He taught me some moves. He spent a long visit with us, almost a year, until he told my father it was time to go to his people in Oklahoma."

Having finally caught his breath, Willingham spoke. "I have one question, boy. Can you teach the rest of us what he taught you?"

On May 29, Colby had his wife and the slaves who worked in the kitchen prepare an extensive meal. Sam guessed it meant they would soon be sent out, and he wasn't wrong.

"You leave tomorrow," Colby said at dinner. "Early, before sunrise. Each of you will ride a different road. Sam, you and Caleb will travel together. You will have papers identifying you as father and son, and you're on your way to see what cattle might be available in Hagerstown, in Maryland, and then Chambersburg in Pennsylvania once you cross the state line.

"In two days, the Army of Northern Virginia will follow. Longstreet, Hill, and Ewell will join together at Hagerstown. Caleb, you and Sam will ride ahead of Lt. General Hill." Colby continued to give them instructions, and then he pulled Caleb aside for a private and very intense conversation. The way both the major and Willingham kept looking over at him, Sam assumed he was the main subject of their conversation.

Sam, expecting a sleepless night, was surprised when Caleb shook him awake. A finger to his lips for silence, he indicated to Sam to gather his things and follow him. They were apparently leaving earlier than the other men.

It was still dark. Alma Colby and a kitchen girl handed them parcels of food for their breakfast and lunch. They filled their canteens. Their saddlebags, packed for them, contained a change of clothes. They would not be wearing uniforms.

"If the Yankees identify us as soldiers, Private McClure," Willingham said as they rode down the street, "we will be shot for wearing civilian clothes." He smiled. "Just so you know."

They rode first to the Confederate camp near Fredericksburg. The camp was in motion; orders had been distributed and the army was beginning its preparations to leave. For the initial move north, Lee was dividing the army into three parts, commanded by Generals Longstreet, Ewell, and Hill. Willingham and Sam would be ahead of General Hill's army by about two to three days. They left the camp on June 1, riding toward Culpepper.

"We won't likely see any Yankee troops for a week to 10 days," Willingham said. "But whenever we do, you remain quiet and let me do the talking. Is that understood?"

Sam nodded.

Their small group initially consisted of six men on horses. At regular intervals, a man would peel off and return to the main army with a report to Gen. Hill. The ride was uneventful.

They passed few people on the roads. The air seemed electric with anticipation, as if nature itself was aware of great military movements afoot.

By the time they reached Sharpsburg in Maryland, Sam began to recognize the terrain.

"I spent a few days in this area when I was seven," Sam said, "hunting with my uncle, particularly the area between Sharpsburg and Hagerstown. I remember the rivers and creeks."

Before entering Sharpsburg, what remained of the unit split up, with Sam and Willingham going on to the town and the others riding around it.

"You and I are staying the night here," Willingham said. "Remember, we're a father and son returning home to Pennsylvania. Our buying trip for livestock in western Virginia was unsuccessful. And don't talk. You sound more like a Yankee than I do, but don't speak unless I tell you it's all right. I expect the townspeople here will still be nervous after the battle last year."

Colby's Rangers were a tough, hard-drinking bunch. Unfailingly polite around Mrs. Colby, the talk turned more than colorful as soon as she was out of earshot. So did the drinking. Evenings after supper meant jaunts to a tavern in a less salubrious part of Richmond. Sam would accompany them but avoided drinking alcohol. He and Nate Cohen had tasted hard liquor once and vowed never to touch it again.

In Sharpsburg, Caleb and Sam found a small hotel with a stable yard, the Jacob Rohrbach Inn. The town had recovered somewhat from the battle of less than a year before, but the nearby battlefield still bore the marks of the carnage. The battle had been to the north and the east of the town, but the Confederate Army had occupied the town itself, with all that occupation implied. Caleb and Sam found the people at the hotel quiet and suspicious, with the clerk owner asking detailed questions about who they were and where they were going. Sam thought to himself that the man was right to be suspicious; little did he and other townspeople know that the Confederate Army would be returning in a matter of days, passing through as it headed north.

The clerk also said that General Lee had used the hotel for his war council during the battle the previous September. Sam didn't miss the slight hint of pride in the man's voice.

After depositing their saddlebags in their room, Caleb said his stomach could no longer be ignored. "We need to find some dinner."

What they found was the only open place in Sharpsburg that served meals. And the Sharpsburg Tavern had a sizeable sign in the front window: "No Women & No Children Under 16."

Caleb stared for a moment. "You wait out here, and I'll bring you some food and something to drink." He went inside, and Sam sat on one of three available benches, none of them currently occupied.

Almost an hour passed before Caleb returned, handing Sam a thick sandwich containing a slab of ham and one of cheese and a tall glass of what turned out to be something that tasted like root beer. He could see that Caleb's face was already flushed, reminding Sam of the forays the man and his fellow Rangers made to Richmond's taverns.

The sandwich was good, but then Sam was so hungry that anything would have tasted good. He was about halfway through it when two soldiers in blue, one an officer, rode up.

The officer tied his horse to the hitching post and immediately addressed Sam. "Boy," he said, "have you seen any strangers come through town? We've had reports of Rebel spies."

Sam, wide-eyed, shook his head. "The strangers might be me and my papa," he said. "We're passing through on our way to Chambersburg, up in Pennsylvania."

"And what might your business be?" the officer said. The soldier at his side was listening intently and had his hand near a pistol.

"Papa's been trying to find milk cows," Sam said. "Our good one was taken for the war and the one they left us with was sickly and is likely to have died before we get back." Sam hoped that Caleb wasn't too far gone in drink to remember the story they'd rehearsed.

"Your father's here?" the officer said.

"Yes, sir," Sam said. "He's the one with the bushy eyebrows and sideburns and handlebar mustache. He wears his farmer's hat toward the back of his head. And might you tell him that he's had enough to drink? My mama asked me to keep my eye on him and she and I would both appreciate it."

Both Union soldiers smiled and entered the tavern.

Sam continued eating his sandwich, although his stomach was in an uproar. He took some deep breaths to calm himself.

Some minutes later, the Union soldiers reappeared, followed by Caleb, who gave Sam an angry look.

"I decide when I've had too much to drink," Caleb said, almost with a snarl.

"Papa," Sam said, "you know I can't lie to Mama, and she's going to ask me for an accounting of everywhere we stop."

The Union soldiers laughed. "I'd listen to your son if I were you, farmer," the officer said.

Caleb mumbled something incoherent and hauled Sam roughly up by his arm. "Come on, boy."

The soldiers mounted their horses and left the way they came. Caleb didn't speak until they were back in their room.

"You were brilliant," he said quietly. "I believed you myself and I knew better. You were so good you should be on the stage."

17

The tumult of each sacked and burning village;
The shout that every prayer for mercy drowns;
The soldiers revel in the midst of pillage;
The wail of famine in beleaguered towns.

—from "The Arsenal at Springfield"

October 1915

"Now," Sam said, "it's late, and the children, not to mention us old people, need our rest."

Elizabeth looked around the table. No one looked tired or ready for bed. Every face displayed deep interest in Sam's story. She glanced at her notebook and saw that she had almost reached the last page.

"I'll need to buy new notebooks tomorrow," she said. "I've almost completely filled this one."

"I'll check tomorrow at the general store," Young Sam said. "They should be able to find something there. Or the school might have some extras."

"If you're expecting me to describe the battles I was involved in, Miss Putnam," Sam said, "I'm afraid I'll disappoint you. The fact is, I was directly involved in very few, and then it was primarily as a messenger boy or some other non-soldier capacity. I saw very little of the Battle of Gettysburg, and then it was only the aftermath of each day. For the first two days, Caleb and Major Colby ran me near ragged carrying messages from General Lee to his field officers, and then the third day I was ordered to melt into the Union lines and find a unit to attach myself to. My primary assignment was to figure out a way to get myself behind Union lines. It helped that the lines were ever-changing.

"And now, to bed."

Young Sam walked with her to the front of the house. "I'll come by about three. We could take the car, but it'll be crowded. The fair is about a five-block walk from here, if that meets with your agreement."

"That'll be fine," Elizabeth said. "Thank you."

"And I'll bring by some notebooks first thing." Young Sam smiled and, with a nod, left through the front door.

Waking early the next morning, Elizabeth made her way to the kitchen, hoping to find coffee on the stove. Which she did, with Sophie already up and preparing the family breakfast.

"You make the best coffee, Miss Sophie," Elizabeth said, taking a sip.

The woman smiled. "Taught by my mother, God rest her soul."

"When did you come to work for Mr. McClure?"

"Fifty years ago this past month," she said. "September of 1865. But I first met him that April."

"How did you meet?"

"It's a long story, Miss Putnam. It's a story about things happening that never should have. If you have time, I'll tell you."

"I have time. Can I help with anything?"

"You can put the plates on the table. We usually have about eight for breakfast, but set out 12, Some of the family might be coming by before heading for the fairgrounds later."

Sophie talked while Elizabeth set the table.

"It was in Greensboro, North Carolina, April of 1865. The word had spread of Lee's surrender, and then Johnston surrendering to Sherman right near town. The city was in chaos. Union troops were ransacking businesses and homes, looking for valuables but mostly drink. I had my two children with me, Belle and Daniel. We'd left Southwind Plantation, a few miles east of town. I'd come with the other slaves, freed when Gen. Sherman's army arrived. We were looking for a freedwoman I knew, Sadie Beechum. She'd always told me to look her up when I needed help.

"The Butler family owned Southwind. They weren't one of the old families. Mr. Butler's father had been a dirt-poor farmer, until somehow he managed to work himself into speculating. He made a fortune, and one of the things he did was buy Southwind. The family that had owned it had gone bankrupt, and Mr. Butler bought it. And that included the slaves. I'd been fortunate; I was a house slave, working in the kitchen. The previous owner had allowed me and my husband, Mac Boy, to marry. We had two children, Belle, born in 1853, and Daniel, born in 1857. We even had our own cabin. It wasn't much, ramshackle and cold as ice in the winter even with a fire, but it was ours. Here, sit yourself down. You look like you need another cup of coffee."

Young Sam cleared his throat. "I don't mean to startle you, but I have some notebooks for Miss Putnam."

"Wonderful," Elizabeth said. "Thank you so much. What

do I owe you?"

"We can settle up later. Unexpectedly, I have to be in court in an hour. I'll see you at 3 p.m., Miss Putnam." And he was gone.

Sophie laughed. "That young man is something. Always bustling about and some place to go." She smiled. "But he's a good man, with a good heart. Now, here's your coffee. Where was I? Oh, yes, The cabin.

"Mr. Butler and his overseer were not kind men. For whatever reason, the overseer, whose name I won't repeat even today, took it into his head to sell Mac Boy off. And he did. Right at Christmas of 1862. Sold him and two others to a man who had a plantation near Vicksburg and needed field hands. The only things I had to hold on to were the children and the promise Big Mac made to me right before they dragged him away. And that was, if we were ever free, to find him in Vicksburg. At the time, it sounded like China. I'd never been any farther from Southwind than the five miles or so to Greensboro. I didn't know if I would ever see him again or not.

"There I was with Belle and Daniel, trying to find Sadie Beechum in all that looting and chaos. It seemed everyone had gotten themselves drunk. First silly drunk and then dangerous drunk. We got directions to Sadie's place, and just as we turned down an alleyway by a general store, we ran smack into a group of drunken soldiers." She stopped and sat at the table. "They thought they'd have some fun. They began to bully and make lewd suggestions. Daniel rushed at the worst of the lot, but they just grabbed him and held him, telling him he could watch. They were laughing and drinking. Belle was terrified. They ripped my blouse and pushed me down on the ground.

They started to do the same with Belle when we all heard a voice break through.

"'Uncle Ned, can you stop this? Please stop this.' It was a young voice; you could tell it was the new voice a boy gets when he's maturing. There was a kind of silence. And then one of the soldiers, an officer, says, 'Sam? What are you doing here?'

"It was Sam McClure. He was trying to find medicine for Miss Janie's grandmother and happened upon us there in the alleyway. You can't imagine the chaos that was going on. Fires, looting, men fighting, it was terrible. Mr. Sam happened to recognize his uncle, a captain in Sherman's army.

"There was a kind of silence after that, and then his uncle told the others to let us go. And they did. We ran out of there as fast as our feet would carry us. I don't know what happened after that. But a couple of hours or so later, I found Sadie's house. It was locked up tighter than a drum, and Sadie was gone. At that, I just sat on the ground and cried. And who should come along but Sam McClure. He recognized us and asked what was wrong. I poured out my whole story. He asked if we had anywhere to stay, and I said no. He offered the plantation house where Miss Janie was. He said if I could cook, he'd trade a place to stay until something else came along. He'd pay me what he could, but Confederate money was worthless, and he said he had only a little bit of Union money. We had no other possibilities, so we walked with him a mile or so out of town to where Miss Janie was.

"Miss Janie saw us, she was but a slip of a girl, and she started fussing at Mr. Sam about three more mouths they couldn't feed." Sophie laughed. "He had a way with words. All he had to say was, 'She can cook.' And Miss Janie stormed off, but there were no more objections. He found a room for us off the kitchen, it had been the one for the cook who'd worked there but left, and I got to work.

"The first problem was how little food there was. Mr. Sam took me to a place behind the slave cabins where some food had been hidden, some tinned goods and even some real wheat flour. And then he went off to hunt, and he came back with a couple of rabbits and a duck. Belle helped me with the meal; Mr. Sam told me to save some of the meat stock for a broth for Miss Janie's grandmother. She was in a poor way. I took her tray to her room, but it was Mr. Sam who spoon-fed her. Miss Janie was barely 14, and she was still learning how to dress herself. She'd always had slaves to dress her, bathe her, and do her hair. She wanted me to help her with that, and I would've been willing, but Mr. Sam said no, she had to learn how to do that for herself now. She called him a bunch of names and flounced out of the room, but she heeded what he said."

Sophie laughed. "I thought they'd known each other for years. Turned out that it had only been a week, that he'd been trying to get home to Mississippi, but ran smack into the barrel of a gun with Miss Janie at the other end. He'll tell you that story, I expect.

"But that first night we were there, he sat us all down at the kitchen table, all of us except the grandmother. She was close to dying. And he laid out a plan. He said that he would see Miss Janie and her cousin Honeybee to her home in Alabama. It was something he'd promised her grandmother, even though he had no connection to that family at all. And he told me he would see me, Belle, and Daniel to Vicksburg, it wasn't much farther than where he was from, in Brookhaven." She laughed. "It wasn't all doing a poor family a kindness. He needed to have someone who knew how to cook, and who could make do with whatever might be at hand. Miss Janie was lost in the kitchen; she eventually learned some things, but a cook she wasn't.

"He saw Miss Janie and her cousin to Alabama, and then we rode to Brookhaven. We stayed for a couple of days, and then he drove us to Vicksburg."

"Did you find your husband?" Elizabeth said.

"Oh, we found him all right," Sophie said. "He'd endured the siege of the city, he and a bunch of other slaves being used to fortify the fields, dig trenches, make earthworks, and anything else the Rebel troops needed. When the city fell, he became a free man. When I found him, that no-account scoundrel had himself a new wife, with one child born and another on the way. And he told me I needed to go back to North Carolina, that we weren't his family anymore."

The room grew quiet and still. Elizabeth could only imagine what this woman she was sitting with had experienced, to have traveled all that way to find out not only her husband was alive but married to someone else.

"Mr. Sam brought me and the children back here. He said his sister Martha needed help in the kitchen, and that we could live in the small room right off the kitchen, for however long we needed and permanently if it suited us." Sophie shook her head. "I call him a man. He was just a boy. He paid me for my work, and he did a lot more than that. When the Freedman's Bureau opened a school here, Belle and Daniel attended. The

Yankee teachers were well intentioned, but there were too few of them and too many children who needed schooling. Belle in particular became real discouraged. Mr. Sam talked to Miss O'Brien. She'd been the schoolteacher but had had to quit when she married the doctor, and she agreed to teach Belle and Daniel while she taught the children in the McClure family. He even had me join them to learn reading and writing, and she worked hard to teach us."

That explained Sophie's educated bearing, Elizabeth thought.

"Miss O'Brien told Mr. Sam that both Belle and Daniel were very, very bright. When the time came, he sent Belle to a normal school for Black teachers in Atlanta. And four years later, he took Daniel to Philadelphia, where he enrolled in the university there and went on to medical school. Belle still teaches grade-school children in Atlanta; she never married. Daniel is a doctor in Philadelphia, married, and given me four grandchildren. My two children, both born slaves, were given opportunities I'd never even dreamed of. And Mr. Sam has always paid me well."

"Sophie," Elizabeth said, "if you don't mind me asking, how old are you?

"I'll be 75 next January."

Sam McClure stood in the kitchen doorway. "You're telling some of your stories, Sophie?"

She laughed. "You know I don't speak anything but the truth, Mr. Sam. Nothing but the truth."

"Breakfast about ready?"

"It is, indeed, so sit yourself," Sophie said. "I'll get some coffee."

Sam smiled at Elizabeth. "And good morning, Miss Putnam. I trust you slept well?"

"I did, Mr. McClure. Very well."

"I think I left off with Antietam last night," he said. "You can read about the Battle of Gettysburg. Any good history book will tell you what happened. What I remember are the sounds—rifle shots, cannons, men screaming as they charged. I'd never seen a battle before, and this one, well, this one was an awful revelation. Any notion of the romance of war and battle left my head for good. I spent almost all my time running messages between General Lee and his corps commanders, and sometimes directly between the commanders. Most of that was on foot, which was probably a good thing. I would have made a proper target on horseback. The battle raged three days, stopping only when night fell. For a boy of 13, I saw too much, the worst being the slaughter they called Pickett's Charge.

"The nights were bad. You'd hear soldiers screaming in the medical tents. Outside of one I saw a pile of arms and legs. You don't ever forget that kind of sight. Or the smell."

"Now don't provide details, Mr. Sam," Sophie said. "You'll put all of us right off our breakfast."

"You're right as usual, Sophie." Sam took a sip of his coffee. "Major Colby gave me two assignments. The first was to strategically lose some fake messages and orders. We found a dead Confederate soldier and placed a messenger bag around him, like he'd been shot while delivering orders. We placed him to the side of the road Lee was retreating along, pursued by some the Union scouts and trackers. The orders were in such a rudimentary code that a schoolboy could have figured it out. Which was by design. They indicated General Longstreet was approaching from the south and would soon plant his army between Lee's and Meade's. It wasn't true, of course, but we hoped it would buy Lee enough time to escape.

"The second assignment started as soon as we dragged the body to the side of the road. I melted into the woods and waited. The federals soon arrived, found the body, and halted until they could get the orders read. I backtracked toward the town of Gettysburg and the battlefield to the south. There was a lot of mopping up to do, and troops were used to help bury the dead. I walked up to one unit and said I would help. Remember that I still looked like a boy, tall, but nonetheless a boy. A sergeant handed me a shovel, and I helped identify and bury the dead soldiers. I must have impressed them with my efforts, because they shared some food with me. I knew enough about the area, so I had my story about who I was and where I lived.

"It was a calculated risk. No one had seen me, and I had no papers on me identifying who I was. At supper that night, a lieutenant was a little suspicious, so I offered to recite some Longfellow for him. It was the poems on slavery. I must have done well because, when I finished, there was a silence, the only sound being the lieutenant wiping his eyes.

"The soldiers I attached myself to were the Iron Brigade. I picked them because I liked their black hats. I knew none of their history or war service. It was weeks later when Major Colby and Caleb Willingham told me about them. You can do your own research here, but let's say for now that they were among the bravest and most ferocious soldiers any Confederate army faced. They were mostly farm boys from Wisconsin, Indiana, and Michigan, many of them only a few years older than I was. They kind of adopted me like a pet, and I stayed with them for the next three weeks. I marched with them, talked with them, joked with them, and ate with them. At night around the campfire, they always wanted to hear some poetry recited, and they didn't mind that all I knew was Longfellow. Their favorite was 'The Courtship of Miles Standish.'

"After three weeks, I told them I needed to make my way home, because I knew my parents would be worried. By that time, Meade's army was back in Virginia. I headed north from the camp, all the way back into Maryland in case anyone followed me to be sure. Then I circled my way back into Virginia, generally following the road Caleb and I had taken north.

"I got to Major Colby and told him what I knew. Militarily, it wasn't a lot. I knew where they were headed. I also had a take on morale, what they thought of their officers, the state of their ammunition and food supplies, and what Gettysburg had cost them." Sam shook his head. "I didn't like it, what I was doing, I mean. I liked those Iron Brigade boys. They'd become my friends, and they treated me better than well. What I think I learned there, Miss Putnam, was that the soldiers on both sides weren't so very different, and they would likely be friends if it wasn't for that dang war."

Sam paused. Elizabeth looked around the room and saw that she'd been so wrapped up in Sam's narrative that she'd been unaware of family coming in, getting their breakfast and sitting to listen. She saw Young Sam had returned from his law work.

It was Young Sam who broke the silence. "If she hadn't come, Papa, we never would've heard these stories."

"Every soldier has his stories, Sam," Sam said. "A lot of them sound the same. Some of mine are a bit different because of the work I did. But I will tell you that I still can't read or recite Longfellow without thinking of those boys of the Iron Brigade."

"You may have felt like you were presenting yourself as something you weren't," Elizabeth said, "but your recitations of Longfellow probably did more good for them than you might imagine. For a short time, they could forget the war, the death, the maiming, and probably their own fears, and escape into the worlds of John and Priscilla, and Evangeline, and Hiawatha. I think, Papa Sam, you likely helped them forget their own mortality, if but for a short time."

Elizabeth had surprised herself. She called him by the name his grandchildren called him, and she hadn't expected to insert her own responses into his story. But that's what she had done, and she wondered what kind of story, or stories, she could fairly write about this man.

She'd also surprised everyone else around the table. Young Sam was looking at her with a thoughtful but almost undefinable expression. Sophie and Beatrice were smiling, as were Cora Beth and Seamus. Even a few of the older grandchildren were looking at her with a bit of wonder on their faces.

"I have never thought of those recitations in quite that way, Miss Putnam," Sam said. "That's a very generous, and a very kind, insight. And from what I remember, I believe there may be considerable truth in what you've said."

He looked down the table where Sophie was sitting. "Sophie, might I trouble you for a sandwich I can take with me? I believe I'd like to spend some time in the woods."

At that, chairs were pushed back from the table, and almost everyone stood. Amid a small hum of conversation, they slowly made their way from the kitchen to the back door or other parts of the house. Only Elizabeth and Young Sam were left in the kitchen with Sophie.

"Did I upset Mr. McClure?" she said.

"You did not," Sophie said. "Not at all. What you did, Miss Putnam, was to touch his heart. He's not used to that, except in a different way with his grandchildren, but not in quite that way since Miss Janie died. What you told him was that, even as compromised as he felt being a spy, something noble came out of it, that he had given those soldiers a gift they couldn't have gotten any other way.

"My grandfather gives so much of himself to others," Young Sam said, "that he wasn't quite prepared for the gift you gave him. And it was a gift, Miss Putnam, a beautiful gift. And a blessing. More than that, it was a blessing for all of us. I know it was for me. The Civil War is forever a part of my grandfather, and I think you just taught him that he did others some good." He cleared his throat. "Now, I have one last visit to the courthouse today, and I'll be done. I'll be here at 3 to escort you to the fair." Young Sam nodded to her, hugged Sophie, and left.

Sophie sat beside Elizabeth, who was feeling a bit shaken.

"You appear to have touched the hearts of both McClure men here today," she said.

"Sophie," Elizabeth said, "they both have touched mine. This was about the last thing I expected to happen. Why do I feel almost frightened?"

"Perhaps change is blowing itself in your face, Miss Put-nam, and in your heart. Change can do that."

18

I have you fast in my fortress,
And will not let you depart,
But put you down into the dungeon
In the round-tower of my heart.

And there will I keep you forever,
Yes, forever and a day,
Till the walls shall crumble to ruin,
And moulder in dust away!

—from "The Children's Hour"

October 1915

Elizabeth ate a light lunch at 1 p.m.; Sophie had left a tray of finger sandwiches for all and sundry to help themselves.

She dressed carefully for the fair. Although no one had said anything, she fully expected that Brookhaven's women would be mindful of how they looked for the opening of Lincoln County's annual party, as Young Sam called it. She'd selected a blue serge skirt of very light wool, a collared white blouse lightly embroidered in a white floral design, and a crème-colored Panama hat with a dark blue underbrim and a swath of similarly colored material around the crown. A light blue serge jacket completed the ensemble. From the front window at the midpoint of the curving stairs, she saw Young Sam striding from his bungalow across the street.

They met at the front door. Sam was dressed in a light, almost crème-colored suit, his Panama hat with its dark blue band pushed back on his head, and a blue bow tie. A matching handkerchief was in his jacket pocket.

"You look lovely," he said, handing her a single white rose.

She smelled the rose. "It's heavenly," she said. "And you look rather lovely yourself. Do I take the rose with me?"

"No. It would just be in the way. I'll find a vase for it." Sam walked to the kitchen and quickly returned with a narrow vase holding water. He placed the vase with the rose on a side table in the hall.

Leaving the house, they turned right on Cherry Street. "Like I said, it's about five or six blocks to the fairgrounds." He offered her his arm, which she accepted.

"When I was a boy, there were a few times when my mother would bring me and then my brothers when they were old enough to the fair here. It was a real treat; she'd pull us out of school, and we'd take the train all the way from Gettysburg, just to come to the fair. My grandfather loved having us visit."

"Did your father come as well?"

Young Sam shook his head. "After my grandmother brought him to Gettysburg in 1873, my father returned once, when he was 15, so that would have been about 1883. From what I understand, the visit did not go well. He was supposed to be here for a week, but the visit lasted all of two days. It's hard to explain, and probably even harder to understand, but as you've already heard, my father is, well, he's different.

"He's a brilliant mathematician, but it's as if his social skills never developed. He blurts out the obvious when polite company would never mention it. He asks questions that everyone would like to ask but are too considerate to say aloud. He holds himself in what seems a very stiff way; he can't seem to turn his head without turning his entire upper body. My mother has worked very, very hard with him, and she's taught him many needed social graces. But he doesn't always successfully use them. He and my grandmother, who died the year I was born, did not get along at all. She was, according to my Aunt Cora Beth, all about social manners, as if they were her refuge and defense against the collapse of everything she knew as a girl. My father, her firstborn, was almost the antithesis of social manners, especially as a young boy. His behavior perplexed everyone, and that last visit was a disaster. He did not return even for her funeral, and he has not spoken to my grandfather since."

"That's 33 years, Sam."

"I know."

They'd come to a cross street. Sam looked both ways, and they crossed. Elizabeth could see other people walking in the same direction.

"For his part, my grandfather has tried to reach out to my father, but it's been mostly by letter. My father has chosen to not respond."

"So," Elizabeth said, "when you turned down the job in Boston to come to Brookhaven, your father saw it as you choosing your grandfather."

"That's part of it, of course," Young Sam said, "but there's more. I was born when my parents had been married less than a year. My father was still at a stage where he was unprepared for the sight, sounds, and smells of a new baby. He'd have very little to do with me, apparently, taking refuge in his study. My mother would talk with him at length, but the result was that we were never close. By the time my younger brothers arrived, as I said before, he was better. He had reached a new stage, and he actually welcomed them both, held them, played with them, and did many of the things fathers are expected to do. At some point, he realized he had not done that with me, and he tried to make amends. But it was awkward and usually ended in one of us becoming frustrated or angry. He would say something he meant as a statement of fact, but he didn't understand how his words could stab a young boy. I chose Brookhaven because this is where I felt I belonged, where I was accepted by family, and where I never doubted the love of my grandfather. We are alike in many ways, and not just the hunting and the horses.

"The fact is, Miss Putnam, I love Brookhaven. Yes, it's a small town, and it's far from perfect, but no place is. But this is where I determined to make my life. It's my home."

Elizabeth knew he was telling her this for a reason, not because he needed something to talk about. She sensed he wanted her to know, and she'd eventually find out why.

"Could I ask you a favor?" she said.

"Of course."

"Could you call me Elizabeth?"

He smiled. "Only if you call me Sam. We can always sort out which Sam you mean."

"It's a deal."

They walked in silence for a time.

"You have two brothers, I believe you said?"

"I have two brilliant brothers," Sam said. "Stephen is now 16, and the last I heard, he's planning on studying engineering at Cornell. He's got a fine mind for it. Michael is 15, and he's always been the prankster and comedian in the family. He has a marvelous way with words, young as he is, and I fully expect that one day he'll be a top-tier writer." He paused. "And you have two brothers as well?"

She nodded. "Charles Jr. is an attorney working in my father's firm."

"I met him on several occasions when I was an intern."

"He and his wife have three children, whom I absolutely adore. Edward is two years younger than Charles and is a doctor. He's married, but there are no children yet. I came later; there's a seven-year gap between me and Edward. I'm afraid I am my mother's despair; most of the girls I grew up with are married and have made brilliant matches, as my mother's so fond of pointing out. She's reluctantly accepted my ambition to work in journalism. My father is more understanding, but I think he, too, hopes that someday I'll settle down, as he puts it."

"And in the meantime, you're chasing after old stories about the Gray Wisp in the Civil War."

She grinned. "I am. I have to say, Sam, I'm enjoying every minute. I'm not sure what I expected, but I've fallen in love with your family, the whole extended clan, and in only three days, no less. Your grandfather is a dear, your Aunt Bea and Uncle Littleton most gracious, and Seamus O'Brien is one of the most original people I've ever met, and believe me when I say I knew plenty of Irish people in Boston. And you—"

She stopped herself. She almost said something that

would embarrass them both.

"And me?" he said, a grin on his face.

"I was going to say you've been most kind. I know I must be a nuisance, and you've been welcoming, friendly, helpful, and you don't seem to mind chauffeuring me all over town. And helping me go horseback riding."

She felt her cheeks redden. She remembered the touch of his hands as he lifted her to the mare. She hoped he wasn't looking at her.

"It's been my pleasure, Elizabeth. I didn't know what to expect when Papa Sam told me a journalist was coming, and that he might have need to call upon my driving and escort skills. But this has been a pure pleasure."

She felt mildly disappointed. She knew he couldn't really say anything else, but it sounded more like he was doing this for his grandfather.

"I should point out," he said, "that neither Papa Sam nor anyone else suggested I take you to the fair. That was all my doing, because I discovered how much I enjoyed your company."

She was no longer mildly disappointed. She felt herself blushing again.

"And we're here."

The Lincoln County Fair surprised her, considerably larger than she'd expected. Young Sam had explained that the state fair was held in Jackson in July, and for southern Mississippi, the Lincoln County Fair was the fall event.

It was already crowded. They entered through the main gateway, which opened into what Sam called the midway. And she agreed to his suggestion to simply stroll and see what was there, and then they could return to anything that might look interesting. Elizabeth saw food booths, games of chance and skill, puppet shows, pony rides for the children, wandering jugglers and acrobats, minstrels and singers, and larger tents with seating for meals. One particularly large tent, Sam said, was for the serious entertainment presentations and lectures, usually on agricultural topics. Another was devoted to the judging of animals, and still another to the sale of food produced on regional farms.

"You'll have to see the tomato girls," he said.

"The tomato girls?"

"About 12 years ago, two girls' clubs were organized, one in Lincoln County and one in Copiah County, just to our north. I think the original purpose was to teach farm girls some of the basics of food production and marketing. The product was tomatoes; we're the tomato-producing capital of Mississippi. The girls plant gardens, tend them, harvest their crops, and then do a lot of canning. Some of their efforts are quite creative. The clubs spread and just recently became part of the National 4-H program. As you might imagine, the tomato girls can be fiercely competitive. The star is one Emmeline Flood, who not only was the 1912 Lincoln County and Mississippi champion but the national champion as well. She was so successful that she used the profits she made to send herself to Mississippi Normal College." He smiled. "She set the bar for performance, and now every farm girl for miles around aims to match or surpass what she did."

"That's a wonderful story," Elizabeth said. "You may have to introduce me to this year's tomato girls. I might find something to write about."

"And we have a pie contest, a cake contest, a jam and preserves contest, a watermelon and pumpkin weight contest, and all kinds of animal judging competitions. Everything happens over the next four days, with the big awards announced on Saturday afternoon, followed by a dance and fireworks Saturday night. Friday night, I am scheduled with a couple from church to escort the church youth group on a hayride. We leave from here, ride to a clearing near the river, have a bonfire and a discussion time, and then return. You would be most welcome to join us, and I suspect the young people would be thrilled to have an official New York newspaper reporter along for the ride."

"Growing up in Boston, hayrides were something I never experienced. I'd love to come."

"Wonderful," Sam said. "Oh, look, there's Aunt Bea and Aunt Cora, which means Seamus must be somewhere around. Do you mind if we chat for a few minutes?"

They greeted the two women and were soon discussing pies, pickles, and the singing troupe scheduled to perform that evening, "the ones with the daring necklines," Aunt Bea said. Seamus showed up with his sparkling commentary, and Elizabeth was so charmed and more than slightly entertained that she didn't realize that Sam wasn't part of the conversation.

"Oh, my," Seamus suddenly said. "There's Margaret Barnett nee Biddle, and somehow she has her claws into Sam."

Elizabeth turned to where the others were looking. Sam was talking to a couple, or rather it was more a case of the woman in the couple talking at Sam. Her husband was smiling blandly, but even from a distance of 20 feet, Elizabeth could see that Sam looked worse than uncomfortable. And the woman seemed to know it and be enjoying it.

"Who are they?" she said.

"Sam and Margaret were thought to be an item for years," Aunt Bea said. "They'd been childhood friends, from the time Sam was about 10. They'd met at church, and by the time they were 14, it was a long-distance love affair. When Sam got his law degree and came to Brookhaven two years ago, I think everyone thought they might marry someday. But Margaret Biddle had no intention of living in Brookhaven. Sam discovered he was supposed to be her one-way ticket out of town, and when he told her he was settling here, she dropped him like he had the plague. He realized she'd never been interested in him but only in what she perceived as his ability to get her out of Brookhaven. Five months later, she married Hiram Barnett; they live in Jackson, where he's some kind of functionary in state government."

Seamus glanced at his wife. "And there's one great-aunt who'd love nothing better than to give Mrs. Barnett what-for."

Elizabeth could see Cora Beth's pressed lips and angry expression as she stared at the threesome across the way.

"I'm afraid she's trying to rub Sam's face into what she considers her great success," Aunt Bea said. "I hope he realizes one day what a narrow escape he had. Those Biddles were always social climbers."

Elizabeth watched a moment longer, and then, almost without thinking, she walked quickly and stood next to Sam. She tucked her hand around Sam's upper arm.

"Hello," she said, smiling, "I'm Elizabeth Putnam. I'm visiting with the McClures for the fair. Sam was so gracious to have invited me. And you are?"

Sam, momentarily surprised, introduced Margaret and Hiram. Margaret looked totally perplexed. Elizabeth could see she was an attractive woman, with high cheekbones and what she was coming to see as "Southern-shaped" green eyes. And the woman carried herself well, dressed in a stylish if slightly ostentatious dress designed to draw attention.

"Sam worked as a legal intern for my father in Boston," Elizabeth said. "In fact, he worked for two summers with the firm, and my father just thinks the world of him. You know, of course, that Sam was editor of the *Harvard Law Review*?"

Margaret sputtered something like "Sam never mentioned it."

"Modest as he is, he wouldn't, would he?" Elizabeth said. She was surprising herself at how easily she was slipping into the character of exactly the kind of girl she'd grown up with, and the kind she disliked. "I believe I just about have him convinced to visit my family for Thanksgiving." She momentarily leaned her head against his shoulder. "My father's not the only one who thinks the world of him. Sam's been nothing but kindness and hospitality since I arrived Monday." She looked up into his face, which was turned toward her. She saw in his eyes he understood exactly what she was doing. Or almost exactly.

They talked for a few more minutes, and then Margaret made their excuses and said they needed to find her mother. Elizabeth and Sam watched them quickly walk away.

Sam glanced across to where his aunts and uncle were standing. They were too far away to have heard the conversation, but they could see what had happened. Aunt Bea was trying to refrain from laughing; Uncle Seamus tried but finally couldn't stand it and let loose with a loud guffaw.

Sam and Elizabeth walked over to them.

"That may have been the highlight of this year's fair," Seamus said, wiping the tears from his eyes. Cora Beth was grinning.

Aunt Bea was giggling. "I don't think I've ever seen Margaret Barnett nee Biddle so flummoxed. I don't know what you said, Miss Putnam, but you clearly one-upped her."

"I'm going to take Elizabeth here and find the root beer booth," Sam said, and he guided her away from his relatives.

"I'm sorry," Elizabeth said as they walked. "That was horrid of me. I should probably apologize."

"I take it my family told you some of the story of Margaret and me."

"They did. And I think I should apologize to you as well. That was uncalled for. I hope I didn't embarrass you."

"I am, frankly, amazed. And tickled. You were completely misleading and yet you never spoke a mistruth. Did you learn how to do that in journalism?"

"I saw red," Elizabeth said. "I don't like bullies, and I really don't like the ones who bully the people I care for. Yet I should've known that you're perfectly capable of taking care of yourself. I am sorry. And I didn't learn that in journalism, but in my school days and Smith College."

"Don't apologize," Sam said. And then he paused. "Do you know my favorite part?"

She shook her head.

"It was when you leaned your head against my shoulder. And here's the tent where we should find the root beer. I think you'll really enjoy it."

They continued to explore the fair. While she tried to digest what Sam had said, he tried his hand at the milk can pitch and the strength test, winning a small stuffed teddy bear which he promptly offered to Elizabeth. They sat with hundreds of others in the food tent, eating fried chicken, corn on the cob, green beans, and apple pie for dessert. They listened to what Sam called a "mountain music band," which seemed all about banjos and guitars, including women fiddle players with the plunging necklines.

Shortly before 9 p.m., at the close of the fair's first day, Sam and Elizabeth walked slowly back to Cherry Street. It had turned cool, and Elizabeth was glad she had her jacket. But she still shivered.

"Here," Sam said, slipping off his coat. "You seem a bit chilled."

"I loved the fair," she said. "You were more than gracious to be my escort today. And thank you for the coat."

"I was planning to escort you tomorrow morning," he said, "but I have to go to Jackson to file a court brief for a client in New Orleans. Unfortunately, that will likely last all day. But I'm hoping you're available to see more of the fair on Friday, and then we have our hayride Friday evening."

"That sounds lovely, Sam. I'm hoping your grandfather is available to talk. I still have more questions, and he has more stories."

"Whatever stories he tells," Sam said, "please give me the summaries. It's such an unbelievable treat to hear him talk about the war, because he so rarely does." He paused as they reached the front door of his grandfather's house. "Something happened to him, something in the war's last year. And I don't mean something like a close brush with death or some awful experience. Aunt Cora has occasionally referred to it. She herself is not sure what it might be, and he may not be willing to talk about it at all. But it was something that affected him deeply, and by extension it affected the rest of the family as well.

"Now, Elizabeth, thank you for a lovely day. It's been a long time since I enjoyed the fair as much as I did today. It's rather fun to see it through new eyes." He took her hand and raised it to his lips. "It would not be proper to do what I'd really like to do, so I'll leave with a kiss on your hand." He smiled and turned, quickly walking down the drive to his bungalow across the street.

Elizabeth stood there a moment, surprised and almost disappointed that it was just her hand he'd kissed.

I've known him less than three days, she thought. *And I'm falling head over heels.*

As she went upstairs to her room, she began to list all the reasons that any thought of a romance was crazy. Her life and career were in New York. She barely knew him. He'd made clear his life was in Brookhaven, and she'd be leaving in a few days, undoubtedly never to return. She had no idea what his immediate family was like, only that the Gettysburg clan didn't speak with the Brookhaven clan. She was meant for New York or Boston, not a small town in Mississippi.

She thought she was in for a sleepless night, but she fell asleep almost immediately.

19

A hurry of hoofs in a village street,
A shape in the moonlight, a bulk in the dark,
And beneath, from the pebbles, in passing, a spark
Struck out by a steed flying fearless and fleet:
That was all! And yet, through the gloom and the light,
The fate of a nation was riding that night;
And the spark struck out by that steed, in his flight,
Kindled the land into flame with its heat.

—from "Tales of a Wayside Inn, the Landlord's Tale"
(better known as "The Midnight Ride of Paul Revere")

October 1915

When Elizabeth came down to the kitchen for breakfast in the morning, Papa Sam, as she now thought of him, was sitting alone at the table, drinking his coffee. He stood when she entered the room.

"Ah, Miss Putnam," he said, smiling, "I'm afraid it's just you, me, and Sophie here this morning. Everyone's off running errands, preparing animals for the judging today, or, like Bea, at one of the churches, helping out or supervising the preparation and baking of pies."

Wishing him and Sophie a good morning, Elizabeth poured herself a cup of coffee from the pot on the stove and sat down next to him. "I hope I didn't upset you yesterday with my comment about reciting the poems to the soldiers."

"Not at all. To be honest, your word moved me to such an extent that I rode out to the woods and spent most of my day there, just thinking. I find the woods calm my spirit. Always have. I've spent more than half a century regretting how I misled those men, until you pointed out that I'd imparted a gift. I didn't mention this, but I attended the 50th anniversary of Gettysburg in 1913. It was the last time I saw David's two younger boys; David had conveniently made other plans for that week. Young Sam had just made his decision about coming to Brookhaven, and David believed I'd put him up to it. But I went to the ceremony, even sleeping in one of the tents they'd set up."

"Did you find anyone you knew?" she said.

"Quite a few, more than I'd expected. There were but a handful left from the original First Wisconsin, and I talked with them for a time. Precious few survived the war, and new people kept being added to it. But there were a few who were there when I was. I shared a few beers, and they started talking. They eventually got around to talking about the young boy who recited Longfellow. I didn't tell them it was me; they probably wouldn't have believed it, thinking he should still be a young Pennsylvania farm boy. After you said what you did, my first thought was that I should have told them. And then I thought no, perhaps not. It was better that they remembered a boy who recited Evangeline, Hiawatha, and The Courtship of Miles Standish, not some Confederate spy who had completely misled them. Telling them would have taken away the meaning and memory of it."

They were both quiet for a time.

"After that time," Sam said, "what I remember is one long series of battles separated by a lot of horse riding and boredom. Second Manassas, small battles like Auburn and Bristoe Station, Rappahannock Station. I was the last official recruit for Colby's Rangers, and one by one they were dying in battle, or getting hung for being a spy. Caleb Willingham was caught and hung, and Major Colby himself died in the early hours of the Battle of the Wilderness. I'd been there a year, and I was the only one left. General Lee had me officially report to one of his staff officers; privates didn't report to army commanders. But I was Lee's man, or Lee's boy. If he needed something, I did it.

"Of all the battles, I think The Wilderness was the worst. It was second- and third-growth forest, more scrub than anything else. And dense. The weather had been dry for weeks. General Grant was now in charge of the Army of the Potomac, and he'd dog Lee all the way to Appomattox. But for years afterward, The Wilderness gave me nightmares. It wasn't a vision of hell; it was hell itself, if you'll pardon the expression. More than two full days of hell itself. And no one could claim victory, although the Union boys seemed to have caught the worst of it. I always hoped that the Union artillery didn't know what they were doing when they fired into the scrub forest. They probably killed more of their own men than anything the Confederates did. And the men hit by artillery fire were the lucky ones."

May 1864

Wearing civilian clothes, Sam's main assignment was messenger boy, carrying orders and messages from Lee to different generals, including the messages telling them to gather on the side of the Orange Plank Road by the area called The Wilderness, north of Richmond. As they met, what the officers didn't notice was a troop of Union soldiers suddenly emerging from the trees and scrub not 50 yards away. Oblivious, Lee and his generals kept talking until Sam on his horse physically inserted himself into the conversation.

"General Lee," he said, "I don't wish to be insubordinate, but you and the commanders here need to quietly get on your horses and disperse."

Lee's eyes flashed anger at Sam until he saw the soldiers. Sam almost stopped breathing until Lee mounted Traveler and moved away. The other commanders quietly did the same. Sam trailed after Lee, and then cut through the woods on the opposite of the road. If those federals had just been slightly more alert, he thought, the whole war might have ended right there.

When the artillery fire started, Sam was given a message to bring to General Longstreet. It was by word of mouth; Lee wanted nothing written. Sam had brought enough messages to and from Longstreet to be trusted with an oral command. After giving Longstreet the orders and leaving his horse with Longstreet's men, Sam melted back into the scrub.

The melting almost became literal.

Sam heard the artillery shells overhead and threw himself into a very shallow ditch. He didn't know how close the explosions were, and he didn't care to find out. Crouching low, he was half-running through the scrub forest when he smelled smoke. And then he saw the fire. He zigzagged away from it, but the dryness of the woods ignited by sparks from the artillery shells was soon cutting off all escape routes except backwards. He could hear men screaming, and he realized there were wounded men yelling for help. He was stunned to see bodies in blue uniforms; these were Union dead and wounded.

Another shell came whistling through and exploded not 100 feet away. The woods around it ignited. The artillery, firing from the direction of the Union lines, was killing their own men.

He began to hear pistol shots, and he tripped over the reason why. A wounded man couldn't walk, the fire was approaching, and rather than burn to death, the man killed himself.

He tripped over the legs of what he thought through the smoke was a dead man. When he sat up, he saw a pistol aimed directly at him.

An officer was seated against a small tree.

"Tell me why I shouldn't shoot you, boy," the man said.

Sam stared, and then fell back on his standard story. "My mama sent me to find a doctor. My sister over the ridge is in a bad way in childbirth, and I got to find a doctor."

"What you're going to do instead is help me get out of here. Help me up, or I'll blow your head off."

Sam nodded and stood. The fire was getting closer, and artillery shells were still flying overhead. He lifted the man to his feet, and the man put his arm around Sam's shoulders. Sam could see the wetness in the man's right leg.

"You're shot," Sam said.

"Yes, I'm shot, boy. And I need your blouse to tie a tourniquet."

Sam stripped off his shirt, knelt, and tied a tight tourniquet around the man's leg. Before the man could say anything, Sam started moving toward the only path not threatened by fire. The man grunted in pain at almost every step.

The way through the burning woods was treacherous. While he was unfamiliar with the Wilderness, as it was called, his head for the woods worked even in this poor excuse for a forest. Twice they had to sidestep snakes, desperate as the men around them to find a way out.

They stopped in a small clearing. The air was smoky, but Sam thought they might have outrun the fire, at least for a time. They were both trying to catch their breath.

"You've got the makings of a beard on your face," the man said. "The last time I saw you was in McClure's store in Brookhaven. What the heck are you doing here, Sam? You sure aren't trying to find a doctor for your sister."

Sam stared. For the first time, he took a hard look at the man's face. It was John Haygood.

He was stunned. What was the chance of this?

Finally, Sam spoke. "I ran away and enlisted after Grierson's Raid."

"What happened with your grandfather was an accident," Haygood said. "I never meant him harm."

"That's not why I enlisted."

Haygood looked at him quizzically. "Then why?"

"I heard you and Mama talking on the porch. I heard what you both said."

Before Haygood could respond, an explosion with a resulting fire erupted in a tree at the side of the clearing. Sam lifted the man's arm over his shoulder. "We have to get out of here."

The pair moved forward through the smoky scrub as fast as they could. Sam knew they were in the general vicinity of the Union line, if it could be called that, and they could easily be mistaken for Rebels and shot. Their movement was slowed by the hilly landscape. Just as Sam thought he might never breathe clear air again, they broke through the scrub woods and found themselves in the middle of what looked like a sea of blue uniforms.

Two soldiers rushed immediately to them and took charge of Haygood. "What do we do with the boy? He's local, ain't he?"

"He saved my life," Haygood said. "He got me through the fire. He comes with me. And tell them to stop the artillery. They're killing our own men."

The soldier pointed a gun at Sam and told him to follow. They reached a medical tent, where Haygood was placed on a stretcher, his leg checked by an orderly, and then carried to a wagon.

"Come with me to the field hospital," Haygood said from the wagon. "I'll explain how to get out of here."

He was the only casualty in the wagon, and the wagon driver told Sam to hop on board.

"Sam," Haygood said in a voice low enough that the driver couldn't hear, "I loved your mother. I still love your mother. We're both married now to other people, and I have a young daughter. But I never stopped loving Louisa. We weren't sup-posed to go to Brookhaven, but I told Major Grierson about the recruitment camp there and he decided to make a visit. The truth is I wanted to see Louisa, and I knew she was liv-ing there. It was wrong in so many ways, but I had to see her.

And I am most heartily sorry about your grandfather." He paused, grimacing with the pain in his leg. "I wish I could have known you. Maybe there will be some time after the war, if we both don't die first."

The wagon pulled up to the field hospital, a series of large tents with doctors, orderlies, and soldiers scurrying back and forth, and other wagons arriving with the wounded.

"Here's what you do," Haygood said. "You head south-east. You'll need to go about two miles to get completely around our armies. I don't think the lines will have changed that much, unless our artillery has managed to kill more of our men than I think. Stay alive and out of harm's way. And thank you for saving my life. I didn't deserve it."

Sam nodded. And then he turned and left, moving in the direction Haygood indicated. He looked back once, and he could still see the man looking after him.

20

And I saw in a vision how far and fleet
That fatal bullet went speeding forth,
Till it reached a town in the distant North,
Till it reached a house in a sunny street,
Till it reached a heart that ceased to beat
Without a murmur, without a cry;
And a bell was tolled, in that far-off town,
For one who had passed from crown to crown,
And the neighbors wondered that she should die.

—from "Killed at the Ford"

October 1915

"The Wilderness battle itself let up by early the next day," Sam said. "But the overall battle didn't really stop for quite some time. The Wilderness took a terrible toll on both armies, and it was greater for Grant. But he had one thing Lee didn't, and that was access to more men. He wasn't going to stop, and he didn't care how many soldiers' deaths it would take. He kept hammering away, and The Wilderness turned into the Battle of Spotsylvania Courthouse. It seemed like weeks of fighting and death. I did finally make it back to General Lee."

"And you did see Captain Haygood again?" Elizabeth said.

He nodded. "Once more. It was the Battle of Petersburg, a few days before Appomattox. General Lee's army was in a poor way, with rations barely enough to sustain life and men disappearing into the woods and headed home. The army was in full flight after the fall of Richmond; Lee was aiming to meet up with General Johnston. And, well, you know how it ended.

"The siege of Petersburg had been going on for some time; the city was a target because of the rail junction. Burnside was coming at the city from the east, with General Beauregard defending. It was famous for that mining operation and big explosion. But Captain Haygood's superior ordered a cavalry charge, and they came right against the Confederate line. I'd delivered a message to Beauregard from General Lee, and I was headed back down to the Appomattox River, to try to reach Lee with Beauregard's response, when everything seemed to explode around me. I was in some woods, and I could see the cavalry charge. It had to be the most foolhardy thing I'd seen in the war. Down they came toward the Confederate line, and they were slaughtered.

"A wounded horse, carrying a wounded rider, came into the woods and collapsed right next to where I was hiding. The man was thrown right at my feet. At first, I thought he was dead. His chest was a mass of blood, and his eyes were closed. And I realized who it was. It was as if Captain Haygood and I had another date with fate."

April 1865

John Haygood opened his eyes and at first thought he'd died. He was staring once again into the face of the boy. Sam McClure.

He shook his head to try to clear his thoughts. "Sam?"

Sam nodded. "We meet again, Captain Haygood. If I try to get you back to the Union line this time, we'll both die in the attempt."

"I'm not making it through this one, Sam." The man grimaced in pain. His ragged breathing was more like short gasps. "I have to ask a favor, and I don't know how you'll get it done. My saddlebag has my wallet and some letters. If you can find a Union officer to give them to, I'd be more than obliged."

"I could look for a medic or an orderly," Sam said.

Haygood shook his head, and then he coughed. Blood trickled from his mouth. "Sam, I have moments left. It's God's provision alone that it's with you. I need to tell you I'm sorry, sorry for all of it. I'm sorry for what happened to Louisa. My father thought he was protecting the family name, and all he did was destroy something that mattered. If you ever see him, tell him I forgive him. Tell him he needs to do right. And in the end, the joke's on him." He gave a short laugh and winced.

"But if you can, get those letters to an officer to see them delivered. Someone you think you can trust." He reached up and touched his palm to Sam's face. "It's like looking at—"

Haygood's head fell to the side. Sam stared, stunned. And then he reached and closed Haygood's eyes.

Part of the horse's weight was holding the saddlebag in place, and Sam had a difficult time working it free. He could hear the sounds of battle drawing closer. With one last look at the dead man, he started running through the woods to the west, skirting the river until he reached Petersburg.

The city was in chaos. Confederate troops were trying to

maintain order but failing, as people were loading household goods and food on anything that might move. The rail station was a nightmare of too many people trying to board the last train out. Fights were breaking out; women were screaming at men and each other.

He saw an unattended horse tethered to a post. Without thinking twice, he freed the tether, lifted himself into the saddle, and headed west. He knew that at some point he'd have to cross the river to get to Lee's army, but for now, he needed to get clear from Petersburg with the message from Beauregard.

Several miles west, he found a sign pointing to a ferry crossing, and he knew God had blessed him when he found the ferry still operating. Once across the river, he rode north, until he found the first scouts of Lee's army, riding hard west for Appomattox Courthouse.

When the bulk of what was now Lee's army arrived, chased by Grant's forward troops, he met Lee and gave him Beauregard's message.

Lee smiled at him. "Faithful to the end, Sam. I could not have asked for better." He motioned to one his staff officers. "I want this noted in the official records," he said to the man. "Private McClure, I'm appointing you as Corporal, which likely makes you the youngest junior officer in the Army of Northern Virginia, or what's left of it. My orders to you now are to find a unit from Mississippi and stay with them."

Sam saluted.

As he walked away from Lee and his officers, the day still looked the same. The sun was shining. He could hear birds in the trees. He'd expected something more dramatic for the collapse of a cause, a belief, a hope, a would-be nation.

But all he heard were the birds.

21

The day is done, and the darkness
Falls from the wings of Night,
As a feather is wafted downward
From an eagle in its flight.

—from "The Day Is Done"

October 1915

"A lot of people claimed to have been present for the signing of the surrender," Sam said, "but there were only two Confederates—General Lee and a staff officer. Grant had all of his staff officers, but there was no one else. Over the years, there must have been 15 or 20 people who claimed to be eyewitnesses. Some who were kept remembering new details as the years passed, or more likely just kept working it into a better story."

"Mr. Sam," Sophie said, "I've laid some sandwiches and fixings on the sideboard here, and you and Miss Putnam can help yourselves to some dinner. And I've got some fresh coffee in the pot. I intend to join some of my church ladies at the fair this afternoon, and Miss Cora will be here to lay out some supper." And she was gone.

"This afternoon," Sam said, "the fair is open to the black folks. It's ridiculous to segregate people like that, but it's Mississippi, and it's what people do. Everyone is welcome, though, for the fireworks on Saturday night."

"Captain Haygood's daughter married my editor at the *World*," Elizabeth said. "Papa Sam, if I'm understanding all of what you've told me so far, and what you've implied, I don't think the story of Captain Haygood will be part of the story or stories I write. I understand his role in your mother's life, in your own, and what happened during the war, but I want to assure you that he won't be part of what I write for the *World*."

"I appreciate that, Miss Putnam."

"This is part of what you meant when we first talked," she said. "You said that it was a story that really couldn't be told chronologically, that no life really can be."

"What I find," he said, "is that the story of the Gray Wisp, like anyone's story, keeps being written. Things I thought I understood or knew turn out to be different. Or they change. Just like your remark about what the soldiers heard when I recited my poems, and what it likely meant to them. That lifted a sense of guilt I've felt for 50 years. And that's why I was in the woods yesterday, working out that the gift I gave them was likely of more benefit than any intelligence I gathered."

She stood. "Can I get you some coffee or one of Sophie's sandwiches?"

"That would be lovely, thank you."

She brought their food and coffee to the table.

"You know," he said, "it's only after the war ended that the story of the Gray Wisp really becomes interesting."

April 1865

Sam stared at the dying embers of the campfire. He'd eaten his breakfast of hard tack, after picking off the moldy parts. This was what his meals had been for most of the last year, except for what he could shoot or forage on his own. Three days of rations, and a parole and travel pass, were supposed to be distributed by the federals at mustering out, but no one had seen any sign of rations or pass, and today was mustering out day. Perhaps he should have disappeared into the woods, like so many others already had. But he thought of his last conversation with General Lee two days before, and he stayed.

General Lee's message to his army had already been passed around, read, and read aloud.

"...The Army of Northern Virginia has been compelled to yield..."

Sam's horse had been taken by a Union officer. Had Sam been a senior officer, they would've let him keep him. But not many corporals had their own horses, and the animal, after all, was originally someone's horse in Petersburg.

The air was smoky from other campfires and the light morning fog. It was cold for early April, likely because they were not far from the mountains. Sam pulled his threadbare khaki jacket closer around him and huddled closer to what was left of the fire. In an hour, they'd be assembled in a parade line for the official surrender. And then, the mustering out. What was left of the Army of Northern Virginia, 27,000 men, would stand at attention, salute their commanding officers, and then disperse for home. Soldiers would be allowed to keep their rifles, but fewer than half the troops still had weapons, and fewer still had any ammunition to speak of. Sam was more fortunate in that regard. He still had the hunting rifle he enlisted with, and the pistol he'd been given, along with a supply of ammunition for both.

From conversations in their camp, he knew many of his fellow soldiers were planning to get to Norfolk and find boat transportation to Mobile, New Orleans, or Galveston. Others were trying the railroads, but everyone knew how difficult that would be, with so many railroad tracks and bridges destroyed. Their passes would supposedly allow them free travel home, but they wouldn't be of much use if the rail lines were damaged.

The army had been larger, but it had been melting away in the night ever since the flight from Richmond began. The melting had accelerated once they'd arrived in Appomattox. Even before the surrender had been officially announced, the soldiers knew. Sam had heard the talk of heading to the mountains and continuing the war from there or even Texas.

"…the brave survivors of so many hard-fought battles…"

Men had been slipping away for days now, some thinking they could still get home in time for planting. And hoping there was still a home to go to. Sam knew his home in Mississippi had been mostly under federal control, ever since Vicksburg.

Union guards stood near the perimeter of their camp, one of dozens scattered in the countryside around Appomattox, but no one stopped men from leaving. The guards joked, laughed, and ridiculed. They looked well fed; the Confederates did not. Sam knew he'd lost considerable weight from the time he joined up two years ago, and he didn't amount to much to start with. He was considered tall at 5 foot 10, and right now he'd be surprised if he weighed more than 130 pounds.

Sam hadn't seen any of the men he'd originally enlisted with, and especially his best friend Nate Cohen, for almost two years. Well, to call them men might be stretching it. Most had been teens. Boys, really. Like himself. Boys old and wise before their time. And too many dead boys. He prayed that Nate had survived.

Today was his 15th birthday. It didn't seem a time to celebrate.

"...I determined to avoid the useless sacrifice of those who past services endeared them..."

Like thousands of other Confederate soldiers, he was now waiting for the mustering out, thinking about how he was to get home and wondering what if anything was left of home. Until he ran out of paper, he'd sent letters to his mother, but there had been no response for more than a year, or at least a response that had caught up with him.

He heard his name being called.

"Corporal Sam McClure! Corporal Sam McClure!"

He looked up. A Confederate captain, accompanied by a federal counterpart, was calling his name.

He stood among hundreds of sitting and sleeping soldiers.

"You've been summoned," said the Confederate captain, "to the house." Sam noticed that the captain's coat had a button missing and a stain on the left arm that looked like dried blood, but the man held himself well. The Union captain, in his sparkling uniform, looked like he had just dressed for a ball.

"...officers and men can return to their homes and remain..."

They began to walk. The federal guards grew quiet when they saw Sam walking between the two captains.

They walked through fields of Confederate soldiers, and then into the federal camp, finally passing the blue-uniformed guards stationed in front of the two-story farmhouse that was General Grant's headquarters. The Confederate captain took Sam's rifle and pistol and motioned for him to enter.

Waiting inside were Grant, Lee, several Union officers, and one Confederate colonel. The official surrender document, now signed, had been placed on a nearby table. Sam noticed that Lee still had his sword.

Sam halted and saluted.

"At rest, Corporal," Lee said. "How are you, Sam?"

"I'm fine, sir, thank you," Sam said.

"Sam," Lee said, "General Grant here specifically asked to meet you."

Sam felt his throat go dry, wondering if he'd been summoned to be shot.

Grant stared at Sam for a full minute before he spoke. "There are stories," he said finally, "of a phantom that could move through dense woods as easily as on an open road. This phantom was said to have been employed by General Lee here, as a scout, a messenger, and a spy. One of Colby's Rangers. He could mix as easily with federal soldiers as he could with his own Rebels. His speech was said to be closer to Northern than Southern. And he had an uncanny ability to sense where troops were headed, to ferret out the best terrain for fighting, and to find paths through woods that even local farmers didn't know about. Had you heard any of those stories, soldier?"

"I might have, sir," Sam said. "I've heard a lot of stories, true and untrue."

"He was called the Will o' the Wisp," Grant said, "or, more simply, the Gray Wisp. He appeared suddenly around the time of Gettysburg, and it's said he was first sighted during the battle, riding a ghost horse behind General Lee and General Pickett. He was reportedly almost captured on three different occasions but somehow was able to make his escape. Some said he was an Indian, a Cherokee. Another story said he was Mexican, getting revenge for the Mexican War. All the stories agreed that he moved as fast as lightning and was as silent as a graveyard. When we signed the surrender, I asked General Lee if I might meet the men he used as scouts and messengers. He told me that of the original five rangers, only one was left, and that was you."

Sam said nothing but kept his eyes on General Grant's face.

"And now I find out that the Wisp is a boy," Grant said. "You don't look old enough to be a soldier."

"I'm going on 17, sir," Sam said. "Well, close enough."

"I expected someone older," Grant said. "I have to say, soldier, you don't look old enough or experienced enough, to be considered capable of prolonging this war by a year and a half. At least that's what some have claimed." He glanced at his officers and turned back to Sam. "A bit of exaggeration, perhaps, but no question that you ran circles around us."

The officers with Grant shifted uneasily; they did not appear pleased with the general's words.

"You give me too much credit, sir," Sam said. "My official duty was to run messages between General Lee and his officers in the field."

"…you will take with you the…consciousness of duty faithfully per-

formed…"

Everyone else in the room, including Lee, remained silent.

"I note that you explain your official duty, but we all have more than our official duties, do we not, soldier?" He paused. "If Billy Sherman was here, he'd insist on having you shot. Or he might just do it himself."

"I hear, sir, that General Sherman would shoot his mother if he thought it might be a boon for the war," Sam said.

Two of the Union officers coughed to stifle their laughter. Lee looked down and smiled. Grant laughed out loud.

"You might well be right, boy," Grant said, still chuckling. "You might be right. Where are you from?"

"Brookhaven, Mississippi, sir," Sam said.

"Brookhaven's been under federal control since we took Jackson," Grant said. "How many slaves does your daddy own, or should I say *did* own?"

"None, sir," said Sam. "He owns the general store, the grist mill, and the sawmill, and we have a small farm outside of town. We don't own slaves."

"Then why were you fighting, son?" Grant said.

"If your state calls you to fight, sir," Sam said, "you fight." He paused. "And there was Grierson's Raid."

"Ah, Grierson's Raid," Grant said, and was quiet for a time. "The slight distraction before Vicksburg. Was your family harmed?"

"The federals raided Brookhaven, burned the courthouse, some stores, and a few houses. One man died defending his store from the looting. That was my grandfather."

"…an increasing admiration of your constancy and devotion to your country…"

The memory was seared in Sam's mind, a scar that might fade in time but never disappear. It was not good to think about it.

"War's a terrible thing, Sam. For everyone. Can you tell me what you think this war was about?"

"A lot of things, sir," Sam said. "Politicians who got too angry or scared for their own good, or anybody else's. Slavery first, most likely. A way of life. Defending what we knew, sir."

"How old were you when you joined up?" Grant said.

"Fourteen, sir." That wasn't strictly true. "Well, almost 14."

"Based upon the time the Gray Wisp has been operating, you would've been closer to 13. They weren't calling them up that young back then," Grant said.

"No, sir, they weren't," Sam said.

Grant nodded. "What'd your mama say when you told her you were joining up?"

"She didn't know until I was gone, sir." He could imagine what happened.

"His father is Franklin McClure," General Lee said. "We served with him in Mexico."

"...and a grateful remembrance of your kind and generous consideration for myself..."

Grant stared at Sam for a moment. "I knew your father. He didn't serve with the Confederates?"

Sam shook his head. "No, sir. He said he wouldn't fight against the United States, and he wouldn't fight against Mississippi."

Grant was silent for a moment. "Where'd you learn to track and scout?"

"My uncle, sir," Sam said, "my mother's brother. He lives near Gettysburg; he's a captain in Sherman's army. And my grandfather, the one who died. He taught me how to hunt and track."

"They taught you well," Grant said. "Do you know how many times you were almost caught?"

Sam looked at Lee, who nodded.

"Twenty-seven, sir, give or take," Sam said.

Grant looked stunned. "I was going to say three. You mean to tell me that we almost caught General Lee's Gray Wisp 27 times?"

"Well, sir," Sam said. "I did have three of my horses shot out from underneath me, so maybe that's why you thought it was only three."

"Fifteen years old," Grant said. "Scout, spy, messenger boy, and who knows what all else. You had something to do with General Meade missing his chance to catch General Lee after Gettysburg?"

Sam glanced again at Lee, seeking Lee's permission to speak.

Lee nodded. "You can tell him, Sam. We're the same country again, or will be soon."

"I was sent from Jackson to Richmond," Sam said. "I got there just as the Army was preparing to leave for Maryland and Pennsylvania. General Lee needed a scout, and I knew the area. After the battle at Gettysburg, we made sure the federals got some bad intelligence, sir."

"General Meade thought a corps was prepared to attack him," Grant said, "a corps that turned out to be non-existent. So, he slowed down and chased General Lee here rather cautiously."

"Yes, sir," Sam said. "We worked hard to make sure he thought that, to give us time to escape across the river."

"If I'd had another soldier like Sam, General Grant," Lee said, "you and I might be in very different places this April morning."

"I believe it, General Lee," Grant said. He turned back to Sam. "I expect you're going back to Mississippi?"

"Yes, sir," Sam said, pulling his saddle bag from his shoulder. "Sir, I have this pouch here I need to leave with you or another officer. That cavalry charge, right before we left Petersburg, this federal officer was shot and his horse pitched into the woods, right where I was trying to stay out of the line of fire. I had a message for General Lee that had to be delivered, and my horse had taken a stray bullet. The officer was in a bad way, and he asked me a favor, if I would get this to someone who could get it back to his family. He was a Captain John Haygood, and he was from Philadelphia, Pennsylvania. I think at first he thought I'd shoot him, but there wasn't any need or purpose. In a saddlebag was his wallet, a photograph of his family, and letters for his family. I promised him I would get them delivered somehow. And then he was gone."

Sam handed the bag to General Grant, who accepted it, running his rough hands over the leather. He opened it, extracted the wallet, and saw the dollars inside. "His money's still here. There must be close to a hundred dollars." He looked at Sam. "We'd heard he'd deserted, but I see those reports were wrong. I will see that it gets delivered, soldier. Thank you." He paused. "Can you tell me where his body is?"

Sam gave him the directions, and the general nodded to

one of his officers.

"You'll likely have to walk most of the way home," Grant said. "Not much running on rail, and not much rail, either." He opened a box on the table next to him. "Here, corporal, take this. You're going to need it. And you may need all of your scouting and tracking skills just to stay alive between here and that general store in Brookhaven, Mississippi."

Sam looked at what Grant had placed in his hand. A small, leather pouch, filled with what felt like coins.

"And this as well," Grant said, as he signed a document on the table and handed it to him. A safe-conduct pass.

"Thank you, sir," Sam said, "but I'm not sure why—"

Grant interrupted him. "You'll need it. Your Confederate money, if you have any, is worthless. And even if it wasn't, General Lee doesn't have anything to pay you with. Your president has run off somewhere in the woods south of here with what's left of the Confederate treasury."

"I expect that just about anything Confederate is worthless now, sir," Sam said.

"I expect you're right, son," Grant said, standing up. He offered his hand, and Sam shook it. "Now you best go on and head back home."

Lee walked Sam to the door and the front porch.

"You did some extraordinary work, Corporal McClure," Lee said. "About that federal officer. That was a kindness on your part, and on General Grant's part."

"Thank you, sir," Sam said. "Why did he give me this?"

"Because he recognized what you did," Lee said. "Because he recognized the brilliance of your work as the Gray Wisp, Sam, and the service you rendered one of his dying men. That was pure grace. And he wished he'd had a soldier like you." He shook Sam's hand. "Now go home to Mississippi, Sam, and find yourself a nice young woman to marry, raise a family, and start building a life. Put this war behind you."

"I'll try, sir," Sam said. "But I expect the war will be with all of us for a long time to come."

"...I bid you a fond farewell..."

Grant and his officers followed them to the porch, preparing to mount for the parade. General Lee and his colonel did the same. There wasn't time for Sam to return to the camp, so he walked out to the road and waited with some federal soldiers. They stepped away from him; he saw their looks of disdain. In their eyes, he thought he was still a rebel, and one whose clothes were not exactly presentable.

The officers began their ride. Sam saluted as they passed him. He saw General Lee give him a nod and a smile, and then he turned away from Grant, directing his horse in the opposite direction. For a moment, Sam watched the solitary figure, heading off for home, alone.

General Grant saluted him, surprising the federal soldiers next to him. Sam returned the salute.

After they'd passed, he gradually made his way to where he's been sleeping with the other soldiers. It had been a group from Georgia and South Carolina; they'd talked of going home to what they'd heard was close to total destruction, hoping to find family still alive.

Stations had been set up to distribute the rations. Sam knew it would take weeks and possibly months for him to reach Brookhaven; soldiers were already hearing that the ships wouldn't take any more Confederates. Three days of rations wouldn't take anyone very far, unless they lived close to Appomattox.

He considered what it would likely mean for 27,000 Confederate soldiers, each soldier trying to get home, to be set loose upon the land. Add hundreds of thousands of emancipated slaves and hordes of deserters and criminals from emptied jails preying upon one and all. General Johnston's army somewhere in the vicinity. And law and order broken down everywhere, except where there might be federal troops. He'd have to work hard to make sure that, surviving the war, the immediate peace didn't kill him.

He got into the line to receive his rations. With the rations came travel passes. Sam already had the one from General Grant, but he accepted the regular pass as well. He didn't see any of the soldiers he'd been camping with.

He stepped to the side and discreetly looked at the bag of coins. Grant had given him five one-dollar U.S. coins. In gold.

An hour later, his rations in hand and stowed in his saddlebag, he joined the stream of soldiers heading west and south from Appomattox. A few continued westward toward the mountains. Sam turned southward with the larger part of the group. They made camp just to the north of Chatham, Virginia, in Pittsylvania County. He ate sparingly of his rations, hoping to make them last a fourth or fifth day. He was hopeful they'd make the North Carolina border by sometime tomorrow. And somewhere, somehow, he'd have to find some better boots. His own were the same ones he'd brought with him when he joined up, and both had holes in the soles.

And he'd have to figure out food.

22

This is the forest primeval.
The murmuring pines and the hemlocks.
Bearded with moss, and in garments green,
indistinct in the twilight,
Stand like Druids of eld, with voices sad and prophetic,
Stand like harpers hoar, with beards that rest
on their bosoms.
Loud from its rocky caverns, the deep-voiced
neighboring ocean
Speaks, and in accents disconsolate answers
the wail of the forest.

—from "Evangeline"

October 1915

Her food eaten, Elizabeth sat quietly at the table, staring at Mr. Sam's face. He was looking down at the floor, but she knew it wasn't the floor he was concerned with but the 15-year-old boy beginning a journey that could well end in his death. A boy wondering what kind of home might be left to come to and hoping there was something still intact. A boy carrying the burden of sitting with a dying man who had loved his mother.

Sam looked up from the floor and smiled. "Brings back a lot of strong feelings."

"I can't imagine, Papa Sam," she said. "But you tell a story that seems far more real than anything I've read in history books."

"It's lived experience," he said. "Well, to be precise, it's lived experience fused with memory, which may or may not be exact."

"But the feelings associated with the experience come back."

He nodded. "They do indeed. If you'll oblige, Miss Putnam, I think I might like to take a short nap. All this remembering is physically tiring."

"Of course. I could use the time to sort through my notes. Or I might take a walk downtown. I find walking helps me sort through my head, and you've given me a lot to sort."

"Stop in at the store, there, the one that used to be the general store and is now the farm and feed emporium. One of the O'Brien grandsons will provide you a cup of coffee or perhaps a Coca-Cola. And let's plan to meet at 4 p.m. back here."

April 1865

In the morning, Sam woke with a crick in his neck and a sore backside. He stretched, trying to ease the hurt in his muscles. In the past two years, he'd slept more nights with a tree canopy for a roof than anything manmade. He hadn't minded, except when it rained or snowed. Sam felt more at home in the woods than he did in a house. Men began to wake and prepare to leave, and he joined a group headed for South Carolina.

They followed the main road into Chatham, a small Southern town typical of its kind. The smithy and stable, the general store, and a few other establishments lined the town's main street. Also lining the street were townspeople with rifles and pistols.

"Just keep on moving through," said a large man in clothes worn but still presentable and sporting a sheriff's badge. "We don't mean to be inhospitable, but we've had too much trouble with soldiers and others. Keep moving and we'll all get along right well."

A few soldiers looked as if they were ready to be less than accommodating but were stopped by others. Sam kept walking, wondering if this is what returning soldiers would find everywhere—frightened people trying to protect what little they had left.

They were five miles south of the town when the rain began. At first, it was light, no more than a sprinkle. Sam and the others were used to worse than this, so everyone kept walking. And then the heavens seemed to open, and the light rain became a proper storm. They rushed for the nearby woods to get some protection. Nearly a hundred people took refuge among the trees.

The rain continued. Sam and the rest of the men made what shelters they could, but they were all soaked. The storm abated, but a steady rain continued through most of the night.

Sam woke early. It was still dark but beginning to edge toward dawn. The other soldiers were still asleep, so he made his way through the woods to find a place to relieve himself. It was then he heard a kind of muffled singing. Curiosity got the better of him and he followed the sound. Going deeper into the woods, he could see a small light as he got closer to the sound. He stepped into a clearing and saw some 20 people clustered around a campfire. They stopped singing when they saw him.

Sam's father hadn't owned any slaves, but Sam knew these people had been slaves. He'd never known any slave or freedman well; he had none to count as friends back home. He knew many by name, but he'd only associated with them when it involved the store or one of the mills. But both of his parents had taught him always to be polite to friend and stranger, free and slave alike.

The people here were men, women, and children of varying ages. They'd been singing "Go Down, Moses" when Sam stepped into the clearing.

Three of the men stood and faced Sam.

"What you want here, Reb?" one said.

"I heard the singing," Sam said. 'We'd been sleeping under the trees because of the rain."

"There are more of you?"

Sam nodded. "About 100 of us, heading home."

The group around the fire exchanged glances.

"I mean you no harm," Sam said. "I just heard the singing."

An older man stood. "We are having worship before we go on our way," an older man said. "You are welcome to join us."

Of all the decisions Sam would make on his journey home, this was the first and, as it happened, possibly the most consequential. It set into motion all that would follow.

"I would like that, sir," Sam said. He walked to the group and sat down next to an older woman. Her hair was gray; her skin was a soft, light brown.

She nodded as he sat. "You're a young man," she said,

looking at him closely, "younger than you first appeared."

"Yes, ma'am," Sam said. "I'm 15."

She said no more; the group continued its worship service around the campfire. The older man who'd welcomed him gave a short message from the Book of Exodus, which was Sam's first solid evidence that this was a group of slaves or former slaves who'd left their master.

They sang a few more spirituals and a hymn that Sam knew, "What a Friend We Have in Jesus." He knew the words, and the group sang as if the music was coming from their souls.

They finished in prayer, yet no one moved when the worship ended. They were waiting for something, Sam thought.

"Are you headed to, or from, the war?" the older man asked.

"From," Sam said. "I'm headed home to Mississippi."

The man nodded. "Discharged or deserted?"

"Mustered out," Sam said. "The army disbanded yesterday." The entire group, including the children, stared at Sam. "General Lee surrendered to General Grant, and his army has been sent home."

The group broke into excited chatter. "Praise God!" the older man said. "Praise the Lord! We are free!"

People were hugging each other. Two of the women were crying.

"General Johnston's army is still in the field," Sam said. "Somewhere in South or North Carolina. They're headed this way, thinking to join up with General Lee. But I expect they'll likely surrender as well."

"We will eat," the older man said. "You will eat with us.

What is your name?"

"My name is Sam McClure, sir," Sam said. "But I only have a little food to share, and it has to last me some time."

"You already shared the blessing with us, Mr. McClure," the older man said. "You gave us the news. We left where we lived four days ago, to walk north to the federal troops. There are many like us, leaving to find the troops. We are not going back. Do you have a cup for soup?"

Sam nodded. He pulled his tin cup from his pack, and soon it was filled with a soup so thick that it was more a stew than a soup. A woman handed him a piece of bread.

Sam ate slowly.

The older man did most of the talking for the group. "We were slaves on a plantation near Greensboro," he said. "The master had died in a battle. The mistress died in childbirth, leaving behind a young child, a girl. The mistress's mother had come from down Alabama way to help with the birth, and she had a granddaughter with her. They and the little girl were all who were left. Food was getting poor. The field hands left first, and then we left as well. The grandmother wants to go home, but the railroads have stopped. She is sick, though she will not speak about it, I think because it would frighten the girl."

The story pained Sam, but he supposed it was being duplicated all over the South. Dead masters, workers leaving, fields lying fallow, children abandoned. The very old and the very young, left to fend for themselves. It was a world in ruins, made up of thousands of stories like this one.

When they finished, he could see they were starting preparations to leave.

"Thank you," he said, standing up. "This is the best food I've eaten in a year. Thank you."

The older man walked up to him. "You may know this, but if you're headed south, travel with others, or travel in the woods by the road. Satan is walking these roads, and sometimes he looks like a white man, and sometimes like a black man. And sometimes both. We promise to pray for you, the young man who brought us the news."

Sam nodded his thanks and then re-entered the woods, making his way back toward the place he and others had slept to get out of the rain.

He walked quickly through the woods. Judging by the sun, it must be about 7 a.m. The group of soldiers would be stirring and preparing to leave.

When he reached where they had camped, he saw it was empty. Everyone was gone. He was alone.

23

Enjoy the Spring of Love and Youth
To some good angel leave the rest;
For time will teach thee soon the truth,
There are no birds in last year's nest!

—from "It Is Not Always May"

October 1915

It was after 5. Sam had been talking for an hour, and Elizabeth sat fascinated. They'd gotten together in the kitchen at 4. Everyone else was still gone, either at the fair like Sophie or off doing errands or work. Elizabeth had had this wonderful man to herself for the entire day. And she felt incredibly blessed. He was right; his story became even more interesting after the end of the war.

"After that meeting in the woods," he said, "I walked for three days, mostly by myself. When I could, I heeded that advice and stayed in the woods. But it was eerie. I met very few people, and almost no soldiers. It was as if the world had emptied. The few homesteads I passed were empty and abandoned. Fields had been left untended.

"I was right at the end of my rations." He stopped and looked up. Cora Beth was standing at the back door, listening. She smiled and set her bag and umbrella down.

"And speaking of rations, we are mighty glad to see you,

dear sister. I expect Seamus is seeing to the horses?"

Elizabeth stood. "Let me help." She and Cora Beth were soon laying out the food left by Sophie.

Just as they sat to say grace, they heard the front door open, and Young Sam joined them. "I see I scheduled my return precisely right," he said, sitting down. "I hope there's enough to share with the conquering attorney returning from battle in the capital?"

Elizabeth set a plate and utensils before him and poured a glass of water. Papa Sam and Cora Beth watched Young Sam follow her movements with his eyes, and the brother and sister smiled at each other.

After small talk and Young Sam recounting his day ("A client in New Orleans needed a motion filed in Jackson, and he needed it done today"), they ate while Papa Sam continued his story.

April 1865

The soldiers Sam had left Appomattox with had said Greensboro was about 150 miles. He figured he could walk at least 15 miles a day, weather permitting. He didn't have a compass, but he knew he could use the sun to guide him to the southeast. After the day with the torrential downpour and meeting with the former slaves in the woods, the skies cleared for the next week. After three days of meeting virtually no one, he got used to the solitude.

His rations were just about gone. He had taken to foraging in woods, where he'd spied and shot a rabbit. The sound from his rifle seemed so loud in the silence of the woods that he jumped. For the first time in a very long time, he went to sleep that night with a full stomach.

After a week, he figured he was making at least 15 miles a day, and longer on two days. He was being as frugal as possible with his bullets. He occupied his mind while walking with trying to figure out how to get the materials he needed to make a bow and arrow.

He started seeing a few people, mostly a family or two heading north. They'd trade information, and now he knew he'd crossed into North Carolina and was two or three days from Greensboro. Two miles north of Greensboro, he stopped for the night in a wooded area of dense trees. He could hear a stream, and after a short walk, he found it. He went looking for something to eat and couldn't believe his good fortune when he spotted and shot a wild turkey.

While the bird roasted on a spit about the campfire, Sam stripped off his clothes and washed in the stream, using a piece of lye soap he'd held on to, hoping he'd never have to use it. Now, it smelled like a sweet perfume compared to how he smelled himself. The weather was warm, and he washed his underclothes, socks, and shirt. As they dried, he turned the bird on the spit.

He felt completely blessed. He had food to eat and some to save, relatively clean clothes, and no sign of rain.

While the sun gradually set, Sam sat by the campfire, grateful for the warmth and light. From his saddlebag, he pulled the copy of *The Song of Hiawatha* he'd brought with him from Brookhaven. It was something of a miracle that the book had survived. Other than his rifle, just about everything else had long since disappeared, was lost or stolen, or thrown away.

He'd gotten the revolver from a dead Yankee soldier he'd tripped over in The Wilderness, minutes before he met John Haygood.

He wondered about John Haygood and his family in Philadelphia, and whether they'd heard of his death. He knew it would be some time before the man's wallet and letters made it home, but he felt assured that General Grant would ensure it happened. He wondered about his own family, and how they were faring under federal occupation.

He began to read. Longfellow's lines were a familiar and well-loved friend. The poet would never know how much his poems had inspired and comforted a Southern boy far from home.

> Ye who love a nation's legends,
> Love the ballads of a people,
> That like voices from afar off
> Call to us to pause and listen,
> Speak in tones so plain and childlike,
> Scarcely can the ear distinguish
> Whether they are sung or spoken;
> Listen to this Indian legend,
> To this Song of Hiawatha!

After reading for a while, he closed the book and reached for the other book in his saddlebag, a Confederate New Testament printed by the Tennessee Bible Society. Major Colby's wife had given it to him when they were leaving the Colbys' house in Richmond for the camp in Fredericksburg. It was looking as worn as *The Song of Hiawatha*, and he reckoned he'd spent more time reading it than he had Longfellow's poem. He turned to his favorite book, the Gospel of John. He liked that John described Jesus as the Word, and that John called himself the disciple that Jesus loved.

It was dark, and the campfire was burning low. His thin blanket didn't smell too bad, and he covered himself as best he could, using his saddlebag for a pillow. Facing the fire, he was soon asleep.

Something was pushing at his foot. He opened his eyes and stared into the barrel of a rifle.

"Are you dead?" a little girl's voice said.

He decided it was safer not to move. "I'm not dead. I was asleep."

Standing before him were two girls. The one who'd spoken looked about five years old, with blonde hair, blue eyes, and a square-looking face with cheeks that should have looked rosy but were drawn and pale, most likely from hunger. The girl holding the rifle looked only slightly younger than Sam himself. She was thin, but then everybody he saw these days was thin. Her hair was blonde as well, and she had large brown eyes that looked rather fiery. Her dress, what his mother would call a day dress, was of good quality, but it was wrinkled and stained.

"You are trespassing on our property," she said. "I should shoot you."

In one swift motion, he grabbed the gun by the barrel and pulled it away from the girl. "If you're going to threaten to shoot somebody, you need to have your finger on the trigger." He checked the rifle. "And it would also help if it had a bullet in it. I mean no harm; I was merely spending the night, and I'd planned on leaving as soon as I was awake." He stood up, securing his own rifle in the process. He handed her rifle back.

The older girl stood trembling. She looked angry enough to spit. Instead, she burst into tears.

Sam was flummoxed. She'd changed from potential assassin to damsel in distress in one movement.

"We're hungry," the little girl said. "Do you have any food? And we need some for my great-grandmother. And some medicine. She's sick."

Something clicked in Sam's mind. He remembered the freed slaves in the woods.

"I think I met your former slaves a few days ago, in Virginia," he said. "They were on their way to find General Grant's army."

"They left us," the older girl said. "They took all our food, and they left us. They left us to die." She collapsed on the ground while great sobs poured out.

He glanced at the little girl, whose blue eyes were filling with tears. He knelt in front of her. "What's your name, little missy?"

"I'm Honeybee," she said.

"Do you live near here?"

She nodded, pointing back behind her. "It's a big house called Fairhope. I used to sleep in the nursery, but there's no nurse now, so I sleep with Octavia Jane in Grandmother's room."

"I don't have much food," Sam said, "but I can offer you a bit of roast turkey I shot yesterday. When did you last eat?"

The older girl stopped crying and answered for them.

"Yesterday morning," she said. "We found some old pecans in the pantry."

From his saddle bag, Sam retrieved the roasted turkey, wrapped in an old sheet of thick paper that had been used to line the saddlebag. "It tasted better when I roasted it, but I think it will still be sufficient." He handed a piece to each girl. "Eat it slowly. If your stomach isn't used to it, you can get sick. So, eat slowly."

He was surprised when they both heeded his instructions. The three sat in silence. Sam pulled a small piece for himself and began to eat.

"I presume you're Octavia Jane?" he said to the older girl.

"I am Octavia Jane Montgomery of Windhaven, Alabama. You may call me Miss Octavia or Miss Montgomery."

"And I am Samuel David McClure of Brookhaven, Mississippi, late of the Army of Northern Virginia. You may call me Your Royal Highness."

Almost in spite of herself, Octavia Jane smiled. Then she frowned. "So, it's true, then? General Lee surrendered?"

"It's true. On April 9th, which also happened to be my birthday."

"But General Johnston is still in the field? There's still hope?"

"The last I heard, Johnston was still in the field. But with Lee's surrender, he'll be forced to do the same. Richmond's fallen, as has Petersburg. I also heard that Sherman was chasing Johnston in this direction." He paused. "Tell me about your grandmother."

"She's sick," Honeybee said.

Octavia Jane nodded. "I came with her from our home in

Alabama a year ago. My sister, Honeybee's mother, was with child, and my grandmother determined she would come to help her. At the time, my brother-in-law was with General Bragg in Tennessee. We learned that he'd been killed in a battle near Nashville. And then my sister, my sister—" She stopped, gathered herself together, and looked up almost defiantly. "My sister died in childbirth, as did the child. My grandmother was already ailing; she never should have traveled here. It was the reason my mother insisted she bring me with her."

"Is there any other family here?"

Octavia Jane shook her head. "Not here. Charleston, where my grandmother is from, and Windhaven in Alabama, where my mother and father are. And my brothers." She paused. "Can you look at my grandmother? I don't know how to find a doctor, and I'm afraid to leave her alone for too long."

Sam considered the request. He needed to keep walking toward home. He felt a sense of foreboding about what Sherman might be up to, and right near this area. On the other hand, a sick old lady, with a young girl and a child by themselves, was a recipe for disaster.

"All right," he said. "I'll come and see how she's doing. But I really need to be making my way for home. It's going to take weeks as it is."

He gathered up his belongings, made sure the campfire was completely out by dumping creek water on it, and then left with the two girls.

24

Oh, though oft depressed and lonely,
All my fears are laid aside,
If I remember only
Such as these have lived and died.

—from "Footsteps of Angels"

October 1915

"That was how you met Grandmother," Young Sam said.

"Yes, it was," Sam said. "We didn't know it then, of course. Meeting someone at the wrong end of a rifle barrel isn't exactly conducive to romance."

"She sounds feisty and vulnerable," Elizabeth said.

"That is precisely what she was," Sam said. "In fact, she pretty much stayed that way the rest of her life." He shook his head. "She was scared to death, and she was trying to be brave for Honeybee. The little girl was all that was left of her own family, father killed, mother dead. And their grandmother, Lucinda Hawkins Montgomery, of the Charleston Hawkins, as she liked to say, was in a bad way. The girls took me straight to her room, and I could see immediately that she wouldn't last much longer. She was one of those grand old Southern matriarchs, and she was enduring a terrific amount of pain in her stomach. I was no doctor, but it sounded like a cancer.

"I could see she was suffering and trying not to show it.

We talked for a while, and then I had Honeybee sit with her while I took Octavia Jane back to the stream. I told her we were going to harvest some willow bark, and I'd show her how to do it.

"We gathered as many new shoots from the willow trees as we could carry. Back at the house, I told Octavia Jane to start a fire in the stove while I skinned out bark from the shoots. She just stood there."

April 1865

"I don't know how," she said. "That's what slaves do."

"Alright," Sam said, "then it's time you learned, since there are no more slaves." He told her to gather some kindling, and he brought in several small logs from the large pile outside the kitchen. He got the fire started, showing her each step, and soon the stove was hot.

"Can you get some water from the well?" he said.

"I'm not completely useless," she said.

Sam had his doubts but kept them to himself.

Soon they had some water set on the stove for boiling. Sam handed her a few of the skinned willow shoots, their exposed bark a pale white. "Take these to your grandmother and tell her to start chewing on one. And no matter how bad it tastes, and it'll be bitter, she needs to keep chewing. I'll brew some willow bark tea. Is there a piece of cloth to strain out the bits of bark?"

"Will this help her?" Octavia Jane said, handing him a linen cloth from a drawer.

"This should help ease the pain," Sam said. "It won't make

it go away, but it'll ease it a bit."

Carrying the skinned shoots, the girl headed upstairs. Sam finally got the tea brewed and strained, and found a cup to pour some in. Carefully holding the cup and a saucer underneath it, he made his way upstairs. He found Mrs. Montgomery grimacing but chewing.

"This is an old folk remedy," she said. "You haven't heard of modern medicine?"

"I have, ma'am," he said, "but when modern medicine is not available, those old folk remedies might suffice for a time."

"It tastes like it came out the mule," she said.

"I have some willow tea," Sam said, "and it'll taste only a little bit less bitter, but it will help even more."

He held the cup to her lips as she sipped the tea.

"It's slightly better than chewing the shoots," the woman said. "But not much."

"Just keep sipping," he said.

When she finished the tea, she laid back on her pillow. "As bad as that tasted," she said, "it helped. The pain's still there, but it's considerably eased. Thank you, young man." She eyed him closely. "My granddaughter tells me you were a soldier in General Lee's army. You seem too young to have served, but your eyes tell a different story."

"I enlisted young, Miss Montgomery, two years ago. I'm making my way home to Mississippi."

"You started from Appomattox?" she said.

"Yes, ma'am."

"I might rest for a time. I thank you for your ministrations here. This is the best I've felt in weeks. If you'll excuse us, Octavia Jane will help me with my necessaries."

Sam and Honeybee quickly left the bedroom, making their way downstairs.

"This is a beautiful place," he said, admiring the portraits on the walls and the grand staircase, which needed dusting.

"Some soldiers came and took things," the little girl said. "A few days ago."

"What color were their uniforms?"

"Gray. They wanted food, but we didn't have any. We were scared, but they left us alone. But they took stuff, like Mama's bracelets."

Sam considered that, for surviving family, this little girl had a young aunt who was more a child herself, plus a dying grandmother. "Does Octavia Jane have a large family in Alabama?"

"She has her mama and daddy, and three brothers," Honeybee said. "Her mama is at home, and her daddy and brothers are all fighting in the war."

Octavia Jane joined them. "She's asleep." She looked at Sam. "Thank you for helping her. I wouldn't have known what to do."

"The willow bark will work for a couple of days, maybe a little longer," Sam said. "But she's going to need something like morphine or opium pills. I don't know where we can find it. Even the army was on short supplies, and most days didn't have any. In the meantime, keep with the willow bark chews and tea. Try to make that last as long as possible."

The girl looked alarmed. "You're leaving? Can't you stay?"

"I'm trying to get home to Mississippi," he said.

"Can you stay just a day or two?" Octavia Jane said. "I don't know how to do anything. I can embroider. I can play piano. I can recite poetry. I can dance. But I don't know how to do anything that matters now. I can't cook. I can't mend that tear you have on your shirt. I don't know how to take care of sick grandmothers. I can't even dress myself properly. I've been brought up to make an advantageous match to better the family's position, and none of that matters now. Can you at least teach me a little about cooking before you go? I know I have no call upon you, and if you were smart, you'd walk out the door and not look back. But, please. I just don't know what to do."

Honeybee took Sam's hand. "Can you help us?"

Sam decided he could stay for a couple of days, which eventually became two weeks. He went into Greensboro to look for some kind of painkiller for Mrs. Montgomery. Octavia Jane was petrified he wouldn't come back come back, so he left his saddlebag and rifle to reassure her.

Greensboro was in chaos. Johnston had surrendered to Sherman, and hungry Confederate soldiers and hungry townspeople were raiding government warehouses. Then federal troops showed up, and the chaos doubled. Soldiers on both sides were looking for whisky and drunkenness seemed out of control. Stepping down an alley to avoid a horde of drunken soldiers singing and shouting their way down the street, he happened upon his uncle Ned Williamson and the other soldiers fondling and planning worse for Sophie and her daughter.

"Uncle Ned? Will you stop this?" Sam said, bringing the actions of the soldiers to an abrupt halt.

His uncle was shocked. "Sam? What on God's green earth

are you doing here?"

The black woman and her children needed no encouragement. They ran down the alley toward the rear of the buildings and vanished.

"I'm trying to find some painkiller. An old lady is dying and suffering a world of pain."

Edward Williamson hugged his nephew. "The circumstances are awful, but it's wonderful to see you. And I apologize for that behavior you just witnessed. There was no call for them to do what they were doing, and no call for me to allow it."

Behind the building next to the alley, they found a tree that sheltered them from the sun while they talked. Sam explained how he came to be in Greensboro.

"So, we were fighting on opposite sides," his uncle said. "But you were too young to enlist."

Sam nodded. "Didn't matter, Uncle Ned. They needed men. And then I found myself shipped off to Richmond for special duty."

"Don't tell me what it was. I don't need to know. My guess would be it was related to your hunting and tracking skills and how you could make yourself at home in the woods. All those times we hunted together, I really didn't have to teach you anything. You already knew. Were you at The Wilderness?"

Sam nodded again.

"If anyone could survive that, it was you, Sam," Ned said. "I have to be back at field headquarters in an hour. Let's see if we can find you some painkiller."

While the Confederate doctors and the Greensboro doctors had little to none, the federal physicians were awash in painkiller. Ned and Sam found a surgeon friend of his uncle's, who was happy to provide a bottle of morphine and a week's supply of opium pills.

When they took their leave, Ned and Sam hugged each other again. His uncle also insisted Sam take most of the Union money he had on him. "You'll need some greenbacks to see you home, and I get paid tomorrow," Ned said. He handed Sam more than $75. "You take care of yourself getting home, Sam, and you give Louisa a big hug from me when you do."

As Sam was leaving Greensboro on his way back to Fairhope, he happened upon Sophie and her children again. When she told him she'd been a cook, he made her a proposition—in return for shelter and some food, she'd cook and teach Octavia Jane.

October 1915

"Mrs. Montgomery was fading fast, but the painkillers eased the way," Sam told the group at the Cherry Street house. "We had to dole them out carefully, because we didn't know how long they'd be needed. The day before she died, she sent for me to come to her room, just the two of us. She offered me her jewelry if I would take Octavia Jane and Honeybee to Windhaven in Alabama. I told her I'd take the girls, but that I'd leave the jewelry with Janie. She squeezed my hand, saying I was one of those gentlemen who didn't have to be taught but came by it naturally, which I took to mean I wasn't born to it like the Charleston Hawkinses or the Alabama Montgomerys. Then she asked me to call for the girls.

"Octavia Jane stayed with her until she died. I found some old pine boards in a shed and was able to make a rough sort of coffin. It wasn't what a high-born lady from Charleston would've expected, but it seemed better than just wrapping her in a sheet and covering her with dirt. I dug her grave in the family plot well behind the house near some oak trees, and we had a burial service for her. There was no minister, but I read some passages from my Confederate New Testament, Octavia Jane shared some reminiscences, and then I said a prayer.

"Now I had to figure out how to transport a former slave, her two children, two girls, and myself. Octavia Jane told me about a buckboard stored in a barn, and three horses kept hidden in an upper pasture. No one would go near the animals; there was a stallion and two geldings, and the stallion was infamous for allowing only Fairhope's master, Honeybee's father, to ride him.

"We all walked up to the far pasture, and I thought, well, there's nothing for it except to go up to the stallion and introduce myself. The horse had a reputation, but he was fine with me. He and the two geldings were well fed; they were the only animals for a pasture that could have accommodated 30 or 40 horses. Honeybee said his name was Tag, for a white patch right between his eyes. He was black as a dark night, and he made quite the formidable sight. The barn had a saddle for him, and I was half-expecting him to give me what-for over it, but he was docile as a lamb. Once we were on the road, people would see him and generally leave us alone.

"We spent several days planning our departure. Honeybee told me I could avail myself of her father's clothes, and he was about my size, only a little shorter and a little broader. Sophie sewed some of the pants and other clothes to fit me, and Janie packed some of her dead sister's clothes as well as her own. We found some clothes for Sophie as well, and she was able to cut some of the others down to size for her children. We took some legal papers, the title to the Fairhope, the family bible, and some birth certificates and wills and such. We stopped in Greensboro and met with the family attorney, who said he'd file the papers and keep Honeybee's address in Alabama until some order was restored and he could file death notices and open probate with the courthouse. By that time, Greensboro had calmed down, but a lot of the town was a wreck. And we began our journey south."

Sam smiled. "Those first days out of Greensboro, there was considerable movement on the roads. People going north, soldiers headed south and toward home, it seemed the whole countryside was on the move. Octavia Jane finally became confident enough to guide the geldings, and I'd ride alongside on Tag. Sometimes we gave women and children a ride on the wagon; we had enough room to accommodate two or three, four at a pinch. And their husbands or brothers would walk alongside.

"It was slow going. With women and children along, we made frequent stops. And we had to find better overnight accommodation than a clearing in the woods or a tree canopy. Usually, it was someone's barn. I'd swap helping to plant or doing other work for a meal or two and a hayloft to sleep. We had a mishap or two, but Octavia Jane became quite adept at making a campfire. Sophie was a good teacher."

Sam looked at his watch. "Well, it's 9 o'clock, and I need my beauty rest. We can pick up again tomorrow, and I'll tell you about what happened right before we got to Charlotte."

The group around the table stood and stretched. Elizabeth wasn't sure when Seamus and Bea had slipped in the door, but they'd been sitting with Cora Beth.

Young Sam nodded at his aunt and uncle. "I'll take you home in the car."

Sam and Bea made their way up the stairs, and Elizabeth walked with Young Sam and his great-aunt and uncle to the front door.

"I love these stories," Young Sam said. "I've only heard bits and snatches before."

Cora Beth spoke in sign language.

"Aunt Cora said she knew some of them, but she's never heard all the details he's providing now."

"He's a wonderful storyteller," Elizabeth said. "My hand aches from taking so many notes. And he knows how to end each session in a way that makes you come back for the next one."

"By the way," Young Sam said, "I remembered something from yesterday. And I wanted you to know that I accept your invitation."

"My invitation?" Elizabeth said.

Grinning, Sam nodded. "You told Margaret Biddle that you almost had me convinced to come to Boston for Thanksgiving. And I wanted you to know that I've considered it carefully and seriously, and I accept. Or was that the one mistruth you told her?" His eyes were twinkling.

"Well, I, um, I did say that, didn't I," Elizabeth said, clearly thrown. "Are you serious?"

"Absolutely, I'm serious," Sam said. "I haven't had a

Boston Thanksgiving since a classmate invited me my senior year at Harvard. And that's about as close to the original site of Thanksgiving as I could get."

"Of course, I'm thrilled that you'd accept," she said. "And you should know that we imitate the original Thanksgiving, so you'll eat a small piece of turkey and a considerable amount of maize."

He wrinkled his brow, and then he laughed. "Which means the food would never detract from experiencing the fine mind and beauty of the New York *World's* foremost reporter."

Elizabeth blushed. "I see that trying to play one-upmanship with you should have been a failure foreseen. I'll let my mother know as soon as I return home. She'll want to extend a formal invitation." She stopped. "My mother. Oh, my. I didn't think about her. She'll likely misinterpret everything and think, well, she'll misinterpret the invitation."

He grinned again. "Maybe she won't misinterpret at all."

With Seamus laughing, Young Sam escorted his aunt and uncle through the door and down the steps. Elizabeth stood on the porch, watching them get into the Buick and the car drive away.

"I've known him all of four days," she said to herself. "And I've invited him home to meet my family?"

25

If thou art worn and hard beset
With sorrows, that thou wouldst forget,
If thou wouldst read a lesson, that will keep
Thy heart from fainting and thy soul from sleep,
Go to the woods and Hill!   No tears
Dim the sweet look that Nature wears.

—from "Sunrise on the Hills"

October 1915

After breakfast the next morning, Elizabeth stood with Sam on the McClures' porch as Young Sam drove up in the Oldsmobile.

"I have to get fuel," he shouted above the din of the engine. "I'll be back in two shakes."

"Two shakes?" Elizabeth said, as they watched the car reach the street and turn toward town.

"Two shakes of a lamb's tail," Sam said. "An expression meaning 'shortly.' He'll be about a quarter of an hour. The fueling takes three or four minutes, but he'll likely have to wait for Amos at the garage to amble out from his breakfast and share a little gossip. I think we should sit here on the porch and enjoy this fine fall morning."

When Young Sam returned, they'd be driving to the sawmill. Sam had a meeting with his managers about the expansion, and Young Sam would then take Elizabeth to the McClure farm next to the woods his grandfather loved so much.

"Young Sam was something of a hellion when he was a boy," Sam said. "Starting about 9, he would drive his parents to total distraction. It coincided with the arrival of his first younger brother, and then the second. He was constantly in trouble there in Gettysburg, most of it pranks and general mischief, but a couple of times the sheriff brought him home. It might have been boyish high spirits, and it might have been acting out, trying to get his father's attention. That was when, in desperation, Amy, that's his mother, prevailed upon David, and she brought Young Sam here to Brookhaven to spend the summer. The next year, he rode the train by himself, from Gettysburg all the way here.

"We never had a lick of trouble with him. It was as if he was a different boy, behaved, polite, fun to be around, and teachable. He was like a little sponge, and bright as a new copper penny. Amy wanted him to stay here permanently, but David wouldn't hear of it. The idea, I think, brought back painful memories of how he was taken away to Gettysburg.

"Somehow, Young Sam made it through school, courting academic disaster at every turn. At first, David was determined that Young Sam would go into the army, that no self-respecting secondary school would accept him with the school record he had. The boy they knew and the boy I knew were very different people. That's when I wrote them a letter and made an offer to pay for his tuition and board.

"His sophomore year in school in Gettysburg, he transformed himself. A D student became an A student, and usually an $A+$ student. His teachers, Amy told me, were stunned. So were Amy and David. He was accepted into the study abroad program and went to Germany. Has he mentioned that?"

"Yes," Elizabeth said, "he has."

"When he came back from Germany, he sat for an entry test for Harvard and wrote an essay that was a marvel. He was accepted, much to his father's shock, and he never looked back. It turned out that the hellion had a first-class, razor-sharp mind. He also had an unbelievably tender heart. Still does, in fact." Sam shook his head. "But he and his father, it's like the relationship between his father and grandfather. Different times, different reasons, but the same result. They aren't close. Sam invited the family to his graduation when he received his B.A. in history. His mother came with his brothers. And, of course, he had the Brookhaven contingent—Cora Beth and Seamus, Leorinda, Seamus, Sophie, and myself. Two years later, it was the same group for his law school graduation. First in his class at the Harvard Law School." He paused. "And his father didn't go."

Sam smiled. "During his first year in law school, his classmates took bets on whether he could pass the Massachusetts bar examination. He hadn't even finished his first year. Young Sam took it and passed it, stunning everyone, including the bar officials when they found out he was still a first-year student. But he was duly admitted to the bar. He's also a member of the bars in Mississippi and Louisiana, and he's waiting on his certification from the U.S. Supreme Court. In the meantime, he's studying for the New York bar exam. His firm here, Foster Perkins, is a small-town law office, but after only two years, Sam has already put them on the legal map. That's why he has clients in New Orleans, Jackson, and Mobile."

"You're telling me this for a reason, Papa Sam," Elizabeth said.

"I am. The first day he arrived in Brookhaven after his law school graduation, Margaret Biddle discovered he intended to stay here. She immediately broke off whatever understanding they had, and he learned that he wasn't what he thought he was in her mind, what he'd understood for years, but instead he was to be a train ticket out of town. Margaret wanted what she thought were the bright lights of New York or Chicago or Boston. She was less interested in Sam and far more interested in escaping what she thought was some little backwater town in Mississippi. Imagine her shock when she found out her train ticket had determined to live in the very place she was trying to escape from.

"So that was the end of that. She might have broken his heart, and in a way not unlike what had happened between Sam and his father. What I think I'm saying is that anyone who might be conceivably interested in Sam should know that he considers himself a Brookhaven man."

Elizabeth felt her cheeks blushing. "Are you suggesting I might be interested in your grandson?"

"I can't say whether you are or aren't, Elizabeth. The two of you have known each other only five days now. But I can already see the regard he has for you, and it appears to me to be a regard that's reciprocated. If your intent is to make a career in New York or up east, then you should tell him that. All I ask is that you not break his heart."

They were saved from further conversation with Young

Sam returning in the Oldsmobile, blowing the car's horn and waving as he entered the drive. Once they settled in the car for the drive to the sawmill, Sam spoke.

"I believe we left off last night with us leaving Fairhope for the journey to Alabama and Mississippi. And what was running through my mind was what happened before Charlotte."

May 1865

It had been no more than four weeks since Appomattox, and now Sam found himself driving a buckboard, with two young girls and three former slaves, two of them children. He'd tethered Tag to the side, and the horse trotted calmly next to the wagon.

He knew he had to be crazy to be doing this. They had better than an even chance of getting killed before they made it to their destinations.

Sam had thought it might take six weeks to get to Windhaven in Alabama and another two weeks to reach Brookhaven. What he hadn't figured into his calculations was, first, he didn't have a map; second, traveling with two women and three children meant more frequent and longer stops; and, third, he'd be bartering his physical labor in return for food, pasture for the horses, and a place for them all to sleep, usually a barn.

It would be four months before he saw Brookhaven.

The labor took the form of moving hay bales, plowing fields with mules, sowing seed, and doing repairs. It was invariably younger women with children whom he helped;

he began to see the toll the war had taken by the widows it'd left in its wake. Two days out from Greensboro, one widow offered to marry Sam and provide a home for the entire group if he would stay.

During the first 10 days, any traveling companions usually meant Confederate soldiers headed home. More than one asked why he was carrying Sophie and her two children, but they were usually left alone. Whenever they encountered former slaves on the road, it was Sophie who told them to mind their own business, that "this young man is taking me and my children to my husband and their father in Mississippi." Everyone they passed eyed their horses, but one look at Tag's fiery eyes and nervous legs was enough of an argument to let the group alone.

Even with the buckboard, it was slow going. But as each day passed, Sam felt more confident that the journey might succeed. Road signs were nearly non-existent, many removed as a war-time measure, and having to stop and ask directions slowed them down more. Octavia Jane rode in the back with Sophie and her children, while Honeybee sat next to Sam on the buckboard's seat.

They were approaching the city of Charlotte when they met serious, and deadly, trouble.

They found a small clearing in dense woods off the road and set up their camp. Sam had gone hunting and shot two rabbits; Sophie quickly skinned them and set some rabbit stew to cooking over a campfire. He'd also found a large pond where they could draw water. They had some cornbread made from meal they'd bought from a farmer where they stayed the previous night, and all of them slept well.

Sam had told them, and often repeated, he had one rule for travel: no wandering off by themselves.

It was early the next day when Sophie and Octavia Jane awakened, along with the children. Sam was still asleep, tired after the journey and two days of plowing and sowing a field.

The scream suddenly woke him up.

He saw the three children sitting together, terrified. They'd heard the scream, too.

"Where's Sophie and Janie?" he said.

Daniel and Belle were too scared to speak. It was Honeybee who pointed to a path in the woods. "They went to take a bath in the pond."

Sam grabbed his rifle and his pistol. "Stay here and don't budge," he said, and he dashed into the woods toward the pond.

He ran as quietly as he could. He figured it must be something like a bear or some other animal.

As Sam neared the pond, he stopped running and crept forward more slowly.

It was animals, all right, but of the human variety.

Octavia Jane and Sophie were both crouched down in the pond, water up to their shoulders. They were moving backward, trying to get away from two men, soldiers from the looks of the dirty gray uniforms left at the pond's edge. One had reached Octavia Jane, and the other was two feet away from Sophie. Octavia Jane screamed again as the man grabbed her wrist.

Sam didn't hesitate. The bullet from the rifle caught the man in the back of the head, and gore flew into the water all around the girl. Sam dropped the rifle and cocked the pistol, firing just as the second man turned to look back toward Sam.

Both men's bodies were floating in the water, blood seeping into what had been fairly clear water.

Octavia Jane was shaking and whimpering. Sophie was wide-eyed in shock. But both began to move around the men's bodies and toward Sam.

"Stop," Sam said, "right there. I'm going to turn my back, and you're going to get yourselves dressed and get back to the wagon." He'd seen their clothes, all of their clothes, folded on a rock by the pond's edge.

Sam turned around. What had been a surge of feeling when he fired the guns was giving way to a white-hot anger. And he knew he had to calm himself.

"We're ready," Octavia Jane said after a few minutes.

"You walk ahead of me, and don't say a word. There may be more of them in the woods, and the sounds of shots will have roused any others."

Both fairly flew up the trail. Their clothes were wet from their bodies, and both had sodden hair.

When the three of them reached the children, Sam grabbed a spade from the back of the wagon.

"I'll be a while," he said. "You fix them their breakfast and then put the fire out. I'll be back."

They waited for two hours. When Sam came up the trail, they could see his pants were drying and dirty.

"We should leave," he said. "And you should consider yourselves blessed by these children here, because otherwise I would have left you to fend for yourselves."

"We just wanted to feel clean," Octavia Jane said.

He looked at her, and the expression on his face was stormy.

"I told you not to go off by yourselves. I told you over and over. We're all dirty. We all smell. We all want to get clean. But I suspect Sophie here could explain to you, Miss Octavia Jane Montgomery of Windhaven Plantation, what almost happened to you back there. I saw it happen often enough with both Confederate and Union troops. You were both worse than stupid." He felt the anger rising and tried to deliberately calm himself yet again. "In all of the two years I was in the war, I never killed a man. Not once. My job didn't require me to shoot at other people. And now, in the space of about five seconds, I killed two men because you did what I told you not to do. Don't talk to me about wanting to feel clean. I have two men's deaths on my conscience now. Scum that they may have been, they were still men and made in God's image. And I killed them."

Sam didn't speak again until they reached Charlotte. The city had been spared from the war, but it was full of refugees from other parts of North Carolina, Columbia, South Carolina, which had been burned by Sherman's army, and even Atlanta. Hotels were full, but Sam had the group wait while he found a widow operating a rooming house with bathing facilities and servants' quarters where Sophie and her children could stay, and even a stable with hay for the horses. Sam inspected everything before agreeing to the woman's price of four dollars in greenbacks. He used some of the money his uncle had given him in Greensboro.

They all had a bath and slept in beds for the first time in two weeks. Sam shared a room with two beds with Octavia Jane and Honeybee. Sophie, Daniel, and Belle had a bed each in the servants' dormitory. They ate separately; the rooming house woman wouldn't hear of whites and blacks eating together. But they enjoyed the same food.

By early afternoon, they'd come close to the South Carolina-North Carolina border.

"The lady at the boarding house suggested we stay on the more northern route across South Carolina," Sam said. "The southerly route would take us near Columbia, and the city was destroyed by Sherman's army. We won't find housing or rooms there, nor any food. She said we'd encounter more hills this way but it's likely safer with food more available."

The lady had been right. They passed few people, and usually only those headed north toward Charlotte. They were now far behind the mass of soldiers headed home from both Lee's and Johnston's armies. Sam hoped the soldiers had behaved themselves; stealing and worse would make the local people more suspicious of anyone passing through.

Both Sophie and Octavia Jane sat in the back of the buckboard. Belle and Honeybee also seemed to have become afraid of Sam. Daniel, however, chose not to sit with his mother and sister but next to Sam on the front seat. Four days out of Charlotte, and some 50 or 60 miles from the Georgia border as he reckoned, Sam shocked the boy when he handed him the reins.

"All you have to do is hold them steady," Sam said. "The horses know what they're doing, and they'll teach you." It might have been his imagination, but the boy, immediately wide-eyed, sat up straighter and concentrated on the horses. Sam showed him how to guide, how to rein in, and how to give the horses a nudge when they slowed too early.

Finding a place to stay and food to eat wasn't so much a

problem as a condition. The area was one of small farms, the people on the clannish side and suspicious of strangers. Sam's willingness to work and shoot for rabbits and game went a long way with the people living there. The usual accommodation was a barn or shed; most weren't thrilled with the idea of accommodating a black family.

Somehow, they managed. Sam would accept any gift of food, provided in appreciation for chopping wood, hoeing garden plots, fixing a leaning porch, mending a leaking roof, and other work.

In late May, right before they reached the South Carolina and Georgia border, they passed through the small town of Hickory Falls. Sam had intended, based upon helpful suggestions from travelers going the other way, to make for the town of Athens and travel across Georgia well south of Atlanta. Occupying his mind was how to cross roughly 50 miles, three or four days of travel with good weather, that Sherman's army columns had left devastated. Most travelers they talked with had not passed that way; the very few who had just shook their heads and wished him luck.

In Hickory Falls, they stopped by a general store that was open and had food to sell.

Sam spent some three dollars to buy what was a considerable amount. The store owner was thrilled when Sam offered American dollars.

"If you need a place to stay," the man said when Sam told him they were planning to cross Georgia for Alabama, "you might try the Widow Hawkins. She's ornery but fair. Her place is about two miles toward the river; you'd be passing it on your way. The widow lost her husband and all three sons in the war." The man nodded toward the buckboard outside. "She won't lodge former slaves, but she might let you stay in her barn."

Sam thanked the man. Less than an hour later, they were at the small farm comprising the widow's home. The widow herself came out on her porch, holding a shotgun.

"Your business might be what?" she said. "And stay right there in your seat until I tell you to get down."

Sam eyed the woman holding the gun. She wasn't aiming at him, which was good, but he recognized that she knew how to use it and wouldn't hesitate.

"My name is Sam McClure, ma'am. I'm escorting my companions to Alabama and then making my way to Mississippi. The man at the general store in town said you might have a barn where we could stay the night."

She looked over the group in the wagon. "You're all a mite young to be traveling by yourselves."

"Yes, ma'am," Sam said. "We started near Greensboro, North Carolina. I was paroled from General Lee's army at Appomattox and met up with them in Greensboro."

"You look too young to be a soldier," she said.

"I was mostly a messenger boy, ma'am."

She stared at him for a moment. "You have your own blankets and food?"

"Yes, ma'am."

"One dollar for the barn and access to my well. That's one greenback dollar."

Sam hadn't realized how much tension he was feeling until he felt himself relax. "Yes, ma'am, fair enough. I'm also available to help you with any chores."

She smiled. "If you can help me plow up my vegetable garden, I'll forget about the greenback."

What neither she nor Sam anticipated was that they would stay with her nearly three weeks.

26

Let us, then, be up and doing,
With a heart for any fate;
Still achieving, still pursuing,
Learn to labor and to wait.

—from "A Psalm of Life"

October 1915

They'd arrived at the sawmill some time before and sat in the car while Sam continued with his story.

"Miss Putnam, I will be here for several hours," he said. "I suppose we should plan to resume our discussion tomorrow at breakfast. I understand you and Young Sam here have that hayride tonight."

Elizabeth glanced at Young Sam. "Yes, sir, I believe we do."

"Papa Sam," Young Sam said, "I'm going to show Elizabeth the farm and a little bit of the woods, and then take her by the stores."

Sam smiled. "Busy afternoon. Well, you two need to get going, and I have my meeting with the managers."

On the way, Young Sam explained that the farm was largely a vegetable farm at the moment, with the corn already harvested along with most of the vegetables. "It's managed by one of Uncle Seamus and Aunt Cora Beth's grandsons and his wife. They have four children, ages 14 to six. And they know to expect us, so I'm hoping for some lunch, too."

"A lot of family life seems to revolve around food," Elizabeth said.

"It's the South. Meals are something like rituals or ceremonies, not in a formal sense, of course, but important times of the day. The high food ceremony, though, you'll find out about Sunday. It's after-church Sunday dinner. As far as food and family are concerned, it's the highlight of the week."

Young Sam was right; lunch was indeed waiting for them in a large and airy kitchen. The four children were in school, so it was just their parents they visited with. Daniel O'Brien explained the operation of the farm, what was grown, and how the management revolved around the seasons. Tomatoes were almost as big a crop as corn, in terms of acreage.

Afterward, Young Sam walked Elizabeth a short way in the nearby woods and then stopped.

"These woods aren't much different from the way they were in the 1860s," he said. "It was about this spot where Papa Sam and Uncle Litt spotted that deer he told us about."

They were far enough into the woods where the farmhouse wasn't visible. For a moment, they both stood without speaking. For Elizabeth, the silence of the woods was almost overwhelming.

"It's remarkable, isn't it?" Young Sam said. "The silence, I mean."

She nodded. "I think I understand why your grandfather comes here. There's really nothing else you should do but listen."

"And occasionally hunt."

Thirty minutes later, they were in town, and Elizabeth entered the McClures' farm-and-feed store on Railroad Street, across from the train station.

"This was the general store when Papa Sam was a boy," Young Sam said. "This was where—"

"—his grandfather was struck down," Elizabeth said, finishing the statement.

"The very same counter, in fact," Young Sam said.

As Elizabeth ran her hand along the counter edge, the store manager introduced himself as Silas Broughton.

"Silas manages the store here," Young Sam said. "He's a local Brookhaven man, married to my cousin Alice. She's one of my Aunt Helen's children, Helen and Edith being my father's two sisters."

"That's right," Elizabeth said. "I remember your grandfather mentioning it the other day."

Silas showed them around the store, and then they left for the food store a few blocks away, McClure's Grocery.

It was larger than she expected, as large, in fact, as the store where her family shopped in Boston. The manager was one of the sons of Seamus and Cora Beth; Patrick O'Brien was in his 50s and strongly resembled his father.

"I'm going to need a genealogy chart," Elizabeth said, "just to keep the family sorted. I've met O'Briens, Seales, a Broughton, and only two McClures. It's a sizeable extended family."

"You should see it in July," Young Sam said, "when the family comes for the annual reunion. Papa Sam rents out most of the Brookhaven Hotel. My mother and brothers stay with me, or at least they did until two years ago; some stay with

Aunt Cora Beth, Papa Sam's place is packed, and he still has to reserve many of the rooms at the hotel." He smiled. "He loves it, of course. We have games, long talks into the night, swimming in the Bogue Chitto River, and all kinds of activities for the children. It usually lasts three or four days over the Fourth of July weekend."

"I understand your father doesn't come?" Elizabeth said.

Young Sam shook his head. "Not once over all the years we've had it. Next summer will mark the 30th anniversary." He smiled. "But Sophie's children and grandchildren come. Belle still teaches in Atlanta, and Daniel is still practicing medicine in Philadelphia."

They drove up the front drive of the house. Young Sam hopped out and helped Elizabeth step down. "We'll leave about 5:30," he said, "so you have time to rest. We have a kind of evening picnic, with the food provided by the parents. We'll have a time for singing and sharing, and we finish up with a marshmallow roast."

"I've heard about them," she said, "but I've never been to one."

"I'll take some credit for introducing them here," Young Sam said. "They started back east about 12 years ago, New Jersey, I think, and we had them in Gettysburg. I even introduced them to the Mittelsteins in Germany, and they were a major if sticky hit. So, until about 5:30?"

She smiled. "Thank you for the lovely afternoon. I feel a bit guilty, knowing I'm keeping you from your work."

"As Uncle Seamus would say, I'm having a grand time, Elizabeth," he said. "A grand time."

The hayride was a major success. Some 20 young people from Brookhaven Presbyterian rode the hay wagon from the parking area of the fair to a clearing near the river. Elizabeth was more than charmed. They sang hymns and popular songs, laughed, pulled pranks on each other, and, at the picnic site, listened intently as Young Sam spoke from a passage in the Epistle to the Philippians.

While they ate, Elizabeth was plied with questions from the girls as well as the boys. They wanted to know about her work as a reporter, life in New York and Boston, what she thought of Brookhaven, her college years, and more. And she loved the marshmallow roast, sticky fingers and all.

They returned to the house on Cherry Street a little after 10. It was getting late, and it had been a long day, but Elizabeth felt nowhere close to sleep. Nor did Young Sam.

"I bet we could find a piece of pie or cake in the kitchen if we looked for it," he said, grinning.

What they found was that Sam had gotten there ahead of them.

"There's some apple pie in the pie safe," he said. "And Sophie's not back yet to fuss, so you help yourself."

They laughed. Young Sam got their slices of pie.

"If you're not too sleepy," Sam said, "we can pick up where we left off."

"I have my notebook in my jacket," Elizabeth said, reaching to retrieve it.

Young Sam sat next to her with their pie plates.

"I believe I stopped with our arrival at the Widow Hawkins' place," he said. "We intended to stay two nights, but that's not quite how things worked out."

May-June 1865

They slept hard that night, even if it was in a barn. Sam was up early the next morning. Before breakfast, he was working the vegetable garden behind the house with a hoe the widow had given him. He could see it was good soil, but the large plot had been left untended for some time.

He'd been at it for three hours when the widow brought him some eggs and even two strips of bacon.

"I'm at the end of the hog I slaughtered," she said. "Why are you putting it in your pocket?"

"For the children," he said. "We have food, or what I can shoot each day, but I'm running low on bullets. Do you have anything like a sturdy carving knife I can use to fashion a bow and arrow?"

She nodded and fetched a knife, handing it to him.

"When I finish here, I'll go into those woods and find me a sapling for a bow. I'm much obliged."

Two hours later, the plot freshly turned, he saw the widow talking with Janie and Sophie at the barn. The children were standing nearby, half-listening but more focused on watching him with the hoe.

"Daniel, I need your help," Sam said, and the boy rushed over. Together, they went into the woods to cut saplings.

"Miz Hawkins gave us bacon," the boy said.

Sam smiled. "She did, did she? That sounds a real treat."

Back at the house, Sam got all three of the children to help apportion sections of the plot for various vegetables.

The widow had seed for carrots, corn, tomatoes, various greens, cucumbers, and even for watermelon. Sam remembered what he'd learned from his brother James at the farm in Mississippi, how to make the right amount of room for the vine crops and where to plant the corn so it wouldn't block the sun for the other vegetables.

Under the widow's watchful eye, they planted the seeds. Sam showed the children how he cut the seed potatoes into pieces, noting the eye would sprout roots. "Potatoes grow fast," he said.

"You've done this before," Widow Hawkins said.

"With my brother James. He managed the family farm for my father."

"I expect he'll be glad to see you home."

"He died at Shiloh," Sam said, "with my brother-in-law."

She was quiet for a time, then spoke. "My husband died at Bull Run, my oldest boy at Antietam, my middle boy at Chancellorsville, and my youngest at Spotsylvania Courthouse. The dying stopped because there were no boys left."

"I was at The Wilderness and Spotsylvania," Sam said. "They were bad. I'm sorry, ma'am."

"None of them had a lick of sense," she said. "They had to go off and do their duty. And they all died. It was all a waste, and their deaths were for nothing. Do you have any brothers left?"

"The oldest, my brother Hugh, may still be," Sam said, "but I haven't heard anything from the family in well over a year. He was with Johnston in Tennessee, and they're likely dispersed from North Carolina now."

"Why are you traveling with that slave woman and her

children?"

"There's no connection," Sam said, "except she came to stay with us near Greensboro and she knows how to cook. I said I'd see her to Vicksburg, where her husband was sold. It's only a few miles beyond where I live."

"And the white girls?"

"The little one, Honeybee, is all that's left of her family. Janie's her cousin. She's taking her back to Alabama. I promised her grandmother I'd see them both home to Alabama." He paused. "We buried the grandmother in Greensboro."

"So much death," the woman said, shaking her head. "Do you fish?"

Sam nodded.

"I should but I don't. There's a good stream about a fifth of mile from here; it's part of my property. It's late in the day, but some shady spots might supply a catfish, a bass, and even a trout. Several poles are on the wall in the barn. If you catch anything, I'll cook it up and we all can share."

"That's a deal," Sam said.

With Daniel alongside, the pair of them caught two trout and two bass. Sam was almost shocked that they'd caught anything at all.

Dinner that night was a feast. The widow brought out some canned beans and even spiced peaches. They all ate carefully and slowly, enjoying every morsel. The widow played the harmonica, and they all sang songs that had been popular for years; they avoided war-related songs.

It was a lighthearted moment, a blessing Sam thought that night, as he prepared his bed in the hay in the barn. He could make out Tag and the other two horses in the darkness, sleeping contentedly after a day of no riding and full stomachs. They planned to leave in the morning; the widow said she'd give them directions and suggestions for what she was hearing about crossing Georgia.

It was an hour before dawn when Sam awakened to the sound of moaning. It was little Honeybee. Everyone else was still asleep, so Sam crawled over to the little girl and felt her forehead. She felt on fire.

"Janie," he said aloud. "Get up. Honeybee has a fever."

Half-awake, Janie sat up, rubbing her eyes.

"Honeybee has a fever. I need you to fetch the Widow."

Sophie, Daniel, and Belle were stirring. Sophie heard Sam's words, and she went first to Belle, who felt fine, and then to Daniel, who did not.

"His forehead's so hot it burns my hand," Sophie said.

"Janie!" Sam said, nearly shouting. "Now. Run to the Widow. Hurry!"

Janie ran for the house. A few minutes later, she was back with the Widow.

The woman looked at both children and felt their foreheads. "They have something," she said. "It's early so I don't know for sure, and I'm half-afraid to guess. You need get to town and find Doc Bigelow. Go to Main Street just past the blacksmith's, turn right and his house is about a half-block."

Widow Hawkins had provided good directions; riding Tag hard, Sam found the doctor's house straight away.

Dr. Albert Bigelow was about 60, a little shorter than Sam, with a bushy beard and sideburns. He looked none-too-pleased to be awakened with the sun barely peeping out. Mrs. Bigelow had followed him down the stairs, and she said she'd get the coffee on.

Sam explained the situation.

"Could be anything," the doctor said, "but with two of them with a fever, it's likely something contagious. Where are you coming from and going to?"

"North Carolina," Sam said, "north of Greensboro, and first to Alabama and then Mississippi."

"Were these children raised on a plantation?"

Sam nodded. "Different ones, but both plantations."

"We're seeing an uptick in children's diseases," Dr. Bigelow said, "and it's starting with the ones raised largely on isolated farms, big and small. The war has uprooted a lot of people, and that means children and adults both are being exposed more to diseases."

Mrs. Bigelow brought them both a cup of coffee. "It's more chicory than coffee," she said, apologizing.

"Anything warm will do fine, ma'am, thank you," Sam said.

"I'll need to harness the horse and buggy, and then I'll be on directly," the doctor said.

"I'll be glad to do that for you," Sam said.

"My stallion isn't too fond of strangers."

"He will be with me," Sam said.

The doctor arched his eyebrows. "We'll see. By the way, my fee is a dollar for house calls. That's an American dollar."

Sam nodded. "That will be fine, sir."

If the doctor was surprised by his horse's response to Sam, he didn't say but he did slightly nod his head in acknowledgement. Sam rode next to the buggy to the Widow's.

When they reached the barn, a wild-eyed Janie met them. "They're both coughing and have a runny nose. And Belle has a slight fever."

"Ah," was all the doctor said.

He stopped inside the barn and saw the widow, Sophie, and the three children. "I don't treat slaves."

Sophie looked panicked.

"They're children, Dr. Bigelow," Sam said.

"I understand, but the people here would object. Maybe not in a year, but right now they would."

"The people here don't have to know," Sam said. "I'll triple your fee."

The doctor hesitated a moment longer, and then he looked at Mrs. Hawkins. "Not a word of this, Widow," he said.

"I don't carry tales, Dr. Bigelow, as you well know," she said.

He grunted and then turned to examine the children.

After a time, he looked up at Janie and Sophie. "I need to see their chests and backs. Can you undo their blouses?"

Sam could easily see that red spots and blotches were appearing on Honeybee's back; the spots were more obvious on white skin. He watched the doctor peer closely at Daniel and Belle.

"It's measles," Dr. Bigelow said. "Has everyone else here had it?"

Widow Hawkins and Sam both nodded. Janie and Sophie shook their heads.

"You both have been exposed, and now all you can do is

wait. You may or may not get it. By South Carolina law, as-suming the law is still functioning, I have to quarantine the farm. Can the children stay in the house?"

The Widow spoke. "Yes. I have three beds in what was the boys' room."

"They need to stay warm but not hot. Keep them quiet and resting. They'll need to drink considerable water. When the itching starts, and it will start, use the calamine. I'll leave some with you." He pointed to Janie and Sophie. "If either of you apply it, use a clean rag that can be washed in hot water. Better still, have this young man or the Widow do it. When the red spots fully emerge, the fever usually falls. For the next few days, I'll come by in the morning and evening to check on them. If their condition gets worse, come get me." He looked at Sam. "I need to speak with you and the Widow outside." They followed the doctor into the barnyard.

"I think the Widow already knows," he said, "but measles can be fatal to children. The older the child, the better the chances for making it. The little girl and the boy are at the greatest risk, but all three are in for a rough spell. Whites seem to have been around measles longer, and we're better able to cope. But it felled Indians like a plague, and blacks are more susceptible than whites. If they haven't had it, the older girl and the black woman will likely get it. Because of the fever, the children may become delirious at times; just talk to them in a soothing, calming voice. Cold compresses will help keep the fever down, but you two will have your hands full. I'll be back this evening." He opened his bag and handed Sam a bottle of calamine lotion. "Remember, use it sparingly, and only when they complain about itching. That usually doesn't show up for a day or two. As for food, try to keep them nourished. They won't want to eat for two or three days, until the fever abates, but make sure to give them water." He paused. "When I return this evening, I'll have a quarantine sign to post."

With that, he nodded, stepped up into his buggy, and left.

"He's a bit abrupt," the Widow said, "But he knows his medicine."

"We're dreadfully imposing on your hospitality, Mrs. Hawkins," Sam said.

"You are," she said, "but we have sick children to tend to. The boys' room is clean, but let me check the linens before we bring the children in."

"You sound like you have some experience with children and measles."

"I had five children, Sam. The measles hit all of them at the same time. The three boys were the oldest, and they made it through. My two girls were six and four, and they both died. Dr. Bigelow tended to all of them, and he nearly moved in, he was here so much. It's a wicked mean disease for children to get."

Sam carried each of the children to the bedroom in the house. All three were feverish hot, and they divided the labor of cold compresses, Sam taking Daniel, Sophie with Belle, and Janie with Honeybee. Sam would take breaks to find food, while the Widow kept herself occupied with preparing meals and fetching cold water in a bucket from the well.

Two days later, Belle's fever broke first, about the same time that Janie began to feel poorly. That night, her fever raged, and Sam took over cold compress duty with her while Sophie looked after Daniel. The next afternoon, Honeybee's fever broke, and she asked for something to eat. The Widow looked after the two recovering girls, while Sophie stayed with Daniel and Sam with Janie. Sam and Sophie slept on the floor next to their patients, rotating shifts so that each could get a few hours of sleep.

Dr. Bigelow continued to call twice a day. He also checked Sophie, but she seemed to have somehow avoided it.

"I suspect," he said to her, "you probably did have measles, but a mild case. Sometimes, it's a cough and a runny nose only, maybe a slight fever, and it seems like a common cold. But our four patients here had a pretty strong case of it." He told Sam privately that he was amazed that Daniel and Honeybee had survived. Both were still weak, but they were eating and strong enough to take themselves to the privy.

Sam did what he could to repay the Widow. He repaired a leak in the roof, fixed the sagging front porch, made sure the vegetable garden was properly watered, fed the Widow's old horse as well as their own, and replaced a broken windowpane in the parlor. After a few days, when the three children were strong enough, he brought them outside to sit under a shady elm tree to enjoy the fresh air.

On the fifth day since the measles had first started, Janie's fever broke. They'd been at the Widow's a full week. The doctor left another bottle of calamine, and Janie's itching started not long afterward.

"I'll tell you what I told the children," Dr. Bigelow said to the girl. "Don't scratch. It'll feel unbearable at times, but the lotion should help. You'll leave scars if you scratch." He told Sam and Sophie that they might consider getting the four patients down to the stream and let them idle in the cool water.

"But no swimming. It's going to take some time for their strength to recover." He thought that they might consider resuming their journey in about 10 days, "assuming the Widow is willing to accommodate you that long."

"I have no problem with that, Dr. Bigelow," the Widow said. "Sam here's fixing leaks, broken windows, my front porch, and a lot of other things I haven't been able to get done since my family went off to war."

"My house calls here are finished," the doctor said.

"We should settle up, then," Sam said.

The two sat in the Widow's parlor as they settled the account. The doctor asked for $5 American; Sam insisted on $10, "given how many times you came out here."

"You've done the Widow Hawkins a world of good," Dr. Bigelow said "even with the measles. She has a caring heart, and she doesn't have anyone to lavish it on anymore."

"Well," Sam said, "she's certainly lavished it on us. I don't know what we would have done without her willingness to see us through. And I thank you for your care and attention. Without it, I'm afraid I would have been digging graves."

They shook hands, the doctor told his patients goodbye, and he left.

27

For the one face I looked for was not there,
The one low voice was mute;
Only an unseen presence filled the air,
And baffled my pursuit.

—from "Hawthorne"

October 1915

"It's after midnight," Sam said. "We all need to get our rest."

"I'd lost all track of the time," Elizabeth said. "You tell a wonderful story, Papa Sam."

"Sophie stayed well?" Young Sam said.

"She did," Sam said. "The doctor, I think, had a point. She'd probably had a mild case sometime in the past, and it protected her from getting it again."

"I had measles when I was 11," Young Sam said, "and it was pretty miserable."

Elizabeth nodded. "I was 10. I thought the itchiness would never go away." She paused. "I have a question. You skipped over it rather lightly, but what was it like to care for the children's measles, and Janie's?"

"Hard," Sam said. "Exhausting. Constantly doing something. But something happened I didn't expect. Pressing cool cloths to Janie's face, I had the strangest sense I should be doing this the rest of my life. Which, by the way, I at first attributed to exhaustion. She was delirious at times from the fever. I'd wipe her brow, and looking into her eyes, I'd see the fever. And I'd see something else. At one point, she grabbed on to me and clung, saying over and over how much she needed Sam, he saved her life, she needed Sam, could I find Sam. That night, I did something I never expected. I fell in love with her. I knew it was impossible; our stations in life were too different and her family would never allow it. But I fell in love with her. Right there in the Widow Hawkins' house near Hickory Falls, South Carolina. That moment of delirium changed my life forever."

Young Sam and Elizabeth stared at the old man. Elizabeth saw the years peel away; she saw that 15-year-old boy holding a delirious 14-year-old girl, telling her he was there, telling her she'd be fine, rocking her gently as she fought the fever of measles, knowing that she'd remember nothing of what she'd said, falling in love with a girl he believed he could never have.

She felt her heart breaking. She glanced at Young Sam and saw tears in his eyes.

The three of them sat silently for a few minutes.

"We'll plan for a leisurely morning," Young Sam said, breaking the silence. "I have some errands, and I might sleep in a bit. I'll take you both to the fair at lunchtime. We can find something to eat and then head to the tents. All the final judging events are in the afternoon. And then the barbeque dinner and the fireworks. Is that agreeable?"

"That sounds more than agreeable," Elizabeth said.

Sam nodded. "And now this old man needs his rest." He bade them a good evening and left the room.

Young Sam, still sitting next to Elizabeth, placed his hand over hers.

"I'm not trying to be forward," he said. "Right at this moment, I need to feel a human touch, and particularly yours. He's never told that story before. Never. Yet he told it to you."

She lifted his hand and entwined her own fingers into his. "I think he told it to us."

They stared at one another. He leaned toward her and kissed her gently on the lips. They touched foreheads.

"We barely know each other," she said.

"That's true. And yet it seems we've always known each other."

They heard the back door open and quickly separated.

"Are you eating my apple pie, Young Sam?" Sophie said, coming into the kitchen.

"I plead not guilty by association," Young Sam said. "Papa Sam was here before us."

Elizabeth smiled. "He was here before us, and I'm afraid he rather paved the way."

The next morning after breakfast, Sam and Elizabeth sat by themselves in Sam's office.

"Littleton arrived near midnight last night," Sam said, "so I expect he's sleeping in. The train was crowded, and it was late starting from Oxford. But it'll be good to have a visit."

He looked down as he gathered his thoughts. "Ah, yes, the measles." He cleared his throat.

"Janie improved rather quickly," he said, "faster than the children. We stayed another 10 days, until everyone seemed strong enough. I did more work than I can tell for Widow

Hawkins, and Sophie helped, too. All of us shed a few tears when we left; she'd been more than kind to us, and I hope we left her feeling blessed as much as she blessed us.

"A ferry took us across the river into Georgia, and we made good time to Athens, only three days. People there told us it was better, but Athens had been a major sanctuary for refugees fleeing Atlanta, or evicted from Atlanta, the year before, with another wave coming after Sherman's march. I'm not sure what worse would have looked like, but the city was still packed with people, including many living in classrooms at the university, prices of everything were sky high, and Confederate money was worthless. We didn't stay there even a full day but left early the afternoon the same day we arrived. We made camp near a stream about 10 miles south of Athens. We still had food packed by the Widow, and I had my bow and some arrows and a fishing pole she let me have.

"A couple of families traveling north camped nearby, and I caught enough fish to share. We sat around a common campfire and traded stories and information, us about Athens and northward and them about southward. They confirmed that we'd need to cross a swath of destruction, two to three days of travel, the same destruction one of the families had come from. Sherman's armies, they told me, had moved in several columns southeast from Atlanta to Savannah, and had burned or picked the countrywide pretty well clean. What I'd noticed about them and other families we met was how there were no men between the ages of 17 and 50. Not a one.

"They did say that just about every farmer was desperate for labor. People could plant vegetable patches, enough to keep a family alive, but to grow cash crops like cotton and corn, you had to have labor.

"A few days later, we reached the northern edge of Sherman's path."

June 1865

The night before they'd reach the town of Madison, by Sam's estimation and helpful directions from other travelers, Sam held a group powwow around the campfire.

"Tomorrow we'll reach where Sherman's army marched," he said. "I don't know what we'll find. Whatever it is, it won't likely be normal. The only town he burned was Atlanta, but there was a lot of destruction in towns, farms, plantations, and villages. The army went faster than its supply trains, so 60,000 men were turned loose on the land. They had orders not to loot or harm civilians, but from all reports those orders were often ignored. We're going to keep our heads down, be respectful, and show some sympathy. My hope is that we'll get across quickly, but food is going to be a problem. Anybody with a gun will be hunting rabbits, squirrels, birds, and anything else that moves. And we may run across ruffians, so we'll just have to deal with it."

The road to Madison ran through thick woods. Sam appointed the children to watch the woods closely, even woods they'd just passed. Janie sat next to him on the buckboard seat. She was holding the reins and guiding the horses. Sam had his pistol on his belt, within easy reach, and his rifle behind him out of sight. He and Janie were chatting about their respective homes, North Carolina, the Widow Hawkins, how Sam had fared with the measles when he was 8, and other general topics, to stay calm and keep the children calm.

He had just started to recite aloud from *Evangeline* when two riders emerged suddenly from the woods to their right. They were dressed in dirty Confederate pants, blue Yankee jackets, brown hats that had seen better days, and what appeared to be brand-new boots. They were both holding guns, aimed directly at Sam. They looked like brothers, with one about 25 and the other a bit younger. The younger one had an almost crazed grin on his face.

"Well, what do we have here this fine June morning?" the older one said. "A nice friendly group traveling through our woods. Well, here's what's going to happen, boy. You're going to drop that pistol you're toting on the ground, step down from the wagon, and take those three children into the woods, escorted by my brother here."

"Can I shoot 'em, Fred?" the younger said. "Can I shoot 'em in the woods?"

"All in good time, Eli, all in good time. As I said, boy, you drop that pistol and get down where I can see you. The girl and the black woman stay in the wagon, and I thank you kindly for providing the entertainment for the next several days. Now move."

Sam had heard a slight movement behind him. What happened next happened so quickly that it almost seemed a dream.

"Tag, bite," Sam said.

The horse was inches from the younger brother's horse. Tag moved his head and bit the horse hard on the neck, causing the horse to rear and pitch the man off.

The rifle suddenly appeared between Sam and Janie and

fired, hitting the older brother straight in the chest and tumbling him to the ground. Sam grabbed his pistol from his belt and shot the younger brother just as he picked himself up.

Sam turned and looked at the children. The force of the rifle had knocked the shooter backwards. It was Honeybee.

For the next hour, they parked on the side of the road. Not a soul passed them in either direction. It was as if the world turned elsewhere while the little group clustered by the buckboard, calmed down, and made sense of what had happened.

Sam himself was shaking, Janie was sobbing in relief, and Sophie was pacing up and down on the road. "I'm thanking the Lord for our deliverance," she said, walking back and forth. "That child saved our lives and saved us from worse." Daniel and Belle were sitting on the ground watching, holding each other and not saying a word.

"After my aunt died," Janie said, drying her tears, "my grandmother taught both me and Honeybee how to fire a gun. She said we'd likely need to know how. She used one of my uncle's rifles, that one I aimed at you that day we met and that's in the traveling case in the back, under my dresses."

Sam tried to imagine Lucinda Hawkins Montgomery of the Charleston Hawkins shooting a rifle and teaching two young girls how to do the same.

Honeybee had a large kickback bruise from the rifle on her right shoulder that would likely feel worse before it felt better. Janie had her arm around her; the little girl was teary-eyed. "He was a bad man," she said, "and I shot him. I used Sam's rifle, and I shot him dead." She suddenly broke into tears. "Am I going to hell?"

Sam sat next to the girl. "I don't think that's how God works it, Miss Honeybee. It's a bad thing to kill someone, but sometimes you have to defend yourself, your family, and your friends. That's what you did. If you hadn't, every one of us would be dead right now. You never do it because you want to, or for what you think you'll gain from it, but only when you have to. I saw enough killing of all kinds in the war to last a thousand lifetimes, and I saw brave men on both sides kill each other and die."

"Did our soldiers defend us, Sam?" Honeybee said.

"They thought so, Honeybee, but I think it was a lot more complicated than that. War is always complicated. You fight for what you think is right. Sometimes it is, and sometimes it isn't. But in what happened here today, I'm going to say it was right to do what you did. You saved Janie's life, and Daniel's, and Belle's, and Sophie's, and mine. And your own."

"You helped, too."

"I did. But you were the one with the courage to take the first and most important step. Don't forget that." He was still feeling the effects of the rifle shot. He hoped the hearing in his right ear would come back.

Sam stood and walked over to where the bodies were, with their horses standing nearby. He considered what he should do. If he buried them here, no one might know, at least for a while. He suspected the two had been terrorizing the countryside, waylaying travelers and locals alike. People in Madison would need to know.

"Sophie," he said, "I may need your help."

An hour later, it was a strange procession that rode into the small Georgia town of Madison. Janie held the reins of the buckboard, with Sophie sitting next to her and the three children standing behind the seat. Tied with reins to the back of the wagon were the two outlaws' horses, carrying the bodies of their masters slung over the saddles. Sam was riding Tag alongside the wagon.

The town had sustained damage from Sherman's march; windows of houses and stores were boarded up, and the general store still showed signs of looting, although some repairs had been made. Few people were on the street, but Sam stopped a woman and asked if they might be directed to the sheriff.

The woman they asked eyed the two dead men. "My word!" she said. "You got them! Yes, sir, follow me." And she dashed up the street, shouting "The Bates are dead! The Bates are dead!"

Her shouts brought people in the street. By the time they reached the sheriff's office, some 50 townspeople were walking with them, chattering happily and some even singing. Whatever Sam had expected, it wasn't a hero's welcome.

The sheriff came out of his office, looked over Sam's group, and then inspected the dead men.

He turned to Sam. "I don't know how you did it, young man, but you have rid the region of the two varmints plaguing us for the last year-and-a-half, before and after Sherman. They're responsible for a string of deaths and untold outrages. We've sent dozens of riders after them, and time and time again, they always managed to slip away. We owe you a great debt."

"Well," Sam said, pointing to Honeybee, "it was Little Missy here who got off the first shot and killed the older one."

The crowd quieted and stared at the girl. "And a little child shall lead them," the sheriff said.

Sam and his group spent the night in Madison. Townspeople shared what food they had and provided accommodations at no charge. The sheriff and others told them what they knew about the road ahead, what had happened during the march, and what they might expect. They also recounted stories of the Bates Brothers, and Sam soon understood the reign of terror that had existed.

"They didn't dare come into town," the sheriff said. "But no guarantee of safety existed outside, even with regular armed patrols. Travelers were especially at risk, because they'd come through with no advance warning, like yourselves. The Union army, when it came through, looted and stole anything that wasn't nailed down, but they didn't indiscriminately slaughter old people, women, and children like the Bates did."

Early the next morning, as they prepared to leave, the sheriff took Sam aside.

"About 20 miles south, on the road to Monticello, there's a German farmer named Mundt." He handed Sam a letter. "Give him this, and he will take care of you. He has a small but prosperous farm, never had any slaves, and Sherman's men thought they'd taken all of his livestock, but he'd hidden a good number of pigs and chickens and a cow in the woods. The Bates Brothers killed his wife and youngest children, and he may or may not tell you that story. But he will take care of you."

28

There is no flock, however watched and tended,
But one dead lamb is there!
There is no fireside, howsoe'er defended,
But has one vacant chair!

—from "Resignation"

October 1915

"Is Sam telling you stories?" a woman's voice said.

Elizabeth turned toward the door of the study and saw Beatrice and Littleton.

"He is," Elizabeth said, smiling. "I'm learning that Annie Oakley may have had some competition."

"Pshaw," Beatrice said. "He has a tendency to exaggerate."

"Not in this case," Sam said, standing up. "Although Honeybee here might be more of a Calamity Jane than an Annie Oakley."

They all laughed.

"It's good to see you, Litt," Sam said, walking to embrace his nephew. "Long train ride?"

"Too long," Littleton said. "Students and legislators heading for New Orleans, not knowing they're missing the county fair here. They were in a rather raucous mood, likely fueled by the eager anticipation of escaping the dry laws and a few discreetly hidden flasks. The train was late from Memphis, but we got here. May we join you?"

"You certainly may," Sam said. "Pull in some chairs from the hall."

When they were settled, Sam began to speak.

"The sheriff told us to look for two fenceposts with an eagle carved on them. The Yankees had left them alone, thinking they indicated Union sympathies. Actually, Mr. Mundt had carved them as a reminder of his home in Germany. The sheriff had also given us the Bates Brothers' horses, to bring to the man. 'He should have them,' was what he said, offering no explanation.

"We passed almost no travelers. The area was eerily quiet, as if even the birds knew to stay away. The road and the woods we passed through seemed normal, we didn't see signs of anything burned or destroyed, but the quiet was strange. We made decent time, and it was late afternoon when Janie spotted the fenceposts."

June 1865

The road to the Mundt farmhouse was about 100 yards long, wending its way through fallow fields and then shallow woods.

Whatever Sam had been expecting, the Mundt homestead wasn't it. The two-story clapboard farmhouse was what later generations would call an "A-frame," painted white with black shutters. A short picket fence surrounded a well-tended front flower garden filled with roses and a variety of blooming flowers. The house seemed neither southern nor northern, with its steeply pitched roof and a façade dressed with wooden crosspieces.

"It's beautiful," Janie said, "like a storybook."

The front door opened, and a man stepped out, holding a rifle aimed generally in their direction. He was of middling height, brown but graying hair, and Sam guessed his age to be near 50. Behind him, in the doorway, Sam could see two boys, the older one about 12 and the other a year or two younger.

"You may leave," the man said in English with a German accent. "You have no business here."

"Sir," said Sam, "my name is Sam McClure, and we're traveling through on our way to Alabama and Mississippi. The sheriff in Madison told me you might be willing to allow us to spend the night in your barn, and he told me to give you this letter." Sam pulled the envelope from his coat pocket.

The man didn't move but kept staring. "Lucas," he said finally, "get the envelope."

The younger boy darted out to the wagon and took the envelope, racing back and handing it to his father. The man held the gun in his right hand while he opened the envelope with his left. He began to read silently.

The man dropped his rifle and fell to his knees, a howl of great anguish pouring from his throat. The older boy ran to his father's side, retrieved the letter, and read it aloud.

"The sheriff says you killed the Bates Brothers," the boy said. He looked at his father, still sobbing in great anguished cries. He looked back at Sam. "You are welcome in our house."

Honeybee, as if she could bear the man's cries no longer, jumped from the wagon and ran to the man, throwing her arms around his neck. The man hugged the little girl.

He looked up at Sam. "You do not sleep in the barn," he said in a ragged breath. "You sleep in our house. You as well," he nodded to Sophie.

The man led Sam to the pasture next to barn, helping him unhitch the horses. "There is plenty of grass," he said. "Some of my horses were taken by the Confederates, and the rest by Sherman."

"The sheriff said to bring these two horses to you," Sam said. "They were the ones ridden by the Bates."

Augustus Mundt stared at the two animals, now in the pasture foraging among the grass. "Let us get something to eat. The children are likely hungry."

They all sat at the kitchen table. Sam noticed that the two boys were quiet and kept watching their father. The room felt saturated with sadness.

"Anna and I came from Germany in 1848," Mundt said. "I was older, 38, and she was 17. I was leaving because of the, what do you say, the politics, the revolutions in Europe. I had been on the wrong side, and I decided to leave for America. Anna heard I was leaving, and she came and asked me to marry her and take her with me. It was something of a scandal for our families, and not only the difference in age.

"She wanted to live where it was warmer, so we decided on Georgia. I preferred Indiana or Illinois, but she convinced me to go south. We went first to Savannah, and then we heard about farms for sale to the west. We had some money, and we bought this farm, a small place surrounded by plantations with slaves. The two closest landowners would have bought it, but both families were having money problems, so we bought it to farm it ourselves. I would not have slaves. We hired a free woman to help with the food and house when the babies came. And I hired two free men to help with the farming. Using free laborers didn't make us popular, I think, but people seemed to like having Germans in the area. We gave them something to talk about.

"We had five children, first the two boys, Lucas and Robert here, and then three girls, Abigail, Emma, and Dorothy. Anna wanted them all to have American names, 'because they're born in America,' she said.

"We thought the worst was over," he said, "when Sherman passed through. His army was like grasshoppers, stripping the countryside of anything that was food or looked valuable. We had some warning, and we hid some of our pigs, our milk cow, and the chickens in the woods. They wrecked Anna's kitchen, taking the food that hadn't been hidden.

"After the army left, we waited until it was safe, and then we brought back the animals a few at a time. About two weeks later, we heard reports of more soldiers, and the two boys and I ran the animals back to the woods. We stayed a few hours to keep the animals calm and fed.

"But it wasn't soldiers. It was the Bates."

Mundt paused, as if gathering strength to tell Sam the rest of the story.

"When we returned to the farm, we found Emma and Dorothy in the farmyard. They'd been shot in the back, killed outright. Abigail, who was seven, was just inside the door of the kitchen, shot dead as well. Jessie, the hired woman, and Anna were dead in the parlor. They'd been, they'd been—"

Sam put his hand on Mundt's arm. "I know. I know what

the Bates intended for Sophie and Janie here. I saw enough of it during the war."

Mundt nodded. The man had tears on his cheeks, and he was rocking back and forth.

"We buried them near an oak tree at the end of the upper pasture. I couldn't speak; I could not say a prayer for them. I still cannot. Evil was loosed upon us and killed my wife and my girls.

"The sheriff came and told me a posse had been formed to find them. They looked everywhere but failed. The Bates had done similar things to other families. You bring the welcome news that they are dead."

Sam explained what had happened.

Mundt smiled and looked at Honeybee. "The little girl shot the older Bates? There is some justice in that."

Sam's group slept in beds that night. Sam and Daniel shared the boys' bedroom, while Sophie, Janie, Belle, and Honeybee had what had been the girls' bedroom. Mr. Mundt and his two sons stayed in the father's bedroom.

In the morning, Mundt fed them a good breakfast and refused to accept any payment.

"Your news is payment enough," he said. "The two horses will help us plow and get some corn planted."

Mundt suggested they try to reach Macon. "Sherman's soldiers sacked Monticello. They tried to take Macon but were fought off. They headed east. Macon had some shelling, but the city is mostly whole. You should find accommodation there." He paused. "I wish you safe travel. The boys and I will pray for you all, the young man who brought us news of justice."

Sam rode Tag next to the wagon. Janie held the reins, becoming quite proficient in driving the horses. Sophie sat next to her, with the three children behind them.

For the first two hours, they traveled in silence, surprising Sam because Sophie was usually chattering away about something and Janie talking more and more of her mother, the closer they got to Alabama. But the first two hours after leaving the Mundts were silent ones.

Janie reined in the horses and stopped. "We need to stop," she said. "At least, I do." Sophie nodded as well. Sam and Daniel waited while the four went a short way into the woods next to the road. Then they took a turn while the young women waited with the wagon.

As they resumed the journey, Janie spoke.

"Sam," she said, "how do you live your life after something like that, after you find your wife and children murdered?"

"I've seen a lot of death, Janie," Sam said, "but I haven't seen what Mr. Mundt and his boys saw. I haven't had to bury murdered family members. I haven't had to look at every stranger I meet as a possible killer."

"I loved my grandmother," Janie said, "but she was an old woman. She lived a full life, even if the end was marked by hardship and sickness. Those little girls were just starting their lives, and they were killed for no reason."

"Witnesses," Sam said. "They were witnesses. They could identify the Bates, even if the men's reputation was known. If the Bates had been caught, they would have been killed immediately, likely hung." He shook his head. "It's like the world has gone crazy, everything's upside down, and nothing works the way it used to."

"You're risking your life, aren't you?" she said. "It would be a whole lot easier if you didn't have us to worry about. We make you a target. And you probably would be home by now without us to worry after." Not looking at him, she wiped a tear from her eye." I didn't even thank you and Sophie for taking care of us with the measles. So, I thank you now, and I thank you for watching out for us and seeing us home."

Sam smiled. "I really don't mind, Miss Octavia Jane Montgomery. I've grown a little fond of the whole passel of you."

They rode through Monticello, stopping only to ask a man for the right road to Macon. The town had not recovered from the visit of Sherman's troops, even more than six months later. Every commercial establishment looked vandalized and looted, and the houses showed signs of the same.

They reached Macon in the late afternoon. Mundt had told them it was a town of 8,000 before the war, swelling as the war progressed, and finally shrinking back to its pre-war size. It had surrendered to Union troops in mid-April, who largely spared the town and used it as a base. "There are still troops there keeping order," Mundt had told them.

Sam stopped the group outside a general store, asking the shopkeeper if any rooms were to be had in town. The man looked out the door at the group, eyeing Sophie and her children. "Go down Forsyth St. to the rifle factory, or what used to be the rifle factory. Turn right and it's just a few yards to Short Street. Go down Short to the point where it ends, it's not far, and turn right. That'll put you on Ross Street. There's a boardinghouse right there on Ross. Ask for Eula May Dalrymple; she's a widow who runs the place. There's a servant quarters in back where she might allow your slaves to stay."

Sam nodded his thanks. "Much obliged." He bought several tinned cans of food, some carrots, and a sack of potatoes.

Miss Eula May Dalrymple turned out to be more than accommodating and gracious, especially when Sam offered her three federal dollars for two rooms for the night. She included a basic dinner and breakfast the next morning. She required Sophie and her children to eat at an outside table, but it was the same food Sam, Janie, and Honeybee had. Sam slept in a chair in the room, while Janie and Honeybee shared the bed. Sophie, Belle, and Daniel shared a bed in a small but clean room in what had once been the servant or slave quarters.

The next morning after breakfast, Sam asked Mrs. Dalrymple for directions to Columbus.

"You've two to three days ride ahead of you," she said. "Go back around the rifle factory to Forsyth and turn south on Pine. After about seven or eight blocks, you'll see the train station. Follow the streets by the track; they'll become a road that more or less follows the railroad and will take you to Fort Valley. The rail track splits there, with a line going south and one going west. Follow the road to the west, to Butler. That's the last town of any size before Columbus. If you leave Butler early enough, you'll be in Columbus by nightfall."

She eyed him, considering if she should say more and finally deciding to do so. "Columbus is a mess. The federals battled us on the Alabama side of the Chattahoochee River. We burned the southern bridge, but they captured the northern one. The town was shelled, and the destruction from that and the occupation and looting were significant. My husband's family were from there, and they stayed here with me when they fled the town. And Girard, just across the river from Columbus, is worse, I hear."

"So, we might consider stopping before Columbus and make it through there and Girard and keep moving," Sam said.

She nodded. "I would. There's some rebuilding, but there's no place for travelers to stay in Columbus or Girard. And Yankee troops still occupy the area. Are you bound for Montgomery?"

"No, ma'am. Actually, we're headed first to Troy, or just to the north of there. That's where Janie's family lives."

"She's not your wife?"

"No, ma'am. I'm escorting her, Sophie, and the children to their families."

The woman nodded. "Well, you've got two days to Columbus, and another two down to Troy. Another route is heading south from Fort Valley down to Oglethorpe, and west from there to the ferry that crosses to Fort Mitchell. You'll bypass Columbus altogether. But keep an eye out. I hear we've got everything imaginable roaming the countryside." She smiled. "Another week, and you should reach Troy."

29

I see the long procession
Still passing to and fro,
The young heart hot and restless,
And the old subdued and slow!

—from "The Bridge"

October 1915

"We were blessed," Sam said. "We'd had decent weather up
to then. But the rains set in once we left Macon, and it considerably slowed us. It didn't take a week, but more like three."
He looked around his study. "I think it's time we made our
way to the fairgrounds and found ourselves something to eat."

Fifteen minutes later, Young Sam was chauffeuring Sam,
Elizabeth, Littleton, and Bea to the fair. The parking area was
crowded, more than on the other days, with both automobiles
and wagons. After a hearty lunch in one of the food tents,
Sam indicated his desire to hear the results of the livestock
contests, and Littleton and Bea made their way to the final
judging of pies.

"It appears you're once again stuck with the lawyer,"
Young Sam said.

Elizabeth took his arm. "And I hope he shows me the
highlights of the final day of the Lincoln County Fair."

They sat for a while in the livestock tent, listening to the awarding of places for pigs, milk cows, and bulls. Then Young Sam led her to a smaller tent nearby, where they watched the final judging and awarding of places to the young livestock raised by children.

"The little calves and lambs are wonderful," Elizabeth said.

Young Sam smiled. "The children have worked very hard the last several months with their animals. This is a big event for the children, including some who don't live on farms but have animals in the back of their houses."

She left him and walked over to a man and a boy standing by a calf with a blue ribbon on its lead. He watched her as she sat on a bale of hay and talked with the boy, pausing to remove her notebook from her handbag. Young Sam could see she was asking the boy questions, and he was responding. She looked up and asked the man something, who smiled and answered her. She shook their hands, and then Elizabeth walked over to a little girl, standing next to her father, and holding a lamb by its lead. Elizabeth repeated the same process.

Smiling, she rejoined him.

"You were interviewing our prizewinners?" he said.

She nodded. "There's more to Brookhaven than the Gray Wisp," she said. "I've written several stories on the fair. Mr. Fenchurch at the Brookhaven *Eagle* has been very gracious to allow me to use the Western Union transmission facility he has to send them to New York. The one on the tomato girls has already been published. My editor, Mr. Osborne, is mailing several copies to the printed papers with the stories here." She paused. "They won't arrive until after I've left, so I'm having him mail them to you, hoping to impose upon you to deliver them to the people in the stories."

"When do you have time to write them?"

"At night, before I go to bed."

They stopped briefly at the pies and preserves tent and watched three judges taste the pies and three others taste the canned preserves. The places would be announced after the judges conferred. "It's a blind judging," Young Sam said. "Each pie and jar of preserves are entered by a number, to keep the judges honest and ensure fairness." Elizabeth repeated her interviews, with the winners and one of the judges.

They wandered to the games area, which was crowded with adults and young people, trying their hands at milk can toss, darts, weight guessing, ring toss, horseshoes, and other games. Young Sam talked her into playing horseshoes, and she discovered she had a terrible aim.

Less crowded was the music tent, and Young Sam explained. "Brookhaven's Baptists and Pentecostals frown on dancing and music, while the Presbyterians, Methodists, Episcopalians, Catholics, and Jews are glad for the thinner crowds, so they listen and dance. And I assume you're—"

"Episcopal," Elizabeth said, "so count me among the latter group."

The band of the hour was playing a waltz, and Young Sam led her to the floor.

"You're a beautiful dancer," Elizabeth said as they danced around the floor. "Is there anything you don't do well?"

"Nothing," Young Sam said, grinning, "when I am accompanied by a beautiful young partner."

She blushed, and he covered her embarrassment by moving them into a wide sweep.

They danced to two more selections, and then he found the punch bowl and a table away from the dance floor.

"This is delightful," she said. "And you don't mind escorting the journalist?"

"I don't mind one bit," he said "It's been a while since I enjoyed myself so much. And I apologize for putting you on the spot about Thanksgiving. And if you'd prefer, I'll release you from the invitation."

Her eyes full of merriment, she smiled. "Perhaps I will hold you to your acceptance. Yes, my invitation stands."

"So, your intention is to leave Brookhaven soon?"

She nodded. "Likely Tuesday. I've written the introductory article, and Mr. Osborne is holding it until I have the rest of them done. He's going to publish it as a series, the start depending on when I have the stories completed."

"Do you have to leave?" Young Sam said.

She looked into his handsome face with the beautiful dark blue eyes.

"I do have to go back to New York," she said softly, "but there's nothing to say I can't return. And I will say the exact kind of thing that drives my mother to distraction. 'You're too outspoken, Elizabeth. No one wants to be around a woman who always speaks exactly what's on her mind.' And what's on my mind is this, Samuel David McClure III. I came to Brookhaven for a story, and I discovered the good story I expected it to be. What I didn't expect was to have my life turned upside down."

He covered her hand, resting on the table, with his own. "When you stepped down from that train on Monday, and I saw you looking surprised and a bit flustered, I knew a new door had opened in my life, one I wasn't expecting. And I knew nothing would be the same again. In a little more than five days, I believe I walked into the rest of my life." He smiled. "And your mother was wrong. There are some men who want to be around a woman who speaks her mind and find it absolutely attractive. But before we go any further, I'm going to ask you to consider a question, and I don't want an answer now or next week, but only when you're ready to give it. Could you see yourself living in a small town in Mississippi?"

She started to answer, but he stopped her by putting a finger to her lips. "I want you to take the time to consider it seriously. I don't want you influenced by the music of the night, or the fair, or my grandfather who could charm the Kaiser and the Tsar three times over just by reciting one of Longfellow's poems. I want you to consider it when you're away from here, away from us, and away from me, when you're back in New York and thinking about your career and possibly becoming the first woman correspondent to cover the war in Europe. Then you'll have the answer that's right for you and also right for me."

She touched her hand to his face. And then she nodded. "Alright. That's what I will do."

They made their way to the food tent, Young Sam buying them a dinner of fried chicken, corn, string beans, with a slice of spice cake for dessert. They ate together, but in silence. They were soon joined by Seamus and Cora Beth, Littleton and Bea, and Sam himself. After they ate, they made their way with the crowd to the large open area next to fairgrounds to watch the fireworks. Elizabeth had seen bigger firework displays in Boston, especially on the Fourth of July, but watching the rockets and explosions of fiery stars made the night seem almost magical.

Sam continued the conversation at breakfast the next morning.

"We have a couple of hours before church," he said, "so we should keep an eye on the time. As I mentioned yesterday, we encountered rain after we left Macon, which slowed our journey considerably. The children were restless, and Janie was fit to be tied as she wanted to reach home. It seemed just within reach, but there was the rain.

"She really wanted to see her mama. I think she believed that, if she could see her mama and feel those arms around her, it would all be all right. She'd talk about Windhaven, that was her home, telling stories of the people, the area, the fancy balls, all the girls with their beaus, picnics and barbeques. It was an entirely different world from the one I knew.

"The plantation was about 10 miles north of Troy and about 40 or so miles south of Montgomery. I was a little nervous at what we might find; Miss Eula May in Macon had pulled me aside and said Grierson's Raiders, the same Union troop that had come through Mississippi, had done the same with Alabama, and they had camped near Troy on their way east. They'd left Troy alone, but they'd pillaged the countryside.

"What would have been about four days travel in dry weather became more like 11. Even when the rain stopped, we had to wait out the roads drying so we could move. We'd pass the time telling stories, Janie talking about Windhaven, and me reciting from Longfellow."

"I was never one for poetry," Sophie said, "but Mr. Sam's recitations helped pass a lot of rainy days." She'd been standing at the oven, listening.

"I nearly exhausted my entire repertoire in those two weeks," Sam said. "I was beginning to fear I'd have to start over again. When we finally reached the Chattahoochee River, the border with Alabama, it was almost as if the ferry had been waiting for us. We crossed with no problems and made our way to Fort Mitchell. And the weather cleared as if by magic, which Janie took as a good omen. Two days later, we reached Windhaven."

30

Southward, forever southward,
They drift through dark and day;
And like a dream, in the Gulf Stream
Sinking, vanish all away.

—from "Sir Humphrey Gilbert"

August 1865

They were 20 miles from Windhaven when Sam knew what was coming wouldn't be what Janie expected. They passed two plantation homes where Janie knew the families. They stopped at the first one, which she called The Pines, and the big house was mostly a charred ruin. The place was deserted.

"This was Colonel and Mrs. Parker's place," she said, shock registering on her face. "But there's no one here, not even slaves."

"The slaves likely left, Janie," Sam said. "It happened whenever Yankee soldiers came through. It happened at Fairhope, too, remember?"

They passed what had been another large cotton plantation, named Riverview, Janie said. It was much the same. The big house burned, and not a soul or an animal around.

Sam was directing the horses, and Janie took his arm. He could see apprehension written all over her face. "I know my mama must be all right. I know she must be."

It was mid-afternoon when they reached Windhaven. The big house wasn't visible from the road, but Janie pointed to the arch between gated posts with the plantation's name.

"We're home," she said, tears in her eyes. "Honeybee, we've reached home."

It was about a half-mile from the road to the house. Dense piney woods stretched on either side of them, but Sam could see that the road had been maintained, at least until recently. When they made the final curve, Sam was almost shocked to see the house was intact. And it was huge. Thick, rounded white columns extended all around the house, covering wide porches on both the main and second levels. A third story had six dormer windows extending from the front.

As they pulled up closer to the front door, Sam could see something else. The war had come to Windhaven.

Broken flower urns were on either side of the front door. Many of the windows had been broken. Shutters were askew. Flower beds had been trampled down.

Janie jumped down from the wagon and ran through the front door, calling for her mother. Sam, Sophie, and the children followed.

The center hall was a wreck. Large portraits on the walls had been slashed. Furniture was broken but curiously set upright. Bullet holes could be seen in the walls, and the railing on the stairs bore signs of slash marks. Sam realized that someone, or more than one someone, had ridden a horse up the wide staircase.

A tall, elderly black man with almost snow-white hair appeared from the back.

He stared at Janie for a moment.

"Henry?" she said.

"Miss Jane! Welcome home. How was your visit to Elmwood?"

Frowning, Janie stared at the man. "Henry, where's mama? Is Father here?"

Henry furrowed his brow. "Your mama, Miss Jane, went to North Carolina to care for Miss Charlotte in her confinement, as you'll recall. Miss Octavia accompanied her, but they haven't returned as of yet. Your daddy is still with General Johnston; the last word was there would be a spirited defense against General Sherman outside Atlanta." The man smiled, as if proud he remembered the details.

Sam could see that Janie was becoming aware that something was wrong with the man.

"Has anyone else returned, Henry?" she said.

"Mr. Wallace is back. He's gone into Troy for some supplies. He's expected to return by sundown. The house servants have been granted a holiday, and the field laborers have been loaned to Colonel Parker to get a second cotton crop planted."

Sam touched Janie's arm and looked at Henry. "Mr. Henry, my name is Sam McClure, and I've escorted Jane here and young Honeybee home from their visit. Sophie and her children came along for the ride. Might there be some refreshment for the ladies?"

"Of course, sir. I am remiss. I will attend to getting some water for tea. I'll bring it to the parlor. Miss Jane, you might want to show your guests the house. Because the servants are on holiday, I'm afraid the rooms have not been attended to as usual." He bowed, turned, and disappeared through a doorway at the back of the hall.

Sophie was staring wide-eyed. "Didn't we pass that place called The Pines?"

As Sam nodded, Janie grabbed his arm. "What's wrong with Henry? He seems he's not in his right mind. He thinks I'm my mother."

"Who is he, Janie?" Sam said.

"He's the house butler. He's been here since Mama and Father married. He was given to Mama when she was a little girl, and he was part of her dowry when she married. But where's Mama? He thinks she went to her childhood home in Elmwood. And I don't know if Wallace is here or if he's just imagined it."

"Wallace is your brother?"

She nodded. "My middle brother. Laurence is the oldest, then Wallace, then James. I came five years after James."

Janie left the hall, turning to the left. The rest of them followed. Walking through what Sam guessed had been a ballroom, she walked through a series of rooms, all bearing signs of upheaval and destruction. She stopped when she reached a library.

The room would have been a small showplace before the war, Sam thought, but it could only be described now as a wreck. Books with polished leather bindings were scattered across the room. Papers were everywhere. Some books were partially burned, and Sam could see someone had used them for a campfire; the ornate ceiling bore smoke stains. A curio cabinet, much like the one his father and mother had, stood in muted and broken splendor, its glass sides smashed, the contents scattered or stolen. Paintings had been slashed, including one of a beautiful young woman.

Janie saw Sam staring at it. "That's my mother." She bit her lip. "She's dead, isn't she? Henry doesn't want to say, or can't say, but she's dead." Sam held her while she cried. "My father loves this room. And they destroyed it."

Composed, Janie led them back the way they'd come to the other side of the house. She stopped when they reached a room that, despite its upset, still looked like a ladies' parlor.

Henry was pouring tea into porcelain cups, using an intricately decorated teapot.

"When we knew the soldiers were coming," he said, "you'll remember you had me hide the china and silver. I made sure no one saw me, even the house servants. And I'm proud to say, Miss Jane, that it survived intact. The tea, however, is hibiscus. With the war and the shortage of supplies, we've had to make do. But I was able to sweeten it with a bit of sugar the soldiers missed."

Sam could see Henry was moving back and forth between the real present and the past, creating explanations for the reality he was living in. Something had confused the man's mind; Sam had seen enough of people with senility to know this was something different.

Janie seemed to understand and had stopped asking questions. "Thank you, Henry. This is most kind."

"If you need me, Miss Jane, I'll be in the kitchen." He bowed and left.

"Do you think he imagined Wallace being here?" she said.

Sam shrugged. "We'll have to wait and see, I reckon."

An hour later, they heard a young man's voice calling

Henry's name.

"Henry! Do we have company?"

Janie raced to the entry hall.

When Sam and the others arrived, they found her holding a thin-faced young man of about 20. Medium height, he had almost jet-black hair and dark brown eyes. He was dressed simply, in pants, boots, and what Sam recognized as an army-issued blouse.

His arms around Janie, the young man kept murmuring "OJ. It's you." Sam smiled at the use of the letters of Janie's name.

After a lot of tears, and introductions, they returned to the parlor. Henry brought another teacup. With a few of the supplies Wallace had brought from Troy and some of the food they had with them on the wagon, Sophie and Henry left to prepare a meal. The three children followed them.

"Not much of the family is left, OJ," Wallace said. "In fact, you, Honeybee, and myself may be the Montgomerys of Windhaven. That's terrible news about Grandmother, Sister, and her family." He paused. "Hugh was taken prisoner at Vicksburg. We hoped for a parole, but that never happened. Mother received one letter from him, months after it was written, over a year ago now. He'd been taken to a prison camp in New York State, some place called Elmira."

Sam visibly started.

Wallace turned to him. "You've heard of it?"

Sam nodded. "Soldiers in Lee's army called it Hellmira."

Wallace shook his head. "There's been no message or letter since. James was with John Bell's Hood Army, and he died in the Battle of Franklin."

Sam felt chilled. His own brother Hugh had been with Hood's army. He knew the Confederates had lost, and there had been a lot of deaths, but he knew nothing specifically about Hugh.

"OJ, Father was wounded in one of the many skirmishes and battles before Atlanta. He died during Sherman's attack on the city. They couldn't get all the wounded out in time, but he died before Atlanta fell, according to what his fellow officers told us in a letter they sent. The dead were buried in a mass grave by Sherman's troops."

"Wallace, where's Mama?" Janie said. "Henry believes I'm her."

"Henry was here when it happened. It was during Grierson's Raid."

"Grierson was here, too?" Sam said. "My grandfather died in Brookhaven during Grierson's Raid. It was right after that I enlisted."

Wallace nodded. "He cut a swath through Alabama in April. They intended to destroy any possible Confederate supplies in this part of the state and across the river in Georgia. One of the columns came through here on its way to Troy and then went on to Eufala. They tried to lay a siege at Troy, but it fell apart. They were here at Windhaven for a day, from what I've heard from people in town.

"Henry can't talk about it; he's blocked it from his mind. He wakes up screaming in the night. This is going to be hard to hear, OJ, so I'll tell it once and then I can't talk about it anymore."

The girl nodded.

"The county sheriff pieced it together for me. The advance troops for the column came riding down the Wind-haven Road. Mama was waiting on the front porch with her rifle. She was all the family that was left here, with Henry to help her. He was old, but he still struck terror into the hearts of the other slaves. Mama had been managing what she could with the field hands and the house, even with the gradual disappearance of the field slaves.

"The Union troops came riding up, and Henry was standing next to Mama, with a few of the house slaves behind them. She ordered them off the property. I can just picture her doing precisely that. One of the soldiers, a sergeant from what Henry said, pulled out a pistol and told her to get out of the way. She refused, and he shot her dead, right there on the front porch." He paused, trying to collect himself. "When the sheriff came, hours later, he found Henry still sitting on the front porch where he was holding Mama's body. He was covered in blood."

Janie, sitting next to Sam, gasped and grabbed Sam's arm.

"Grierson had reportedly given his men strict orders that private property wasn't to be molested. The order was ignored. You probably saw The Pines or what's left of it. They told the slaves they were free. When the slaves here said they didn't know where to go, the Yankees chased them back down the road, threatening to kill anyone who returned. They ransacked the house, looking for liquor, valuables, and food, in that order. They found little of anything, which made them mad. So, they turned to wrecking the house.

"Grierson himself arrived a few hours later and saw Henry holding Mama's body on the porch. To the man's credit, he found the sergeant who'd shot her, held a court-martial right here in front of the house, and had the man hung from the oak tree closest to the house. He also had soldiers remove Mama's body from Henry's arms and bury her in the family cemetery.

"Henry never left, and the Yankees probably left him alone because of his age. He directed them to the cemetery up on the ridge. When the soldiers left, some of the slaves returned, and they finished the ransacking the soldiers hadn't gotten to. And they all left, following Grierson's troops or at least walking east where the soldiers had gone. Not a one has been seen since.

"I got home about a month ago, after Bragg's army surrendered. I'd hoped you and Grandmother were safe with Sister at Fairhope." Wallace looked at Sam. "You've brought them all the way from Greensboro?"

Sam nodded. "We've been on the road since late April."

"Sam, you're welcome to stay here as long as you need. Henry and I have been cleaning up what we can, and somehow the troops and the slaves left the mattresses alone. So, we have beds. Mama had Henry hide her jewelry and the family silver, and that's what we've been using for currency and to buy supplies. But I can't pry the china loose from his grasp." Wallace smiled and held up his teacup.

"That reminds me," Sam said, reaching to his pack and pulling out a large leather bag. "Mrs. Montgomery offered me her jewelry to see Janie and Honeybee here to Windhaven. I told her I wouldn't accept it, but I'd get them here. She asked me to give the bag to your mother." He handed the bag to Wallace.

31

Such is the cross I wear upon my breast
These eighteen years, through all the changing scenes
And Seasons, changeless since the day she died.

—from "The Cross of Snow"

October 1915

"We stayed at Windhaven for 10 days," Sam said, as the group walked home from church. "We helped Wallace and Henry straighten up what could be in the house, and we plowed up a few acres to get some late corn planted. I don't know where Wallace found the seed, but he did. The geldings needed a break from the journey, and the pastures had plenty of grass."

"Was it hard to leave?" Elizabeth said.

Sam was silent for a time. "It nearly killed me. I'd fallen hard for Miss Octavia Jane Montgomery of Windhaven Plantation. The two of us worked in her father's library, trying to get the mess cleaned up. She told me that her father had banned any of the books by Mr. Longfellow from crossing the threshold, calling him a 'black abolitionist,' and that was why she so enjoyed my recitations, because she'd never heard the poems before. She asked me if Mr. Longfellow was an abolitionist, and I told her he most certainly leaned that way. I recited some of his poems on slavery, and she listened very intently. She told me she now understood her father's ban on the man's books.

"But we did finally leave. I had to get home, and Sophie was itching to find her husband. Janie, Honeybee, Wallace, and Henry all saw us off." He shook his head. "She kissed me on the cheek and told me I had to write. I told her I would. As we started down the road, I looked back. She was crying on her brother's shoulder.

"It took about a week's worth of travel to reach Brookhaven. Nothing of note happened, other than being stopped twice by Yankee troops on patrol. But that happened with everyone. I've already told you about finding my family at church."

Elizabeth nodded.

"And Sophie's already spoken of what happened when she found her husband in Vicksburg."

She nodded again.

They'd reached the house on Cherry Street. Littleton and Bea walked up the steps, while Sam, Elizabeth, and Young Sam lingered on the drive.

"So, are we finished with the story of the Gray Wisp?" Sam said. "Do you have what you need for your stories?"

"I do, Papa Sam. In fact, I mentioned to Young Sam here that I've already been writing them and sent the first one on to New York. But I have one question remaining, about how you and Janie came to be married." She had another question, but she stopped herself from asking it. She knew something had happened when John Haygood's wife, daughter, and parents visited after the war. She decided to wait and decide later whether to ask it or not.

"I can answer your question at Sunday dinner, which I can tell from the smell Sophie's been preparing." He suddenly turned and walked up the steps and into the house.

As Elizabeth and Young Sam followed, he touched her arm. They stopped at the door.

"You were going to ask him something else," Young Sam said. "I could see it on the tip of your tongue."

She nodded.

"Let me guess. Your unspoken question is the family mystery. Papa has never talked about the Haygoods. There's been a great deal of speculation, because Uncle Litt was there and saw much of what happened. But Mr. Haygood asked Papa to take him to the woods, and they spent most of a day there. Only Papa knows what they talked about. The family believes that Jacob Haygood was the unknown benefactor behind the investments in the sawmill and the racing stables, but Papa has refused to talk about it."

He smiled. "What the past week has taught me about Papa is that his recitations of poetry have a point; he invites you to become part of the stories he's telling. He's done something similar with your interviews. He's been inviting you, and whoever else might be hearing them, to become part of his story. I suspect that if you ask and he answers your unspoken question, his answer may change everything you've already heard. I hope he allows me to be part of that conversation, if it happens."

Being Sunday dinner, the table was crowded, mostly with O'Briens. Young Sam brought extra chairs from the dining room to accommodate everyone.

They were eating dessert when Sam tapped his water glass.

"I promised Miss Putnam to answer a question she had. Some of you have heard the story before, and Bea and Littleton here were witnesses at the creation. If I recall correctly, Cora Beth came in right at the end." Sam looked around. Every face around the table was riveted on his. "It's the story of how Janie and I came to be married."

Not a person moved to leave the table. Seamus, sitting next to Cora Beth, smiled thoughtfully and put his hand on his wife's.

"I'd kept my promise to write her," Sam said. "Miss Octavia Jane Montgomery at Windhaven Plantation, Pike County, Alabama. And she wrote back. We were exchanging letters about once a month or every three weeks. I would tell her what was happening with the family here, like trying to get the businesses functioning and, later, the plans for the double wedding of Cora Beth and Leorinda to two rascals from Ireland. And she would tell me what was happening at Windhaven, up to a point. She'd mention the personal, but not any specifics about the plantation itself.

"We were both very reserved about our feelings, although I suspect she could read between the lines and see my heart on my sleeve. I turned 16 and she turned 15, and for her birthday I sent her a little carved dove I'd made. She sent me a photograph of her, Wallace, Honeybee, and Henry, and it's still there on the wall of my study.

"And then a month went by with no letter. It was October. I hadn't seen her in more than a year. It had been a hard year for her family and for mine. And I began to worry."

October 1865

It was a Saturday, a busy day for McClure's store on Railroad

Street. Life was still slowly returning to something approaching normal, but it was a very different normal from anything the McClure family and Brookhaven had known.

Franklin McClure was still somewhat incapacitated from his stroke. Sam was dividing his time between the store, the grist mill, and the sawmill; today, because of the crush of customers, he was working at the store all day.

Seamus O'Brien, engaged to Cora Beth, was working at the grist mill and occasionally talking with Sam about the idea of raising racehorses. Now that the grist mill was returning to operation in a reunited country, they were learning that the war had brought considerable changes in industry and manufacturing in the North. Large national millers were emerging, and Sam and Seamus could see that the Brookhaven mill would, in a few years, be out of business. Racehorses, Seamus said, might be a substitute, pointing out the rather extensive land holdings around the mill, land unencumbered by woods. Even if Sam had been so inclined, he had no idea where they might find the money for it.

Cora Beth and Martha were handling the register and helping fill customers' orders; Sam was opening boxes and moving food tins and other items to add to the shelves. He was in the storeroom, opening a box of tinned yams, when he heard Martha call his name.

"Sam," she said, "you have a visitor."

It was Wallace Montgomery. The two young men embraced.

"Wallace! It's wonderful to see you! What on earth are you doing in Brookhaven?"

"Good to see you, too, Sam. I'm passing through on my

way to New Orleans, and I need to talk with you."

"There's a small office in the back. Come on through."

When they were seated, Wallace explained.

"I've accepted a position with a farming operation in Brazil," he said. "We've sold Windhaven. There's no money to invest in it, and it's not competitive without slaves. It was devastating, but it was the best thing for us. A man I served with in the war wrote and asked if I'd be interested in working with him down in South America. At first, I couldn't see it, but the more I thought about it, the more it made sense. I hated to leave Windhaven, but the temporary government was already set to levy ruinous taxes. And everything we knew, Sam, everything, is gone. I finally had to admit to myself that we were trying to keep a dead dream alive, and it was time to let go.

"We auctioned what furniture we could, and quite a few of the books from the library. I sold what little livestock there was. Henry crated up Mama's china service; as you might imagine, neither he nor OJ were going to part with that. That's being shipped by rail; Henry is toting the silver service in his bags. What we made from selling Windhaven, and after taxes it wasn't much, the demand isn't strong for large fallow plantations, but the proceeds and the auction will cover passage to Brazil and setting up a household there."

"Where was Janie in all of this?" Sam said.

"Well," Wallace said, "that's why we stopped. My sister, who has a will of iron when she wants to, is not keen on going to Brazil." He paused, and Sam could see he was struggling to say what he had to. "Sam, she said that she would prefer to come to Brookhaven."

Sam felt his ears grow warm. He hoped he wasn't blushing.

"The truth is, Sam, she wants to come to you. I don't know what all happened on your journey to Windhaven. She hasn't said much, other than you saved her life more than once and her honor as well. We don't know what your situation here might be, but Honeybee will have to stay with OJ, and Henry won't think of going anywhere she's not. He still calls her Miss Jane and thinks she's our mother. He's not any worse than what you saw at Windhaven, but he's also not any better. I told her I simply didn't feel right about saddling you with the responsibility for three more people. But she's insistent that they will stay in Brookhaven regardless and she will take care of Henry and Honeybee on her own if she has to."

"She's here?" Sam said.

"She's outside in the carriage. It and the horses are what's left of the Windhaven Plantation. And Mama's china and silver, of course, and a few clothes that somehow survived the Yankees and the slaves."

Sam stood. "I'll talk with her." He quickly moved from the office and through the store, with Wallace trailing after him. Martha, Cora Beth, and several customers stared as Sam acknowledged no one as he hurried through the door.

"Sam!" Honeybee said with a squeal of delight. The little girl jumped down from the carriage and ran to him, throwing her arms around him. He picked her up and gave her a big hug. Still carrying her, he walked over to the carriage, where Janie sat in a simple yet beautiful white dress and holding a parasol against the sun. She had a small white hat with short ribbons trailing in the back.

Holding her head very straight, she turned to him in acknowledgement. "Mr. McClure."

"Miss Octavia Jane Montgomery, you may call me your royal highness," Sam said.

Janie, trying to look so regal and mature, tried to control her laugh but finally couldn't.

"Janie, I am asking you to give me the honor of spending the rest of our lives together."

He saw the tears form in her yes and her lip began to quiver.

"Yes, I believe I would like that very much, your royal highness."

Still holding Honeybee, Sam leaned into the carriage and kissed her.

October 1915

"Oh," Bea, said, tears in her eyes, "I remember it like it was yesterday. I thought my little heart was going to burst." She dabbed her eyes with her napkin. "Only Wallace was keen for Brazil. The rest of us were terrified at the prospect. Janie put her foot down and said that if Sam wouldn't have her, she'd figure it out on her own."

"We married in February of 1867," Sam said. "Janie, Honeybee, and Henry moved in with the Widow Pettigrew. It must have seemed crowded, with Dr. O'Brien and Leorinda already living there, but it was only a few weeks. The real surprise was how Henry and Mrs. Pettigrew took to each other. She gave him his own room off the kitchen. After we were married and took the little house across the street, where Young Sam is now, Henry divided his time between our house and hers." He smiled and shook his head. "They grew very fond of each other. I think each reminded the other of old times, and they found comfort in that. He attended to her as she became sick and eventually confined to her bed, and he held her hand as she passed, that would have been May of 1871. A few days later, he went to sleep in the chair in his room and never woke up. But to the end he believed Janie was her mother.

"Mrs. Pettigrew caused a scandal in Brookhaven over the burial arrangements. She was buried next to her husband, of course, but she made a provision in her will for Henry to be buried next to them. I don't know what Doc Pettigrew might have thought if he'd known, but I suspect he would have accepted her decision. She had the kind of determination that brooked no opposition when she wanted something to happen."

At that, people began to stand from the table. The children began clearing the dishes and washing up, while the adults went on various pursuits. Sam announced he intended to take his Sunday nap.

Young Sam and Elizabeth joined Littleton and Bea on the porch, taking seats to enjoy the coolness of October coupled with afternoon sunshine.

"Mrs. Seale," Elizabeth said, "what happened with Janie? This isn't for my story, and if it's something best left unsaid, then please tell me."

"Well," Bea said, "Sam did say we were to answer your questions, didn't he? Where do I start? Give me a minute to collect my thoughts."

She finally began to speak. "I believe the first thing you

should know is how much she loved Sam, and he her. Had the war not changed everything, Janie would have been matched to someone of wealth and influence, the son of another large planter, most likely. As would I have been. But so much wealth was destroyed, and so many young men dead, that world changed, whether we liked it or not.

"It was easier for me because I was just a young child. Janie was older, right at the age when the possibilities for marriage would be opening up. She had been prepared for exactly that. And she liked to read. Her father had all of Sir Walter Scott's novels in his library. And she loved Charles Dickens; she saw herself as Lucy Manette in *A Tale of Two Cities*. She would talk about how much she was like the long-suffering Agnes Wickfield in *David Copperfield*, but, in truth, she was more like Dora Spenlow, David's frail first wife who dies. I think what I'm trying to say is that she was a romantic at heart. And she saw the world as a romantic place, even with the war."

Bea reached for her husband's hand. "She romanticized herself and Sam, I think. They were a young couple in a world that had collapsed around them. Sam was determined to live in that new world, and he would be successful at it. Janie always wanted to turn the clock back to before 1861.

"When she was carrying David, she had these images of what motherhood and babyhood would be, mostly influenced by the romance novels she'd read. And that's not what happened, of course. From the moment he was born in early 1868, he was difficult. He had colic. He'd spit up all over the beautiful clothes she'd had made for him. And by the time he was three, we could all see that something was very different, and often strange, about him. He'd become hysterical when most people tried to touch him or hold him, almost as if human touch burned his skin. Many people thought he was a mental defective; I know Janie worried. About the only person he'd allow to touch him was Belle, curiously enough, and even she was limited in what she could do. They had him examined by doctors in Jackson and New Orleans; Belle would travel with them to manage David.

"In meantime, the two girls had been born. David would watch them, a smile on his face, but he never came close. He would take delight in repetitive tasks, like arranging and rearranging his toy soldiers or stacking books on the shelves. Sam tried taking him to the woods, but the boy was terrified. All of this, of course, put a terrible strain on Sam and Janie's marriage. She saw herself as a failure as a mother, utterly unlike her own or my mother, her older sister.

"When David was six, that would be the summer of 1874, Sam's mother Louisa visited for the first time since she'd left in 1866. It turned out to be hugely consequential for the family. It was the oddest thing, but David took to his grandmother immediately. She had no sooner walked in the door when he walked up to her and took her hand. When she awakened that first morning, she found him sleeping on the floor at the foot of her bed. It was uncanny. Louisa was, I might say, a difficult personality. Martha was almost hostile to her, and even Cora Beth, who loved everyone, kept her distance.

"Louisa proposed that she take David back with her to Pennsylvania. Sam was opposed, almost adamantly so, but I think Janie saw it as something like a deliverance. Louisa talked about taking him to specialists at the medical school in

Philadelphia, and even Dr. O'Brien thought it might be a good idea. Janie was utterly convinced; she probably saw it as a way to achieve some peace in the household. She finally convinced Sam, or perhaps wore him down. And David left with Louisa. He seemed happy enough to go, and Louisa wrote later that he adored the train ride.

"David didn't return for a visit until 1883. He was 15, and he looked so much like his father it was astounding. Sam and Janie would travel every summer to Gettysburg to see him and Sam's mother. But David only returned the once. And it wasn't a good visit. He was certainly better than he had been as a child, but he could be mercilessly blunt. He said or did something that infuriated Janie, and she ended up screaming at him. All he did was crouch into a ball and hold his ears. Louisa refused to speak to Janie, and she barely talked to Sam before they left. And neither of them ever returned.

"Life here went on. The girls married, both to good husbands. Janie kept herself busy with work around the house and church activities. Sam was expanding the general store business and the sawmill, and the horseracing venture turned out to be surprisingly successful. We don't know where Sam or Seamus found the money; all either of them would say was that it was an investor who wished to remain anonymous.

"Janie's brother Wallace visited from Brazil in 1879, bringing his wife and three children. They spoke a fair amount of English; the little girl looked more like Janie than her own daughters did. Sam and Janie returned the visit in 1885. Janie said they still had slavery in Brazil, it reminded her of Windhaven, but Wallace was already taking steps to free the slaves. He'd been the manager of the plantation for his wife's parents; that's how they met.

"It was in 1893, I think, that Littleton and I returned with our four boys for a visit. We were living in Oxford, and Littleton had been teaching for several years. As soon as I saw Janie, I knew she was seriously ill. She denied it, of course, but Sam knew something was seriously wrong. But she refused to see any doctor, and even stopped doing regular visits with Dr. O'Brien. She died the next year; the doctor said all the signs suggested a cancer.

"Sam was more than heartbroken. The family thought for a time he'd lose his mind. The day of her funeral, he disappeared into his woods, and he didn't come back for three weeks. And only then because Cora Beth wired Littleton and asked him to come here to get Sam home."

"It took two days of talk and argument," Littleton said, "but I finally convinced him. He was filthy. We rigged up a water spray from the cistern, and Seamus and I stripped him down and scrubbed. Sam said nothing; it was as if he was numb. We got him to the barber for a haircut and shave; his beard and hair were tangled and matted. We sat him down in his study, and we told him that the family needed him, the businesses needed him, and we needed him. It took another day, and I think Sophie's cooking might have been what finally did it, but he came back to being his old self. That is, almost his old self. Something was missing, a certain joy or sprint in his step, or enthusiasm. Call it what you will, I don't think I've ever seen a man or woman who was so grieved. In many ways, Miss Putnam, he's still grieving."

"Papa Sam never thought of remarrying?" Elizabeth said.

Bea shook her head. "If you'd seen them together, you'd

know that they both knew they were only for each other. I don't think the idea ever entered Sam's head."

"They were a lovely couple," Littleton said. "You could tell they liked being around each other. The one troublesome spot was David; having the boy grow up away from them, even with all his problems, broke Sam's heart."

"Father doesn't talk about Papa Sam," Young Sam said. "When Papa came up for the big Gettysburg Reunion in 1913, Father announced he had to be at a mathematics conference in New York. Papa Sam had hoped for an additional reunion besides Gettysburg, but it never happened. Papa talked with Mother and my two brothers, and she begged him to stay with them, but he said sleeping in the tents provided was all part of the reunion plan." He paused. "I'd remained here. I'd just started my new job, and I was not in Father's good graces because of my decision about Brookhaven."

"We haven't seen David since he was 15," Littleton said. "That's what, 32 years ago? He's 47 now?"

Young Sam nodded.

"Sam," Bea said, "you remind me so much of your father and grandfather, it's just amazing. That black wavy hair, dark blue eyes, you could pass for both of them."

After Bea and Littleton went inside, Young Sam convinced Elizabeth to accompany him on a walk. He guided them toward the downtown area.

"So, you're going to be really leaving?" he said.

"Tuesday," she said. "The 8 a.m. to Jackson."

"We're still on for Thanksgiving," he said. "I will be arriving in Boston, likely the Monday or Tuesday before. Can you recommend a good hotel? I remember a few from law school but hotels often change."

"Yes, I can," she said. "The Putnam residence. First-class accommodations and what I know will be my mother's almost undivided interest and attention. Seriously, my parents have plenty of room, especially since my brothers married and set up their own homes. As I think I mentioned, Charles Jr. and his wife Ann have two children, a boy and a girl. Edward and his wife Sarah have a boy. Both of my sisters-in-law are expecting. Everyone will be there for Thanksgiving dinner." She paused. "I've never invited a young man home before. Just so you're aware, it will likely be a family sensation."

He laughed. "Will I have to meet high expectations?"

"No. If anything, the fact that you're single and breathing will be sufficient for my mother."

32

And we stand from day to day,
Like the dwarfs of times gone by,
Who, as Northern legends say,
On their shoulders held the sky.

—from "Something Left Undone"

October 1915

At breakfast the next morning, it was only Sam, Elizabeth, and Young Sam. Bea and Littleton had left early to visit Seamus and Cora Beth, and Sophie had announced she needed to run an errand with her church.

"I understand you're leaving us tomorrow, Miss Putnam?" Sam said, glancing at his grandson before turning his full attention upon his guest.

"I am, Papa Sam," she said. "I have considerable writing to do, and I hope to use the train ride to make some headway. You've gone out of your way to welcome me, house and feed me, and answer all my questions. And I'll never be able to thank you enough."

"And I hear my grandson here will paying you a visit in Boston come Thanksgiving."

Elizabeth felt herself blushing and hoped no one noticed. "He is. I offered to show him the sights, but he reminded me that he lived there for two years. I told him there was more to Boston than the Harvard Law Library."

Sam laughed and Young Sam grinned.

"I hope everyone has answered all of your questions," Sam said.

She nodded. "They have. Everyone's been most gracious and forthcoming." She hesitated.

"You have something on your mind," Sam said.

"I know the story of the Gray Wisp," she said. "I know when he enlisted, how he came to work in a select group of spies for General Lee, what his significant experiences were, and how his life became even more interesting after the war. I learned about how he met his wife, what happened to his family, and how he became a pillar, if not *the* pillar, of the Brookhaven community. I know about the businesses he took over or helped create. And I know he loves the poetry of Longfellow and is famous for his recitations."

Sam smiled.

"But I don't know why he enlisted in the first place," she said. "I sense that something happened. It might have been the accidental death of his grandfather during Grierson's Raid, or the raid itself, but I sense there's something else. And it's rather rude and almost ungrateful of me to even mention it."

Young Sam looked at his grandfather, who had looked away toward the kitchen window.

She decided to take the plunge. "I think it's connected to John Haygood and his family."

Sam turned to her so suddenly and sharply that at first she thought she would be harshly reprimanded. He stared before he finally spoke.

"You are a perceptive young woman, Miss Putnam. If I say anything else, I must have your assurance, and your word, that you will not use it in your stories. Saying that it was because of the accidental death of my grandfather during the raid should be sufficient, and not untrue."

"You have my word, Papa Sam." Elizabeth laid down her pen and closed her notebook. "But you should tell me only if you believe me when I say I won't use it. If you have any doubt, you should hold back."

Sam looked at Young Sam and turned back to her. "I also trust my grandson's good judgment."

Elizabeth knew she was blushing for real this time.

"I will tell you of the Haygood family's visit to Brookhaven two years after the war. I believe that will answer your question."

September 1867

Sam was at the sawmill that Thursday morning, along with a group of men struggling with the mill's main engine. It had been damaged by the soldiers during Grierson's Raid, but not to the point of being completely broken. Sam had taken a considerable amount of the profits from the corn mill and the store to bring a mechanic from Birmingham with spare parts.

All of them assembled around the engine, including Seamus, Ben Cohen, and several others, knew what was really needed was an entirely new engine. But no one had the money for it.

Since Nate's recent return to St. Louis and Franklin's death after another stroke, Sam and Ben had developed a close friendship. Ben had the wisdom of life to help guide the young McClure, and Sam was almost taking the place of Ben's son, whom no one expected to return from St. Louis. Even Mrs. Cohen always had a welcome smile when Sam came around.

Twelve-year-old Littleton suddenly burst into the mill's operations room.

"Sam," he said, "you have visitors at the house asking for you. They're Yankees."

Sam's eyebrows shot up in surprise; the rest of the group were equally taken aback.

"Soldiers?" Sam said.

Littleton shook his head. "A man, two women, and a little girl. Mama sent me to come get you."

Sam grinned, knowing Littleton would have leapt for the opportunity to escape his school lessons with Mrs. O'Brien, his sisters, and Sophie's Belle and Daniel. They rode back to the house.

After tethering their horses in the house stable, Sam and Littleton walked into the kitchen, where Sophie was working on refreshments for the guests. She shrugged her shoulders at Sam. "I don't know who they might be, but you need a little sprucing up." Removing his hat, she flicked a few pieces of sawdust from his longish hair, pulled on his vest to straighten it, and puffed the sleeves of his work shirt. As a final step, she straightened his tie.

"There," she said. "You look almost presentable. Your sister Martha and Janie have been talking with them while they wait." Janie was carrying their first child and showing. She'd been through about three months of morning sickness, but that seemed to have passed.

Littleton made to follow Sam to the parlor but was stopped by Sophie. "I need some firewood for supper and a little help with tea for our guests." The boy was not thrilled, but he dutifully headed for the back door to fetch the wood.

Sam walked to the front parlor. He saw a distinguished-looking man in his late 50s, a woman likely of the same age, a younger woman in her late 20s, and a little girl. They were all dressed in what only could be called Eastern finery, the clothes of wealthy people.

When they saw him, the younger woman gasped, clutching her throat. The man gaped at him. The older woman seemed shocked speechless.

But it was the little girl who had the most surprising reaction. She jumped up and ran across the room, throwing her arms around Sam's waist and yelling "Daddy!"

In the stunned silence that followed, Sam did the only thing he knew to do. He knelt in front of the little girl.

"What's your name, young lady?"

"I'm Adelaide," she said.

"Do you go by Adelaide or Addy?"

"My friends call me Addy, and you can, too."

"Well, Addy," Sam said, "I'm glad to make your acquaintance, and I welcome you to our home, but I'm not your daddy. You look about six years old, and I'm only 17, so I would have been 11 when you were born."

"But you're just like the picture on Mama's bed table."

Sam was saved from further conversation when the man cleared his throat.

"Mr. McClure, I do apologize. My name is Jacob Haygood. This is my wife, Amelia, and our daughter-in-law Julia.

You've been introduced to our granddaughter Adelaide. We're all somewhat taken aback, as you bear an extraordinarily strong resemblance to my late son."

"John Haygood," Sam said, just as Sophie and Littleton entered the room, Sophie carrying the tea tray and Littleton a plate of tea biscuits.

For a moment the man stared. "General Grant visited us in Philadelphia about a year ago," he said. "He brought Jack's saddle bag and wallet, and he told us of a young Rebel soldier who gave it to him—that somehow Jack had prevailed upon the young man to get it to a Union officer, and the young man had done that. The bag contained letters to Julia here, and Adelaide, and to his mother and myself. General Grant said he'd never known an enemy soldier of any kind to leave a dead man's wallet intact, but you had done that."

"Captain Haygood was seriously wounded, sir," Sam said, "but he was able to talk for a short time. I'd been on my way with a message, and his horse crashed into the woods right where I was trying to stay out of sight."

"What did he say?" Julia Haygood asked.

"He was in serious pain from his wounds," Sam said, "so some of what he said didn't make sense to me. He said that he was sorry, that he didn't know. I'm not sure what that meant." Sam knew exactly what he'd meant, but, for some strange reason, he felt he needed to spare these people, and especially Julia Haygood, additional pain on top of what they had already likely endured.

"In his letter to me," Haygood said, "which of course he'd written before Petersburg, he mentioned that he had met you twice."

Sam stood there, almost trembling. Janie stood and walked over to him. She took his hand.

"Yes, sir, we'd met before."

"He wrote that you had saved his life in The Wilderness, that he'd been wounded in the leg, and you carried him to Union lines, at no small peril to yourself."

Sam nodded.

"And before that, he'd met you in 1863."

"Grierson's Raid, right here in Brookhaven," Sam said.

"He told me," Haygood said, "that he had accidentally pushed your grandfather in your general store, and he'd fallen, striking his head. And that the old man died in your arms."

The room had become completely still. Sam felt he could barely breathe, that the only thing keeping him upright was Janie's hand in his. Sam simply nodded, remembering the awfulness of his grandfather's death. And the blood.

"Your mother," Julia said, in a faltering voice, "your mother is Louisa Williamson."

"Yes, ma'am," Sam said. "Louisa Williamson McClure. She's currently with her parents in Gettysburg."

The young woman retrieved a handkerchief from her purse. She'd begun to cry softly.

It was Sophie who broke the silence. "Mr. Haygood, we will be having supper in an hour or so. You and your family are welcome to join us, if you don't mind plain, simple food."

Jacob Haygood looked at Sam.

"Yes, sir," Sam said, "you'd be most welcome."

As Sam's extended family and the Haygoods crowded around the kitchen table, Sam said the blessing and then it seemed all cheerful noise. Seamus and a pregnant Cora Beth were there, as were Martha and Ellen and their children, Janie and Honeybee, and Dr. O'Brien and Leorinda. At first the Haygoods seemed almost bewildered, but Honeybee took quickly to Adelaide and the two little girls began whispering to each other and laughing. And soon the Haygoods seemed to relax and enjoy the conversation. Sam guessed that their meals at home in Philadelphia, for that was where they lived, must be very formal and very quiet, with servants attending to the meal.

Afterward, the men made their way to the front porch to enjoy the evening, with Seamus, Sean, and Mr. Haygood smoking cigars and Seamus and Jacob enjoying a glass of after-dinner brandy, both brought by Mr. Haygood.

"My late son loved to hunt," Mr. Haygood said. "I often said that he was more at home in the woods than in our house. He said in his letter that you were known as quite the woodsman, Sam."

"I do enjoy the woods, sir. I often hunted with my grandfather and with my Uncle Ned, my mother's brother, when we would visit Pennsylvania."

"Might I prevail upon you for a short visit to your woods tomorrow? Not to hunt, but just to see them? I think Jack had inherited his love of the woods from me, and I'd done quite a bit of hunting when I was a boy. If it's an imposition or you have other plans, I would fully understand."

"I'll be glad to, Mr. Haygood. After church, we'll ride out to the farm, and the woods are right there. I have a horse you can ride, and I'll meet you at the hotel at 9 o'clock, if that suits."

"That suits fine," Haygood said.

Sam knew that the point wouldn't be to see the woods; the point would be for the two of them to have time together to talk.

The next morning at the farm, they tethered their horses, and then they made their way into the woods. Sam didn't expect to run across any animals they shouldn't, but he had a rifle slung across his back just in case.

They came to a small clearing, and Haygood sat on a large fallen tree trunk. Sam joined him.

"It's beautiful here," Haygood said. "I could bask a long time in the quiet and not miss the world, I think. How much of this does your family own?"

"The farm has about 30 acres cleared," Sam said. "The woods are another 150. My father resisted every effort or scheme to cut the trees and turn it into agricultural land. The soil wouldn't be sufficient for more than a season or two without the constant addition of fertilizer."

"You should always keep these woods," Haygood said. "Not that I'm telling you how to run your business, but the beauty here could never be replicated." He stopped speaking for a few minutes, and the two of them enjoyed the morning and the woods.

"Jack actually wrote me two letters, tucking one inside the other," the older man said. "I'm the only person who's read the second one; I haven't even shown Amelia. He told me what happened during Grierson's Raid, how he convinced Grierson to divert to Brookhaven with some made-up reasoning. What he really wanted was to see your mother."

Sam said nothing; he knew his purpose at this moment

was to listen.

"What he didn't expect was to find was you. He told me it was like looking at himself in the mirror, and he was horrified that he'd been the cause of your grandfather's death, that his death would always be the event which first brought the two of you together. Did you know about him and your mother?"

"No, sir, not when we first saw each other. As you might expect, my mother had never mentioned him. My father knew; he shocked the family when he unexpectedly brought home not only a wife, but a wife in the early months of carrying a child. He always claimed me for his own, he treated me like a son, and I didn't know any better until that day I met your son. I saw how he and my mother recognized each other, and even as young as I was, I could see it was more than just old two friends renewing their acquaintance."

"When she was 16 and he was 17, they eloped," Haygood said. "They took a train down to Maryland and were married by a justice of the peace. I had detectives track them down." He paused. "Jack was an impetuous boy. If he saw something he wanted, nothing was going to stand in his way to get it. He'd met your mother at a ball in Philadelphia; the Williamsons were renting a townhouse for a few months, and we met them through various friends. We didn't run in the same social circles. We were the Haygoods of Haygood's Department Store and a number of other enterprises in Philadelphia, and we did not see your mother as a suitable match. But Jack believed otherwise. He was head over heels in love. When he told me he would marry her, I said no.

"It took a considerable investment, you could call it a

bribe and not be wrong, but the justice who married them not only annulled the marriage but also destroyed any record of it. The detectives took Jack, leaving Louisa sufficient funds to return to Gettysburg and $500 for her trouble. I'm not proud of my actions, Sam, but it's what I did and what happened.

"Jack was taken to England and essentially held under a kind of house arrest at an estate in Yorkshire. It was owned by some people we'd met on our travels who'd become good friends, and they were more than accommodating, having had their own problems with children.

"Three months later, he managed to escape, get himself to Liverpool, signed on as a sailor on a merchant ship, and came home. He went straight to Gettysburg to find your mother, and the Williamsons told him she'd married and gone to live in Mississippi. He was devastated; he was so angry he barely spoke to me and his mother for two years. He attended and graduated from Yale, and a few years later married Julia. Adelaide was born in 1861. We thought there would be other children, but of course the war had started, and he enlisted. We thought he'd put Louisa behind him, but it turned out that she'd kept in touch with a girlfriend who knew Jack, and the friend told him that Louisa was living in Brookhaven. And you know the rest. When did he tell you about their marriage?"

"He didn't," Sam said. "He met with Mother the night of the raid. They were sitting right where we were last night, on the front porch in the darkness. I'd crept around the side of the house and listened to them talk. He told her what had happened. He said he'd had no idea she was carrying his child, and I figured out who that child had turned out to be. It turned everything upside down in my mind."

"It was why you enlisted, wasn't it?" Haygood said. "Everything you thought you knew was wrong. Everything you understood had turned out to be a house of cards, and it all came crashing in. And you a 13-year-old boy whose grandfather had just died in his arms. Enlisting must have offered an escape, and perhaps a way to find a new place." Haygood's voice was shaking. "My boy, I can't even imagine what you experienced, and I was the cause behind it all. I hope you can forgive me one day."

The man was weeping. Sam put his hand on his shoulder. "There's nothing to forgive here, Mr. Haygood. It happened, and things changed. I will say that it was a difficult thing for me when I learned that all three of my brothers had died in the war. I was the last McClure left. My father knew the story, of course; we talked during the time after his stroke and before he died. I realized what he had done for my mother and for me."

"What is funny here, Sam, is that we'd always hoped for more grandchildren, and especially for Addy to have a little brother. There will be no one to carry on the direct line of the Haygood name and the Haygood Department Store. It's a kind of justice that there was indeed a brother, as it turns out, a brother who because of his grandfather's stupidity was given another man's name."

October 1915

Elizabeth saw the stunned expression on Young Sam's face. The look on his grandfather's was that of a man looking back, remembering, and still feeling the pain of what had happened in his family.

"Did you ever talk with your mother about this?" she said.

Sam nodded. "When she visited in 1874. I hadn't seen her in almost eight years. She'd never written, or at least I thought she hadn't. Her father had gotten sick; in fact, he'd die that year. He was bedridden, and one of his daily chores fell to my mother, which was to deliver and pick up mail at the general store, which was also the post office. The postmistress had expressed concern about her father, and then made a comment about what a faithful letter writer her son was.

"The postmistress was actually commenting on what she believed she knew, that my mother was receiving all these letters from me and not responding to a one. It turned out that her father, my Grandpa Williamson, had been collecting the letters and never giving them to her. She thought we'd cut her off completely. She went home in a state and proceeded to scream at her father in his bed. She told me that all he said was that I was dead to him, and no one in his family should be reading my letters.

"She tore the room apart until she found them, tied neatly with a ribbon in a box in his armoire. He'd kept every single one of them, unopened and unread. Her mother was shocked; she'd no idea of what he'd been doing. There were 40 or 50 letters from me, and a few from Cora Beth. In a single afternoon, she discovered that her husband had had a stroke and died, that her stepdaughter was married with two children, that a step-grandson was at Yale, that her son was married with two children and another on the way, and that the Haygoods had visited Brookhaven. And she knew I now understood the story of John Haygood.

"She read every letter to her father and mother. She left the next morning on the train to return to Mississippi. When she got to Brookhaven, she came directly to the house, shocking Martha. Word was sent to me at the former grist mill, what was becoming the stables. I hurried home, and she explained in almost hysterical tears. It was hard to believe he would do such a cruel thing. I told her what I hadn't said in the letter about the Haygoods, that I was with John Haygood when he died. When I told her what he said, I didn't think she'd stop crying.

"A few days later, her mother sent a telegram, saying her father had died. Mama did not attend his funeral, but waited another month before she went back."

33

I breathed a song into the air,
It fell to earth, I know not where;
For who has sight so keen and strong,
That it can follow the flight of song?

—from "The Arrow and The Song"

October 1915

Elizabeth and Young Sam sat on the platform, waiting for the 8 a.m. train to Jackson. After Sam had finished his story the day before, Young Sam had taken her to the Brookhaven Hotel for lunch. They'd both been quiet, saying little. That night, the entire family had showed up for what was essentially a farewell dinner for Elizabeth. And, out of earshot of everyone else including his grandson, Papa Sam had taken her aside.

"I have a favor to ask, Miss Putnam. If it's not possible or too much, you're free to refuse, of course. But I hope you'll say yes." And he'd told her what he was asking her to do. She told him she would give it serious thought.

"Would it be too forward of me to ask if I might hold your hand?" Young Sam said, as they waited for the train.

"Yes," she said, "it would be, but you may do it anyway. I was hoping you might ask."

"Thanksgiving seems like an eternity away," he said, as he folded her hand inside his own.

"We can write," she said.

"Yes, we can. I will. I may have to write more than once a day, so I'll number the letters."

Why did she feel such a rush of strong feeling when he talked like this, she thought to herself. She'd always been put off by similar sentiments before. What made this so different? She knew the answer, and it felt like she was stepping into the great unknown. Everything before had seemed so set in stone —her job, her career, her future, her causes, what she wanted to do. And now everything had become so uncertain, like she was walking into a mystery.

"In eight days, Sam," she said, "my life changed."

"I thought I was doing my grandfather a favor," he said, "when I agreed to pick you and Aunt Bea up at the station. I saw you, and I felt my heart fly out of my chest."

They heard the train whistle.

"Well, darn. Right on schedule," Young Sam said. "The porter will make sure your trunks are stowed. You have your ticket?"

She nodded. And suddenly she didn't want to leave. She wanted to stay right there with him, never leaving his side.

It was as if he could read her mind. "We'll be together in a few weeks. I've already made my reservations; I'll be arriving in Boston the Tuesday before Thanksgiving. And I intend to talk with your father."

They heard the conductor call for boarding.

They turned to each other.

"I'll miss you, Samuel David McClure III," she said. "I'll miss you more than I can possibly say."

"I'm with you wherever you are," he said. He took her

face in his hands and kissed her.

He helped her step up into the car. She found a seat next to the window, right where he was standing outside. He put his hand to the window, and she matched it with hers.

The train began to move. For a few seconds he ran alongside the car. And then the train picked up speed. She looked back for as long as she could, until the track rounded a bend.

Elizabeth changed trains in Jackson, checking to make sure her trunks made it to the train for Atlanta.

She'd gone to the expense of a small, private compartment. She'd done the same for the Atlanta to Philadelphia run. For the hop to New York City, she'd booked a regular seat.

She arrived in Philadelphia early Thursday, and it was there she changed her plans. She sent her trunks to storage in the Philadelphia station and carried a small overnight bag for a quick ride to Gettysburg.

It was noon when she arrived at the Gettysburg station. She found a cab to take her to Gettysburg College. There, she sought directions to the Department of Mathematics. She kept herself focused on the task at hand; otherwise, she would have bolted back to the train station. But she was determined to do this for Papa Sam, as he asked her, even if it might end badly, as it likely would.

She was told that Professor David McClure was currently teaching a large class in Glatfelter Hall and given directions, after being cautioned not to interrupt the class. She made her way there. Through a small window in the door, she could see the room was large and crowded; she slipped in easily and took a seat in the back without anyone noticing.

She almost gasped when she saw Professor McClure. It was almost like looking at a Young Sam who was 20 years older. The physical resemblance was uncanny. But everything else was different.

David McClure spoke in a kind of stilted language. His movement, when he lectured and walked in front of the blackboard, seemed jerky. No one else in the room seemed bothered by it; they must be used to it, she thought.

She shook her head. *And what is it about me and this family? I seem to have a habit of showing up in college classrooms, trying to corral professors.*

Mathematics had never been her strong suit. She tried listening to the lecture, but it was well beyond what she called her meager arithmetic skills. As she looked around the lecture hall, she saw faces in rapt attention and people furiously taking notes. Then she saw there were also a few men dressed in professor gowns, who were listening and writing as intently as the students.

The class ended; she expected to see students flock to the front to ask questions, as they had with Professor Seale in Mississippi. But no one did. Instead, students and professors alike talked among themselves as they filed past her out of the lecture hall.

She walked to the front. "Dr. McClure?"

He turned abruptly from where he'd been erasing complicated symbols on the blackboard.

"Yes?" He peered closely at her. "You're not a student."

The resemblance to his son was even stronger closeup. For a moment, she felt disconcerted.

"No, sir, I'm not. My name is Elizabeth Putnam, and I'm

a reporter for the New York *World*."

"A reporter?"

"Yes. I wondered if I might talk with you about your father. I've just spent more than a week with him and your family in Brookhaven, interviewing him on a series of stories for the newspaper about his work in the Civil War. There is still considerable interest in the man who was known as the Gray Wisp."

He held his hands in front of him, one cupped inside the other. He was forward-and-back swaying, which then intensified. Most disconcerting was that his facial expression never changed, making him seem almost machine-like.

"I know nothing about his service in the Civil War," he said. "If you spent eight days there, then you would know my father and I do not speak. I can add nothing to your investigation. I must go." He turned and began to walk away.

"Professor McClure, I spent almost every waking moment of those eight days in the presence of your son. And the rift between you has broken his heart."

He stopped and turned back to her, staring at her intently. He seemed a bundle of intensity, as if an explosion was imminent.

"The rift with my son has left me heartbroken as well, and it was my fault." He stared. "I presume you're staying at the Gettysburg Hotel."

She nodded.

"We have dinner at 6:30 p.m. My sons Stephen and Michael will call for you at the hotel at 5:30 and drive you to our home in the automobile. I do not like driving, but they seem to find some enjoyment in it."

He turned away, picked up his briefcase, and left.

Elizabeth made her way out of the hall and back to the hotel.

She was waiting in the lobby at 5:25. A few minutes later, a teenaged boy walked in, dressed in slacks, a white dress shirt, and bow tie, with a boater pushed jauntily back on his head. He was tall, with light brown hair and dark blue eyes.

This has to be Sam's brother, she thought. *The shape of the face, the eyes, and the boater must be a family trait.*

He caught sight of her, smiled, and walked over, introducing himself.

"Miss Putnam? I'm Michael McClure, but you can call me Mike. Welcome to Gettysburg, home of famous battles and eccentric mathematicians."

"You must be the youngest of the McClure boys," Elizabeth said. "The one known as the family jokester and prankster, who has a way with words and will likely become a famous writer one day?"

"Someone's been talking about me," he said, grinning. "My reputation for jokes and pranks is much exaggerated, I'm glad to say. I'll escort you to your waiting carriage, milady; your driver, also known as Stephen, awaits."

Outside, Stephen McClure sat behind the wheel of a Ford Model T touring car, with its roof fastened to the windscreen. Michael introduced his brother, helped Elizabeth into the front seat, and they were off.

"I hear you're planning to study engineering at Cornell," she said to Stephen over the loud engine noise.

The young man nodded. "I am. I've been accepted for the

1916 freshmen class."

"Be careful, Steve," Michael said from the back seat, "she has the inside dope on all of us. I suspect a certain older brother has been telling her a mixture of truths and outright lies."

"You've talked to our brother?" Stephen said.

She nodded. "Yes. And he says he misses you both."

A serious look covered Stephen's face. "We miss him fiercely. And we miss Papa Sam. My father says you saw them in Brookhaven?"

"I did. I spent eight days at your grandfather's house, and your brother served as my tour guide, chauffeur, escort to the county fair, and horseback riding instructor."

"When we arrive home," Michael said from the back seat, "you must tell us everything. And don't let my father's frowns stop you."

They'd driven only a short time when Stephen guided the Ford onto a carefully maintained gravel road leading up to a Victorian-style farmhouse. Despite the gathering dusk, she could see it was an imposing structure, with two floors and an attic, a wide front porch, and a turret at the corner. Waiting on the porch was an attractive woman in her 40s, dressed simply but stylishly in a long skirt and a white blouse with a lace collar.

"Miss Putnam," she said, smiling, as they walked up the stairs and reached the porch, "welcome to our home." She took Elizabeth's hand and gave it a slight squeeze with both of her own.

"Thank you, Mrs. McClure. I know it must have been unexpected to hear of a dinner guest."

"My dear, we're used to it. With David, one is always prepared for surprises. With three boys, surprises are commonplace. David's in his study and will join us shortly. And please call me Amy."

As they walked into the parlor, Amy touched her arm to stop them. "And how is Sam?"

The woman's tone and the look in her eyes told Elizabeth this was a mother hungry for information about her oldest son.

"He's doing well. He loves his law practice, and he's already making a name for himself far beyond Brookhaven. He has clients in New Orleans and Mobile, he's passed both the Mississippi and Louisiana bars, he's studying for the New York bar exam, and he's waiting to hear if he's passed his certification for the U.S. Supreme Court."

"That's wonderful. I'm so proud of him. Is he still seeing that Biddle girl?"

"Ah, no. When she learned that he had come to Brookhaven to stay, she broke it off. Her plans extended beyond her hometown, I believe. She has since married and moved to Jackson. I met her and her husband at the Lincoln County Fair."

Amy sighed and took Elizabeth's arm. "I shouldn't say this, but it's welcome news and the lifting of a great burden on my mind. Come, let's go to the dining room."

The two boys and their father were waiting. The room seemed almost sparkling. Elizabeth could see that someone, which turned out to be two servant girls, had set out the good china, silver, and crystal. Fresh flowers occupied the table's center.

Elizabeth nodded at David McClure. "Professor."

He nodded back with the upper half of his body. "Miss Putnam."

"You should come more often, Miss Putnam," Michael said. "We don't usually eat this fancy on a weeknight."

Amy rolled her eyes, while her husband's long stare at his youngest son silenced the boy, at least temporarily.

"Why don't we sit," Amy said. She sat at her husband's left, with Jamie next to her. Elizabeth was directed to the chair at David McClure's right, with Stephen next to her.

"We have reduced the chance of a table upset significantly," Dr. McClure said, "by placing Michael next to his mother instead of our guest." And he stared at his youngest again.

Michael grinned. "Pa, no vinegar tonight. We want to hear everything Miss Putnam has to tell us. And I promise no jokes or pranks." He paused. "Until after dinner, of course."

Stephen helped with Elizabeth's chair. David McClure gave the blessing, and the two girls began to serve the food.

At first, Elizabeth was hesitant to answer the family's questions. Amy, Stephen, and Michael were like sponges. How was Sam? Was Papa still hunting? Had she tried Sophie's raisin cake? Was Uncle Seamus still telling jokes? It was a never-ending stream from people hungry for information and cut off from it for more than two years. She told them all about her eight days in Brookhaven, her interviews with Papa Sam, and all of the things she'd done with Young Sam.

David McClure sat quietly listening, not saying anything.

"Did Sam say anything about the family here?" Amy said.

Elizabeth smiled. "He told me all about his brothers."

Both boys beamed. "He talked about growing up in Gettysburg, his time at Harvard. And his two years in Germany. And I didn't know that he had interned at my father's law offices in Boston."

"Of course," Amy said. "Putnam was one of the partners."

"Sam worked with Mr. Frost and his staff primarily," Elizabeth said, "but he'd met both my father and my oldest brother, who's also an attorney there." Then she moved toward the subject on her mind and likely on David's and Amy's minds. "I understand from Sam that it was the offer from Stevens, Frost, & Putnam that caused some upset."

Amy glanced at her husband, who had suddenly sat up even straighter in his chair, if that was possible.

"He told me," Elizabeth said carefully, "why he'd chosen to work in Brookhaven over a place like Boston or New York or even Chicago and St. Louis. The longer I was there, the more I understood his reasoning. It has to do with family, with community, with being grounded in a specific place."

David finally spoke. "Miss Putnam, did my son ask you to visit us?"

"No, he didn't, Mr. McClure. In fact, he doesn't even know I'm here."

"You decided on your own to come?"

"Not exactly," she said. "Your father asked me if I might consider a visit to your family, because, he said, he didn't want to see Sam estranged from his family like his father was estranged from his."

Everything went silent; everyone sat motionless.

"I suspect my father had another reason," David said. "He knew you had fallen in love with Sam. Does Sam reciprocate your feelings?"

Amy and the boys gaped.

"David!" Amy said. "You don't say such things to a guest."

"But she has the same tone in her voice whenever she talks about Sam that you have whenever you talk about me." He looked back at Elizabeth.

"If that was indeed his second reason, Mr. McClure," Elizabeth said, "then I believe Papa Sam read the feelings of both Sam's feelings and my own correctly."

On the train the next day to Philadelphia and the connection to New York, Elizabeth considered the conversation. She remembered little of what happened after. David had nodded, Amy was still red with embarrassment, and the boys were wide-eyed, saying nothing but grinning up a storm. They'd driven her back to the hotel, mercifully saying nothing about the dinner conversation.

Arriving in New York, she had her trunks dispatched to the women's hotel, and she made her way to the New York *World*. She went directly to John Osborne's offices, greeting people she knew along the way. He was standing at his office door, talking with his secretary, when he spotted her.

"Elizabeth Putnam!" he said, in nearly a shout. "Back from the sunny South! That tomato girl story was priceless. I'm hoping you have some additional stories for me?"

She smiled and handed him a raft of paper all in her handwriting. "I do. And I need to talk with you. About Mrs. Osborne."

They talked for an hour. The upshot was an invitation that night to dinner at his apartment on Fifth Avenue.

"I won't say anything to Addy before you arrive," he said. "To be honest, I don't know how she'll react. I don't know how anyone in this position would react. Surprise? Shock? Relief? Wondering how well you knew your own parents and grandparents?"

"She was just a little girl, Mr. Osborne. She was only six."

"She often talks about her grandparents. She adored them both, and especially Jacob Haygood. I think she'll be rethinking things, especially regarding her grandfather."

"Miss Putnam," Adelaide Osborne said, "John said you had something to talk with me about."

They had finished dinner. The table had been cleared but they were still sitting and talking. Elizabeth had been quietly amazed at how much Mrs. Osborne's eyes resembled those of Papa Sam.

Elizabeth told her the story of the Gray Wisp.

"It wasn't a figment of my imagination, then," Mrs. Osborne said. "It wasn't my father I saw on that journey; it was someone who *looked* like my father because he was my father's son."

Elizabeth nodded. John Osborne was watching his wife closely.

"I have a half-brother."

The woman looked down. She seemed almost talking to herself. "My grandfather lied, because he was ashamed of what he'd done. Jacob Haygood, the founder of Haygood's Department Store, destroyed two lives because he believed the girl wasn't suitable. I take it the woman my father first married isn't still alive?"

"She died in 1895, Mr. McClure said."

"The same year my mother died." She shook her head. "Neither of them deserved what they got. One had a husband snatched away, and she was left carrying his child. The other, my mother, all she ever wanted was to be cherished, to be the love of someone's life. She told me that when she was dying, and I told her that Father had loved her. She shook her head and said that she felt he had respected and cared for her, but someone else had been the love of his life."

"I'm sorry, Mrs. Osborne; I've upset you."

"No, dear. I'm upset, yes, but it's always better to know the truth, isn't it? My entire life, I've believed my grandfather was a saint, an angel, the man who took the place of my father after he died. And he wasn't that at all, not at all, was he?"

"No one is, Addy," John Osborne said. "No one is. We're all frail, imperfect creatures, and we too often do stupid things."

She nodded and reached for his hand. "I'd like to meet him, John. I'd like to meet my half-brother."

In the taxi back to her hotel, Elizabeth thought about how her story, or the story about the Gray Wisp, was having such an impact on people's lives, and it hadn't even been published yet. That's what stories do, she thought, the true ones, anyway. They pull you into other lives, and when you come out again, you're different, and the world becomes different. She was glad that Mr. Osborne had prevailed upon his wife to wait, to let some time pass before she met her half-brother.

She was asleep as soon as her head touched the pillow.

34

The book is completed,
And closed, like the day;
And the hand that has written it
Lays it away.

—from "Curfew"

November 1915

It had been a busy two weeks. John Osborne had assigned one of his top editors to work with Elizabeth on what would now be a week-long series about the Gray Wisp. It would begin this Sunday and run through Friday. A photographer had been hired, and the photographs of Papa Sam, the McClure house in Brookhaven, and the businesses were now on a large table while she and the editor pored over them.

Osborne had walked in and picked up three photographs of Papa Sam and his grandson. "The family resemblance is extraordinary," he said. "Might I have a copy of one?"

With the work on the series and a few additional assignments completed, Elizabeth was leaving that evening and spending tomorrow and Sunday in Boston, returning to New York Sunday evening. She wanted to see her family, and she had a Thanksgiving invitation to arrange with her parents.

She and Sam had written daily, sometimes twice a day, and one day, three times. Sam's suggestion that they number their letters proved a helpful one. He'd also telephoned twice at her apartment hotel, "just to hear your voice," he said.

She'd also written to Papa Sam, to let him know his half-sister wanted to meet him.

Saturday evening, she bathed and dressed for what her mother had called an unofficial celebration dinner for her newspaper series and to welcome her home even for a short weekend stay. She had just reached downstairs when Edward and his family arrived, with Charles Jr. and his clan closely behind.

Growing up, the gap in their ages hadn't deterred either of the Putnam boys from doting on their little sister. She loved them both, as different as they were. She also liked both of her sisters-in-law; Edward's wife now expecting in February. Charlie had a girl, a boy, and a new baby girl, and Elizabeth dearly loved all three of them.

The one problem she'd been wrestling with was how to tell her family about Sam, and how to explain her invitation to him for Thanksgiving. As it so happened, Edward solved the problem for her.

As they were eating, Edward cleared his throat. "Mother, Jen's sister will be staying with us over the holidays, and I hope one more place at the table won't be any trouble? She's going to be staying with us through the birth and help with the baby."

"Of course not, dear," Mrs. Putnam said. "I love a crowd, and she's a lovely girl."

"Mother," Elizabeth said, "I've also invited a guest for Thanksgiving, if that's all right."

"Of course, Elizabeth," her mother said. "Is it a colleague

from work or one of your friends from the hotel? Have we met her?"

Moment of truth, Elizabeth thought. Her lack of an immediate answer had caught the table's attention.

"Well," she said, "Father and Charlie have." Seeing the puzzled looks exchanged, she plunged. "His name is Sam Mc-Clure. Samuel David McClure III, to be precise. He's the grandson of the man I wrote about in my series, the Gray Wisp, and he lives and works in Brookhaven."

Silence engulfed the table, until Charlie spoke. "Wait. That's Sam McClure, who interned with us a couple of years ago or so? Oh my, he's a marvel. He was the first-year law student who accepted a dare to take the Massachusetts bar exam, and he aced it. He's absolutely brilliant. Please tell me he's coming to talk with father about a position with the firm?"

"He does want to talk with Father," Elizabeth said, "but it's not about a position at the firm." She saw comprehension dawning on the faces of her sisters-in-law, while her father, brothers, and mother were frowning in puzzlement.

"We've known each only a few weeks," Elizabeth said. "But we spent almost every waking moment together in Brookhaven. He chauffeured me everywhere, he escorted me to the county fair, we went horseback riding, and he sat with me and Papa Sam, I mean Mr. McClure, for almost all the interviews. And, well, um, things happened. Very quickly. I think we were both rather shocked how fast it all developed. We've been writing every day, sometimes twice a day, and he's telephoned twice. And if it's all right, he'll arrive the Tuesday before Thanksgiving and stay until Sunday."

She'd gotten it all out in a rush. She was looking down,

almost afraid to look at her parents. She finally risked a glance at her brothers and saw both of them grinning.

"Joan of Arc has been captured by a knight on a horse," Charlie said, almost chortling. "Tell me it's a white horse!"

"It's raven black," Elizabeth said, pretending to be snappy when all she wanted to do was laugh.

"Dora?" her father said.

Elizabeth turned toward her parents. Her father had placed his hand on her mother's. Her mother, staring at Elizabeth, was making slight jerks with her head and making little puffing breaths, as if she couldn't speak.

'Mother?" Elizabeth said. "Are you all right?"

Her mother finally calmed, and then turned to Mr. Putnam. "Charles, we need to replace the wallpaper in the guest room. And I may need new bed linens, and a proper cover. And new pillows, of course."

Mr. Putnam smiled at his wife. "Dora, you had the guest room repapered less than a year ago."

"I know," she said, "but that was then, and this is now. We want Mr. McClure's stay to be comfortable and memorable. Oh, Elizabeth, you must provide me with his address, so I can extend a proper invitation."

Elizabeth thought she'd never loved her mother so much as in that moment. "Mother, I know I have been a source of agitation and vexation for you, and on this very subject. What happened in Brookhaven was the last thing I expected. He's unlike anyone I've ever met. And if he asks, I will tell him that I will spend the rest of my life with him. And that will mean moving to Brookhaven."

Both Elizabeth and her mother woke early on the Tuesday before Thanksgiving. By 6 a.m., Mrs. Putnam had roused the servants, ordered one more dusting of the parlor, dining room, Mr. Putnam's library, and the guest room.

Elizabeth's series on the Gray Wisp had been published to great success. Even ordering an extended print run wasn't sufficient to meet demand. In fact, requests for copies were so great, both in New York and more broadly cross the country, that the *World's* publisher had decided to reprint the entire series as an oversized pamphlet. It was already in production.

Each day the story was published, Elizabeth made sure to send five copies by expedited post to Brookhaven. Papa Sam had responded with a short telegram that meant more to her than all the other kudos and congratulations combined. "You told my story. Stop. And you told it very well indeed. Stop. Thank you. Stop. And I owe you a recitation. Stop."

Elizabeth dressed. Her father had checked with the railroad to verify that the 8:30 non-stop train from New York to Boston was on time. It was. Sam had told her he would take a taxi to the house in case the train was delayed.

By 7, Mrs. Putnam had roused her husband, almost dragging him out of bed and pushing him toward the bathroom.

"Why are we up so early?" he said grumpily.

"It may well be one of the most important days in your daughter's life, and it's time you were up."

Elizabeth sat by a front window, watching the street. She jumped up every time an automobile appeared, which fortunately wasn't often.

It was going on 11 when she saw the vehicle stop in front of their house and beep its horn. She grabbed a shawl and dashed through the front door and down the steps. Mrs. Putnam made to dash after her, but her husband stopped her.

"Give Elizabeth a chance to welcome him first, and then you can greet him in your best hostess manner, stately and serene, when he comes through the door."

They both watched from the window.

"Do you think she might have misread or overinterpreted his intentions?" Mrs. Putnam said to her husband.

Elizabeth had stopped a couple of feet away while Sam paid the driver. A bouquet of roses in his arms, he turned to her with a huge smile on his face.

"I'm going to do something completely improper for Boston," Sam said. He stepped forward, roses in his left arm, drew Elizabeth to him with his right arm, and kissed her. Passionately.

"No, dear," Mr. Putnam said, "I don't think she misread his intentions at all."

The End

Author's Note

When I was seven years old, my mother took me to see the movie *The Horse Soldiers*, starring John Wayne and William Holden. It's the story of a Union cavalry troop of almost 2,000 soldiers who slice their way across Confederate territory. Little did I know that it was based on a true story, called Grierson's Raid, and that the raid had been experienced by my ancestors in 1863, when they lived in the Brookhaven, Mississippi area.

Brookhaven began as a family story about my great-grandfather, handed down by my grandfather to my father to me. The story was accompanied by the family bible, passed down in the same way.

The story was that my great-grandfather Samuel had been a messenger boy in the Civil War. He'd been too young to serve as a soldier. When the war ended, he was stranded somewhere in the eastern United States, with Robert E. Lee's army in Virginia or William Johnston's army in North Carolina. He made his way home to Brookhaven, Mississippi, mostly on foot, to discover that the family had left for Texas to escape federal occupation, so he continued his journey until he found them.

It was a great story, but it turned out to be mostly invented. An example: my great-grandfather had been a messenger boy, but not in the army. Messenger boys were the young teens who brought telegrams to families telling them of their relative's death in battle. They were not involved in military battles.

But the larger story was what my family believed and went

to their graves believing. (My grandmother was still fighting the Civil War, or what she called the War of Northern Aggression, when she died in 1984.) The real story wasn't anywhere near as interesting as the invented one, and it was the invented one that I imagined for *Brookhaven*. That invented story, however, is based on years of research, study, and reading. The characters are all fictitious, but what they experience in the story really happened to people during and after the war.

Books don't appear by themselves, and L.L. Barkat and Sara Barkat at T. S. Poetry Press were instrumental in making this book happen. My family, including my wife Janet, has put up with a lot while I was writing. I've had numerous private conversations with people about battles, historical figures, the Civil War, and the Reconstruction period. A special thanks goes to the writers and editors of the Emerging Civil War website.

I learned something important through this book. Our ancestors may not be the great heroes we thought they were, but living through a cataclysm like the Civil War and its aftermath is a heroic act all by itself.

—*Glynn Young, St. Louis, Missouri, November 2024*

List of Characters

The Franklin McClure Family, Brookhaven

Franklin McClure, father and Mexican War veteran
Margaret Fletcher, Franklin's first wife
  Hugh McClure, died at Battle of Franklin
  James McClure, died at Battle of Shiloh
    Married to Emily McClure; 2 daughters
  Martha McClure Seale, widow of Jarvis Seale
    Littleton Seale, her son
    4 daughters
  Cora Beth McClure O'Brien, married to Seamus
Louisa Williamson McClure, Franklin's second wife
  Samuel David McClure, son of Franklin and Louisa

Samuel David McClure, Franklin's son and Civil War veteran
Octavia Jane Montgomery, Samuel's wife
  David McClure, professor of mathematics at Gettysburg College
  Edith McClure and Helen McClure, daughters

Sophie, housekeeper and cook for the McClures in Brookhaven
  Belle, her daughter
  Daniel, her son

Other Brookhaven Characters

Nathan Cohen, Sam's best friend
Ben Cohen, Nathan's father
Sean O'Brien, doctor and Confederate veteran
Seamus O'Brien, Sean's brother and Union veteran
Leorinda Russell, schoolteacher

Mrs. Pettigrew, widow of the previous doctor

The David McClure family, Gettysburg

David McClure, son of Samuel and Octavia, mathematics
professor at Gettysburg College
Amy McClure, David's wife
  Samuel David McClure III, Brookhaven attorney
  Stephen McClure
  Michael McClure

**The Montgomery Family, Greensboro,
N.C. and Windhaven Plantation, Alabama**

Lucinda Montgomery, family matriarch
Beatrice (Honeybee), her granddaughter
Wallace Montgomery, surviving son at Windhaven Planta-
tion
Octavia Jane Montgomery, Lucinda's granddaughter and
Sam McClure's wife

Henry, Montgomery family retainer

**The Jacob Haygood Family, Philadelphia,
Pennsylvania**

Jacob Haygood, founder of the department store
Amelia Haygood, Jacob's wife
John Haygood, Jacob and Amelia's son
Julia Haygood, John's wife
Adelaide Haygood, daughter of John and Julia

Colby's Raiders

Major Colby
Caleb Willingham

Historical Figures

Robert E. Lee
Ulysses S. Grant
Jefferson Davis

New York *World*

John Osborne, managing editor, married to Adelaide Haygood

The Putnam Family, Boston, Massachusetts

Charles Putnam, Sr., attorney
Dora Putnam, his wife
  Charles Putnam, Jr., attorney
  James Putnam, physician
  Emily Putnam, reporter for the New York *World*

Bibliography

Poems by Henry Wadsworth Longfellow

All quotations by Longfellow included in the text are taken from one
of three collections:

The Complete Poetical Works by Henry Wadsworth Longfellow, Household
Edition; Houghton, Mifflin and Company, 1898.

The Poems of Longfellow, Illustrated Modern Library, New York, 1944.

Longfellow: Poems & Other Writings, edited by J.D. McClatchy; The Library
of America, 2000.

For general biographical information

Basbanes, Nicholas A., *Cross of Snow: A Life of Henry Wadsworth Longfellow*. New York: Alfred A. Knopf, 2020.

General Civil War History

Ash, Stephen, *A Year in the South*. New York: Harper Perennial, 2002.

Bateson, Catherine, *Irish American Civil War Songs: Identity, Loyalty, and
Nationhood*. Baton Rouge: Louisiana State University Press, 2022.

Calkin, Chris, "No One Wants to Be the Last to Die": *The Battles of Appomattox April 8-9, 1865*. El Dorado Hills, California: Savas Beatie,
2023.

Catton, Bruce, *The Army of the Potomac Trilogy*. New York: Library of
America, 2022.

Clarke, Frances M. and Plant, Rebecca Jo, *Of Age: Boy Soldiers and Military Power in the Civil War Era*. New York: Oxford University Press, 2023.

Cushman, Stephen, *Belligerent Muse: Five Northern Writers and How They Shaped Our Perceptions of the Civil War*. Chapel Hill: University of North Carolina Press, 2014.

Delbanco, Andrew, *The War Before the War: Fugitive Slaves and the Struggle for America's Soul from the Revolution to the Civil War*. New York: Penguin Press, 2018.

Dollar, Jr., Ernest A., *Hearts Torn Asunder: Trauma in the Civil War's Final Campaign in North Carolina*. El Dorado Hills, California: Savas Beatie, 2022.

Dunkerly, Robert M., *The Confederate Surrender at Greensboro: The Final Days of the Army of the Tennessee, April 1865*. Jefferson, North Carolina: McFarland and Company, 2013.

Gorra, Michael, *The Saddest Words: William Faulkner's Civil War*. New York: Liveright Publishing, 2020.

Gwynne, S.C., *Hymns of the Republic: The Story of the Final Year of the American Civil War*. New York: Scribner, 2019.

Holzer, Harold, *President Lincoln Assassinated!! The Firsthand Story of the Murder, Manhunt, Trial, and Mourning*. New York: Library of America, 2014.

Hopkins, John L., *The World Will Never See the Like: The Gettysburg Reunion of 1913*. El Dorado Hills, California: Savas Beatie, 2024.

Janney, Caroline E., *Ends of War: The Unfinished Fight of Lee's Army after*

Appomattox. Chapel Hill: University of North Carolina Press, 2021.

Johnson, Ludwell H., *North Against South: The American Iliad 1848-1877*. Columbia: Foundation for American Education, 1993.

Kagan, Neil and Hyslop, Stephen, *Eyewitness to the Civil War: The Complete History from Secession to Reconstruction*. Washington, D.C.: National Geographic Society, 2006.

Kagan, Neil and Hyslop, Stephen, *Atlas of the Civil War*. Washington, D.C.: National Geographic Society, 2009.

Keller, David, *The Story of Camp Douglas, Chicago's Forgotten Civil War Prison*. Charleston, South Carolina: The History Press, 2015.

Marszalek, John F., *Sherman's March to the Sea*. Abilene: McWhiney Foundation Press, McMurry University, 2005.

Mazur, Louis, *The Civil War: A Concise History*. New York: Oxford University Press, 2011.

McIvor, Hames, *God Rest Ye Merry, Soldiers: A True Civil War Christmas Story*. New York: Penguin, 2006.

McPherson, James, *Battle Cry of Freedom: The Civil War Era*. New York: Ballantine Books, 1988.

Mitchell, Patricia, introduction, *Confederate Receipt Book: Recipes, Cures, and Camp & Household Hints*. Richmond, Virginia, 1863.

Phillips, David, *Maps of the Civil War: The Roads They Took*. New York: Metro Books, 1999.

Power, Tracy J., *Lee's Miserables: Life in the Army of Northern Virginia from the Wilderness to Appomattox*. Chapel Hill: University of North Carolina Press, 1998.

Ward, Geoffrey C. with Burns, Rick and Burns, Ken, *The Civil War: An Illustrated History*. New York: Knopf, 1990.

Woodward, C. Vann, *Origins of the New South 1877-1913*. Baton Rouge: Louisiana State University Press, 1951.

Williams, Harry T., *Lincoln and His Generals*. New York: Knopf, 1952.

Civil War in Mississippi

Ballard, Michael, *The Civil War in Mississippi: Major Battles and Campaigns*. Jackson: University of Mississippi Press, 2011.

Brown, Dee, *Grierson's Raid*. New York: Curtis Books, 1954.

Garner, James Wilford, *Reconstruction in Mississippi*. Charleston, South Carolina: Legare Street Press, Ph.D thesis, 1901.

Harris, William C., *Presidential Reconstruction in Mississippi*. Baton Rouge: Louisiana State University Press, 1967.

Mackowski, Chris, *The Battle of Jackson, Mississippi May 14, 1863*. El Dorado Hills, California: Savas Beatie Battles & Leaders Series, 2022.

Mills, Charles A., *War and Reconstruction in Mississippi 1861-1875: A Portrait*; self-published, 2010.

Roberts, Bobby and Moneyhon, Carl, *Portraits of Conflict: A Photographic History of Mississippi in the Civil War*. Fayetteville: University of Arkansas Press, 1993.

Ruminski, Jaret, *The Limits of Loyalty: Ordinary People in Civil War Mississippi*. Jackson: University Press of Mississippi, 2017.

Smith, Timothy B., *Mississippi in the Civil War: The Home Front*. Jackson: University Press of Mississippi, 2010.

Smith, Timothy B., *The Real Horse Soldiers: Benjamin Grierson's Epic 1863 Civil War Raid Through Mississippi*. El Dorado Hills, California: Savas Beatie, 2018.

Woodrick, Jim, *The Civil War Siege of Jackson, Mississippi*. Charleston, South Carolina: The History Press, 2016.

Biographies, Letters, and Memoirs

Alleman, Matilda Pierce, *At Gettysburg: Or, What a Girl Saw and Heard of the Battle*. New York: W.L. Borland, 1889; republished in 2016.

Berry, Col. Thomas F., *Four Years with Morgan and Forrest*. Oklahoma City: The Harlow-Ratliff Company, 1914; republished in 2017.

Catton, Bruce, *Waiting for the Morning Train: An American Boyhood*. Detroit, Michigan: Wayne State University Press, 1972.

Chernow, Ron: *Grant*. New York: Penguin Press, 2017.

Fuller, Theodore Albert and Knight, Daniel Thomas, editors, *Contemners and Serpents: The James Wilson Family Civil War Correspondence*. Macon, Georgia: Mercer University Press, 2023.

Grant, Ulysses S., *My Dearest Julia: The Wartime Letters of Ulysses S. Grant to His Wife*. New York: Library of America, 2018.

Grant, Ulysses S., *Personal Memoirs of U.S. Grant in Two Volumes*. New

York: Charles Webster & Co., 1885.

Guelzo, Allen, Robert E. Lee: *A Life*. New York: Knopf, 2021.

Hague, Parthenia Antoinette, *A Blockaded Family: Life in Southern Alabama During the Civil War*. New York: Houghton, Mifflin and Company, 1888; republished in 2019.

Jackson, Mary Anna, *The Life and Letters of General Thomas J. Jackson*. New
York: Harper & Brothers, 1892; republished in 2019.

Korda, Michael, *Clouds of Glory: The Life and Legend of Robert E. Lee*. New
York: Harper, 2014.

Leubke, Peter C., *From Western Virginia with Jackson to Spotsylvania with
Lee: The Civil War Diaries and Letters of St. Joseph Tucker Randolph*.
Charleston, West Virginia: 35th Star Publishing, 2023.

Maxfield, Derek D., *Man of Fire: William Tecumseh Sherman in the Civil
War*. El Dorado Hills, California: Savas Beatie Emerging Civil War
Series, 2018.

Page, James Madison, *The True Story of Andersonville Prison: A Defense of
Major Henry Wirz*. New York: The Neale Publishing Company,
1908; republished 2017.

Random, John, Andersonville *Diary*. New York: Roland Books, 2016;
first published in 1883.

Reed, Thomas Benton, *A Private in Gray: Life in the Army of Northern
Virginia from 1862 to 1865*. Self-published in 1905; republished in
2019.

Simpson, Brooks D. et al, *The Civil War Told by Those Who Lived It, 4 vol-*

umes. New York: Library of America, 2011.

Sorrell, G. Moxley, *Recollections of a Confederate Staff Officer*. New York: The Neale Publishing Company, 1905; republished 2016.

Williams, T. Harry, P.G.T. *Beauregard: Napoleon in Gray*. Baton Rouge: Louisiana State University Press, 1955.

Williamson, James Joseph *Mosby's Rangers: A Record of the Operations of the Forty-Third Battalion Virginia Cavalry*. New York: Sturgis & Walton. 1909; republished 2018.

Fiction and Poetry

Alcott, Louisa May, *Hospital Classics*. Public domain.

Alcott, Louisa May, *Little Women*. Public domain.

Ashley, Robert, *The Stolen Train*. New York: Scholastic Book Services, 1971.

Benet, Stephen Vincent, *John Brown's Body*. New York: Rinehart & Co., New York, 1954 (originally published 1928).

Crane, Stephen, *The Red Badge of Courage and Selected Stories*. New York: Signet Classic / Penguin Books USA, 1980.

Doctorow, E.L., *The March, a Novel*. New York: Random House, 2005.

Foote, Shelby, *Shiloh, a Novel*. New York: Random House, 1952.

Garner, Stephen, *The Civil War World of Herman Melville*. Lawrence, Kansas: University Press of Kansas, 1993.

Hunt, Irene, *Across Five Aprils*. New York: Berkley, 2023.

McClatchy, J.D., editor, *Poets of the Civil War*. New York: Library of America, 2005.

Peterson, A.S., *The Battle of Franklin: A Tale of a House Divided*. Nashville: Rabbit Room Press, 2016.

Whitman, Walt, *Drum Taps: The Complete Civil War Poems*. Kennebunkport, Maine: Cider Mill Press, 2015.

Civil War Battles

Alexander, Edward S., *Dawn of Victory: Breakthrough at Petersburg, March 25-April 2, 1865*. El Dorado Hills California: Savas Beatie Civil War Series, 2015.

Cushman, Stephen, *Bloody Promenade: Reflections on a Civil War Battle*. Charlottesville: University Press of Virginia, 1999.

Mackowski, Chris, *Hell Itself: The Battle of the Wilderness, May 5-7, 1864*. El Dorado Hills, California: Savas Beatie Emerging Civil War Series, 2016.

Mackowski, Chris and White, Kristopher D., *A Season of Slaughter: The Battle of Spotsylvania Court House May 8-21, 1864*. El Dorado Hills, California: Savas Beatie Emerging Civil War Series, 2013.

Mertz, Gregory A., *Attack at Daylight and Whip Them: The Battle of Shiloh April 6-7, 1862*. El Dorado Hills, California: Savas Beatie Emerging Civil War Series, 2019.

Mingus, Sr., Scott L and Wittenberg, Eric J., "If We Are Striking for Pennsylvania": *The Army of Northern Virginia and the Army of the Potomac March to Gettysburg, Vols. 1 and 2*. El Dorado Hills, California: Savas Beatie, 2023.

Orrison, Robert and Welsh, Dan, *The Last Road North: A Guide to the Gettysburg Campaign, 1863*. El Dorado Hills, California: Savas Beatie Emerging Civil War Series, 2016.

Rhea, Gordon C., *The Battle of the Wilderness, May 5-6, 1864*. Baton Rouge: Louisiana State University Press, 1994.

Waldermer, Donald E., *Bear in the Wilderness: The Battle of the Wilderness May 5, 6, 7 1864*. Mansfield, Ohio: Book Masters, Inc., 2001.

Web Sites

Emerging Civil War: https://emergingcivilwar.com

Civil War Books and Authors: https://cwba.blogspot.com

Also from T. S. Poetry Press

The Shivering Ground & Other Stories

by Sara Barkat

a national indie excellence awards finalist